# DESCENT INTO HELL

Garrett held his breath, battling desperately to maintain his equilibrium. Over and over he whirled as the vessel plummeted crazily down into the black ocean depths. Objects floated through the water, penlights and drink containers, instrument handles and oxygen packs.

Down, down, down: . . . The sense of descent was overwhelming; there seemed no end to it, as if the chasm into which he had plunged reached deep into the earth's innermost core.

Directly in front, the bodies of the three cosmonauts, strapped securely in their seats, floundered like a trio of rag dolls. The fourth had torn loose from its safety harness and was whirling around the cabin like a demented ghost.

Suddenly, Garrett heard a clang, and with a spine-numbing jerk, the spacecraft shuddered to a halt. He hung for a moment, dazed, as the cabin swiveled into alignment. The Soviet spacecraft had jammed on a projectile further down the underwater cliff. Like a bug on the side of a wall, it was clinging tentatively to the precipice.

But for how long?

# BOB LANGLEY
# PRECIPICE

BANTAM BOOKS

NEW YORK • TORONTO • LONDON • SYDNEY • AUCKLAND

PRECIPICE
*A Bantam Book / March 1991*

*FALCON and the portrayal of a boxed ''f'' are trademarks of Bantam Books, a division of Bantam Doubleday Dell Publishing Group, Inc.*

ISBN 0-553-28934-9

*Published simultaneously in the United States and Canada*

*Bantam Books are published by Bantam Books, a division of Bantam Doubleday Dell Publishing Group, Inc. Its trademark, consisting of the words ''Bantam Books'' and the portrayal of a rooster, is Registered in U.S. Patent and Trademark Office and in other countries. Marca Registrada. Bantam Books, 666 Fifth Avenue, New York, New York 10103*

PRINTED IN THE UNITED STATES OF AMERICA

RAD      0 9 8 7 6 5 4 3 2

# PROLOGUE

Suvluv didn't see the missile's approach, but he felt its impact. One hundred miles above the Atlantic, on an orbital incline of 49.5 degrees, Suvluv shuddered as a series of violent tremors shook his vessel's titanium hull. Barely an hour had passed since the launch tower at Baikonur had hurled them into space, and both the flight indicator and the *vzor* screen for optical orientation remained disarmingly clear. There was nothing to suggest the presence of impending danger, but as a young man serving in Afghanistan, Suvluv had twice been shot down by Mujahidin guerrillas, and he possessed an inborn sense of calamity.

He glanced at his three companions strapped in their padded ejector seats, their bodies obscured beneath their coolant-fluid spacesuits. "We've been hit," he said simply.

Sunlight from the viewing ports gleamed on the shaded visors as their helmets tilted in his direction.

"Hit?" Ryomin echoed.

"Somebody's using us for target practice."

When the second blast came, the spacecraft vibrated as though seized by a giant hand, and a series of deafening explosions echoed through Suvluv's skull. He clenched his teeth, grasping the control panel as the vessel reeled dizzily from side to side. Objects rose into the air, floating around the tiny cabin: drink containers, empty food packages, sleeping masks. Turning on its axis, the craft rotated in a ponderous, disorienting fashion. Freed from the earth's atmosphere, Suvluv experienced no physical discomfort, but a terrible dread settled in his stomach. Through the porthole window, he saw the thermal tiles of their detachable instrument console charred and blackened like a piece of crumpled carbon paper.

"My God!" Timofeevna howled.

He yelled into the radio microphone: "Mayday... Mayday... This is *Suchko Twenty-three* to Flight Control. Can you read me?... Mayday..."

The spacecraft whirled wildly, its momentum picking up speed as the seconds lengthened. Through the orientation visor, Suvluv saw the spherical outline of the earth below, its surface violet in the sunlight.

He felt another shock wave and realized they had been hit a third time. Suddenly, they were out of control, careering dizzily through the firmament. Sweat streaming, Suvluv caught glimpses of the world flashing by, like a film viewed slowly, frame by frame.

"Descent velocity gauge indicates we are reentering the atmosphere!" Teledyn shouted.

Suvluv fought back the confusion threatening to engulf him. He knew if they failed to penetrate the earth's oxygen sheath at just the right angle, their vessel would flare up like a shooting star. "Hang on," he said, "I'm switching to manual for reentry."

Instinctively, Ryomin and Timofeevna reached down to inflate their spacesuit legs. Special bladders around the thighs and calves squeezed their flesh to prevent blood from gathering there during deceleration.

Suvluv brought the orbiter around, pumping the foot-pedals to control the rudder for yaw. Descending tailfirst, the spacecraft smashed through the atmosphere's upper molecules. Flames licked around the porthole windows.

"Can't you stabilize her?" Ryomin shouted. "We'll burn to cinder at this rate. Use the thrusters."

"The thrusters aren't working," Suvluv told him. "I'm going for separation from the service module."

He released the vehicle's equipment-and-electronic section, watching it float eerily into the stratosphere. The cabin pressure intensified as their weightlessness began to dissipate, and he permitted himself a momentary glance away from the controls. For the next few minutes, ionized particles would shut off their contact with Baikonur, but they had to be ready to reestablish contact as soon as the opportunity arose.

"Ryomin, see if you can fix the radio. That was no meteorite shower back there. We're being shot at."

Ryomin's gloved hands fumbled at the instrument panel.

Suddenly, to Suvluv's amazement, Teledyn swiveled sideways, seizing his companion violently from behind and dragging him away from the controls. The act was so unexpected, so illogical, that for a moment, Suvluv could only sit and watch.

The two men struggled, fighting the accelerating pressure of the atmosphere, then Teledyn, jamming his forearm against Ryomin's throat, reached out with his heavy glove, and deliberately ripped the communications console to shreds. Suvluv couldn't believe his eyes. His mouth opened in protest as he watched Teledyn shatter their last hope of contact with Flight Control.

"Stop him, damn it!" Suvluv shouted.

Straining at his seat belt, Timofeevna hurled himself across Teledyn's shoulders, pushing him savagely against the chair. Without hesitating, Ryomin, freed from constraint, drove his fist into Teledyn's stomach, and Teledyn jerked forward, groaning. As he did so, his bulbous helmet clicked loose in the struggle, floating wildly across the cabin.

Suvluv blinked in astonishment. The face staring back at them was not Teledyn's but that of a total stranger.

Tugging the heavy handgrip from the instrument panel, Ryomin hit the intruder across the left temple, and he sagged into unconsciousness, his head lolling against the padded neckrest.

Suvluv examined the man's features with disbelief. Had they really been accompanied throughout the entire flight by an imposter? True, the helmet visor had obscured the man's face and the microphone had distorted his voice, but how in God's name had he infiltrated the takeoff procedures at Baikonur?

Suvluv squinted at his companions. "Who is he?"

"I don't know," Ryomin croaked. "I never saw him before."

"How the hell did he get in here? Timo, you were with Teledyn in the kitting-up room. What happened?"

"Nothing happened. We got on the bus to the launchpad, that's all."

"Did you leave him at any point?"

"Only for a minute. I went to call my wife."

Suvluv felt the mounting overload pinning him against the headrest. Glancing through the porthole window, he saw flames engulfing their outer hull. They were descending like a stone, wrapped in a blinding ball of fire. Forget the intruder. Concentrate on survival.

"Back to your seats," he ordered. "We're going in."

"Control panel indicates we're down to seventy thousand feet," Timofeevna said. "According to our position, we're crashing somewhere over the Antarctic."

"I'll try to engage the parachute," Ryomin said.

He was silent for a moment, then Suvluv saw him slap the instrument panel in disgust. "Nothing is functioning, Vladimir. Shall we trigger the ejector seats?"

"In the Antarctic? Without shelter, without warmth? How long do you think we'll last?"

"Then what are we going to do?"

Suvluv sighed as he leaned back in his chair, his aluminized body casting ripples of refracted light across his domed helmet. He felt weary, bitter, and defeated.

"The only thing we can do. Pray."

In a sealed chamber deep inside the hollowed-out 4.5-acre military complex that housed NORAD's Cheyenne Mountain headquarters, the U.S. missile crew followed the spacecraft's progress on a panel of visual-display screens. They had been tracking it for almost an hour, and precisely seventeen minutes earlier, after calculating the vessel's orbital incline, had detonated their fly-by F-22 antisatellite warheads, blasting it out of the sky.

There was no sense of triumph or elation in the massive steel-lined chamber. The observers were low-keyed and businesslike, their voices husky with strain. Each man present realized that the operation they had just carried out represented an act of war.

Grim-faced and unblinking, NORAD's duty commander, Lieutenant General Leo D. Culver, watched the blip gradually approaching ground level and steeled himself for the moment of impact. The blip dropped, touched, and vanished—and a murmur rippled through the men present.

"Signature no longer moving," a voice announced. "Repeat—signature no longer moving. Everything consistent with earth contact."

"Map it," Culver commanded.

The officer engaged his computer, fingers dancing lightly over the keys. "Sir, reading is somewhere in the area of seventy-nine degrees, sixty-two minutes south, forty-four degrees, twelve minutes west. No further signals. Source presumed terminated."

Culver filled his lungs with air and gradually exhaled. His cheeks looked pale, his eyes strained, and he was conscious of a debilitating lassitude spreading through his limbs. "Keep watching," he commanded. "I'll call General Weir."

Walking into a tiny office, he picked up the telephone and punched out a number, squinting in the glow from the shaded desklamp. It wasn't every day of the week a man got to carry out a preemptive strike against the Soviet Union, he reflected.

The line buzzed for a moment, then a voice came on—low, anxious, urgent. "Weir here."

"General, this is Culver."

There was a slight pause, and Culver heard Major General George Stanton Weir breathing heavily at the end of the line. "How did it go, Leo?"

"Bull's-eye."

"Any reaction from the Soviets?"

"Negative, George. They lost contact after the first impact."

"And the *Suchko*?"

"Somewhere in the Antarctic, we estimate. What's left of her."

"We've done it, then."

"I guess so. Congratulations, General."

Weir's voice took on a bitter tone. "For what? Bringing the world to the brink of nuclear war?"

"It was a gamble, we knew that from the beginning. But I think it's paid off, George."

"I wish I had your confidence, Leo. What happens when the Soviets find the wreckage, when they examine the evidence? Only one nation in the world has the capacity to carry out such an attack, and the Russians know it."

Culver's voice was soothing. "It had to be done. It was us or them, George."

"Thanks, Coach. That'll be a great comfort to me when I'm sitting in the fallout shelter."

"Maybe we'll get lucky. Maybe the Russians will put it down to some kind of engineering fault, or even a meteor shower. You did your best, George."

"Anyhow, thanks for the tip-off, Leo. I'll call you in the morning."

"Good night, General. And sleep tight. You deserve it."

"You too, Leo. Good night."

General George Weir put down the telephone and stared at it for a moment, as if expecting it to ring again. Then, walking into the hall, he reached for his overcoat while his bodyguard, Willard Tilbert, studied him anxiously. "I'm going for a drive," Weir said.

"It's late, sir."

"I know it's late. Don't treat me like a simpleton, Tilbert."

"I'm sorry, sir. I'll get the car."

"No. I want to be alone."

Tilbert hesitated. He understood the strain the general had been under and remained carefully respectful. "Sir, the General knows it is my duty . . ."

"To protect me at all hours of the day or night. Yes, yes, Tilbert, I wouldn't dream of interfering with your duty. You may follow in your own car, but if you have any sensitivity at all, which I sometimes doubt, you will keep your distance."

Tilbert accompanied the general outside and trailed him along the deserted Beltway. They saw little traffic in the early morning. A few cars trundled south toward Rock Creek Park and Chevy Chase, but the roads remained surprisingly clear.

Tilbert dreaded the thought of what he had to do tonight. He liked the general, admired him deeply, and in the seven months he had been under Weir's command, he had developed a near reverence for his commanding officer. But he had given his word. He was committed. He would have to see it through.

The lights of the city formed a coppery halo in the cloudy sky as they cruised through Bethesda and took the Great Falls road, following the Potomac. After about twenty minutes, Weir pulled into a registered observation point, and climbing from his car, stood gazing moodily across the sleekly flowing water. The night was dark, the stars vivid, and across the river, Tilbert saw headlamps flashing around Dranesville District Park. Tears streamed down his cheeks. Duty, he thought. It had a lot to answer for.

Tilbert buttoned his raincoat, and opening the glove compartment, took out a .38 Special Colt Cobra. He checked the load, then holding the weapon against his thigh, got out of the car and walked toward Weir across the cindered parking lot. Crickets chirped in the grass. Bullfrogs croaked among the river reeds.

When Weir heard Tilbert's footsteps, he turned. "Willard, is something wrong?"

Tilbert drew to a halt. He tried to speak. "General, I . . ." His words froze in his mouth. What could he say at such a moment?

He seized Weir around the neck, dragging him close. The general's bafflement turned to alarm, and he raised his arms protectively. Tilbert thrust Weir's face against his chest, gripping his body in a suffocating bear hug.

"I'm sorry, General," he croaked. Placing the Colt against Weir's left temple, he squeezed the trigger.

The detonation was muffled in the night, as if the river reeds and the darkness had conspired in some way to absorb his deed. Bone and brain fragments sprayed the air, and Weir crumpled to the ground at Tilbert's feet. Tilbert looked down at him, crying uncontrollably now, his raincoat splattered with blood. He glanced at the empty road behind, and wiping the pistol clean, knelt and placed it tenderly in the general's grasp. For a moment, he remained perfectly still, his head bowed in silent prayer. Then he rose to his feet, and walked back to his car where he picked up the radio telephone.

In a modest room overlooking the courtyard of the Kremlin Arsenal, the thirteen members of the Soviet Politburo faced each other across the mahogany conference table. The atmosphere was heavy with smoke as two stenographers sat recording the proceedings in rapid shorthand.

The chairman of the Central Committee, Mikhail Poskrebyshev—dour, baggy-eyed, caustic, and phlegmatic—stared balefully at Marshal Valisova, the Soviet defense minister, who was explaining, with some trepidation, the events surrounding the spacecraft catastrophe. "The body of cosmonaut Yuri Teledyn was found on the shower-room floor," Valisova was saying. "His skull had been fractured and his neck broken. The attack apparently came from behind, possibly from one of the private cubicles."

"So someone deliberately prevented Teledyn taking his place on board the *Suchko*?" Poskrebyshev asked.

Valisova said, "Which means, of course, one of our cosmonauts was an imposter."

Poskrebyshev toyed absently with a pencil. "An American?"

"Who knows? A spy, certainly."

"You think the United States suspected *Suchko Twenty-three*'s true objective?"

Valisova smiled humorlessly. "If they had, they'd have raised the roof at the United Nations. No, Comrade Chairman, I think our inquisitive friend had something else on his mind."

"Like sabotage?"

"Only a lunatic would destroy his own spacecraft, Comrade Chairman. The more likely explanation is that the man was snooping around when his plans were interrupted by the forces of circumstance."

"Meaning the crash was accidental?"

"What else? Faulty fuel boosters would lead to the separation tanks' detonating after the vessel left the atmosphere."

"What about the communications linkup?" Poskrebyshev said. "Why should it fail at such a relevant moment?"

"Perhaps the antenna got damaged during the explosion."

"That's little more than conjecture."

"Of course. We have no way of verifying it, since *Suchko Twenty-three* has completely disappeared."

Poskrebyshev's face looked bland as he leaned forward to refill his water glass. "Are we to assume it has vanished into thin air? Some curious anomaly from space perhaps, a kind of stardust which causes vessels to melt like butter?"

Valisova was accustomed to Poskrebyshev's sarcasm, but there were times when he found it difficult to take. "Comrade Chairman, you must understand our problem. The point at which the *Suchko* crashed is off the Antarctic Peninsula. The seabed there is a vast submerged mountain range, its deepest valleys lying at levels beyond the reach of man or machine. The region is so remote, so inaccessible, that our ships are finding it almost impossible to operate, and to add to their problems, the ocean surface is covered by a layer of ice nearly six feet thick.''

"Are you suggesting we leave the spacecraft undisturbed, knowing it carried a spy?"

"The man is already dead," Valisova insisted. "He had no time to communicate his findings, and we have little to gain in recovering his unidentifiable corpse. Our inquiries continue at Baikonur, and if our investigators discover who was responsible for murdering Teledyn, then perhaps we'll find some answers to this riddle. Meanwhile, we are wasting valuable time and resources on a wild-goose chase."

"And if the vessel should fall into the wrong hands?"

"Comrade Chairman, since our scanning sonars can find no trace of the *Suchko*'s existence, we can only conclude she must be somewhere deep on the ocean floor. Even if she should be located at some future date—a highly unlikely possibility—her hull will have crumpled like an old tin can. I propose we call off this fruitless search. We can make a gesture to satisfy the people, perhaps scatter a few flowers on the ice-pack's surface, and in view of the cosmonauts' deaths, we might admit them into the pantheon of virtuous Soviet manhood—posthumously, of course. But to continue the operation is both pointless and extravagant."

Poskrebyshev regarded him thoughtfully. In the bright light from the window, his face appeared all angles, lines, and shadows. "You wish to forget we have a time bomb ticking in our laps?"

"Not a time bomb, Comrade Chairman. *Suchko Twenty-three* is as safe on the seabed as she would be on the launchpad at Baikonur. To the Americans, to the entire world, it will be as if she never existed."

Poskrebyshev considered for a moment. "Very well," he agreed at last, "I accept the proposal. The search for the *Suchko* will be discontinued. Order the navy to withdraw their ships."

He paused, his eyes growing cold as he gazed around the silent assemblage. "But for the sake of our future, for the sake of our children, let us pray no one ever discovers what the spacecraft contained."

# PART

## I

# THE HUNT

# ONE

The theater entrance was crowded with people when Nick Koster and Jan Marisa Bowering arrived. Uniformed patrolmen held back the crowds, forming a phalanx along both sides of the lobby steps, and as Koster helped Jan Bowering from the limousine, he caught glimpses of police marksmen studying the throng from the rooftops above. A small group of civil dignitaries waited inside the theater door, looking awkward and uncomfortable.

Koster glanced at his watch. "We're early," he said as the limousine drove off.

Jan Marisa Bowering, gathered her coat more tightly around her. "We're not early," she corrected. "The President's late. He always is." She sniffed as she eyed the uniformed officials waiting on the theater steps. "Two hours of boredom. I don't know why he insists on dragging me along. He knows how I hate opera."

"He's looking for moral support. Randolph Guthrie makes him feel like an intellectual pygmy. With you in tow, he figures he's redressing the balance."

"Thanks, friend. You've just made my evening."

Koster glanced at the spectators milling behind the police lines. "Shall we wait inside?" he suggested.

"Bad form. The President always goes first. That's protocol."

"Then I wish to God he'd hurry up. I'm freezing my buns off out here."

She eyed him with an air of affectionate amusement. Koster's youthful face looked oddly cherubic beneath his sculpted hair, and his slender fingers fluttered nervously up and down his tuxedo jacket.

"Stop worrying, Nicky."

"I can't help it. I keep expecting things to go wrong."

"Nothing will go wrong. Trust me."

Koster had worked for Jan Marisa Bowering for almost a year now, and during that time had found her to be not only a lady of considerable charm but also one of ruthless resolve. Sugar-and-spice she might appear on the outside, but as many a politician had discovered to his cost, she could be cold hard steel beneath.

Jan Bowering was President Clayman's White House chief of staff, and she had established herself indelibly as his strong right hand during his first few weeks in office by adroitly handling a scandal at the Treasury Department. Jan Bowering's meteoric White House career had attracted not only the attention of the nation's press but the interest of the entire world, and at the age of forty-one—slim, elegant, and sophisticated—she had become a role model for women everywhere.

However, the President's favor had earned her many enemies in the administration who often snidely hinted at a more intimate relationship. Koster knew this to be untrue since Jan Bowering had been happily married for the past six years. Still, no one underestimated her power; few people had such direct access to the President, and she had proved her toughness, resilience, and uncompromising attitude a dozen times over.

Koster slipped his hands in his overcoat pockets as they stood waiting patiently in the chill. Across the street, segregated by a group of grim-faced security men, a party of demonstrators chanted rhythmically, their placards catching the streetlights' rays. They were protesting the projected Centaur Program in which the United States, together with the Soviet Union, intended to supply liquid-fuel rockets, specialists, and equipment to the developing countries to help make space research universal. Controversy had dogged the program from the outset; people were acutely conscious that Centaur would cost the American taxpayers billions of dollars, and as the delivery date approached, the issue had split not only Congress, but virtually the entire country.

Jan Marisa Bowering had been the scheme's architect and administrator, but even Nick Koster disagreed with her views on the subject of space cooperation.

"You see that?" he whispered. "You've got a lot of opposition out there, Mrs. Bowering."

Jan Bowering said, "When people change history, there's always opposition, Nicky. That's human nature."

"But just look at them. They're mad because they feel you're squandering money on a lunatic venture, and scared because they think opening up space will make the United States vulnerable to attack from other nations."

"The Russians will be vulnerable too, remember that."

"Who trusts the Russians anymore? Look what happened in the early nineties. We thought the era of confrontation was over, then the hard-liners returned stronger than ever."

"They were only reestablishing control after a period of instability. You can't blame governments for wanting order instead of chaos. And they're still our friends—if not yet our allies."

"Just the same, if anything goes wrong, you'll be crucified by the American people."

"For what? Honoring an agreement started as far back as the mid-nineties? I don't know about you, Nicky, but I'd call that ethics, not betrayal."

"I'm not talking about ethics, ma'am, I'm talking about politics. The universe isn't a playground anymore, it's an arena. We're opening the door to interspace warfare—photo-reconnaissance, electronic intelligence, even, God forbid, missile-carrying satellites. We're placing the U.S. in the trigger sights of every nut on the globe."

"Nicky, we're not supplying these people with warheads, we're simply helping them get into orbit. We can't continue with the policies of the eighties and early nineties. We have to make the heavens safe for people to live under. When we decided to scrap SDI, it was the first step on the road to global sanity. I promised to honor the Centaur Program when I took this job, and I'm not modifying that promise just because a few bleeding-heart liberals start beating their chests. Besides, the President is as committed as I am."

"Even if it means political suicide?"

She smiled thinly. "This may sound kind of strange, but not all politicians place their personal survival above their pledges to the people."

"I hope the people remember that at election time," Koster said dryly.

Jan Bowering studied him in silence for a moment. She could feel his opposition like a shield. He was a good man: loyal, true, and dedicated, but blinded like so many by the fallacies of the past.

"What are we arguing about, Nicky? We've gone through this a million times before. The people will change in time. All they need is a chance to get used to the idea. Remember what happened when oil was discovered in Antarctica? Ecology groups all over the country cited the Antarctic Treaty, reserving Antarctica for scientific research.

"But what kind of people would we be if we didn't make use of Antarctic oil? We can't leave our descendants the legacy of a civilization run dry. We need that oil to give us time to develop new energy sources, and it's the same with space exploration.

"We have to ensure that space is retained for purely peaceful purposes, and the only way to do that is to make it accessible to the entire world. We're on the threshold of a new era. Soon, men will live and work on the moon. They'll have furnaces for melting lunar ore, cell plants for making electricity out of sunlight. We'll be exploring the planets. But we need new blood, new attitudes, new thinking.

"The President wants to fix things so that never again will a Star Wars project be considered viable, or even desirable. He wants to make the universe what it is and always should be—universal—with the danger of interspace warfare totally eradicated."

She paused as the President's motorcade approached. Motorcycle patrolmen flanked each side of the gleaming limousines. An excited shout rose from the waiting crowd.

"Here he comes," Jan Bowering murmured. "Nearly fifteen minutes late. I have a feeling Larry Clayman will go down as the tardiest president in American history."

They watched the cavalcade of limousines draw up at the curb. Then the doors of the lead vehicle sprang open and Secret Service men spilled into the street. On the rooftops, the police marksmen studied the heads below.

A liveried attendant opened the door of the President's car, and the people cheered as Clayman emerged. Tall, dapper, leathery-featured, he clasped his hands above his head in the manner of an Olympic athlete acknowledging the tribute of the crowd.

To the obvious dismay of his security contingent, the President strode to the police barrier and began shaking hands. Lawrence Clayman considered himself a man of the people and rarely missed a chance to make the most of his friendly "guy-next-door" image.

The D.C. police chief spoke softly into the President's ear, and Clayman moved back to the limousine and helped First Lady Lucille Clayman to alight. Clad in a stunning black gown, she looked radiant beneath the streetlights.

Regally, the President and his wife strode toward the theater entrance, and Clayman's eyes twinkled as he passed Jan Marisa Bowering. He gave her a wink. Trailing at his rear, Vice President Randolph Guthrie, accompanied by his wife Theresa, glared at her coldly.

"Doesn't look as though I'll be winning friends and influencing people in that direction," Jan Bowering whispered to Nick Koster.

"Guthrie's jealous. He can't understand why the President regards you so highly."

"Male vanity. I'm used to it. I've been dealing with men like Guthrie all my life."

The presidential party paused for the welcoming ceremony in the theater lobby, surrounded by a tight secret service entourage. When the official introductions had been completed, the party moved toward the auditorium. The audience, clad in tuxedos and evening gowns, rose to give the President a standing ovation.

Wilson came out of the boiler room, clutching the rifle concealed in a plastic garbage bag. He had found it, as instructed, wrapped in cellophane and thrust inside the central heating pipes. It was an M76 sniper's weapon with a slim metal barrel and an elongated sight.

When he reached the theater lobby, he found two security guards standing at the open doorway, eyeing him suspiciously. "Who the hell are you?" one asked.

Wilson felt sweat breaking out between his shoulder blades. Authority unnerved him, always had.

The second man chuckled, recognizing Wilson's features. "It's okay," he said. "It's only the janitor."

"Then where's his security pass, for Chrissake?"

"My pass?" Wilson muttered.

Cursing inwardly, he fumbled in his boiler-suit pocket. He felt sick, there was no other way to describe it; a sour pall of nausea had gathered in his stomach and was sweeping in waves through his entire body. They had warned him to guard against physical reactions. Strain shows, they'd said. Damp cheeks and tense eyes are surefire giveaways to sharp-eyed security men.

Wilson wasn't good at concealing his emotions. His wife read him like a book. He mustn't worry, that was the important thing. Anxiety was his enemy, tension an emasculating force.

Fingers trembling, he clipped the tiny badge to his overall lapel, and the first man nodded, satisfied. "That's better."

Wilson crossed the theater lobby, his heart beating wildly as he reached the stairway. Pausing at the utility room, he inserted his key in the lock and stepped into the stifling darkness, filling his lungs with air. An odor of dust hung in his nostrils as he ran his hand along the wall, flicking the light switch with his finger.

Beneath the shelves and cleaning brooms, he found the ventilator grill, and kneeling down, began to work at the fastenings with a tiny screwdriver. It took him less than three minutes to remove the metal wiring; then, gripping the rifle in front of him, he wriggled into the aluminum shaft. Ahead, he could see a faint glimmer in the darkness and hear the singers' voices echoing clearly from the theater below.

He approached the wire grating, using his screwdriver to pick away at the metal strands. He removed the grill, laid it in the dust at his feet, and looked into the crowded auditorium. He could see the opera performers going through their paces on the brightly lit stage, and directly opposite, in a private box, President Clayman, surrounded by aides, dignitaries, and secret service.

Moistening his lips, Wilson steadied the rifle across the concrete shelf. The stock felt slippery against his cheek, and he fixed his gaze on the blunt outline of the flash eliminator

**dominating the barrel tip. Manipulating the optical-sight lens,**
he brought his target into focus, training the cross hairs on the
President's middle body.

Don't try for a head shot, they had warned, too showy, too
unreliable. Go for the chest or upper stomach. Wilson's finger
slid beneath the trigger guard and gently applied pressure
until he was just short of firing. He tried not to think of the
President as a human being. He had killed people before,
often perfectly innocent people, but that had been in a
different age, a different climate—a time of war.

Yet this too was war, in a way. A war against imprudence.
A war against insanity. Some men never listened, Wilson
thought. They clung to a dream, nurturing it like a secret
obsession until their madness infected everyone around them.
The President was working against the people's wishes. He
had to be eliminated.

Wilson leaned forward to give himself a clearer view, and
in doing so, rested the bulk of his weight against the fragile
plastering on the ventilator frame. He felt the rifle shudder as
the stock slipped loosely from his cheek, and a few flakes of
coating dropped into the theater below. Wilson watched them
fall with a thrill of horror. Faces peered up in his direction,
and a terrible hush settled over the opera stage. Panic seared
Wilson as he realized his momentary carelessness, his fractional error of judgment, had given away his presence.

In the box opposite, security guards stampeded everywhere. A man leapt forward, hurling the President violently
to the floor.

Wilson loosed a shot, knowing instinctively he had missed.
Panic-stricken, he dropped the rifle and scrambled back the
way he had come.

He raced down the landing and barged into the electrician's
office. He vaulted across the work desk to the open window
and clambered onto the concrete ledge outside. He felt the
wind plucking at his hair, but he was careful not to look
down. He had no head for heights, and somewhere below lay
the parking lot, the street, and the people. He would pretend
they didn't exist. He would pretend gravity didn't exist. His
brain worked not on a reasoning level but in the blind,
instinctive manner of a cornered animal. His only hope was to
reach the fire escape leading to the exit alley.

Wilson wriggled breathlessly onto the roof, his stomach

tightening as he glimpsed figures emerging from behind the sloping panels. He started to run, following the line of the drainage funnel to his left. Suddenly there were men everywhere, swarming like vermin across the slippery rooftops— men in uniforms and civilian suits, men in face masks and bulletproof jackets, men wielding weapons of every shape and description.

There was no hope in Wilson now, no last-minute yearning for reprieve. They had warned him from the beginning. No surrender. He felt drained of fear, that was the extraordinary thing; his fear had vanished in the face of imminent oblivion. Suddenly, everything in his life became poignantly and startlingly vivid.

How brightly flared the candle at the moment of extinction, he thought, and with a fluid, elegant motion, dived headlong from the theater roof.

The President sat impatiently in the theater manager's office as the White House doctor bound his twisted wrist. He had been whisked up the private stairway that led from the theater box to the floor above. Now, safely ensconced behind a battered desk, he watched the little knot of security men milling about in the passageway outside.

Jan Bowering came through the doorway, her heels clicking on the carpetless floor. The President studied her approvingly. He knew what his critics thought, but he considered Jan Bowering a formidable lady and trusted her more than almost anyone else in the world.

"They've got him," she said.

"Alive?"

"Suicide. He went off the roof."

The President filled his lungs with air and gently exhaled. "A man would have to be awfully committed to sacrifice his life like that."

"The press wants interviews. I told them the press secretary would issue a statement first thing in the morning."

"Good thinking, Jan."

"In the meantime, the Secret Service want to get you out of here as quickly as possible. They've ordered the motorcade to the rear entrance. There could be backup snipers around."

Clayman winced as the doctor pulled at the bandage. "What are the chances of playing this down?"

"Zero," Jan Bowering told him bluntly. "Too many witnesses. It's world news."

"He had to be an intruder. No one else could have gotten through the security net."

"The theater manager says the man's name was Wilson. He had been working as the janitor here for the past four months. That's about the time this visit was arranged, so he must have had inside knowledge at the highest level."

Clayman grimaced. "Makes me feel a little creepy to think someone in my administration might be setting me up."

"You do realize this is a warning."

"Against the Centaur Program? My God, somebody wants to put a bullet in my head just because I'm trying to make the heavens safe for the future of mankind."

"I wondered if you'd like to slow down a bit?"

"Why? Because some crazy kook takes a shot at me?"

"I couldn't blame you for deciding to wait until the country's a little more ready—I mean, psychologically speaking."

"You know better than that, Jan. In two months' time, I'm going to Moscow to ratify the agreement. It'll be the culmination of everything I've worked for, and no miserable shootist is going to stop me."

"I'm glad you feel that way, Mr. President. I just wanted to make sure."

"Jan, will you ride back to the White House with me? Mrs. Clayman is a little upset, and I feel another woman along might give her moral support."

"I'd be honored, Mr. President."

When the doctor had finished, the chief security aide, Wallace Colton, announced that the rear plaza had been cleared and the motorcade was ready for departure. Surrounded by bodyguards and accompanied by Jan Bowering, the President walked down the private stairway and left via a discreet exit at the rear. Nick Koster walked with Jan Bowering to the limousine door.

"Nicky, tell the press secretary no statement is to be issued until tomorrow morning. Have him call a conference for seven A.M."

"It'll never stick," Koster told her bluntly. "We'll have to say *something*, for Chrissake."

"Say we believe the gunman was a lone wolf and we're

checking out his background now. Deny any suggestion of a conspiracy. They can ask all the questions they want in the morning.''

She ducked into the rear seat of the limousine, slamming the door behind her. ''Nicky,'' she breathed, sliding down the bulletproof window.

''Yes, ma'am?''

''On the space thing. I know you're against it in principle.'' Koster hesitated. ''I never said . . .''

''Don't apologize. I can't expect you to agree with me on everything. But I want you to know I appreciate the way you've stood behind me, in spite of your personal beliefs. I appreciate your loyalty.''

''You'll always have that.''

''I know, Nicky. I know.''

Nick Koster parked his car near the front of the mansion and jogged up the elegant stone stairway to the door. A muscular young guard frisked him expertly before leading the way along a maze of corridors to a sumptuously furnished conference room where a group of men sat around a large table. Several wore military uniforms. The others were conservatively dressed and nondescript in appearance. Only their leader, a thickset bullnecked man with sunbaked muscular features, looked in any way remarkable. He glanced up as Koster entered.

''Trust might, trust constancy,'' Koster said, feeling slightly ridiculous as he did so. The code sign irritated him, always had, but the others seemed to expect it. They studied him in silence, their faces bereft of emotion.

''It was a fiasco,'' Koster reported. ''One of the security guards spotted Wilson from the President's box.''

''It was always a possibility,'' the bullnecked man said. ''Nobody's blaming you, Nicky.''

''At least Wilson had the decency to kill himself,'' an army colonel commented.

''I expected that of Wilson,'' the chairman said. ''It's why I chose him.''

''We can still make another attempt,'' a third man put in. ''Since we have direct access to the President, there'd be no reason to fail again.''

''Out of the question. It has to look like the work of an

outside group; otherwise we achieve nothing. No, the Moscow meeting is less than a couple of months away. Much as I abhor the thought, I believe we only have one recourse left.''

The conference was silent for a moment; then an officer shifted uncomfortably in his chair. "It's a hell of an undertaking, Frank. Supposing we can't pull it off?''

"Why? We've prepared long enough.''

"But you're talking about putting men into space.''

"Not me, Jocko. NASA. Thanks to Dan Connel, the crew is already under training at Houston. Even the launch date has been set. All they need is the go-ahead.''

Nick Koster removed his spectacles, wiping them with his handkerchief. In the light from the window, his too-young face looked curiously unformed, like a plaster sculpture only half completed. "Maybe the price of victory can be too high.''

The chairman frowned. "What are you talking about, Nicky?''

"It's an inhuman concept.''

"What do you take me for, a monster? I'm as appalled by the prospect as you are. But consider the alternative.''

"I have considered it. Goddammit, Frank, we can't justify what we're planning here. It's unthinkable.''

The chairman sighed. "You knew what you were doing, Nicky, you knew from the beginning. We went into this—all of us—with our eyes open.''

"But the *Stallion* was only intended as a last resort.''

"And where do you think we are now? This is the bottom line. The President is about to open the floodgates into space. In his pathetic way, he believes it'll be used for peaceful purposes. He can't seem to grasp that what happens in space is merely an extension of political rivalries on earth. Apart from the bankrupting expense, the military implications are terrifying. When some of the smaller nations get themselves into orbit, we'll be virtually defenseless against surprise attack. Is that what you want, Nicky? To see the U.S. become a third-rate power? Because make no mistake, that is what we are considering here. The *Stallion* is a desperate measure, I agree. In some ways, it is a barbaric measure, but it's the only one which will preserve the sovereignty and sanctity of this country.''

He raised his hand as Koster started to protest. "You know the rules. We abide by the majority decision."

He turned to the others. "Do we abort the operation, or steel ourselves to take the last, irrevocable step? Those wishing to proceed please raise your right hands."

Koster watched the arms rising, felt his stomach churning, hated what he was being forced to accept. It wasn't a fantasy any longer, but cold hard fact, and God knew he was part of it, whether he liked it or not.

He saw the bullnecked man awaiting his response, and Koster lifted his hand. The chairman leaned back in his seat.

"The issue is decided, gentlemen. We have lift-off."

# TWO

Lori Madden, operations controller of the Space Satellite Ops and Signals Tracking Network at Cape Canaveral, Florida, heard the telephone ringing somewhere deep inside her consciousness and blinked in annoyance at the stars still gleaming between her parted curtains. Glancing at the clock, she groped groggily for the receiver.

"Lori?"

"Who is this?"

"Herb Baker."

"Herb, for God's sake, you know what time it is?"

"Things are happening here, Lori. I need somebody who can make decisions."

Lori wriggled up on the pillow. Something in Baker's voice brought her senses alert. Herb was Lori's assistant at the telecommunications center, a branch of the international DOLPAS-POSAT program involved in locating, via satellite, aircraft and vessels in distress. She had worked with him for almost four years and knew he wasn't the type to panic unduly. Her face was tense as she reached for the bedside lamp.

"What's going on Herb?"

"I can't discuss it over the phone."

"What are you talking about? You sound like James Bond, for heaven's sake."

"I've got something here would make James Bond's hair stand on end."

"Are you serious?"

"Never felt more serious in my life."

"This better be good," she warned.

"It's more than good. It'll blow your mind."

Lori showered quickly and tugged on a pair of slacks and a sweatshirt. The stars were still out as she left her Titusville apartment and drove around the promontory to the NASA test range on Merritt Island.

Lori Madden had worked in the space program for almost seven years. She had started at Wernher von Braun's old Redstone rocket factory in Huntsville, Alabama, had transferred to the Johnson Space Center at Houston, and finally, twenty-eight and unmarried, had assumed command of the Ops and Signals tracking station at Cape Canaveral.

She had reached the pinnacle of her career when she had been chosen by NASA to join the crew of the *Fremont* shuttle on a routine flight to launch two new weather satellites, and eight months later had taken part in the historic Salida Mission, which had included two lengthy space walks testing construction techniques for the building of a revolutionary new space station.

An attractive woman with a smattering of freckles across her nose and cheeks, Lori Madden had few interests beyond her job. After two disastrous love affairs that had left her feeling bruised and bewildered, she had decided to ignore all amatory attachments and devote herself solely to her work.

She had become quite adept at resisting the thinly veiled advances of her male colleagues, and she knew that in their disappointment, they had labeled her cold, standoffish, and unresponsive, but Lori Madden cared little what people said or thought. She concentrated on channeling her energies into the one area that gave her fulfillment, and she had to admit that so far at least, her life had proved a satisfying one.

Dawn was breaking as she approached the entrance gates to the plant and launch complex. To the left, she could see the dim outline of the Vehicle Assembly Building, a huge cube-shaped affair 525 feet high, occupying almost eight acres of swampland. Ahead lay the parkway to the Banana River and the now-inactive pads for C-19, once used for the *Gemini* capsules and the *Atlas* rocket launchers.

The uniformed guards seemed surprised to see Lori Madden as she passed through the security checkpoint and made her way to the Ops and Signals Section in the central administration block. She found Herb Baker waiting alone in the deserted office, a thickset man with receding red hair.

"How do I look to you?" he asked by way of greeting, spreading his hands like a vaudeville performer.

"A little baggy around the eyes. That's the night shift, Herb."

"I mean, do I look crazy? I've just spent the last three hours wondering if I'm going crazy or not. Come on in here."

Baffled, she followed him into the signals room. In the dim light from the night bulbs, the computer consoles hummed furiously. Herb pointed at a signature blip on one of the visual-display panels.

"Know what that is?"

"It's a signal."

"Right. It started a little after two, beamed in from our station in Valparaiso. I got some words at first, garbled mostly. Incomprehensible. Then I realized they were in Russian, so I had the message translated. Take a look."

Lori cast her eyes over the typewritten sheet. The words seemed unreal, imbued with an air of eerie theatricality. "Mayday, Mayday, Mayday. This is *Suchko Twenty-three*. Can you hear us? Please respond. Retros destroyed by enemy assault. We cannot move. Repeat—we cannot move. Our oxygen tanks have been damaged by shrapnel, and we are losing atmosphere fast. We are unable to abandon vessel. Repeat—we are unable to abandon vessel. In the name of God, get us out of here. Mayday, Mayday, Mayday."

"This is an SOS," Lori said earnestly. "Did you contact the emergency services?"

Herb hesitated, wiping his palms on the front of his shirt. "Lori, I know this sounds crazy, but there's something weird about that message."

"Weird? In what way?"

"The vessel which transmitted it, *Suchko Twenty-three*, crashed into the Antarctic fourteen years ago."

Lori stared at him. "Is that some kind of joke?"

"Would I joke at six-thirty in the morning? I looked it up in the records. *Suchko Twenty-three* was a Soviet workhorse. During a routine flight to re-man one of the *Salyut* space stations, she got into difficulties above the stratosphere and plunged into the Weddel Sea with four Russian cosmonauts on board. Nobody came out alive."

Lori sucked in her breath. "I remember the incident. I was only a kid at school, but the papers were full of it."

"The Russians tried five times to recover the *Suchko*, but there was ice covering the whole area, and she'd sunk so deep they just couldn't find her, so in the end, they decided to leave the vessel where it was."

Lori looked at the paper in her hand, feeling a breathless sensation gathering in her diaphragm. "Herb, are you telling me a Soviet spacecraft crashed into the Antarctic with a full crew on board, and fourteen years later starts sending out distress signals?"

"Kind of creepy, isn't it? I figured I must be caught in some sort of time warp at first; then I realized there'll be no atmosphere inside *Suchko Twenty-three* any more, nothing to sustain life. What must have happened—and it's the only credible explanation—is that the craft computer *recorded* the distress signals at the time the vessel was crashing, though for some reason—probably because it got damaged during reentry— its radio failed to transmit. Now, fourteen years later, some- thing's jostled the computer into working order again—a fall of ice maybe, a shift on the seabed, who knows? We're picking up messages from a crew who, presumably, died fourteen years ago."

Lori took a deep breath. "That's grotesque, Herb."

"It gets worse." Herb's eyes glittered fiercely. "I ran *Suchko Twenty-three* through the computer, and guess what? It carries a TK-CC—anything connected with the vessel has to be referred directly to the National Security Agency."

"What did you do?"

"Notified Washington, of course."

"And?"

"Nothing. I'm still waiting for a response."

Clutching the message pad, Lori sat down at the computer console. All traces of sleepiness had vanished from her body.

"It's a hoax."

"It's no hoax, Lori, it's real. Part of the problem of recovering the *Suchko* was that nobody knew precisely where she lay. The Soviets kept dragging the seabed with their sonar gear, but nothing registered. Now, for the first time, we've got a fix on the spacecraft's position."

"Herb, these signals may be garbled, but their intimation is clear. Whatever the reason, the people who sent them believed themselves under attack.''

''That's why I called you. Strictly speaking, we should contact Moscow right away. Under the terms of the Drinov Agreement, all information has to be shared immediately with the Soviets. Only I didn't feel like sticking my neck on the block without referring to higher authority.''

''Thanks, sport, you've made my day.''

''What are you going to do?''

She rose to her feet, pushing the message into her slacks pocket.

''What every aspiring young bureaucrat does in the fullness of time. Pass the buck.''

Lori locked her office door before using the direct line to call Francis Schofield, the SSOS director. The phone rang for several minutes before a voice came on the line—gruff, deep, irritable. ''Schofield here.''

''Francis, it's Lori Madden. I think you'd better use the scrambler.''

She heard Schofield grunt with surprise. Then the line clicked as he engaged the electronic device designed to prevent their conversation being overheard. When he spoke again, his truculence had vanished. His voice was sharp and alert. ''What's going on out there?''

''Something very weird's just happened,'' Lori told him, outlining the events of the past few hours. When she had finished, Schofield was silent for a moment.

Then he said, ''You're sure it's not a setup?''

''Herb Baker doesn't think so. He claims everything tallies with our computer records.''

Schofield whistled softly. ''Wow, what have we got here?''

''The question is, do I notify the Soviets? They're bound to pick up the signals themselves sooner or later, but strictly speaking, under the terms of the Drinov Agreement, we should contact them without delay. That's what the rule book says.''

''Any word from Washington yet?''

''Not a murmur, Francis.''

''Then forget the rule book for the moment. Sit tight while I sort things out. I'll be at the center in twenty minutes.''

Lori's lips twitched. ''I had a feeling you might.''

\* \* \*

Lori was sitting in the canteen when she heard the loud-speaker. "Will Miss Madden report to the SSOS director's office at once?"

She tapped lightly on Francis Schofield's door and found him talking to a rotund man in an expensive business suit who glanced at her speculatively as she entered. The newcomer, despite his girth, moved like a dancer, his corpulent frame balanced expertly on the balls of his feet.

"Come in, Lori," Francis Schofield said. "I'd like you to meet Louis Wesker. Mr. Wesker is special consultant for counterespionage and national security at the White House. He's also former CIA."

She frowned in surprise, staring at the visitor's diminutive rotund figure.

Wesker smiled indulgently. "You thought all agents were supposed to be lean and mean. Well, I'm the new model, Miss Madden. Cuddly."

His head barely reached Lori's shoulder. Everything about him looked scrupulously tended and manicured, and she had the feeling he would regard untidiness as the deepest depravity.

"Have there been any further developments this morning?" he asked.

"On the signals, no. The signature's still bleeping, but it's getting weaker by the hour."

"You do have a fix, though, on its position?"

"Right. However, there's a problem. According to our calculations, the transmitter is submerged, under water."

"Any idea how deep?"

"Approximately three thousand feet."

"Three thousand?"

"That's what our computers say."

Wesker breathed deeply. "Well, at least that's an improvement on the Russian view. They figured the spacecraft had sunk beyond reach."

"Mr. Wesker," Lori said, "if this vessel crashed fourteen years ago, what makes it so important today?"

"I'll come to that in a minute. First, I wonder if you can throw any light on this affair?"

She folded her arms. "Well, as far as I can gather from the computer records, *Suchko Twenty-three* was a traditional rocket using an F-One booster based on the SS-Nine, suitable for both long-range and suborbital firings. In those days, the

Soviets scorned the use of shuttles. They relied on an assortment of time-tested heavy-lift vehicles powered by liquid fuel rather than solid propellants. According to our information, *Suchko Twenty-three* was launched at an inclination of forty-nine and a half degrees, thrusting it into a low elliptical orbit of three hundred twenty-five by a hundred thirty-three miles. All things being equal, she should have shed her manned capsule in the vicinity of *Salyut Fifty-six*, but at this stage, we have no way of knowing precisely what went wrong."

"It would be impossible, however, for anyone to have survived in there?"

"After fourteen years under the Antarctic ice? Hardly."

Wesker pursed his lips, his sleek hair giving off slivers of refracted light. "Miss Madden, I understand you've been cleared to a security level of Class G-Three?"

"That's right."

"I'm about to take you far beyond that, so I must emphasize the need for discretion."

Lori glanced at Schofield. "What's going on here, Francis?"

"Let Mr. Wesker explain, Lori."

"I need a consultant," Wesker continued. "Someone familiar with rockets and their design. I've asked Mr. Schofield to transfer you to my department for the next couple of weeks."

"What about Ops and Signals?"

"Herb Baker can handle things until you return," Schofield said. "This is far more important."

"But there must be dozens of scientists you can choose."

"Not with your experience," Wesker maintained. "The situation's kind of delicate, and I don't want to recruit people who aren't already involved."

Lori moved to the open window. It was an intriguing prospect, working for the White House, not one she encountered every day of the week.

"How soon do you need me to start?" she asked.

"What about now? My jet is waiting at the Executive Airport, and there's someone in Washington who very much wants to meet you."

"He's talking about the President, Lori," Schofield interjected.

"What?"

"The President," Wesker confirmed.

She pressed her fingers against her hair. She couldn't

believe what she was hearing here. "I'll have to pinch myself to see if this is real."

"It's no dream, Miss Madden. It's more in the nature of what you might call a command. And I must tell you, we're running against the clock."

Something in Wesker's manner, his air of utter determination, filled Lori with panic. "I'll have to go back to my apartment. I'll need clothes, makeup."

"You can take care of that later."

"I look like something the cat dragged in, for heaven's sake. The President will think he has a scarecrow in the White House."

Wesker's lips twitched as he took her arm, steering her firmly toward the door. She caught a whiff of his cologne, fragrant and expensive.

"If all scarecrows looked like you, Miss Madden," he said, "I reckon I'd never have left the farm."

Washington looked stately in the afternoon sunlight. Sitting in the limousine, Lori gazed through the sun-tinted windows at the majestic marble buildings lining Pennsylvania Avenue. She had scarcely spoken during their brief flight from Titusville, and Louis Wesker had seemed content to leave her to her private thoughts.

She glimpsed Lafayette Square and the familiar outline of the White House, and felt her stomach tense.

Pulling to a halt at the north entrance, Wesker shepherded her past the portico security desk and through a complex labyrinth of corridors. To Lori's surprise, the building was flooded with people; it might have been the headquarters of some major business corporation rather than the residence of the President of the United States.

"How can Mr. Clayman live among such turmoil?" she wondered aloud.

"He doesn't. These are the state rooms, the part of the White House the visitor sees. The President's quarters are on the second floor of the west wing."

He paused at an ordinary-looking door, flanked by two Secret Service men.

"This is where I leave you."

Lori felt a flash of panic. "Aren't you coming in?"

"I've said all I have to say already. The President's secretary will look after you from here."

He waved Lori inside, and she found herself in a spacious anteroom where a crewcut young man appraised her coolly. "You are Miss Lori Madden?"

"Yes."

"Please go in, Miss Madden. The President is expecting you."

Lori paused, her fingers on the door handle, then, taking a deep breath, stepped inside. To her disappointment, she found herself not in the Oval Office, as she'd expected, but in a large airy cabinet room. Light and spacious, it carried a smell that was strangely antiseptic, as if foreign odors would not be tolerated within its confines. Portraits of former presidents lined its walls, and the plush carpet was dominated by a motif of the American Eagle.

A group of people sat around a magnificent mahogany table, framed and to some extent magnified by the beveled green-tinted windows at their rear. Each individual had a name plaque fixed on the back of his chair. Lori recognized Lawrence Clayman, and the Vice President, Randolph Guthrie, but the others were strangers to her. They were mostly men in their late forties and early fifties, conservatively dressed. The only woman present looked elegant and refined in a simple black suit and a polo-necked sweater.

Lori studied the President nervously, noting the wide mouth, the dark compelling eyes. Leaning back in his chair, he lifted his arm to emphasize some point, and Lori noticed that his wrist was heavily bandaged. She remembered that the President had sprained a muscle during an assassination attempt several days before.

Lawrence Clayman paused in midsentence, glancing at the newcomer inquiringly. "You must be Lori Madden?"

"Yes, sir."

"Come in." The President waved Lori to an empty chair. "You'll probably recognize Vice President Guthrie and Secretary of State Dan Edwards. This is Secretary of Defense Dave Richner, Director of Central Intelligence Phil Howell, and the Chairman of the Joint Chiefs of Staff, Admiral John Reeves. You already know Hal McCafferty, director of NASA. And this is my chief of staff, Jan Marisa Bowering."

Lori nodded uncomfortably as she settled herself in the seat.

"Would you care for something to drink, Miss Madden?" Clayman asked. "Coffee?"

"Nothing, thank you. I . . . I guess I'm a little unglued by what's going on today."

"I can understand that. If you want the truth, I'm a little unglued myself."

The President leaned forward, folding his arms on the table. For the second time, Lori became conscious of the almost hypnotic quality in his eyes.

"Those signals you picked up this morning, what do you make of them?"

Lori glanced at the people surrounding her. Like the President, they studied her closely. "Well, it seems beyond human belief that anyone could still be alive inside *Suchko Twenty-three*. Therefore, we're left with the assumption that the spacecraft computer recorded the message at the time of the disaster fourteen years ago, and for some inexplicable reason has suddenly started transmitting them again."

"I was thinking more in terms of the message itself."

"I would assume, based on what I heard, that the vessel was under attack immediately prior to reentering the earth's atmosphere."

The President said, "That is our interpretation precisely."

"Miss Madden." Jan Bowering spoke for the first time. She reminded Lori of the old-time movie star, Joan Crawford. "*Suchko Twenty-three* was a routine spaceflight designed— ostensibly at least—to man the Soviet *Salyut Fifty-six* station orbiting around the earth. Until now, it was always assumed it developed difficulties just above the stratosphere and crashed into the ice pack off the Antarctic coastline."

"I remember the incident," Lori said. "It was headline news at the time."

"Four cosmonauts were trapped inside the *Suchko*'s hull. The Soviets never managed to recover their bodies. They made several attempts to locate the orbiter, but in the end decided to leave it where it was, on the ocean bed."

"You do appreciate," the President broke in, "that what we are discussing here is extremely sensitive?"

Lori's mouth felt dry. "I understand, Mr. President."

Jan Bowering continued, "You were correct in your assumption, Miss Madden. *Suchko Twenty-three was* attacked prior to reentry. In fact, it was deliberately shot down. The attack was carried out by NORAD, the North American Air Defense Command. The operation was conducted from

NORAD's headquarters inside Cheyenne Mountain. *Suchko Twenty-three* was disabled by shrapnel hurled directly into its path by F-Twenty-two antisatellite missiles.''

"The world was different then, Miss Madden," the President said. "We regarded the Russians as our principal enemies, and they felt similarly about us. After the Gorbachev era, things changed dramatically, but in those days, our relationship with the Soviet Union was a precarious one, to say the least. However, here's the unbelievable part. Nobody knows why that attack was carried out. All reference to the *Suchko* operation has been deleted from the computer banks. All files and documents have been systematically shredded.''

*"Suchko Twenty-three,"* Jan Bowering went on gravely, "was neutralized on information received from a Soviet double agent, Alexander Zystev. Apart from that name, we have no evidence—no existing evidence, that is—to suggest why it should have been destroyed.''

"Surely somebody must remember. Fourteen years is hardly a lifetime.''

"The head of NORAD knew, as did the director of Central Intelligence at the time. Unfortunately, both men are now dead, and the personnel taking part in the operation were strictly compartmentalized. They can tell us when and how it was carried out, but not why. The motive behind the attack has been meticulously erased.''

"You do understand my position, Miss Madden?" the President said. "In six weeks' time, I travel to Moscow to finalize details on the last phase of the Centaur Program, promoting the concept of space cooperation. Now I discover that fourteen years ago, American military personnel shot down an apparently innocent Soviet spacecraft with four Russian cosmonauts on board. Not only am I unable to explain this extraordinary act, but I'm equally unable to throw any light on the motives behind it. If the Soviets discover the truth, it could mean everything we've achieved during the past few years will disintegrate.''

Lori was silent for a moment. Her first flush of nervousness had passed. "It's only a matter of time before the Russians pick up the *Suchko*'s signals. And when they do, they're bound to try and recover her.''

The President agreed. "And with the recent advances in underwater technology, they'll probably succeed. Which is why we have to get there first.''

" 'First'?" Lori echoed.

"We've built up a level of trust with the Soviets. Now that the hard-line Communists are back in control, it may be a precarious trust, but it's a trust nevertheless, and I will not sit back and watch it go down the drain. We must beat them to *Suchko Twenty-three* and discover what made the spacecraft so dangerous that we had no alternative but to shoot it out of the sky."

"Thanks to your people," Jan Bowering declared, "we do have a precise location at last, and there are at least eight submersibles that could carry out the job. Unfortunately, they are all at the National Oceanographic Unit in California, and by the time we transport them to the Antarctic, the Soviets will probably already be in position. Also—" she paused gloomily, "there's another critical aspect to consider. *Suchko Twenty-three* is Soviet property, and strictly speaking, we have no right to interfere. If the United States attempts a salvage operation, it could help to compound our guilt. It'll be awfully difficult making a denial stick if American personnel are spotted trying to recover the evidence."

Lori considered the problem for a moment. "Why not ask the British?"

She felt the eyes of the room suddenly center upon her, and her cheeks flushed.

"The British?" the President said.

"Well, we supplied their SAS with submersible equipment more than a year ago, and I know they're using it to protect their oil rigs off the Antarctic Peninsula."

The President considered the suggestion. "But that would mean taking them into our confidence."

"Yes, sir. They are, after all, our allies."

"Just the same, in a situation like this, with such far-reaching implications . . ."

"Implications that also affect Britain. I feel sure that if we explained the delicacy of this mission—" Lori hesitated, wondering if she had overstepped an invisible line, "well, somewhere down there, they must have a man capable of carrying it out."

# THREE

"Bearing?"

"One-one-five, Skipper."

"Starboard two degrees."

Garrett increased pressure on the forward thrusters, and the tiny submersible picked up speed, burrowing its way through the oppressive curtain of slivered light and darkness that hung above the ocean bed. Through the viewing ports, the water looked luminous in places, its silvery columns dotted with tiny shreds of floating matter that brushed against the titanium sphere on the submersible's outer hull. The vessel was small and bulbous, its short marrowlike dimensions almost toylike in comparison with a full-size submarine, but it could plumb depths few naval war vessels could even begin to dream of.

Lieutenant Toby Jeavson, twenty-six, rosy-cheeked and tousled-haired, checked the scanning sonar, his fingers fumbling with the panel buttons. He noticed the intensity in Garrett's face as the major leaned forward, manipulating the controls. In the thin light from the viewing port, Garrett's features looked jagged and uneven, and Jeavson saw his eyes gleaming in the semidarkness.

"Try her again," Garrett ordered. He reached for the hand-operated instrument console that controlled the camera-and-video robot attached to the submersible's hull.

"Spot on," Jeavson muttered.

"Keep her locked on course." Garrett eased the craft gently through the gloom.

A school of penguins darted by, their flashing white bellies dazzlingly bright in the dim translucent current. Despite the insidious chill seeping through the submersible's hull, Jeavson's underclothes felt sticky against his body. He could see Garrett's face creased in concentration, peering through the forward viewing port.

An elephant seal, its ugly snout quivering with curiosity, hovered above them like a floating kite. Jeavson glimpsed the small beady eyes, the yellow teeth, the elongated nose.

Garrett chuckled dryly. "I didn't know your mother-in-law was holidaying here."

Jeavson's mouth felt dry, and Garrett glanced at him sideways. "That was a joke."

"Yes, sir."

"To laugh at, dammit."

Jeavson grimaced. "I don't feel much like laughing today, Skipper."

"You're not going to turn sour on me, are you, Toby? I get enough of that in the Officers' Mess."

"I'm a little edgy, that's all. We could get our heads blown off if this goes wrong."

"That'll be the day."

Garrett was a strange man. Different from anyone Jeavson had met before. In some respects, he wasn't like a soldier at all. Reckless and unpredictable, Garrett didn't relate, didn't conform. Tall, muscular, and athletic, he had a friendly smile and an easy manner, but Jeavson recalled the first time he'd ever set eyes on Major Zachary Paul Garrett, huddled over a table in the Officers' Mess. He'd thought him a dangerous man then, and despite Garrett's geniality, he saw no reason to alter that assessment. Nobody messed with Garrett when Garrett was drunk; that was the first lesson Jeavson had learned on the base. The second was that no one could ask for a better companion when the going got rough.

"Check the atmosphere," Garrett ordered, using his elbow to wipe the Plexiglas.

Jeavson scanned the line of gauges in front of him. "We've another four hours yet, sir."

"Quids-in then."

Beneath the submersible hull, the ocean bed bobbed and

dipped. Jagged outcrops loomed through the eddying current, cluttered with clouds of breeding krill. Jeavson glimpsed a school of porpoises, their long bodies sublimely graceful as they soared past the submersible's camera robot, vanishing into the encircling gloom.

Jeavson glanced at the sonar panel. "Almost there. Bearing zero-five-two."

Dimly, merging and solidifying amid the rippling shadows in front, something symmetrical was taking shape. As they approached, the outline assumed detail and definition, and Jeavson recognized the base of the Argentine drilling rig.

"We've done it," he hissed, lowering his voice.

Garrett's face was chiseled into a frozen mask. "Lights."

Jeavson reached down to the control panel. For the sake of stealth, they had made the journey blind, but once the lights went on, they faced the risk of being spotted from the platform above. Jeavson flicked the switch, and the lamp beams sliced through the water's fluctuating wall, pinning the rig base in a dazzling phosphorescent glare. Garrett brought the submersible to a crawl and sent the camera robot winging forward on its extended arm, operating the instrument console with his left hand. Jeavson heard a soft purring sound as Garrett's thumb engaged the video machine.

Attached to their hull, the tiny robot explored the foundations of the Argentine oil platform—probing, hovering, taping, recording.

Jeavson struggled to hide his tension as the minutes slowly stretched. Garrett seemed unperturbed. Features taut, he was easing the robot into crevices and hollows, twisting the camera this way and that. There were times, Jeavson had to admit, that he felt very nervous in Garrett's company. There was an air of indomitability in the man; you couldn't stop him. He was like a bulldozer when his mind was set.

A signature on the sonar panel caught Jeavson's attention. "Bandits," he whispered sharply.

Garrett's eyes flickered, but he kept his gaze on the camera robot in front.

"Looks like a motorboat."

Jeavson watched the signature strengthening. "It's circling, Major. We've been tumbled."

"One more shot," Garrett insisted. "I just want to get those couplings registered. They look kind of innovative."

Jeavson's mouth turned even drier. Mesmerized, he watched the sonar panel where the signature was hovering now, its blip ominously stationary. There was no longer any doubt in Jeavson's mind. The bloody Argies knew they were here.

Something dropped into the water, and Jeavson saw it clearly through the starboard viewing port, small, dark, and rectangular—not far distant—a 100, maybe a 150 yards. "Zach," he exclaimed breathlessly, "they're depth-charging!"

Garrett cursed under his breath as he worked the hand-control set. The robot reeled backward. "Bloody fools, what are they trying to do, blow up their own bloody oil well?"

The explosion almost turned the submersible over.

Jeavson saw a blinding flash of light, felt the impact of the detonation shuddering through their hull, held furiously to the control panel as the vessel rocked to port, its rivets squeaking ominously. He heard a hissing sound above his head, and ran his thumb along the panel of dials and gauges in front. A red light flashed in warning.

"Zach, we've got to get out of here! The power module's leaking."

"Easy, Squire," Garrett said in a soothing voice, locking the robot into position. Engaging the reverse thrusters, he sent the craft sliding backward. Jeavson heard the hissing increasing above his head. Garrett's face flushed with excitement.

Jeavson saw a second depth charge drifting through the gloom, and, teeth clenched, braced himself for the impact. The explosion came almost simultaneously, and Jeavson clung dizzily to the insulation pipes. Another explosion followed the first, hurling the submersible into a dizzy sideways spin. Clumps of tangled marine vegetation, ripped up by the roots, bounded around them like whirling tumbleweed. Mushroom sandbursts spurted from the bottom, turning the water into a turbid gray blur.

Garrett flicked off the lights, his hands incredibly steady. A fourth explosion rocked their vessel, and Garrett spun the wheel, his knuckles showing white through the skin. The submersible strained and creaked as the shock waves hit it. Then, in the suffocating fumes, Jeavson heard another sound and for a moment, couldn't believe his ears. His blood chilled as he realized with astonishment he hadn't been mistaken.

Garrett was laughing.

\* \* \*

The roar of the engines lulled Lori's senses. Swathed in her padded duvet jacket, she felt warm and comfortable, despite the ice forming on the aircraft's windshield. With Louis Wesker, she had flown overnight from Washington to Buenos Aires, changing planes for the long hop over the snowcapped Andes to Santiago, Chile. From there, they had taken a series of short hops down the South American coastline, boarding a British transport plane at Tierra del Fuego for the last stage of their journey to Britain's Shackleton oil base on the Antarctic Peninsula.

Wesker looked ludicrous in his padded survival gear. His diminutive height and enormous girth made him seem almost balloonlike in proportion, and she couldn't rid herself of the idea that his body was about to explode at any second. But she had to admit he was an engaging companion, with a wry and infectious sense of humor.

The events of the past twenty-four hours had nearly overwhelmed Lori. It seemed hard to believe that only yesterday she had been a task supervisor at Cape Canaveral. Now, amazingly, she was embarked on a secret mission at the direct orders of the President himself.

Lori's body ached in all the most disagreeable places, and she longed for a chance to stretch out and rest. She gazed down at the sea below, glimpsing a ragged, snowcapped mountain rising directly out of the foam-crested water.

"That's Elephant Island," the pilot told her. "It gets its name because it's populated by huge herds of elephant seals."

Snow coated the mountain's upper peak, but the lower slopes looked gray and black, like volcanic ash. "It's pretty barren," Lori remarked.

"Shackleton's men wintered there in 1917, after their vessel sank in the Weddel Sea. He rowed across Drake's Passage in an open boat to seek help. After a year-and-a-half on the ice, he brought out every one of his men alive."

"How far's the mainland?" Wesker inquired.

"Almost there. You'll see the coastline in a second or two. After that, we start descending. We'll be landing at Shackleton in about fifteen minutes, providing the Argies leave us alone."

He grinned at her over his shoulder. "They've got fighter planes defending their oil installations. They like to buzz us from time to time, just to keep us on our toes."

"You mean we could be in danger here?"

"Not unless the pilots miscalculate. Saber rattling is all it is. The Argies figure the Grahamland Peninsula belongs exclusively to them. We British disagree, but since the last Labor government handed the Falkland Islands over to Argentina, there's precious little we can do. We've no deep-water ports in the South Atlantic to support a retaliatory task force, and the Argies know it. They ruffle our feathers once in a while to demonstrate just how vulnerable we are."

"Terrific. Does anyone get hurt?"

"A few close shaves, but no casualties yet."

Lori glared at Wesker. "Nobody warned me I was dropping into a combat zone."

"Oh, they're great people, really," the pilot said. "When one of our helicopters went down, they sent out a rescue team to pick up the survivors. It's a sort of love-hate relationship. We jostle them a bit, they jostle us."

Lori stared out at the landscape taking shape below. High mountains rose as far as the eye could see, their snowcapped summits framed against the azure sky. In the valleys, black crags towered above jagged ice fissures, and to the east lay the adjacent coastline. She thought she had never seen anything quite so beautiful.

"It's breaktaking. I always thought Antarctica was simply a wilderness of snow and ice."

The pilot raised his voice above the engine's roar. "This is summertime. Everyone's surprised when they see how spectacular the place is in summertime. And it's more than just physical beauty. It's that weird feeling you get when you know you're at the end of the world."

The aircraft descended, picking its way through the twisting sprawl of snowcapped mountain peaks, and Lori gazed in wonder at the serrated ice walls tumbling thousands of feet below. The summits parted as they approached the coast, and there were countless oil rigs scattered across the icebound ocean. To their left, she saw a tiny runway.

The pilot brought them down expertly, taxiing to a halt in front of a corrugated-iron hangar. An army staff car stood on the ice-glazed road where a British officer in survival gear was stamping about in the chill.

"Welcome to Antarctica," the pilot said cheerfully. "That's Major Watson, the admin officer here. He'll look after your creature comforts."

"Thank you for getting us in safely," Lori said.

"Don't thank me. Thank the Argies."

The British officer walked toward them as Lori and Wesker alighted. He was tall and slender with a handlebar moustache.

"Mr. Wesker, Miss Madden, glad to meet you. Any trouble landing?"

"Smooth as a whistle," Wesker muttered.

"Good. I was a little afraid the Argies might start playing silly buggers again. They caught us filming one of their oil rigs the other day. Started a right old row, it has. We're expecting some kind of retaliatory action. I'm relieved you didn't end up on the receiving end."

A corporal in padded combat fatigues collected their baggage from the cargo hold, and they drove into camp along the blacktop roadway. The buildings were stark and austere in the wintry sunlight, the hut rows linked by single corridor units, with larger structures marking the compound's central enclosure. Barbed-wire fences encircled the periphery, punctuated by skeletal machine-gun turrets and sandbagged artillery emplacements.

"Looks like you're expecting trouble," Wesker commented.

The British officer laughed. " 'Train hard, fight easy,' that's the Russian maxim. So far, the most we've had to endure has been a little Argentine breast-beating, but we believe in boxing clever. We've got a lot of oil workers living on this camp, and those rigs represent a considerable investment to the British taxpayer. We'd be a little bonkers if we didn't take steps to protect that."

"Have they told you what we're doing here?"

"Not my sphere, Mr. Wesker. The order came from the very top, which makes you quite a celebrity in these parts."

"What about cooperation?"

"Already assigned. Major Garrett, SAS. You'll find none better, not even for ready money. He specializes in deepwater explorations. Normally, that's the role of the Special Boat Squadron, but Major Garret is an expert in the use of the ANSAAD."

"ANSAAD?"

Watson said, "We use particle-beam technology to locate oil wells on the ocean bed. It's quicker than the traditional method, but the problem lies in focusing its magnetic power. The ANSAAD's complex and difficult to operate, which is why we have to rely on skilled professionals like Garrett."

"Where is Major Garrett?"

"You'll meet him tonight. He'll be in the Officers' Mess."

"What's wrong with now?"

The officer looked surprised. "I thought you'd like to rest. It's quite a haul from Washington, D.C."

"Time's critical, Major. We need to move fast."

Watson hesitated. "I must warn you, Major Garrett can be a little difficult at times."

"Difficult?"

'He's not what you might call the acquiescent type. Don't get me wrong. He's a splendid fellow and all that. Marvelous company when he's in the mood. But as I say, he *can* be difficult."

"Major, we appreciate your concern, but we're racing against the clock."

"Very well. I'll take you directly to his quarters."

They passed through the security gate and skidded to a halt outside a building with a Union Jack fluttering from its roof.

"This is where Major Garrett resides," the British officer said, helping Lori to alight. "He's off duty today, which can mean one of two things. Either he'll be relaxed and delighted to see you, or—" He paused as a resounding crash echoed from inside the hut's interior and they heard a male voice cursing profusely. Watson looked apologetic. "It's not the perfect moment, I'm afraid."

"I'm sure we'll be able to handle Major Garrett," Wesker said.

"Okay, sir. It's *your* funeral."

Watson tapped twice on the hut door, easing it cautiously open. "Zach?"

A metal mug ricocheted off the wall above Watson's head. "Can't you see I'm busy?" a voice thundered.

"Zach, I've brought some people to see you."

Watson swung the door fully open, and Lori glimpsed a narrow bunk, a paneled wardrobe, a bedside locker. The odor of paint filled her nostrils, and in front of an artist's easel, its canvas carefully positioned to catch the light, she saw a man in a paint-smeared smock. He was tall, not unnaturally so but tall enough to dominate the cramped confines of his living quarters. His body looked hard and angular, like a professional athlete's. His face, creased with laughter lines, looked fierce in the dazzling Antarctic sunlight, and his hair, thick and tousled, was streaked with silvery flecks above the temples. He looked—not mad exactly but imbued with some dark restless energy, as if he had a fire smoldering inside. His face was wholly masculine, but amid its rugged contours she discerned something that surprised her—a hint of sensitivity, even aestheticism.

Garrett ran his fingers through his unruly hair as the visitors stepped warily over the threshold. "For God's sake, Felix, bring them back later, will you? I'm up to my armpits here. I've been struggling for hours, and I can't seem to get the bloody thing right."

"What's wrong with it?" Watson asked.

"Something's missing. I don't know what. It lacks force, life."

Lori felt strangely nervous as she moved across the linoleum floor. She sensed the man's anger and frustration, and stepped to one side so she could view the canvas more clearly. Her breath caught in her throat.

The painting depicted the ocean bed, a mystical fusion of light and shade. In the left-hand corner, a hammerhead shark was tearing at the carcass of a dead seal pup, and the artist had tried to contrast the placid tranquillity of the foreground with the macabre activity in the background. The daring composition of his color harmonies aroused Lori's admiration. He had used a light luminous gray to accentuate the clear blues and greens.

There was no denying the painting's vigor and power, but she could see why the man felt dissatisfied.

"You're trying to achieve simplicity by indulging in eccentric color," she told him. "You need to lighten your palette, modify the freshness of the sea."

The man stared at her. There was a smear of paint on his nose, another coating the hollow below his left cheekbone. His eyes, crinkled against the sun, were scarcely discernible beneath his heavy brow.

He threw his paintbrush on the table. "You two," he snapped, jerking his head at Wesker and Watson, "out."

Wesker started to protest, but Watson stopped him with a discreet hand on his forearm.

"She stays," the artist said coolly.

Watson shepherded Wesker to the open door. "Time for a nip, I think, before they close the mess. You'll find us a hospitable lot here. We get so bored with each other's company, we welcome visitors with open arms. Even the Argies."

"But . . ." Wesker protested as Watson shut the hut door.

"Don't interfere. Take my advice and let them thrash it out. I have the happiest feeling at the back of my nostrils that Major Zachary Paul Garrett is about to meet his Waterloo."

Inside the hut, Lori felt the man's eyes upon her. She saw the intelligence in his gaze and a penetrating insight that seemed to bore into her very soul.

"Who are you?" he demanded.

"My name's Lori Madden."

A flash of understanding showed in his face. "The American scientist."

He moved toward her, stepping slightly to one side so that he was standing at an angle to the canvas. "How do you know about painting?"

"I used to paint, myself. A long time ago."

"Then perhaps you can tell me where I'm going wrong."

She had the feeling she was on trial as she examined the picture carefully. It was undeniably brilliant. It carried a unique freshness of style, and she knew it wouldn't take much to put it right.

"What are you hoping to achieve?"

"I don't know. I've been trying to create a feeling of richness by using a diversity of tints, but all I seem to do is destroy the integrity of the lines."

"You've worked too hard," she told him. "You have to remember a picture is composed of rhythms. Break those rhythms and you destroy the harmony. By using complementary shades, you can produce a much more striking effect. You can indicate volume, space, light by using rapid passages of the brush, like this."

She took the paintbrush from where Garrett had thrown it and swiftly added a few delicate touches, reducing the sea to a series of semitransparent nuances that separated the areas of color, underlining their richness.

Garrett stared at her. "By God, I've been trying to achieve that effect for hours, and you capture it in less than a minute."

"Beginner's luck, I guess."

"That was more than just luck."

His face broke into a friendly grin, and suddenly the fierceness disappeared. She was astonished at the transformation. In the twinkling of an eye, he had switched from truculence to sociability. "Do all NASA scientists look like you?" he asked.

"Only the female variety."

"You're not what I expected, not a bit."

"Disappointed?"

"On the contrary. Pleasantly surprised. It's not often we get a woman on the base. Who's your friend? CIA?"

"Mr. Wesker is an intelligence consultant at the White House."

"Well, welcome to our humble outpost. We'll try and make your visit comfortable."

He opened the locker and took out a bottle of whiskey. "Drink?"

"Isn't it a little early in the day?"

"This is Antarctica. Time doesn't have much meaning here."

Filling two glasses, he pushed one into her hand. Lori struggled to steer the conversation to more businesslike lines.

"How much have they told you about this mission?"

"Only that you want me to reach a submerged spacecraft. Three thousand feet, they said."

"That's a conservative estimate. Think you can do it?"

"Why not? We've got the equipment, and we've got the location. The question is . . ."

He tossed down his drink and promptly poured another. "Why? Three thousand feet is a long way down. Anything goes wrong, I might not come out alive. When the odds are stacked against me, I like to know the reason."

"I can't tell you the reason. It's classified."

He laughed shortly. "In that case, get yourself another boy."

"I thought soldiers were supposed to obey orders."

"This is an above-and-beyond job. Strictly voluntary. I go if I'm interested. If not . . ." He shrugged. "Go ahead, interest me."

"Major Garrett, I'd tell you everything if I could, but this is a security matter. We operate strictly on a need-to-know basis. That's the rule."

"Change the rule. I'm not sticking my neck in a noose for some faceless bureaucrat in Washington. Tell me what it's all about, then let me decide if it's worth it. That's the only way we'll operate."

"Major Watson was right. He said you'd be difficult."

"Major Watson's my PR man. You can see why I'm not doing too well on the social scene."

"You do realize you're putting me on the line?"

"Now that, I have to admit, is an intriguing prospect."

"What do I tell Wesker? He's sworn me to secrecy."

"Tell him I wheedled it out of you with my irresistible sex appeal."

Lori sighed. "Well, I guess if you're risking your life, you've got a right to know the truth."

She was disobeying orders, she knew, but without Garrett, what could they hope to achieve?

In a few swift sentences, she outlined the details surrounding *Suchko Twenty-three,* and when she had finished, Garrett said, "You're not seriously suggesting someone could still be alive down there?"

"After fourteen years? Of course not. It has to be a defective computer."

"But you think the Russians will try to reach it too?"

"The *Suchko* is Soviet property. We're not the only ones monitoring those signals. They're bound to be curious."

"And if they discover the vessel didn't crash by accident . . ."

"Will you do it?" she demanded.

Garrett tossed back the remains of his drink. In the sunlight, his eyes looked wild and roguish. "Do it? I wouldn't miss it for the world."

After the quarrel, Sergei Malenov stood on the balcony, the chill night air biting through his flimsy clothing. In the street below, traffic roared along Torsino Avenue toward Jauza and the river. Lights gleamed in the windows of the university buildings, and from where he stood, he could see the streetlights forming a dazzling grid around Gorky Park. Moscow was like a chameleon in winter, he thought; amid the glare and the snow-filled streets, its true nature was hidden.

He noticed his hand was trembling as he rested it on the balcony rim. The wind picked up, scattering snow flurries into his face, and he turned his head against it. Damn fool that he was, standing here in the open. Serve him right if he froze to death, if they found him in the morning, silent and immobile, looking out across a frigid city. Then she'd regret her hasty words. Regret the way she'd stung him. Or would she? That was the awful thing about Elke. You never knew.

Shivering with cold, Malenov stepped back inside the apartment, locking the French windows carefully behind him. As he turned, he heard a sound from the opposite side of the room and saw Elke bending over the cocktail cabinet, dressed in a frilly slip reaching barely halfway down her naked thighs. He felt a thickness in his throat as he glimpsed the outline of her body framed by the lamp. She never failed to have that effect upon him. He loved her, that was the crazy part, loved her in spite of the things she did, in spite of the things she said. He just couldn't help himself.

He moved toward her as she reached for a vodka bottle, and, running his fingers through her hair, let his hand rest lightly on her naked shoulder. The warmth of her skin sent a tingling sensation along his forearm.

He felt her body stiffen.

"Don't touch me," she said without turning her head.

"I'm sorry," he whispered. "I apologize for the things I said. I was angry."

"You had no right to be angry. I'd done nothing, and you know it."

"You're right. I get these ridiculous fantasies. It only happens because I love you so."

He let his arm slide down the steep curve of her chest, cupping her breast in his right palm. He could feel the softness of her flesh, the hard thrust of her nipple through the silky material.

"Take your hand away."

"Elke."

"Do it."

Malenov's arm dropped to his side, and he stood looking at the back of her head.

"Try to see it from my point of view," he pleaded. "You're my whole life. I've given you everything in the world you need, everything you could possibly want, but I must know how you really feel. Can't you tell me, just once in a while, Elke, what you're thinking? Surely I deserve that, after all these years."

She looked calmly at his reflection in the mirror on the opposite wall. "Frankly, Sergei, I think you're a prize shit."

Malenov sucked in his breath as, clutching her drink, she strolled back to the bedroom, slamming the door behind her.

He stood there, gazing dismally at the snow flurries dancing against the windowpanes outside, then slowly exhaled, and with his fingertips, massaged the skin above his left temple. Why was she always so forthright? Lying wasn't a difficult thing. Where would the human race be if men and women didn't lie to each other?

Sergei Malenov was a colonel in the GRU, the intelligence arm of the Red Army. He was also Russia's leading exponent of the ANSAAD particle-beam accelerator. Tall, pale-cheeked, and slim-hipped, he was noted for his air of moody introspection. At 2 Dzerzhinsky Square, headquarters of the KGB where his wife, Elke, worked, he was known disparagingly as Elke's "Mongolian Poet."

The lamplight fell across a photograph standing on the cabinet top, and Malenov's face twisted in distaste. Elke, her lips parted in a mischievous smile. Himself—younger, slimmer, darker, laughing spontaneously. And Zachary Garrett. There was something different in the way Garrett laughed, something animal.

There were few people in the world Malenov hated so murderously. It was hard to believe the man had once been his friend.

He looked over at a painting that faced the window where the light could pick out its subtle nuances of texture and shade. It was a vivid nude study of Elke. Garrett had done it at Baikonur, and Elke steadfastly refused to take it down.

The apartment doorbell rang, and Malenov glanced sourly at his watch. It was almost eleven o'clock.

He found a uniformed sergeant waiting on the landing. The man snapped to attention, saluted smartly. "Colonel, you are required immediately at Section Three."

"Do you know what time it is?" Malenov asked.

"I apologize, Colonel. My orders were to collect you at once."

Another crisis. They occurred almost daily since General Misha Suivesky had taken over as director of Foreign Intelligence. Most of the matters were pointless or trivial, but it was sound policy to humor these people.

"Let me get my coat," Malenov said.

They drove through the almost deserted streets and drew to a halt in Dzerzhinsky Square. Arbatskaya Ploschad, headquarters of the GRU, stood directly opposite Lubianka, home of the KGB, though the two departments were bitter rivals.

At the end of World War II, an attempt had been made to amalgamate them, but so virulent had their antagonism proved that the Kremlin had been forced to abandon the experiment. Further conciliatory approaches had been made during the Gorbachev era when the Russians had tried hard to "humanize" their intelligence services, but the two organizations had proved irreconcilable.

The fact that Malenov's wife worked as a KGB computer operator had led to a good deal of suspicion during Malenov's early years, but his devotion to his work, and in particular his skill with the ANSAAD, had finally allayed his colleagues' misgivings.

The GRU building was divided into halves, one containing the administration offices, the other a detention center for political prisoners. Malenov flashed his identity card at the sentries on duty and made his way to General Suivesky's office on the second floor. The blinds were drawn, and a number of figures sat facing a screen on which images were being beamed from a slide projector. General Suivesky's cropped hair looked spiky in the semidarkness.

"Is that you, Sergei?" he asked as Malenov entered.

"Yes, General."

"Please take a seat. We are almost finished."

Malenov groped his way to an empty chair, staring at the picture on the screen. It showed meaningless splotches of white and gray, a gridwork of cross hairs marking longitude and latitude.

"This photograph was taken by our satellite P-two, three-oh-oh-six," General Suivesky said. "If you look closely, you will observe the outline of the Antarctic Peninsula. Here" —he used a ruler to point out a section in the picture's upper left-hand rim—"is the area in which we are interested."

The camera operator flicked the "proceed" switch, and the image altered. Now there was nothing but varying shades of gray.

"This is the same section, magnified a thousand times," Suivesky said. "It shows the ice cap covering the Weddel Sea. Our experts say it's a comprehensive layer, but relatively thin. It can be breached by a sturdy icebreaker."

He raised his voice. "Lights, please."

Malenov blinked rapidly as the room suddenly brightened. Easing back in his chair, he glanced around him at the high-ranking officers and security men who sat impassively.

"We have an icebreaking vessel stationed at Pavlic Harbor on the western flank of the Antarctic mainland. It carries a deep-sea submersible and deep-water diving gear. Using a particle-beam accelerator, locating the wreck should be a relatively straightforward matter. Arrangements have been made for Colonel Malenov, our leading ANSAAD specialist, to join the vessel and take command of the operation."

Malenov sat up, startled. "General?"

Beneath the fluorescent lamps, General Suivesky's face looked almost paternal. "You remember *Suchko Twenty-three*?"

Malenov thought for a moment. "The spacecraft which crashed into the Weddel Sea?"

Suivesky said, "We've found it at last."

"How?"

"Very simple. It has started transmitting distress signals."

"General, *Suchko Twenty-three* crashed fourteen years ago. How can a dead vessel suddenly spring to life?"

"That," Suivesky answered, "is what you are being sent to find out."

He tossed his ruler on the desk and fumbled in his tunic for a packet of cigarettes. Placing one between his lips, he lit it carefully. His skin looked pale, and somehow its pallor seemed accentuated by his cropped white hair. "The signals have presented us with a difficult dilemma. We thought the spacecraft secure beneath the Antarctic ice cap. Now we discover it is lying at a depth of little more than one thousand meters. Moreover, judging by the communications, it would appear the *Suchko* did not crash by accident as we originally imagined but was the victim of a deliberate attack. Our friends in Washington will undoubtedly have picked up the messages too. They'll be curious, as we are. Though officially we regard them as our friends, they have grown increasingly suspicious since it became necessary to reestablish communist principles in the Kremlin."

He stared at Malenov bleakly, smoke drifting from his nostrils. In the harsh light from the striplamps, his face looked lined and tired. "You understand the danger, Colonel Malenov. Whatever happens, you must reach the *Suchko* before the Americans."

# FOUR

The miniature sea battle had been noisy and exuberant, and the trees above London's Hyde Park echoed with applause as Eli Kozani, operating his radio console from the shoreline, brought his model naval fleet into an impressive "sail-past" finale. Bellman waited until the spectators had begun to disperse, then picked his way through the ducks padding about the concrete foreshore and approached Kozani, who was on his knees, dismantling the complex array of radio equipment. Kozani was a medium-size man, gray-haired and heavyset, one eye slightly out of alignment.

"That was quite a show," Bellman said.

Kozani glanced up at him, his bad eye flickering in the wintry sunlight.

"Simple electronics. The kids love it."

"Not just the kids. Half the population of London, I'd say."

Kozani shrugged. "It amuses me. It may look easy, but it isn't. Those ships are controlled by radio signals. Some of them are quite intricate."

"I know. What a waste of an extraordinary talent."

Kozani eyed him curiously. His eras had detected something familiar in Bellman's speech patterns. "You're an American?"

"Right. John Bellman's my name. Washington, D.C."

Kozani rose to his feet, wiping his palm on the back of his pants. He held out his hand. "Tony Fraser, late of Monroe City, Missouri. I've been living here for damn near eleven years now."

"Correction," Bellman said. "Your name is Eli Kozani, and you were born and raised in Grand Island, Nebraska. You served with the Atlantic Fleet, intercepting Soviet satellite signals."

Kozani's features froze, but he kept his composure well, Bellman noted approvingly. Old habits died hard. "Trust might, trust constancy," Bellman said.

Kozani glanced around, as if fearful their conversation might be overheard. "Who are you?"

"A friend of Frank De Tabley's."

Kozani frowned. "Hey, Sammy!" he shouted to a youth who was winding in the generator wire. "Look after the ships for me, will you?" To Bellman he said, "Let's walk."

Their shoes crunched among the crisp fallen leaves.

"Okay," Kozani said at length. "Forget the double-talk. What's this all about?"

"I've come to take you home again. We need your expertise." Bellman paused, then added softly: "It's for the *Stallion*.

Kozani spat on the ground. "The *Stallion* belongs to the past."

"Wrong. It's the stairway to the future. In six weeks' time, the President will sign the final phase of the Centaur Program. Once it's ratified, our country will be at the mercy of every tinpot dictator who manages to get a vehicle into space. We have to act now, before it's too late."

Kozani moaned softly under his breath. He looked like a man who had just seen his worst fears materialize. "I'm happy here. I married again, did you know that?"

He glanced at Bellman as if seeking confirmation, even approval, but Bellman's face was expressionless.

"My wife's an Englishwoman," Kozani continued. "She's a lawyer in the city. We get on well together. I'm reluctant to see that crumble."

"You took an oath, Mr. Kozani. You are, I take it, still a patriot?"

"You don't have to ask that."

"Then you know where your duty lies."

Kozani halted, staring across the lawns in front. In the

wintry sunshine, they could see the midmorning traffic speeding down Park Lane toward Hyde Park Corner. Bellman watched the conflict of emotions in his face. Then Kozani's shoulders stooped resignedly, and Bellman knew that he had won.

"When do we leave?" Kozani asked.

"I've booked adjoining seats on the overnight plane."

"Give me an hour. I have to say good-bye to my wife."

Claggett knocked twice on the apartment door and stepped quickly into the darkened room. As he stood panting in the shadows, an arc lamp pinned him in a dazzling beam of light. Through its brilliance he discerned the outline of a human head.

"You're late," a voice said.

"Forgive me. I was held up in the city."

"Do not keep me waiting again."

Shielding his eyes against the glare, Claggett groped his way to a chair. The featureless outline regarded him stonily. "You have the information?"

"It wasn't easy, but I have it," Claggett confirmed.

He closed his eyes and began to recite. "There are fourteen ELINT satellites at present on a twenty-two three-hundred-mile circular orbit above the equator. Most are positioned to monitor missile launches from Plesetsk in the USSR, but because of the geosynchronous orbits they occupy, they are virtually useless to us. We should use instead the JAX satellites. They are multifaceted, with six communications antennae, two of which have their beams formed by one hundred forty-six phased microwave transmitters. There are eight in all, each with an orbital apogee of three hundred seventy-three miles."

"And the possibility of interception?"

"Almost none. There are two more satellites in nine-hundred-mile orbits. They were launched piggyback style, by firing on-board engines at midtrajectory. Their purpose is to check antiballistic radar units, but they are too far away to pose any realistic threat."

"You're quite certain of that?"

"I'd stake my life on it."

There was a slight pause, and Claggett heard the sound of a pen scratching on paper. He opened his eyes. Against the shimmering glare, the head was a sphere of impenetrable blackness.

"Now listen carefully. Tonight, when the Colonel has retired to bed, you will telephone this number."

A scrap of paper slid across the table toward Claggett.

"A man's voice will answer and say, 'The Orange Blossom Fruit Company.' You will ask if Uncle Sidney is there. He will reply that Uncle Sidney is attending his annual lodge benefit in Cincinnati. He will then hang up. Tomorrow, after the Colonel has left for the base, you will take a taxicab to the northwest corner of Windego Square and wait under the jeweler's clock. A woman will approach you at eleven-oh-seven and ask if the benefit turned out okay. Then, and only then, you will give her the information on the JAXs. Is that understood?"

Blinking in the lamplight, Claggett picked up the paper, slipped it into his pocket.


Nick Koster arrived at the Pentagon early. The corridors were teeming with people as an MP escorted him across the twenty-nine-acre complex to Major General Dan Connel's office on the third floor. Connel was a large man with the build of a professional football player. His crinkly black hair was brushed back from his forehead to hide a bald patch in the center of his skull.

He shook Koster's hand in the office doorway. "Trust might, trust constancy," he said.

Koster ignored the remark. He found the use of such a code juvenile. Instead, he said, "It's like a menagerie in here. How can you work in such an atmosphere?"

"We've got thirty thousand people in this building, but you get used to it in time." Connel shepherded Koster inside. "Take a seat, Nicky. It's good to see you."

He closed the door, and opening a cabinet on the wall, flicked a tiny button. A red light on the cabinet's lower rim blinked off, and a humming sound, which Koster had assumed to be the air conditioner, abruptly ceased.

"Recording machine," General Connel explained. "Everything said in this office is supposed to go down on tape. Regulations."

He pulled up a chair and settled opposite Koster, facing him across the desk. Koster leaned forward, rubbing his forehead with his fingertips. Beneath his thickly rimmed glasses, his college-boy features looked strained.

"Something wrong?" Connel inquired.

"Bit of a headache, that's all."

Connel stabbed the intercom with his finger. "Ginny, bring me a glass of water and two aspirins."

Sitting back, he examined Koster speculatively. Connel knew Koster's reputation for anxiety, but it was clear the White House aide was suffering an unusual degree of psychological stress. "You weren't happy with the committee's decision, were you, Nicky?"

"I didn't say that."

"You didn't have to. To tell the truth, I was a little surprised myself. I thought the Stallion had been consigned to the garbage heap ages ago."

Koster stared at him. "How can you look so relaxed, knowing what it entails?"

The general shrugged. "Not my responsibility. I'm a cog in the machine, that's all. And I have to admit—I know this sounds a little screwy—but it's kind of intriguing working out how to make the pieces fit."

He paused as the door opened and his secretary came into the room. She handed Koster a paper cup filled with ice water, and two aspirins. Connel watched him slip the tablets into his mouth and swallow them, grimacing.

"Better?" the general asked.

Koster placed his cup on the desktop in front of him, a hint of cognizance entering his eyes. He waited until the woman had left the room before speaking again. His voice now sounded crisp and businesslike. "How many people can you count on?"

"Four positive. Maybe a couple more after I've worked on them a bit."

"Six men? That's all?"

"It's all we need, Koster."

"For God's sake." Koster waved at the bustling corridor outside. "You've got an entire army to deal with."

Connel was patient. Nobody appreciated the delicacy—the intricacy—of deception. It took more than brains, a lot more. It took patience, fastidiousness, care.

"If you want to beat the system," he explained, "all you need to know is how the system works. Remember George

Washington, that paragon of virtue? When it came to cheating on expenses, he was the cleanup hitter in the whole damned lineup. You see, he'd learned the magic formula. Nothing's so small it can afford to be overlooked.''

''I hope you know what you're doing, General. You've got an awful lot of people to convince at NASA.''

''NASA is used to taking orders from the Pentagon. They'll play ball so long as the paperwork's right, and I'll make sure it's right. Bureaucracy's my business.''

He leaned forward, lacing his fingers on the desktop. His lips revealed a line of perfectly formed teeth, and for no reason Koster could clearly explain, he was reminded of a basking shark.

''The shuttle crew have almost completed their training,'' Connel said. ''NASA believes they're being launched into orbit to renovate a disused spy satellite. The entire operation has been funded by the government. However, once we move into the final phase, there can be no pulling back, understand? In the event of a leak, I want you to act as a buffer between the Pentagon and the White House.''

Koster considered for a moment. ''Leave it to me,'' he said.


Jan Bowering got up wearily and switched off the TV set. She had been watching the news reports of demonstrators outside the White House, a scene that was becoming depressingly familiar as the weeks sped by.

''They're objecting to the Centaur Program again,'' she sighed. ''Why doesn't somebody tell them we're simply trying to make the world a safer place to live in?''

Thrusting a drink in her hand, her husband Walter drew her gently back to the sofa. ''You're looking tired, kitten.''

''I feel tired, Walt. Dog-tired.''

She flopped into the cushions, cradling the glass against her chest.

''It's crazy. Here we are trying to protect the future of the human race, and we're being attacked like a bunch of lunatics. Does that make sense to you?''

''Nobody said politics had to make sense.''

Kneeling on the floor, Walter took off her shoes and began to massage her feet, his movements tender and soothing. Walter was Jan Bowering's third husband, a gentle bear of a man who had never raised his voice to her in anger. They had met at a political fund-raiser in Atlanta, and though it hadn't exactly been love at first sight, their relationship had proved a happy and harmonious one. A millionaire several times over, Walter Bowering seemed totally unabashed by the high-powered world in which his spouse existed.

She looked at him tenderly. "You're a good man, Walt. You're my strong right arm. More. You're what makes it all seem worthwhile."

"You'd have done it with or without my help. Nobody can argue with that."

She sipped her drink, her face weary and dispirited. She'd wanted to achieve so much, had planned, hoped, dreamed of the day she could make the President's vision a reality, and now, with success almost in her grasp, she appeared on the brink of losing everything. "Do you think we're right in what we're doing, opening up space?"

"I think you believe you're right, and that's the important thing."

"There has to be a better way, Walt. We can't go on turning the heavens into a battleground, with antisatellite systems everywhere. We've got to call a halt someplace. The Strategic Defense Initiative was threatening the stability of the entire world, which is why it had to be terminated. But suddenly, because of an idiot incident from the past, everything the President has worked toward is being thrown into jeopardy."

"Clayman can't be held responsible for what happened fourteen years ago."

"Tell that to the Russians. What are they going to think of a President who can't even explain why his own people carried out a hostile act?"

"Maybe it won't come to that."

He paused, still clutching her foot, and glanced curiously over his shoulder as the rumble of a car reached them from the drive outside. Doors slammed, and someone tugged at the heavy brass porch bell.

"Who on earth can that be at this hour of night?"

Jan Bowering heard the houseboy's footsteps moving along the passageway, and after a moment, he knocked gently at the door. "It's Mr. Koster, ma'am."

Nick Koster's face looked strangely drawn, despite the youthfulness of his features. "I'm sorry to disturb you, Mrs. Bowering, but I have some papers that need signing."

"Can't they wait until morning, Nicky?"

"Best not. I want to get them moving soonest. Besides, Mr. Brightman would like a word with you."

For the first time, Jan Bowering noticed Caryl Brightman standing behind Koster in the corridor. Brightman was the deputy national security adviser, a wiry man with a pinched, curiously impassive face.

"Caryl," Jan Bowering said, "I thought you'd be tucked up soundly in bed by now."

"I figured I ought to contact you right away. I have a compilation of the FBI's findings on last week's assassination attempt, and they make disturbing reading."

"Well, come in, don't look so somber. Can I offer you a drink?"

"No thank you. This isn't exactly a social call."

Jan Bowering looked at Nick Koster.

"Go ahead," Koster said. "I guess these papers can wait a few more minutes."

Taking the dossier from Brightman's hand, Jan Bowering thumbed through the typewritten pages. "This will take some digesting. Can't you explain it to me, Caryl? My brain is operating in neutral tonight."

Brightman sank onto the couch opposite Jan Bowering's sofa, his face bereft of emotion. "I'm afraid the conspiracy theory probably checks out. The gunman was no isolated screwball. He had guidance at the highest level. The whole thing was meticulously planned and executed."

Jan Bowering glanced meaningfully at Nick Koster. "I was afraid of that."

"It goes further," Brightman said.

"Further?"

"I mean, Mrs. Bowering, it moves into a completely new sphere."

"What are you talking about? The President was targeted because of the Centaur Program, right?"

"Right. However, there's another element involved, one we haven't been able to pinpoint yet. We've come across a number of incidental pieces of information—nothing concrete, you understand, but a little too recurrent to be pure coincidence.''

He crossed his legs, brushing at an imaginary dust speck on his thigh.

''The man who shot at the President was named Charles Wilson. He ran a security business in Alexandria—bugging, street surveillance, that sort of thing. He hired out to the big corporations, or to anyone else with the money to pay.''

''Industrial espionage?''

''Mostly. Sometimes personal—divorce lawyers, outraged husbands, whatever. He was kind of a shady character, our Mr. Wilson. He was also, paradoxically, a hero. A Medal of Honor man.''

'' 'Medal of Honor'?'' Jan Bowering echoed in surprise.

''When he was nineteen, Wilson was Special Forces in Vietnam. He was part of a guerrilla unit that moved up the Mekong River equipped with radios and wiretapping devices, infiltrating hundreds of miles inside the Chinese People's Republic. After the war, Wilson continued in the army for a while—and here's the interesting thing: Fourteen years ago, he was working with NORAD at Colorado Springs. In fact, he must have been at Cheyenne Mountain on the day *Suchko Twenty-three* was blown out of the sky.''

''That *is* strange.''

''A little too strange for me,'' Brightman admitted. ''Wilson wasn't some nut acting on his own initiative. He was part of an organized machine. And his motive appears to have had a direct connection with the shooting down of *Suchko Twenty-three*.''

He fumbled in his pocket and took out a tiny notebook, flipping through the pages. ''We've checked the records, and Wilson was missing for two periods immediately prior to and immediately following the *Suchko* operation. According to his file, he was at his married quarters, home, suffering from recurrent swamp fever, a bug he picked up in the Mekong Delta, but according to his wife, he was taking part, on each occasion, in a high-level army security exercise. We can find no reference to any such exercise in NORAD files.

''And here's the second curious factor. The man who commanded Wilson's unit in Vietnam, Major Frank De Tabley, was a CIA operative. Though attached to Special Forces, he answered to the Department for Secret Operations in Washington. The agency has a file on De Tabley, but it's spotty. There are no photographs, for example, no fingerprints. It's almost as if someone deliberately doctored the dossier so that nothing incriminating, or identifying, would remain.''

"But why is De Tabley so important?'' Nick Koster asked.

"De Tabley was one of our troubleshooters in Nam. It wasn't only wiretapping he specialized in. He was an expert in the dirty tricks department. If you wanted something done—something unsavory—De Tabley was your man. Apparently he had no feelings, as you and I understand that term. No job was too dirty, no action too extreme.''

"A psychopath,'' Jan Bowering said.

"Precisely. When Vietnam ended, De Tabley remained with the agency as a freelance, running his own private espionage network. He was good. He made several sorties into the Soviet Union, we do know that. He worked in Central and South America. Then, in 1993, he turned up in Iran, organizing unrest. De Tabley was a ruthless, brilliant operator.''

"Why does CIA insist on dealing with such people?'' Jan Bowering said.

Fumbling in his pocket, Brightman took out a packet of indigestion tablets, slipped one into his mouth, and began to chew.

"Since the opposition does disagreeable things, Mrs. Bowering, we're sometimes forced to do disagreeable things ourselves. When that becomes necessary, the agency tends to call on freelancers. It makes the source more difficult to trace. The De Tabley network was the best they had. They used them frequently.''

"Where is De Tabley now?''

"Nobody knows. Several years ago, he vanished without a trace. Maybe he's dead, or maybe he retired someplace in South America. The important thing is, immediately prior to the *Suchko* operation, both De Tabley and Wilson were at Cheyenne Mountain, helping reorganize NORAD's internal security.''

"And you think they were involved in the spacecraft shooting?''

"I'd stake my career on it,'' Brightman said.

"So there appears to be a link between the *Suchko* affair and the assassination attempt last week?''

"I think somebody wants Clayman out of the way not for

his current policies but because of an event that took place long before he even came to office.''

Jan Bowering leaned back in the sofa. Running her fingers through the pages on her knee, she nodded wearily. "Thank you, Caryl, you were right to bring me this report. I'll read it tonight and talk to the President first thing in the morning.''

Back at his apartment, Nick Koster hurriedly drew the window shades and punched out a number on the telephone. He stood fidgeting as a voice came on the line. "Hello?"

"It's Koster.''

"Something wrong?''

"Something you may not like.''

The voice took on an irritated tone. "Don't play games with me, Nicky. If you've got something to say, then say it.''

Koster felt a strange unwillingness to proceed, as if he might be held responsible in some way. Pulling up the swivel chair, he sank into it, and taking off his glasses, rubbed his eyelids with his fingertips.

"They've found out about De Tabley.''

There was silence at the end of the line. Then, "What can they do? By the time they check him out, it'll be too late.''

"You don't understand. De Tabley's only the first link in the chain.''

"What chain?''

"Wesker's down in the Antarctic now with that NASA woman. They're sailing from Port Shackleton on the British warship HMS *Ashbourne*.''

"So?''

"Have you considered what might happen if they actually find the *Suchko*?''

# FIVE

"According to our calculations," Louis Wesker said, "*Suchko* sank at approximately eighty degrees, sixty-four minutes south, forty-five degrees, twelve minutes west."

Gathered around the wardroom table, the little group of officers examined the navigation charts thoughtfully. For two days, aboard the icebreaker HMS *Ashbourne,* they had been butting their way south through the floating ice pack on the Weddel Sea.

"The question is," Garrett said as he studied the map contours, "did she go down in a direct line, or did she corkscrew?"

"Does it matter?"

"Well, it would give us some idea of where she might be sitting on the ocean bed."

"We estimate her depth to be around three thousand twenty-four feet. Is that any help?"

Garrett used his finger to indicate the approximate area. "We're floating over a vast submerged mountain range, with valleys several miles deep in places. Sounds as thought the *Suchko* settled on one of its higher peaks."

"Will it make things easier?"

"Let's say it'll make them more attainable, at any rate. However, we still need to know what we're looking for."

Wesker glanced across the table at Lori. "I think Miss Madden can answer that."

Lori sat up in her chair. Conscious of the men's eyes focusing upon her, she assumed a businesslike air. "If everything went according to plan, the *Suchko*'s engines should have triggered reentry when the machine was positioned at exactly the right angle for its homeward journey. The manned capsule would then have separated from its service module and engaged its parachute for the final descent. Accepting that was the case, the spacecraft will look something like a large tennis ball. However, it's just possible the *Suchko* came down with its electronics section intact, which means it probably resembles an overgrown peanut, with antenna, maybe even a nose cone protruding from its hull."

"What effect would crashing through the ice cap have on its outer casing?" Garrett asked.

"It should be badly dented, even smashed—though the signals seem to refute that."

"And if we have to enter her at seabed level?"

"As long as the atmosphere's dispersed, no problem. However—" she paused, "in the days of *Suchko*, Russian cosmonaut crews breathed a mixture of oxygen and nitrogen at a pressure of fourteen point seven pounds per square inch, while our *Apollo* astronauts used pure oxygen at a pressure of five pounds. This meant that moving through a docking tunnel from one machine to another, without any kind of interim break, could prove lethal."

"You think we might be facing a similar situation here?"

"No, I don't. It's inconceivable the air could have lasted for fourteen years. The *Suchko*'s interior will be little more than a vacuum by now."

"Which means the cosmonauts can't be alive?"

"Hardly."

Garrett shook his head. "'Hardly' isn't enough. I'd hate to blow that hatch and find four drowning men on my hands."

Lori shuffled uncomfortably in her seat. She disliked having the decision thrust into her lap. "They're dead. Anything else is beyond human credibility."

"In that case, we'll raise the *Suchko* if we can, penetrate her under water if we can't."

"First, we've got to find her," Wesker interjected.

"No problem. We'll use the ANSAAD. It's a particle-beam device which works by accelerating electrons to high energies and velocities."

"Like sonar?"

"Not exactly."

Garrett leaned forward, using his hands to illustrate. "If you ever played with magnets as a child, you noticed how similar ends tend to repel each other. When the magnets are strong enough, the electromagnetic repulsion can produce enough power to overcome the tug of gravity. Particle beams operate in a similar way. The degree of repulsion they register tells us the nature of the area we're exploring. The beams can be aimed by electrical currents which allow them to sweep from one spot to another in a single instant. When we reach the location, we'll lower our submersible and start mowing the lawn."

" 'Mowing the lawn'?" Lori echoed.

"We just keep moving up and down in parallel rows until we pinpoint what we're looking for."

"Will it be dangerous?"

"Three thousand feet is always dangerous. The ocean is made up of two distinct levels—the upper or surface layer, and the dense, chill bottom layer. Down below, the sea will be inky black. We'll have to use lamps. However, our submersible is the most sophisticated on the market, which means we can descend thousands of feet and return to the surface without needing to decompress. We can also dive as regularly and as frequently as we like. Unlike the old-fashioned submersibles, she uses hydroplanes and trimming tanks, which make her almost as maneuverable as a full-size nuclear sub. She has a hollow steel frame and carries not only the ANSAAD but side-scan sonar and a computerized timing system as well."

"How long before we reach the search area?" Wesker asked.

"Nine hours. Less, if the ice pack gets any thinner. But we do have a courtesy call to make first. Acuna Island. There's a New Zealand oil camp on Mineral Bay. It's protocol for all passing vessels to drop in and pay their respects."

"If we waste time on diplomatic niceties, we'll have the Russians crawling up our backsides," Lori protested.

Garrett said, "We have to maintain appearances, for security's sake. The New Zealanders will have picked up our radio traffic by now. They'll know we're in the area. Any deviation from routine will make them suspicious. If the Russians arrive, they'll find themselves in the same boat.''

Wesker said, "You're right. No point in alerting anyone unduly. We'll observe the formalities just as if we were carrying out a proper survey. Let's hope it doesn't hold us back too long.''

The meeting continued for another hour, and when the officers finally dispersed, Lori watched Garrett tug his padded jacket from the bulkhead peg and make his way to the *Ashbourne*'s fo'c'sle. There, he stood gazing over the endless expanse of ice and snow. Garrett had been conspicuously absent since their departure from Port Shackleton. Most of the time, he'd eaten alone in his cabin, spending long hours sketching the frozen seascape.

Through the porthole window, she saw him take a drawing book from his pocket and begin scribbling, using his pencil to measure dimensions and perspectives. He looked oddly remote, as if he belonged not to the ship with its life and people but to the icebound wastes beyond.

"Garrett's a strange man," she said. "Not a bit like a soldier.''

Commander Henderson laughed. "You're wrong. Garrett's the best damn soldier I ever met. Ask his men—they'd follow him anywhere. He cut his teeth as a second lieutenant during the Falklands War, and since then, he's served in just about every trouble spot in the world.''

"How come he manages to remain so independent? I thought soldiers were supposed to follow orders.''

"Garrett has his own way of doing things, and the brass tend to go along with that. I suppose he's just too valuable to lose. Sometimes, he's downright insubordinate. Five months ago, when Corporal Simms went missing on patrol during the worst blizzards the peninsula had seen in forty years, Garrett ignored the colonel's order for all personnel to remain indoors and set off into the snow alone. Somehow—God knows how he managed it—he found Simms and carried him back alive.

"They say when he emerged out of the storm with Simms across his shoulders, he looked half crazed, furred up with snow and his eyes blazing. The sentries thought he was some kind of monster. Idiots damn near shot him in panic and fright.''

''Is he married?''

''His wife was killed in a plane crash eleven years ago. He has a son at school in England. At one time, there was a rumor he'd become involved with some Russian lady, but whatever happened, he's ended up married to the regiment,'' Henderson said.

''He's a brilliant painter, did you know that?''

''Indeed he is. In fact, the War Office appointed him their official artist for a time, but he couldn't stand the quiet life.''

''Where's he from?''

''Far as I can gather, a little place in Northumberland called Yeavering. His father's supposed to be part of the old aristocracy. Garrett's sort of the black sheep. He could be living like a country gentleman in the Cheviot Hills, except that he'd rather be down here, putting the frights up the poor old Argies.''

Henderson smiled. ''Of course, that's just wardroom gossip. Garrett is the kind of man people make up stories about. He never talks about himself. He's SAS, strictly D and D.''

'' 'D and D'?''

''Deaf and dumb,'' Henderson said.

Garrett was scrawling feverishly now, but even with his face composed, there was a hint of humor in his eyes. He wasn't exactly good-looking, Lori reflected. Not in the conventional sense. Interesting maybe, in a bashed-up sort of way, but hardly a matinee idol. She had never cared much for pretty men. In fact, after her last disastrous encounter with the opposite sex, she had stopped caring for men altogether. Which made it even more confusing why Garrett, of all people, should intrigue her so.

''Will you excuse me?'' she said.

Returning to her cabin, she changed quickly into padded arctic gear and made her way to the lower deck. Garrett was still sketching as she approached. He had drawn an outline of the distant mountains, using the harsh, bright South Atlantic sky to emphasize the volcanic rock formations.

''You've missed the color,'' she said. ''It seems a pity to draw pictures without color.''

He glanced at her in surprise. "It's only a blueprint. I'll do the color later. From memory."

She gazed across the ice pack where giant bergs glistened in the daylight. From a distance, they looked smooth and contourless, but close up, she saw they offered a bewildering complexity of differing hues and textures.

"It's beautiful, isn't it?" she whispered. "I never realized Antarctica could be so beautiful."

"In places, that ice cap's nearly twelve miles thick. Almost a tenth of the world's fresh water lies down here."

"God, imagine what would happen if it ever melted."

"See how green the ice gets near the water surface? That's because it's thousands of years old. Hard to imagine, isn't it? We're accustomed to thinking of ice in perishable terms. In Antarctica, it's eternal."

"You like it here, don't you?"

"Yes, I like it. Man hasn't managed to spoil it yet. Besides . . . It goes with my frosty personality."

"You're not frosty, Major Garrett. As a matter of fact, I think that Neanderthal routine is nothing but an act. Commander Henderson tells me your father is some kind of aristocrat."

"Henderson's nuts. I come from a long line of cattle raiders and sheepstealers."

"Sheepstealers?"

"I grew up just south of the Scottish border. It was once the proving ground for two of the most warlike nations in history. Back in the old days, if a landowner wanted to survive, he had to be a dab hand at brigandry as well as farming and livestock."

"You make it sound very romantic."

His eyes creased with amusement. " 'Romantic' is hardly the word. Plunder and murder were considered an essential part of the social graces. My father has a saber hanging on his study wall. The legend is, when the larder was getting low, the ladies of the household used to serve the saber to their menfolk for supper—to let them know it was time to start raiding again."

"How civilized."

"It went with the land. Americans tend to think of the English countryside as very pastoral, but up in Northumbria where I spent my boyhood, it's raw and primitive."

"Is that why you like it here? Because it reminds you of home?"

"That's why."

She pushed her hands into her anorak pockets, hunching her shoulders against the chill. "You know, if someone had told me a week ago I'd be sitting on a tub in the middle of the Antarctic, competing with the Russians in a race for a sunken spacecraft, I'd have said they were crazy. My life as a rule is peaceful and unencumbered. Some people might call it dull, but speaking personally, I like it that way."

"How did a lady so feminine end up in such a masculine preserve?"

"I grew up in a masculine environment. You're not the only one who knows what it feels like to be isolated. We lived on a cattle ranch in the Bitterroot foothills near Coeur d'Alene. I was the only female for almost thirty miles. In a setting like that, independence becomes sort of a necessity."

"But cattle to rockets, that's quite a switch."

"Well, we were pretty cut off at Lomstoun. I got used to fixing things at a very early age. You'd be surprised at how nifty I can be with a monkey wrench and a screwdriver. By the time I reached college, I knew what I really wanted. Space."

"Ever been up there?"

"Twice," she said.

She saw a hint of envy enter his features, and he whistled softly.

"Wow, that's something I've always dreamed of. Four years ago, I went through a cosmonaut training course in the Soviet Union, part of the United European space program. We did the lot from A to Z, practicing on simulators, but they never actually launched us into orbit."

"You'd like it. It's even emptier than this. And once you've experienced space, it's impossible to look at the world in quite the same way again. It's like pulling back a curtain and gazing through a window at things you never dreamed existed."

"You're a lucky girl," Garrett told her.

"I know. And believe me, I'm grateful. But sometimes I wonder what might have happened if I'd stayed back in Coeur D'Alene, got married, settled down. I know this sounds kind of strange, but after that first leap into the firmament, none of

the ordinary things in life—the good, solid, reliable things—
were enough for me anymore.''

Back in his cabin, Garrett tugged off his jacket and threw
himself on his bunk. He heard ice scraping along the *Ashbourne*'s
hull, felt the harsh, rhythmic vibrations as their bow bit
deeper and deeper into the pack, and knew without being told
that the old pattern was beginning to repeat itself.

The way she'd looked at him had almost taken his breath
away. He thought: Who am I to dream about Lori Madden? I
have my own life, and I've guarded it jealously. I have a
home to retreat to when the feeling takes me, and that home
is filled with the things I treasure. I have my boy and my
painting, and everything else I consider important in this
world, but I would be lying to myself if I didn't admit that
something is missing, and that something can chill a man's
heart if he gave himself up to it.

He hadn't done too badly, all things considered. When
Elaine had died, he'd almost gone crazy for a while, trying to
blot out the pain with drinking. But he'd managed to pull
himself together, by God, and nobody could accuse him of
not facing reality squarely, of not coming to terms with the
truth.

Of course, he had Sean to worry about, and that had proved
a blessing in a way, because a son gave a man solace and
hope; he offered a new direction, a sense of purpose, a reason
for going on. But Sean lived with the family in England (it
had been no life for a growing boy, following the regiment
from one corner of the world to another), so he and Garrett
had grown apart.

After Elaine, Garrett thought he would never look at a
woman again, not in the real sense. He had whored around
some in those early months, but they'd been transitory affairs,
featureless creatures with suppliant bodies whose identities
scarcely registered on his consciousness.

And then he'd met Elke. Garrett's lips twisted wryly at the
thought. Elke. He thought she was expunged from his memory like some forgotten fantasy. But he knew now he could
never forget.

She had reminded him of his wife—that, he supposed, had
been the initial attraction—the same eyes, the same sculpted
cheekbones, the same glacial composure. But there the simi-

larity had ended. Elke was frank and direct. She had a sense
of fun, and something else—something he couldn't quite put
a name to—a kind of recklessness that almost matched his
own. For a while, they'd been blissfully happy. Then had
come the moment of betrayal. . . .

His drinking had started again, just as he'd known it
would, and his brawling and his whoring, yet despite everything, he'd managed to survive a second time around—a little
more frayed at the edges, the scars on his psyche now
indelibly printed—but he'd pulled through intact.

And now, just as he was getting things back into perspective, along came this American girl to fire him up again.
Nothing in life went smoothly, he thought. Nothing that was
worth a damn anyhow. A man learned the pitfalls to watch out
for, learned how to avoid them, recognize the signals of past
follies and past indulgences, yet life, with its maddening
contrarity, somehow managed to confound him.

Still, it was an intriguing notion just the same—he and Lori
Madden—and he hummed softly to himself as the ship
ploughed its way south through the endless sea of ice.

The oil camp stood on the island's western slope, flanked
by ribbons of ice-glazed water. Behind, the land rose into a
series of jagged mountains, arid as far as the snowline, then
sparkling white above. The buildings formed a semicircle, the
somber units linked by centrally heated tunnels. At first
glance, the settlement looked frighteningly vulnerable, a mere
toehold of civilization on the outermost rim of the world.

In a natural harbor created by the promontory and the
adjacent bay, the Soviet vessel *Orlov* lay moored to a rocky
outcrop, her sleek lines contrasting strangely with the harsh
contours of the surrounding countryside.

Clad in padded survival gear, Sergei Malenov strolled
along the wooden catwalk with Maurice Shingleton, the New
Zealand supervisor. Shingleton was a muscular man with a
moonlike face that seemed emphasized by his tangled red
beard.

"You've made some changes since my last visit," Malenov
observed.

Shingleton said, "We've extended the living area. Things
were getting out of hand. We had so many engineers, they
were virtually living on top of each other. When a man came

off duty, he had to jump into the bed of the man replacing him. In the end, we decided to spread out a little."

"It's quite an improvement," Malenov said.

They traced the edge of the cookhouse, making their way toward the administration block, their breath steaming on the afternoon air. Shingleton eyed his companion with amusement. "This is more than just a social call, Colonel Malenov. I can't imagine you traveled all the way from Moscow just to look at our living quarters."

"You're right. The Soviet government, in its wisdom, has decided to explore the bottom of the Weddel Sea. Our scanning sonars suggest the rock formations on the ocean bed could be extremely rich in mineral wealth. Naturally, it will be a long time before the technology exists to utilize such deposits, but it seems good business to at least explore the possibility."

Malenov knew the little New Zealander hadn't believed a word he'd said, but that was irrelevant. The *Suchko*'s recovery took precedence over everything, including diplomatic niceties. Malenov resented the task Suivesky had thrust on him, but he was an ambitious man, dedicated to the cause of self-survival, and whatever happened, he was determined he would not return to Moscow empty-handed.

"You must get lonely here," he said.

"Never get the opportunity. Too much to do just keeping alive, especially during winter. Boredom's a luxury we can't afford. The men work turn and turn about, with little time off. What they do get, they spend in the bar and recreation room."

"How do you bring in your supplies?"

"Air, mostly. We used to rely on twice-monthly visits from the New Zealand Navy, but in winter, the ice pack makes the island virtually inaccessible. In the end, we built an airstrip on the promontory's upper shoulder. It's a slow process, using transport planes, but it's proved more dependable in the long run. Our greatest problem is getting rid of our trash. We can't bury it, because the ground's too frozen, and we can't stick it under the snow because in the Antarctic, nothing ever rots. We have to pack it into steel containers and ferry it out by air. It's a costly business."

Malenov eyed the surrounding peaks, and tried to imagine

living here day in, day out, for months on end. "Don't you ever think about home?"

"All the time. It's seldom far from anyone's mind. But you'll find it a different world inside the complex. We've done the place up with pictures. Lots of greenery—pastures, forests, hillslopes. That's what the men miss most."

"Personally, I find vodka a wonderful substitute when it comes to nostalgia. I've brought you a couple of fresh cases."

"We're still working on your last consignment. However, please accept my thanks on behalf of my companions. I hope you'll join us for dinner tonight, together with the *Orlov*'s captain?"

"We'll be delighted," Malenov said.

He paused as a man shouted from the weather survey tower above. Malenov peered up at him, squinting into the sunlight. The miniscule figure was waving excitedly at the harbor entrance, and Malenov felt a tremor of uneasiness as he turned, gazing at the straits behind. Steaming around the frozen headland was a British warship, its bridge wings bristling with quadruple missile launchers, ice glistening on its steel-gray bow.

A terrible suspicion gathered in Malenov's mind. Could there be a connection, he wondered, between the vessel's arrival and the *Suchko*'s distress signals?

"Ah," Shingleton remarked cheerfully, "looks as though we may have other guests tonight."

Malenov felt his uneasiness deepening as the ship dropped anchor and the deck crane lowered a mechanized landing craft into the ice-glazed water. Pale-faced, he followed Shingleton along the jetty to greet the visitors' arrival. His brain was working furiously as the tiny boat bobbed toward them across the foam-flecked waves. One of the passengers looked strikingly familiar, and for a fractional moment, Malenov thought his eyes were playing tricks, but as the LCN drew closer, a sudden spasm knotted in his chest.

Garrett.

He recognized the heavy shoulders, the spare, angular frame. Garrett stood out in a crowd, always had.

Malenov struggled hard to control himself as old jealousies, forgotten guilts, stirred uncomfortably inside him. He tried to make sense of this inexplicable phenomenon. His ancient antagonist here, in this forgotten end-of-the-world wilderness? Such things didn't happen by accident. There had to be a reason. Garrett was an ANSAAD man, and the ANSAAD was used in underwater analysis.

Suddenly Malenov knew without any shadow of doubt, the British were after the *Suchko*.

He kept his face impassive as the LCM drew alongside and the British captain came ashore, pausing to shake Shingleton's hand. He introduced each of his companions in turn, while Malenov, standing slightly to the rear, examined Garrett in silence. Garrett's face was tanned and healthy, his eyes carrying only a trace of their familiar wildness. If he noticed Malenov's presence, he gave no sign.

When the introductions were complete, Shingleton motioned Malenov forward. "May I present Colonel Sergei Malenov of the Soviet Red Army."

Despite his natural reticence, Malenov could be socially adept when the occasion demanded, and he used his charm to full effect now, shaking hands and speaking pleasantly to each of the guests in turn. When he reached Garrett, he forced himself to remain relaxed.

There was no surprise on Garrett's face. "Like a bad penny, Sergei, sooner or later you always turn up."

Malenov said, "What is it this time, Zachary? Naval maneuvers? Or are you going to throw me that old chestnut about using the ANSAAD to track penguin colonies in the Weddel Sea?"

"That depends on which old chestnut you decide to throw me," Garrett countered.

"Scientific exploration, nothing extraordinary. We are carrying out a survey of geological deposits on the ocean bed for the future benefit of mankind."

"A commendable endeavor," Garrett answered without a pause. Sunlight slanted across his features, setting his eyes alight. "And how is Elke?"

"She speaks of you often," Malenov answered. "About Baikonur, the fun we had in the old days."

Lori, watching, felt the tension like a physical force. On the surface, Garrett and Malenov looked like two old friends greeting each other warmly in a forgotten corner of the world, but something told her things were not as they appeared.

Malenov threw his arm around Garrett's shoulder, escorting him along the narrow gangplank, and Lori followed.

* * *

"There was a time that Antarctica was the last great wilderness," Malenov declared. "A man could believe himself in a different universe, with no people, no sign of human habitation. But that's all changed now. With more and more countries milking Antarctica's oil and mineral deposits, the land and the water are becoming increasingly polluted, and on this continent of continents, pollution is a serious problem. Sooner or later, the nations of the world must get together and draw up new guidelines; otherwise, we'll turn the place into an international garbage can."

"Surely the Soviet Union must take its share of the blame for that?" Lori said. "Aren't you one of the foremost exploiters of the oil fields in the Topchy Gulf?"

Malenov said, "Correct, Miss Madden, the Soviet Union needs energy like everyone else, and we would be fools not to extract it from Antarctica's shores, but we are becoming increasingly conscious of the need for restraint, the need for some kind of policy on conservation and wildlife. In February, at a meeting of the Skvortsov Committee in Leningrad, a blueprint for Antarctica's future was discussed by scientists from all over the Soviet Union. Hopefully, we will place it before the United Nations in early July. Unless we introduce a realistic program of control, we will destroy this continent forever."

Lori had to admit that the Soviet colonel, far from displaying the bullishness she normally associated with military men, appeared intelligent and well informed. He smiled frequently, and when he did, there was a genuine warmth behind his eyes.

"How would you relate the violation of Antarctica," Garrett asked, casually lighting a thin cheroot, "with the sanctity of space?"

Malenov's eyes flickered, and Lori detected a sudden wariness in his manner. He lounged back in his chair, toying with his wineglass. "The two are interchangeable. One lies at the most inaccessible corner of our planet's surface, the other represents the firmament itself. Man may use them for his benefit, but he has a duty to respect their uniqueness, to preserve it for future generations. That was why the Space Arms Control Treaty was signed back in 1964."

"I take it, then, you would be morally opposed to any use of space for military purposes?"

"The idea would be unthinkable. When the United States agreed to terminate its Strategic Defense Initiative, the Soviet Union halted all research into the development of space weapons."

Garrett rolled his cheroot between his fingers, examining it with studied absorption. "On the other hand, though space itself may be squeaky clean these days, there could still be embarrassing skeletons in our political cupboards."

Malenov's eyes narrowed. "What are you taking about?"

"Well, look at this way." Garrett leaned back, the cheroot clenched between his teeth. "It was in this very area that one of your spacecraft crashed in the most tragic circumstances fourteen years ago. I'm sure you'll remember it, Colonel. The *Suchko Twenty-three*. Now just supposing—and I'm simply speculating here—but just supposing the *Suchko* had been carrying something which, in diplomatic terms, might be regarded as political dynamite—a new type of weaponry perhaps for installation on one of the *Salyut* weather satellites, or a revolutionary spying device, capable of homing directly on Washington, D.C. If one accepted that proposition, would it not seem curious that two of the world's leading ANSAAD experts should meet in this particular location at the same specific moment?"

Lori sucked in her breath. Garrett was pushing the situation to the limit. If Malenov hadn't guessed their intention in coming here, he certainly would now.

The Russian colonel said, "You forget one important thing. The *Suchko* crashed into uncharted waters. The search parties at the time could find no trace of her resting place. We decided—and I see no reason to question that decision—that the spacecraft must have plummeted into a chasm on the ocean floor. Since such chasms are believed to extend to depths of several miles, it's clear the *Suchko* is quite beyond the reach of man."

"True," Garrett agreed. "Unless—and again, I'm speculating here—some new evidence had come to light indicating the spacecraft might be lying much higher. If that happened, and if the Soviets kept it a secret whilst trying to carry out a salvage operation, wouldn't it suggest to you they had something they badly wanted to hide?"

Malenov's face paled. Though his eyes looked calm, a tiny pulse on his left temple had begun, almost imperceptibly, to throb. Taking the napkin from his lap, he rubbed it over his cheeks and threw it brusquely across his plate. When he spoke, he did so in Russian, his voice sharp and accusing.

To Lori's astonishment, Garrett answered him fluently, switching languages with scarcely a pause. For a few minutes, the two men quarreled across the table, their voices rising and falling in harsh cadences.

When the exchange ended, Malenov turned to the startled dinner guests.

"Forgive me. That was extremely ill-mannered, and I apologize on behalf of Major Garrett and myself. We will conduct the rest of our conversation in English."

"You speak Russian very well, Major Garrett," Shingleton commented.

"I had a good teacher," Garrett replied, watching Malenov through narrowed eyes.

Lori reached nervously for the vegetables. "A little more celery, Colonel?" she asked, trying to lighten her tone. "I understand that in certain parts of Estonia, the inhabitants eat little else."

Malenov took the dish from her hand. "You are quite right, Miss Madden. Celery is considered a delicacy in Estonia. In fact, among some of the more fanciful residents, it's considered to be a wonderful accompaniment to the pleasures of love."

"Celery an aphrodisiac?" Louis Wesker spoke up. "First time I've heard that."

"They don't eat it—they use it as a splint," Garrett growled, rising to his feet and seizing his jacket as he strode abruptly from the room.

Excusing herself, Lori Madden followed him quickly, tugging on her overcoat. Something odd was happening, something she didn't understand. She wanted an explanation.

The mountains were bathed in a pinkish shroud, and she could see the two ships moored in the harbor among the hazy outlines of floating icebergs. Garrett stood leaning against the wall, one foot propped on the veranda rail.

Lori hesitated, shivering in the chill. "That was quite a performance in there."

"Just warming up. The big scene comes later. That's when Malenov and I get to sing our duet."

"I don't know if anyone ever told you, but you have a facility for annoying people."

"I wondered why I flunked the Dale Carnegie course."

"I suppose you know you've blown the whole thing? He's probably guessed the truth by now. I mean, about what we're doing here."

"He already knows. Whatever else you might say about Malenov, he's nobody's fool. Two ANSAAD experts in the same area—there can be only one explanation. We're both after the *Suchko*."

Lori looked down at the harbor. On the wind-driven snow, she could see the outlines of sleeping seals. "How come I get the feeling that he hates you?"

"He hates me, all right. Probably more than any man alive."

"But why?"

Garrett was silent for a moment, gazing out at the ocean as if he resented her intrusion. "Remember, I told you about Baikonur? The United European Space program? Well, I was the British ANSAAD specialist, Malenov the Soviet."

"You worked together?"

"More than that. Malenov was my best friend."

"Your best friend?"

"It didn't please his superiors. The Russians wanted to turn the whole thing into a duel. They'd ordered Malenov to outdo me at every opportunity."

"That's political, not personal."

"It became personal."

Garrett hesitated. "There was a girl at Baikonur."

"A girl?" Lori sounded almost scornful. She hadn't expected the explanation to be so banal.

Garrett laughed shortly. "You don't understand, there's something primitive about the feeling a man gets in a situation like that. It cuts through the veneer of civilized behavior."

"What happened to her?"

He kicked the post rail with his boot, dislodging some of the snow. "She married Malenov."

Terrific, Lori thought. Now she had a personal vendetta on her hands. She thrust her fists into her anorak pockets, her breath steaming on the chill night air. "I hope you're not going to do anything rash."

Garrett looked at her. "You're missing my point. Sergei Malenov is no ordinary colonel. He's the top ANSAAD specialist in the Soviet Union. Which raises an intriguing question."

"What's that?"

In the hazy twilight, steam from his nostrils hung like a halo around his tousled hair.

"If the Russians are so desperate to get the *Suchko* back, what in God's name was that spacecraft carrying?"

# SIX

Lieutenant Robert Harris, Section III, Administration and Accounts, tapped lightly on Major Wilbur Ardrey's door and stepped inside his office. The major was sitting at his desk, fashioning a paper airplane out of an unused field report; coughing in confusion, he tucked it swiftly into a drawer as Harris entered.

Harris removed his spectacles. "Can I have a word with you, sir?"

Major Ardrey waved him to a chair. "Sit down, Lieutenant. Coffee?"

"No thank you, sir. I'm trying to cut down on my caffeine. I haven't been sleeping too well lately."

Ardrey sat back in his seat, examining the young officer thoughtfully. Harris was an odd type; pale-cheeked and scholarly, he didn't look like army material at all. In fact, if it hadn't been for Harris's analytical mind, he probably would never have made it through West Point. As it was, he had built up quite a reputation for his computerlike mentality.

"Okay," Major Ardrey said, "what's the problem?"

Harris shifted in his chair. "Well, it may be nothing, sir, but I've come across an anomaly which seems to be repeating itself, like a ripple effect, right through the system."

"What kind of anomaly?"

Harris toyed with his spectacles, rubbing the stems nervously together. He seemed unable to meet Ardrey's gaze. "Last Thursday, I received a number of expense sheets for a training program code-named Seneca. The sheets came under the Maximum Secret classification. They contained invoices for an Astra Three satellite communications system, and a coorbital high-energy radio accelerator. I didn't spot anything unusual at first. Then I noticed that Seneca involved two infantry companies from Fort Gaujas, North Carolina."

Major Ardrey looked blank. "So?"

"Major, Fort Gaujas is a cadet training school. There are not now, nor have there ever been, infantry companies based within its confines. I know that because my uncle happens to work there. As a matter of fact—" he hesitated, "when I received the invoices, I called him, just to check."

"You called your uncle about a Maximum Secret training program?"

"Naturally, sir, I did not indicate my reasons for the inquiry."

Major Ardrey picked up his ruler, bending it between his fingers.

"Whose signatures appeared on those invoices?"

"Captain Michael Sepalma's. I ran his name through the computer, and"—Lieutenant Harris shrugged helplessly—"this is where it starts to get weird, Major. Captain Sepalma was killed in a skiing accident near Ouray, Colorado, thirteen months ago."

Major Ardrey blinked. "You're sure?"

"Yes, sir. I called his wife in Oklahoma City."

"Well then, the only explanation is that there must be two Captain Sepalmas."

"No, sir. I also checked his service record. I ran Captain Sepalma's name through the central computer. According to my findings, his signature appears on at least a dozen projects currently in motion, all of them authorized after Captain Sepalma's death. In fact, in one instance, he even spells his name incorrectly. *S-e-p-a-m-l-a* instead of *S-e-p-a-l-m-a*. Naturally, I found this puzzling, so I checked out several of the operations bearing Sepalma's name."

"And were they genuine?"

"Impossible to tell, sir. The computers kept cross-referencing. There's a labyrinth of detail, none of which appears to add up. What's more, when several other names appeared, I was unable to establish either their identities or in some cases even the departments from which they operate."

"Quite a busy bee, you've been, Lieutenant."

"Yes, sir. I thought I ought to bring it to the Major's attention, sir."

"Who else have you told about this?"

"Only Lieutenant Johnson. He's been helping me with the investigation."

"Johnson?"

"He shares my office, sir."

Major Ardrey took a deep breath, filling his lungs with air. Tossing the ruler on the desk, he leaned forward, interlocking his fingers. For a moment, he stared down at his hands, then looked at Harris approvingly.

"Lieutenant," he said, "I want you to know I admire your astuteness."

"Thank you, sir."

"I don't know what you've uncovered here, but I sure as hell intend to find out."

"Yes, sir."

"However, we'll need to proceed delicately."

"Those were my feelings precisely, sir."

"Right now, I want you to return to your office and wait until you hear from me. Say nothing to anyone about your discovery. I'll get back to you as soon as I can. Is that understood?"

"Yes, sir. Perfectly, sir," Harris said with obvious relief.

The pilot grinned as he popped his head through the office door.

"Lieutenants Harris and Johnson?"

"That's right."

"Let's go, gents. The chopper's waiting."

Harris glanced at Johnson. "Hold on a minute. What chopper?"

The newcomer was pink-cheeked and muscular, with a fierce *bandido* mustache. "You're Lieutenant Harris?"

"Yes, I am."

"Lieutenant Robert Harris?"

"Correct."

"Major Ardrey's your section commander?"

"Sure, but—"

"Then you're my passenger, Lieutenant."

Harris waved his hand helplessly. "Passenger to where?"

"Norfolk," the officer announced cheerfully. "Express delivery for the secretary of defense."

"The secretary of defense?" Harris blinked at Johnson. "Jesus."

Harris was an insular young man, unaccustomed to such unusual attention, and the prospect of meeting the secretary of defense filled him with alarm. His mind was swimming as he and Andy Johnson followed the flying officer out to the Pentagon helicopter pad. The chopper's engine roared deafeningly, and Harris caught a glimpse of the navigator watching them through the Plexiglas nose cone. It was not the customary passenger vehicle, but a full-size Sikorsky H-37A *Mojave*, designed to carry thirty-six fully armed troops.

As the machine took off, Harris watched the five-angled Pentagon building gradually diminishing through the porthole window, saw the wide fork of the Potomac and Anacostia Rivers, the oblong sprawl of the Mall topped by Jenkins Hall, and the slender promontory of East Potomac Park. Then the pilot banked westward, and the Washington rooftops faded away swiftly below.

"What do you figure is going on?" he shouted to Johnson above the clatter of the rotor blades.

"Search me. Looks like you put your finger on a bogie, Coach. Maybe they'll pin a medal on your chest."

"Or nail my ass for being too nosy," Harris muttered.

The flat waters of the Chesapeake and the lush Shenandoah pasturelands gave way gradually to the Appalachian foothills, and peering down, Harris glimpsed wooded mountains, sprawling valleys, and scattered starbursts of tiny towns.

After a while, Johnson, sitting directly to Harris's rear, leaned forward, digging his shoulder. "Hey, Bob, Norfolk's to the south, right?"

Harris blinked at him. Johnson's cheeks looked even more freckled in the sunlight. His hair, blown by the wind, lay tangled across his forehead.

"Right," Harris agreed.

"Well, we're heading directly into the sun."

Frowning, Harris gazed across the cloudless blue sky. "Maybe the pilot wants to clear the mountains before altering course."

Johnson shook his head. His eyes looked worried. "Listen, there's something screwy about this whole thing. Did you ever see that pilot before?"

"No, I didn't."

"Did you stop to check his credentials?"

"For Chrissake, Andy, you know I didn't."

"Well, I'm no genius, Coach, but I know enough to realize that whatever we've stumbled into is going to cause somebody a whole lot of pain. Now if my name was on those invoices, I reckon I'd do just about anything to make sure nobody found out, wouldn't you?"

Harris felt his mouth turn dry as a terrible suspicion gathered in his head. Reaching down, he tugged at his safety harness. "Let's check," he said, and with Johnson following, scrambled up the companionway ladder to the flight deck above.

Harris's muscles tensed as he pulled back the connecting curtain. For a moment, he could scarcely believe his eyes as he stared into the cabin speechlessly. There was no sign of the pilot or navigator, no sign of anyone at all except for a disembodied voice issuing from the radio transmitter, giving weather reports for the next twenty-four hours. The flight deck was completely deserted.

"Jesus God, nobody's flying this thing!"

Lights flashed on the instrument panel, and the control column tilted, bringing the machine to a horizontal plane. Harris's fingers chilled as through the windshield he glimpsed mountain peaks ahead.

Johnson was stupefied with terror. "Where have they gone? They were in here when we took off. Pilots don't just disappear, for Chrissake."

"Maybe they baled out."

"Then how come we're still airborne?"

"Some kind of remote control."

"Somebody badly wants us out of the way, Coach, and Ardrey's in on it. Got to be."

Harris looked at him, his cheeks chalky. "Can you fly a helicopter, Andy?"

"Christ, no. Choppers scare the shit out of me."

Johnson was right, Harris thought, gazing at the instrument console. Even a skilled aircraft pilot would have difficulty landing a helicopter untrained, especially in such heavily wooded terrain.

He was filled with a dangerous sense of instability as he tried to instill his voice with confidence. "What the hell, they all work on the same principle, don't they?"

Johnson stared in astonishment as Harris shuffled into the pilot's seat.

"You're crazy, Bob, you don't know a goddamned thing about helicopters."

"I've read the manuals. I know the flight control is effected by changing the direction magnitude of the main rotor thrust."

Harris seized the control column. "If I tilt the cyclic stick back, I change the blade angles, and in theory the machine should slow down."

He felt the lever vibrating against his palms as he eased it gently but firmly toward his chest. There was no response. The helicopter continued its forward surge at the same breakneck speed, and Harris saw the mountains approaching rapidly through the Plexiglas.

"Shit, nothing's happening."

There were rivers below, cutting through the forests like silken thread, wooded valleys with glistening lakes, and rounded summits flanked by boulder-studded pastures; sunlight lay across the timbered slopes, blurring their textures, flashing on isolated torrents and waterfalls.

Ahead, something rose through the glare, chilling Harris's blood. It hovered above them, silhouetted against the sky, a massive rampart of fractured black rock.

Johnson's voice became a hysterical screech. "Bob, for Chrissake, we're never going to clear that ridge."

Harris's muscles twitched, and his diaphragm felt paralyzed. The cliff looked like a monster from some mystic vision, its cracks and crannies lost in a textureless flatness wrought by the sun. He saw slivers of shale forming spidery patterns along its pine-cluttered crest.

Desperately, he scanned the instrument console. "I need the collective pitch control. Find it, goddammit!"

Johnson leaned over Harris's shoulder, his body quivering with fear. His fingers touched a projection to the left of the panel, hinged at the rear. "Here, here."

"Right," Harris declared grimly. "If I rotate the throttle twist-grip, it should give us increased engine power."

A thunderous roar echoed beneath the bulkhead.

"It's working," Johnson yelled.

Harris compressed his lips, focusing his mind on the myriad sensations flitting through his wrists. "Now," he said, "if I tug on the control lever—fingers crossed—we'll start to rise."

There was no immediate response, no dramatic upward surge, but gently, almost imperceptibly, the helicopter began to ascend. Sweat streaming, Harris watched the rock face sliding implacably by, its craggy buttresses blurring into a contourless sprawl. There seemed no end to it; it was like an immeasurable palisade reaching all the way to heaven itself. Up, he thought, his stomach cringing, up, for Chrissake.

"Harder, Bob!" Johnson shouted. "Harder!"

"I'm lifting her as hard as I can, goddammit."

Battling for altitude, the helicopter faltered as the wind hit it, swinging them wildly to starboard, and Johnson stumbled against the navigator's seat, almost toppling to the deck. They were still rising, but Harris knew he couldn't hold it much longer. Twenty seconds, maybe ten.

The cliff whipped by in a bewildering blur. In places, the rock streamed with moisture; in others, its fractured surface lay baking in the sun.

Suddenly, it sheared away. Harris glimpsed the jagged summit crest, felt pine tips brushing their undercarriage. Then the chopper shuddered as it caught the updraft from the wind currents, and they were soaring gracefully through empty sky.

Johnson began pounding his shoulder enthusiastically. "We made it. Sweet God in heaven, we made it!"

Harris felt tears flooding his eyes. Below, the land looked like a rumpled quilt, the timbered hilltops creased by tiny furrows and streams. He heard the *chomp-chomp-chomp* of the rotor blades pounding in his ears.

"See if you can operate the radio," he ordered. "We'll need all the help we can get if we hope to put this mother down."

Suddenly the breath froze in Harris's throat, and his muscles tightened involuntarily. Directly ahead, a second cliff rose in their path, its jagged wall confronting them like the prow of some ancient galleon. Cluttered with slabs and rubble-strewn ledges, it formed an endless barrier of rock.

"Oh, my God!"

He hauled on the control lever, gritting his teeth as the helicopter banked steeply to starboard. The earth seemed to tilt, and he saw the wall streaking up to meet them, its ragged outline blotting out the sun.

Then the nose cone struck, and the helicopter erupted in a blinding flash of smoke and flame.

Nick Koster was seething with anger when he arrived at the Pentagon. Ignoring his MP escort, he stormed along the corridor and barged into General Connel's office.

The general was sitting behind his desk. "Hello, Nicky. You look a little down in the mouth this morning."

Nodding at the MP to withdraw, Connel rose to his feet and carefully locked the door. Walking to the wall cabinet, he switched off the hidden sound recorder, then flopped into his chair and examined Koster appraisingly. "What's the problem, Chief?"

"Have you completely blown your mind?"

Connel considered the question. "I believe, according to my latest psychiatric report, I'm as sane as the next man."

"Who gave you permission to commit murder, for God's sake?"

"Murder? What are you talking about?"

"You know damned well what I'm talking about. Those two young lieutenants, Harris and Johnson."

Connel said, "That was a regrettable accident. Helicopter crashes happen all the time. It's tragic, but it's a simple fact of life."

"You had no right to kill them. You know the rules. We operate on a majority decision."

"There wasn't time to get any kind of decision. Those two young meddlers had their noses stuck firmly in the cookie jar. If I hadn't moved fast, they'd have brought the whole damned operation crashing around our ears. Besides"—He opened a desk drawer—"there was another factor to consider."

"What's that?"

Connel took out an envelope, and opening it, laid two photographs on the desktop. "These pictures just came in from our *Capitan* satellite. This one shows the ocean off the Antarctic Peninsula. Here's the same area magnified a thousand times. That dot you see in the center has been identified

as the British icebreaker HMS *Ashbourne*. The other is the
Soviet vessel the *Orlov*.''

Koster examined the photographs. "How can you be sure
at such a distance?''

The general's lips twisted into a humorless smile. "We
have our methods, Koster.''

Picking up the pictures, he slipped them deftly into the
envelope and returned it to the desk drawer.

"Now you'll understand why it was necessary to deal with
Lieutenant Harris and his colleague. We can't afford screwups
at this critical stage. It looks as if both the British and
Russians are almost at the search area, and you know what
that means.''

His eyes settled on Koster coolly across the desktop. "With
good weather and an equal amount of luck, they could be
inside the *Suchko* within twenty-four hours.''

The sun cast slivers of light across the mountain peaks as
Lori Madden, clad in padded jacket and overtrousers, set off
from the oil camp toward the distant headland. At the invita-
tion of the New Zealanders, both the British and the Soviets
had agreed to remain for one more night to join in the camp's
anniversary celebrations. It would have been churlish not to,
Garrett said. However, as soon as the festivities were at their
height, the *Ashbourne* intended to steal a march on its rival
*Orlov*, a tactic of which Lori herself wholeheartedly approved.

The day felt surprisingly warm as she traced the foreshore,
beating an erratic path along the snowline's lower rim. Seals
basked on the hard volcanic rocks, their oily-sleek bodies
glistening like strips of polished black rubber. She felt glad to
be out on this frosty day, glad to feel the wind on her cheeks,
the sun in her face.

She thought about the evening before, about Malenov's
anger and the strange circumstances that had brought him and
Garrett together. She thought about the curious and indefina-
ble feelings she was experiencing.

Reaching the headland, she clambered up the steep rocky
slope, and cresting the ridge, glimpsed a sprawl of buildings
in the hollow below. It was a deserted Norwegian whaling
station with most of its huts intact. They looked, not knew
exactly but uniform and well tended, as if the occupants
expected to return at any moment. It seemed hard to believe

the place had been abandoned nearly half a century before. Only three things indicated the camp's derelict state—the empty window sockets (the glass had probably been blown out by the Antarctic gales), a collapsed roof (another symptom of the inclement weather), and the huge metal vats, once used for melting whale blubber and now rusted beyond recognition.

Strolling among the scattered shacks, Lori visualized the station at its peak, picturing masculine faces, the odor of fish, and boiling blubber.

One of the doors stood open to the winds, and Lori ventured warily inside. The clapboard walls had cracked in places, and the floor was scattered with feathery snow dunes. The rafters, invaded by generations of Antarctic wildlife, were coated with several layers of bird droppings, and the deck was stacked with cartons of supplies, still meticulously labeled. She picked up a packet of powdered milk, holding it to the light.

Hearing a noise outside, she dropped the packet and stepped back anxiously to the door. Framed in the sunlight was a figure clad in bulky Antarctic gear, stamping snow from its padded leggings. As she looked, the intruder tugged back his fur-lined hood. It took a moment before she recognized Colonel Sergei Malenov.

"I hope I didn't startle you."

She moved into the sunlight. "I thought you were a ghost. It's kind of spooky around here."

He glanced behind him at the derelict buildings. "It's just the way the Norwegians left it. Some of the men from the oil camp use this camp as a retreat when they feel the pressures of Antarctic living beginning to get them down. It can become quite a strain, being locked up at the end of the world."

"Are you speaking from personal experience?"

"No, but I've been coming here for years. It's on a direct line with the Soviet base at Pavlic Harbor, so our ships call in regularly on their voyages home. The oil camp is functional enough in physical terms, but it doesn't do much for the senses."

He smiled at her, shaking the snow from his clothing. "I'm on my way to visit the penguin colonies on Minox Bay. Feel like coming along?"

Lori considered for a moment. Despite the things Garrett had said, she liked the Russian colonel. She'd already heard Garrett's side of the story. Maybe it was time to consider Malenov's.

"I think I'd enjoy that."

They walked through the camp together, their boots crunching on the snow. "You speak English very well," she told him.

"You think so? I learned it at school. Also, I lived in Sweden for a while. English is practically a second language there."

"I was surprised to discover that Major Garrett speaks Russian."

"Zachary's almost bilingual. He has an inherent talent for languages, picks them up at the drop of a hat. He understands Russian, French, Spanish, and Arabic. He can also get along quite comfortably in German, Hebrew, and Portuguese."

"You don't like him much, do you?"

"What makes you say that?"

"Anyone with half an eye can see it."

"You're exaggerating. As a matter of fact, Zachary was once my friend, and it isn't easy to forget that—not entirely. But you are quite right, I do dislike him, for reasons I am not prepared to disclose, even to such an alluring listener."

Lori acknowledged the compliment with a tilt of her head. "I thought Russians considered gallantry frivolous?"

"That's because you don't really know us, Miss Madden. There is nothing more wistful or romantic than the Russian soul."

Lori saw a vehicle standing at the side of the road. It looked like a motorcycle, with broad skilike runners underbracing its central frame. "What's this?"

"It's a Ski-doo. That's another Russian characteristic. We never walk when we can ride."

Lori slid into the saddle as Malenov started up the engine. Opening the throttle, he steered the Ski-doo across the rising snow slope, leaving the whale station behind and tracing the rim of a rippling glacier. Lori felt the wind scouring her cheeks, and with her arms around Malenov's waist, shielded her head against the churned-up ice granules spraying about the Ski-doo's prow.

Fleecy mountains surrounded them on all sides; in places where the surface snow had melted, buttresses of crumbling black rock towered against the sky. She saw the shoreline, and the smooth sugarlike ice apron punctured with cracks as it approached the ocean waves.

They swept over the rise, skirting a cluster of treacherous crevasses, and Lori glimpsed, in the bay ahead, a vast carpet of fluctuating movement. Penguins.

Malenov brought the Ski-doo to a halt, switching off the engine. "Better if we walk the rest of the way. The machine might alarm them."

Lori took Malenov's hand and he helped her down the slippery snowslope. To her surprise, the penguins appeared undisturbed by their approach. They scuttled around, looking like comical waiters at some bizarre brasserie. A pungent fishy smell lingered in her nostrils as Malenov led her deeper into the teeming colony. Curious and unafraid, the red-eyed birds gathered around their feet, peering up at them with inquisitive faces.

"I can't believe they're so tame," she exclaimed.

"Man hasn't harmed them yet, that's the reason. The rest of the animal kingdom has learned what to expect from the human race, but down here, people are probably the most peculiar things these little creatures have ever seen."

"You're a strange one for a professional soldier. You care about animals, you care about conserving wild places. Most of the military men I've met see everything in black and white—*us* and *them*."

"Including Garrett?"

"Not Garrett. He's different."

She was silent for a moment as they strolled among the flurrying colony. Then she said, "He told me what happened between you two. He told me about Elke."

"That doesn't sound like Garrett."

"He said you married her. Is that true?"

His breath steamed on the afternoon air as he stared at the gawking birds. The fish odor was almost overpowering now, but Malenov scarcely seemed to notice. "We're married. In a manner of speaking."

Kicking idly at the snow, he watched the penguins leap, squawking, from his path. "Do we have to talk about Garrett?"

"Not if you don't want to. How about Sergei Malenov for a change?"

"An infinitely more fascinating subject," he agreed.

He came, he told her, from the Serov region in the upper Urals, the son of a poor peasant family, determined from the beginning to rise above the restrictions of his upbringing. An ambitious man, he had graduated seventh in a class of forty-two at the Red Army Academy, and at the age of twenty-eight, an acknowledged expert on the particle beam ANSAAD, had transferred to the GRU on the express instructions of Marshal Vetuiga himself.

Malenov told the story with no attempt to impress. He seemed almost embarrassed by his success, trying to minimize it in small insignificant ways.

It was late afternoon by the time they returned to the oil camp. Malenov skidded to a halt.

"I've had a marvelous day," Lori said. She jumped from the saddle, shaking her hair in the wind. "I hope you've enjoyed it as much as I have."

"Better. You don't know how gratifying it is to have such a lovely companion hanging on my every word."

He examined her thoughtfully for a moment, then pulling back his sleeve, uncoupled his wristwatch.

"An old Soviet custom," he explained. "If you wear it, it means we will meet again.

Lori looked surprised. The watch was exquisitely hand-crafted, its surface studded with high-quality stones. "I can't take this. It's much too valuable."

"Please. I want you to have it. It's also a good-luck piece, designed to protect the wearer from physical harm."

Lori hesitated, then leaned forward and kissed him impulsively on the cheek. "It's beautiful. I'll be delighted to wear it. And thank you for everything."

Malenov watched her strolling down the jetty toward the British cutter, and for a moment he felt almost envious of Garrett. She was, he had to admit, an extraordinarily beautiful young woman.

Reaching inside his jacket, he took out a small radio receiver and using a tiny screwdriver, tinkered with the controls. Lori's voice rose through the crackling, loud and clear.

"I hope I haven't kept anyone waiting," she was saying.

The surveillance transmitter Malenov had planted in the wristwatch worked perfectly. He whistled as he slipped the receiver back inside his jacket pocket and steered the Ski-doo toward the empty vehicle hut.

The oil-camp bar was heavy with smoke. Around the piano, the men stood singing, their voices echoing lustily beneath the raftered ceiling. It was an old New Zealand hunting song Malenov had heard many times before, and he sipped his vodka absently, gazing around the crowded common room. He realized he hadn't seen Garrett for at least an hour. Come to that, he hadn't seen any of the British contingent at all, including the girl.

A vague uneasiness stirred inside him. Frowning, he placed his glass on a nearby table. He was halfway to the door when he saw Gubkin, the Soviet ship captain, approaching from the opposite direction. The stiffness in Gubkin's manner told Malenov something was wrong.

"Comrade Colonel, the British have vanished. Our night watch reports the *Ashbourne* departed almost an hour ago."

Malenov cursed. What a fool he'd been—a stupid, inexcusable fool. He should have realized Garrett would try to outwit him. It was Garrett's way.

If the *Ashbourne* reached the search area first, she would commence diving operations immediately. By the time the Russian ship arrived, Malenov would be relegated to the role of observer. He could hardly explore the same strip of ocean bed without declaring his intentions, which meant he would have to watch and wait until a suitable opportunity arose.

"Call the men," he ordered angrily. "Tell them the party's over. We've wasted enough time here."

# SEVEN

Garrett saw the Russian ship arriving as he climbed into his diving gear. The vessel paused about half a mile to the east, dropping anchor in the lee of a floating berg. Its twin funnels and elongated radar mast looked strangely incongruous against the glacial symmetry of the surrounding ice pack.

Garrett felt a sense of grim satisfaction as he watched the Russians settling into position; it was a petty triumph, he supposed, taking the wind out of Malenov's sails, but he felt childishly gratified.

Whistling softly, he strolled across the deck to Wesker, who was standing beneath the suspended submersible, watching the support team carrying out their final safety check. Dressed in a padded duvet jacket, Wesker looked almost as broad as he was long. His squat body seemed to swell like an overblown balloon, and his pink face, framed by a fur-lined flying helmet, was oddly cherubic.

"Looks like our friends have arrived," Garrett said.

"Didn't take them long to figure out we'd gone." Wesker stamped his feet to get the circulation going. "You'll be tripping over each other's toes down there."

"I doubt that. They'll sit tight and wait. Malenov knows if he appears too anxious, we'll realize he's got something to hide."

"Just the same, can't you hustle things along a bit?"

Garrett liked the plump little American. Wesker's fastidi-ous manner and fleshy appearance reminded him of a rubber ball. "Three thousand feet is a long way down. Making a dive in one of these things is like blasting off at Cape Canaveral. We test everything. And I mean everything."

Wesker eyed the submersible dangling beneath the A-frame at the *Ashbourne*'s stern. "Hard to believe you can get two fully grown men in there."

"Depends on what you mean by fully grown," Garrett said.

"I resent that. It might interest you to know that during my navy days, I took a course in oceanography at the Miami Institute. I'm what you might call a natural diver. I've got built-in protection against the cold."

"Wesker, with you along, we might get down there, but we'd sure as hell never get up."

Lori appeared on the snowswept deck. She looked across at the Russians, shielding her eyes against the Antarctic sun. The smattering of freckles across her nose seemed new and fresh to Garrett.

Easy, he thought. He'd made a fool of himself already over a woman. He didn't want to travel the same route again.

Lori was smiling as she came toward them, thrusting her hands in her anorak pockets. "The Russians have arrived."

"Well, we figured they would, sooner or later."

"Think they'll try to interfere?"

"Not Malenov. He'll bide his time."

Lori gazed up at the tiny submersible suspended beneath the heavy A-frame. The vessel looked squat, unwieldy, its bloated hull clearly built for convenience rather than speed; its upper deck was topped by a miniature turret or conning tower designed to keep water from splashing into its entrance hatch.

"Are you really going down in that thing?"

"Just waiting for the starter's pistol."

"But it's tiny."

"Don't be fooled by appearances. It's the most sophisticat-ed submersible on the market. It will dive deeper than any military craft you can name."

"Can it move independently of the mother ship?"

"Sure. But because we'll be under the ice pack, we keep the dragline attached as a precautionary measure."

"I know we've gone through this a dozen times, but you do know what you're looking for?"

"A launch vehicle with a total length of one hundred and forty feet, if the booster is intact."

"And if the electronics section has been destroyed on reentry?"

"A conical capsule with a cylindrical base twenty feet in length, three cabin ports, plus possible communications antennae and an antenna for attitude correction control from Earth."

She hesitated, suddenly nervous. She didn't know why she felt like this; it was nothing she could put a name to, nothing tangible, but the thought of Garrett vanishing into that murky void disturbed her deeply. "Think you'll be okay?"

"Snug as a bug," he promised.

"I'll be watching from the control room."

"Enjoy the show."

"Bring me back a nice fat snapper." Wesker grinned.

"Boiled or fried?"

"Just make sure it's good-looking."

Garrett nodded to Lieutenant Jeavson, who reached up, hauling himself through the submersible entrance. Garrett followed, taking care to avoid the hatch cover, which was heavily greased to help the seal. The bulkhead seemed to gather around him as he uncoiled his long body inside the cramped little cabin, and he experienced the familiar breathlessness he always got at the start of a major dive. No matter how many times he went through the motions, the sensation was always the same—panic just around the corner, especially when they slammed the hatch shut.

He took his seat at the control panel, switching on the lights, shutting his ears to the rattle of the sailors sealing the airtight cover above. He turned on the oxygen tank and the lithium hydroxide ventilator that would help keep the cabin free of carbon dioxide. The tension was leaving him now, fading amid the simple demands of the moment. His eyes scanned the dazzling array of dials and gauges in front as he recited to Jeavson at his side: "Ballast tanks functioning; accoustic telephone working normally; batteries and thrusters responding okay..."

He heard a creaking sound above his head, feeling his muscles tense as the A-frame swung the bulbous cocoon gently over the deck rail, lowering it inch by inch through the gaping hole in the ice pack. For no reason he could explain, this was always the moment he hated most, as they vanished beneath the water's surface, leaving the world they knew behind, entering a strange and hostile environment. Once under, as the dive commenced, he knew he would be fine again.

Water spumed over the submersible's hull, lapping at the metal rivets that ran like stitching along the titanium shield. Garrett watched the sea swirling around them, over them, above them, a column of bubbles marking their downward route. When the vessel was completely submerged, support-crew divers entered the water and rechecked every inch of the hull. Garrett and Jeavson went through a final instrument appraisal, testing the system under pressure. Then at last they were ready.

"Here we go, Toby. Basement floor next stop."

Jeavson rolled his eyeballs. "Why do I always get the feeling I should have stuck to a nice safe job like tightrope walking?"

Garrett flooded the air-ballast tanks. Through the viewing port, he saw the ragged underbelly of the ice pack, gray in places, green in others, serrated stalactites dripping from its frigid roof casing, formed by concentrated brine from the surface trickling through cracks and freezing in the superchilled seawater. The ocean here was sparklingly clear, lit from above by tiny slivers of sunlight. This was the photic zone, where most of the ocean's creatures lived. Lower would come the twilight euphotic zone, and finally the mysterious, sunless abyss.

Fish shoals darted among the ice floes, and Garrett spotted a porpoise school zooming in to investigate. His eyes studied the depth gauge. They were falling rapidly, the ocean darkening around him. The air was stifling inside the tiny cabin, but Garrett could feel the chill of the surrounding water seeping insidiously through their insulated hull. Condensation from their breathing gathered on the bulkheads, running in trickles down the shiny walls.

For no reason he could explain, he thought fleetingly of Lori Madden, not in any conscious way, but on a separate level, the main part of his brain going through the motions of their dive with a detached, almost intuitive precision. Okay, so he liked her, he wasn't about to argue on that score. She stirred him emotionally—again, nothing to get in a tangle about. But it was more than just looks. It was her air of composure. He wondered what she'd be like if she ever let her defenses slip?

His lips twisted wryly as the memory of another woman entered his head. Elke. Funny, she hadn't been on his mind much lately, not until Malenov had come along. At Baikonur, he'd thought about her every waking moment of the day, but as time passed, so had the pain. Elke had faded into his memory like a hazy dream he could scarcely put a shape to.

Not so, Malenov. He hated the man with a deep and burning passion. It wasn't jealousy—it was what Malenov had done. Something nobody knew about, not even Elke. Nobody except Garrett.

A crackling reached them from the acoustic telephone. A voice, blurred and indistinct, said, "*Ashbourne*-con to submersible, *Ashbourne*-con to submersible, are you receiving us? Over."

Garrett tinkered with the controls. "Garrett here. We're down to nine-hundred feet and still descending. Conditions good, visibility moderate. Over."

A glance at the barometer told him the outside temperature was 28 degrees Fahrenheit, and he tugged on a heavy sweater. Strange shadows loomed through the encircling gloom, drifting planktonic creatures whose outlines were blurred and indistinct. Freezing circumpolar currents formed a barrier around the Antarctic mainland, killing off much of the deep-water life, but a gleaming tentacled arctapodema swayed against the viewing port, its red stomach glowing within its translucent shell.

Soon, the sea darkened more rapidly. They had left the ice cap far behind and were dropping into a well of total blackness. The water seemed to take on different densities, different textures, depth and perspective vanishing in a rippling curtain of varying grays and browns. The tiny organisms that had floated so profusely near the surface had gone now, leaving them suspended in an emptiness devoid of substance, life, or light.

The accoustic telephone crackled again. "*Ashbourne*-con to submersible. State your depth. Over."

Garrett checked the gauges, running his fingers along the

line of luminous dials. "Two thousand eight hundred feet. Still descending. How's the weather up there? Over."

"The weather's fine. Power module holding out?"

"Instrument panel normal. We're approaching the three-thousand-foot mark."

"Slow your descent, Zach. We don't want you bouncing off the bottom."

"Roger that."

Garrett reached down, reducing the intake of seawater into the ballast tanks. He switched on the lights, watching the elongated beams slice through the suffocating wall ahead. The ocean was like a blanket—black, oppressive, pitiless.

"Drifting to starboard," Jeavson announced suddenly.

Garrett blew water from the starboard trimming tank, then, using the propulsion motors, adjusted their attitude angle, bringing the vessel into alignment. They were down to three thousand feet now. Beyond the viewing port, the submersible's manipulator arms protruded from the hull like lobster claws. Garrett felt a tension gathering inside him. The sea had lost its texture completely. There were no ripples, no currents, nothing but solid unrelieved black.

The voice on the telephone spoke again. "*Ashbourne*-con to submersible. Instruments indicate you are approaching search area now. Please state your depth. Over."

"Thirty-two hundred feet." Garrett heard Jeavson's impulsive intake of breath.

Something eased into the circle of light, and Garrett felt his stomach tighten as a jagged ridge rose slowly up to meet them, its shark-tooth spine coated with a million years of sediment. The seabed.

His hands moved across the control console, holding the submersible at neutral buoyancy four feet from the bottom. "We're down," he said into the telephone receiver. "Please mark our position. We'll begin the mowing process in RFQ mode."

"Roger that," the voice replied.

Using the hand-operated control set, Garrett engaged the rear thrusters, propelling the craft gently forward over the rim of the twisting ridge. Holding their course meticulously even, he kept his eyes on the ANSAAD scanner, following the designates at the side of the screen. The seabed bobbed and buckled, its peaks and hollows forming a grotesque obstacle course of treacherous outcrops as he guided their tiny craft through the hazardous labyrinth of rocks.

In the control room, Lori watched the panel of TV screens uneasily. She scarcely knew what she was getting so uptight about. She'd gone through worse moments than this, a thousand times over, those awful buildups at the cape, wondering if the shuttle would fly, wondering if all the painstaking preparation was about to be repaid with one swift dissolving flash. But in a funny sort of way, this was different. Creepier. And whether she liked the idea or not, she was worried about Garrett.

She'd learned to her cost the folly of becoming emotionally involved. Twice now, she'd felt the sting, and after the last time, she'd sworn, never, never again. She wasn't devious enough, that was her problem. When she said something, she usually meant it.

Men said what they liked, especially men like Nick Rodin. It had taken months before she'd realized Nick was married. He had lied from the beginning, and by the time she'd discovered the truth, it had been too late—the anguish had started, the humiliation. She'd left him in the end, but she'd felt as if she'd amputated her soul.

Hank MacIntyre hadn't been much better—too wrapped up in his mother. After seven months, she had discovered a rival too entrenched to compete with. When she'd taken Hank home to Coeur d'Alene, her brothers had laughed at what they considered his effete manners. She grimaced at the memory. Somehow, she couldn't imagine them laughing at Garrett. She couldn't imagine anyone laughing at Garrett— not to his face, at any rate.

Four of the TV screens were totally blank. The other two, picking up images transmitted by the submersible's electronic cameras, followed Garrett's progress through the twisting rock formations peppering the ocean bed. It was a strange sensation, watching the savage spires rearing out of the darkness, their pinnacles softened by centuries of gathering slime.

"You do realize," Commander Henderson remarked at her elbow, "that you're witnessing something never before seen by man?"

Lori heard the radio operator say, "Ship-con to submersible, you're nearing the end of your first sweep. Watch for sudden changes in altitude and try to maintain speed at less than point-five knots. You've got obstacles all around down there. Where the hell do you think you are, Brands Hatch?''

Garrett's voice crackled faintly over the receiver. "Roger that. Keep your shirt on, Andy.''

Commander Henderson carefully lit his pipe. "It's a weary business, I'm afraid. We have to keep crisscrossing the area until our ANSAAD strikes pay dirt. There's simply no other way of doing it.''

Lori followed the submersible's progress over jagged ridges and yawning canyons. "We've waited this long,'' she said. "I guess we can wait a little longer.''

Malenov stood in the *Orlov*'s control room, watching the radio operator manipulate the receiver console, the man's fingers, light as thistledown, delicately adjusting sound and volume. From time to time, garbled words emerged amid the incessant crackling, but the operator would lose contact almost at once, allowing the transmission to dissolve into a babble of static.

Malenov felt his fury intensifying. The fact that the British had beaten him to the search area complicated matters enormously, but he supposed if he were honest with himself, scrupulously and brutally honest, it was Garrett's presence that troubled him most.

Just seeing the man again—those mocking eyes, that insolent grin—had fired Malenov's hatred. It was something deeper than Elke, more intrinsic. Guilt. Yet his feelings, far from weakening his hatred, made it stronger, more virulent, for you seldom hated anyone as much, he reflected, as the man who reminded you of your most unpardonable sin.

The radio operator tensed as he delicately adjusted the background crackle. "Down three meters,'' a voice declared, and Malenov sucked in his breath. Garrett. The sound had come directly from the *Ashbourne*'s control room. The bug he had planted in Lori Madden's wristwatch was capable of transmitting only a short distance; it had been necessary to rig an accoustic probe at the top of the *Orlov*'s mainmast, but to Malenov's satisfaction, the strategy had worked. The tiny microphone was relaying the conversation between the *Ashbourne* and the British submersible.

He touched the operator's shoulder approvingly. "You've got them at last," he said.

Garrett steered the submersible deftly, easing it in and out of the twisting tangle of snags and spurs, surprised at the complexity of the seabed, the way it went rolling and dipping this way and that, full of crevices and bulges, much like the country he'd grown up in, the country he'd trained in. He felt at home here—or could have if it hadn't been for the insufferable gloom.

The route led him along a spine of rock, around a jagged promontory, over a tumbling shale slope, the boulders coated with sediment and slime, and always he was conscious of the breathless void beneath. There were depths even this machine could never hope to penetrate.

Mountain tips reared through the darkness as Garrett nudged their tiny craft skillfully between the spires, operating the control console with a delicacy that had become almost instinctive. Sometimes he felt as if the submersible were part of himself, a second skin responding to the minutest signals of his brain. He experienced no discomfort beyond the inevitable dampness and cold—and the curious metallic odor he was always conscious of at extreme depths. Through the viewing port, he discerned the contours of the seascape, the rocky buttresses and hillslopes, the rolling bulges of forgotten summits—a weird, unreal, unimaginable world.

Their search followed a switchback course, the ANSAAD scanner cutting a swath nearly half a mile wide, and Garrett divided his attention between the screen itself and the control panel in front, picking out the individual signatures, assimilating, appraising, identifying. There was no tension in him now, only the absorption of his job.

"Coffee?" Jeavson asked, filing a plastic cup from a thermos flask in his lap.

Garrett sipped the scalding liquid, a glow of warmth spreading upward through his stomach. The coffee tasted thick and brackish. "Who made this muck?"

"It's hot and wet, isn't it? What more do you want at three thousand feet?"

Garrett was about to answer when a red bulb flashed on the control console.

Almost simultaneously, a shrill ringing sound echoed through the tiny cabin, and Jeavson stared at him with alarm. "The power module! It's flooding again."

Garrett swore. The damned power module hadn't been right since the hammering they'd received from the Argentine depth charges. If enough seawater seeped through the leaks, the entire system could short-circuit.

"We've only just got here," he growled.

"What are we going to do, Zach?"

"What else can we do? We'll have to go up and get the bloody things seen to."

He stabbed the radio transmitter with his finger. "Submersible to ship-con, are you receiving me? Over."

"Hearing you loud and clear, Major Garrett. What's the problem?"

"We've sprung a leak in the power module again. It's filling up with seawater."

"Bad, is it?"

"Bad enough. I don't want to be wallowing about down here if the control section blacks out. Mark our position and bring us up to the surface."

"Understood. Position identified and recorded. Hang on to your underpants, gents."

The submersible rose slowly through the gloom.

Malenov straightened from the radio console, his pale face strangely luminous beneath the overhead striplamps. "They're in trouble."

The Russian captain said: "So it would seem, Comrade Colonel."

"It could take them hours to fix that power module. This is our chance."

Lieutenant Pertsovka, the submersible commander, blanched visibly. Malenov knew Pertsovka didn't relish the prospect of confronting the British on the ocean bed, but he was filled with an uncontrollable excitement. He could still, with luck and good judgment, outwit Garrett at this moment of defeat.

"You want us to dive, with the British so close?" Lieutenant Pertsovka asked dubiously.

"It's our only chance," Malenov said.

"But, Comrade Colonel, you stressed the importance of secrecy. No observers, no intruders."

"The situation has changed. The British already know what we are doing here. Garrett knows. We have to seize our opportunities as they arise."

The captain watched the exchange with a seasoned eye. He said, "If we do find the *Suchko,* how can we raise her in full view of the British warship?"

"We'll worry about that when the moment comes. In the meantime, prepare the submersible for diving."

Malenov had no desire to venture into the ocean depths himself. Diving oppressed him, always had, but hopefully such a move wouldn't be necessary. His particle beams could be directed as effectively from the mother ship.

His voice grew crisp and businesslike. "I will handle the ANSAAD scanner from the control room. Lieutenant Pertsovka, when you reach the search area, you will follow the customary procedure of crisscrossing the seabed in parallel rows."

"If the Comrade Colonel wishes it."

"I do wish it. I also wish you luck, Lieutenant. If you handle this correctly, we stand a chance, a very strong chance, of snatching the prize from under our enemy's nose."

Clad in his diving gear, Garrett stood on the *Ashbourne*'s deck, watching the submersible being cranked up from the water hole. The sailors waited to receive it, shouting instructions as the crane operator, working his gearbox delicately, eased the glistening craft gently over the deck rail and brought it to a rest on the metal ramp.

Standing at Garrett's side, Wesker noticed the frustration in the Englishman's features. "How does it look down there?" he asked.

"Rocks. Mud. Damn all else. Not even fish at that level."

Wesker glanced at the sailors who were pumping seawater out of the submersible's damaged pressure housings. "How long will it take to get the leaks mended?"

"An hour. Two. Maybe all day, if luck goes against us."

Commander Henderson chewed at his pipe stem. "The Russians'll be here then. Like a shot. Bound to."

"Isn't there anything we can do?" Lori asked. She couldn't bear the thought of the Soviets interceding, especially after the President himself had placed his trust in her.

"This is Antarctica," Garrett told her. "Down here, you learn to take things slowly, or you simply don't survive."

He paused as the radar officer appeared, his face taut with concern.

"I'm sorry to intrude, sir, but we've picked up a puzzling signature on the scanner. Something seems to be approaching at seabed level. It's too large for drifting wreckage. It looks—" the man hesitated, "it looks like another submersible."

"My God, they're here already," Lori said.

Garrett's face was expressionless. "How close is he, this intruder?"

"He's nearing the search area now. And there's something else, sir. The vessel's giving off strong electromagnetic impulses."

Garrett frowned. What in God's name was Malenov playing at? Whoever was operating the submersible, it was clear Malenov himself was still on the Soviet warship. Was he looking after his own skin? Garrett knew the Russian to be a devious man, but he would never have called him cowardly.

Garrett began to chuckle, and Lori stared at him in bewilderment.

"What's so funny?"

"Malenov. He's trying to operate the ANSAAD from inside the *Orlov*'s control room. He doesn't relish the idea of crawling around on the ocean bed."

"Does it make a difference?" Wesker asked.

"A big difference. It means we can beat him to the punch."

"How?"

"By placing our ANSAAD transmitter directly over the ice hole. Malenov's trying to control his accelerator from the mother ship, but he's weakening the signals, giving us a chance to intercept and slow them down. The ANSAAD's particle beams are formed by accelerating electrons, or protons, to high energies and velocities. By emitting beams of neutral particles with our own accelerator, we can corrupt the signatures on Malenov's scanner."

"You're sure it'll work?"

"Hell no, not a hundred percent, but I'm going to give it a damned good try."

Garrett slapped Jeavson on the shoulder, trotting toward the dangling submersible. "Come on, Toby, let's get that ANSAAD uncoupled."

* * *

Huddled over the instrument console, Malenov stared at the videoscreen in front of him. The readings were meaningless, senseless hieroglyphics, little else.

Leaning across his shoulder, Captain Gubkin examined the unit, frowning.

"What is wrong, Comrade Colonel?"

Malenov thumped the panel with his fist. "The signatures aren't making sense. Something's corrupting the readings."

"Perhaps you are too far away to operate the machine effectively."

"It has nothing to do with distance. This is some kind of interference, something magnetic getting in the way."

The breath caught in his throat, and his frustration turned to a blind consuming fury. Suddenly he knew the reason, knew it beyond any shadow of doubt.

"It has to be Garrett. He's using the British ANSAAD to intercept our impulses."

Was there no depravity Garrett wouldn't stoop to? Like a nemesis hovering on the fringes of his psyche, the Englishman's image dominated his senses. There could be no peace, no salve for his troubled conscience, until Garrett was dead—he knew that.

Fear welled up inside him. He'd tried to avoid going down with Pertsovka, dreaded the thought of crawling through those dank dark depths below. Space he could take any day, he'd never balked at Baikonur, but the ocean bed was something else. He couldn't bear the prospect of entombment, no matter how transitory.

"What do you want us to do, sir?" the captain asked, eyeing Malenov.

Malenov came to an unwilling decision. "Recall Pertsovka," he ordered brusquely. "I will have to accompany the submersible myself."

Garrett stood at the ship's rail, watching the squat, cylindrical quadrupole injector, strapped to a metal frame wedged across the ice hole, pulsing its signals through the gently lapping water. From above, it looked like an oversize vacuum cleaner, emitting an eerie blue light from its carefully positioned director tube. Back in the eighties, Garrett reflected, an accelerator like the ANSAAD would have filled an entire building.

Holding the instrument panel in front of him, he tinkered with the controls—testing, judging, transmitting. It was a delicate operation, requiring years of skill and experience. He had spent countless hours learning his craft, honing his instinct until he could control those impulses better than any man alive, though he couldn't guarantee his strategy was sound. The ANSAAD was mercurial, to say the least, and maybe Malenov had an ace or two up his own sleeve. Nobody in the West knew how far Soviet technology had advanced during the past four years.

At his rear, the others stood watching, afraid to interrupt in case they broke Garrett's concentration.

Feet clanged on the foredeck as the radar operator emerged running from the lower companionway. "The Russian submersible is returning to its ship!" he shouted jubilantly.

A ragged cheer broke from the watching seamen, and Garrett felt a flush of triumph as he visualized Malenov's face. Twice during the last twelve hours he had outmaneuvered his enemy. The Soviet colonel would be almost demented by now.

Wesker smiled, his plump cheeks pink with cold. "Congratulations, Major. I didn't believe you could pull it off."

"Piece of cake," Garrett told him modestly.

"What happens now?"

"Well, as soon as Malenov gets his ANSAAD on board, he'll be back like a shot. Only this time, he'll find us waiting."

"Without the submersible?"

"Of course not. How else do you expect us to reach the ocean bed?"

"But what about the structural faults?"

"We'll just have to take a chance."

Garrett turned, shouting to the sailors gathered at his rear. "Prepare the vessel for diving."

The chief mechanic looked startled. "She's not ready yet, Major. We've got to plug the power module. Otherwise, she'll blow again."

"Seal it up with Gaskin tape."

"Too dodgy, sir. It'll disintegrate under pressure."

"Not if you do it carefully. Anyhow, it's my neck on the chopping block, so don't argue."

"Right, sir."

Garrett handed the ANSAAD instrument panel to a watching seaman. He placed his arm about Jeavson's shoulder, drawing him gently aside. "Toby, I want you to sit this one out."

"What are you talking about, Skipper?"

"I mean I'm making the dive alone."

Jeavson blinked. "You're nuts."

"That thing's ready to come apart at the seams, and I don't want you getting hurt."

"Developing a conscience, Major?"

"Put it down to my strong moral fiber."

"I know what you're up to," Jeavson accused. "You want to hog all the glory for yourself."

"That's me, Squire. A regular prima donna."

"Nothing doing. You can't operate that machine *and* look after the ANSAAD at the same time. It isn't humanly possible."

"Toby, this is between Malenov and me. Anything happens to you, I'll never forgive myself."

"Zach, stop kidding about. I'm going. It's my job. You need me, and you know it."

"I can order you to back off," Garrett threatened.

Jeavson shook his head. "Make that dive alone, and you'll find yourself in front of a court-martial. And believe me, I'll be delighted to testify."

"That's what I like. The devotion of a true friend."

"Besides, somebody's got to keep you in line down there. You're too bloody wild to be let out alone."

Garrett conceded defeat. "Okay. Don't say you haven't been warned."

The preparations were carried out in double time. Garrett watched impatiently as the submersible was swung quickly into position. When everything was ready, Jeavson slithered through the narrow entrance hatch and Garrett followed, reaching back to close the cover. The sound of Lori's voice made him pause.

"Zachary?" She was peering up at him from the deck rail. "Why are you doing this?"

"Gallantry," he said. "It runs in the family."

Lori ignored the quip. "Is it because of the *Suchko*, or because of Colonel Malenov?"

"What difference does it make? They amount to the same thing, don't they?"

"No Zachary, they don't amount to the same thing at all. You're turning this into a personal vendetta."

In the brilliant sunlight, her face looked pale, despite its tan. She's worried about me, he thought, his spirits lifting. But she didn't understand. Nobody did. Only Malenov. Malenov knew the gravity of his guilt, just as he knew the fierceness of Garrett's hatred.

Reaching down, he squeezed Lori's arm. "Listen, I'm not planning to settle old scores at three thousand feet if that's what you think, but somebody's got to stop those Russians. If Malenov reaches that spacecraft first, this whole escapade will have been for nothing."

Without waiting for her reply, he slammed shut the hatch and slithered into the tiny cabin. Time to go. Time to set the record straight. Vengeance was a purifying thing when a man set his heart on it.

Jeavson's cheeks paled as their midget craft was hoisted into position. The A-frame swung out, suspending them over the jagged ice hole, then with a clanking sound lowered them gently into the water. Garrett waited in a fever as the final safety checks were carried out. When everything was ready, the lead diver gave the thumbs-up signal.

Garrett watched the frantic flurry of bubbles as the sea darkened around them. His body seemed on fire with a burning excitement. It was like the culmination of some long-awaited dream. Everything he'd gone through, the anger, the betrayal, was about to find fulfillment. The girl was right. It wasn't the *Suchko* any more. This was the repaying of old scores, and all the bitterness seemed to flow out of him like pus from some old but freshly reopened wound.

Outside the viewing ports, the water became black as pitch, and soon even Toby was indiscernible. Their only focal point lay in the luminous dials on the control panel. Like an insidious vapor, the cold again seeped through their insulated hull, and Garrett swallowed an antihistamine tablet to clear his lungs and throat.

They were descending more rapidly than prudence demanded, but this was his moment, the confrontation he had hoped and prayed for. No tricks now. Just he and Malenov together. And the ocean. The impervious, unbeatable ocean.

They were past the euphotic zone—dropping, dropping—
the water losing its texture, its substance, darkening against
their viewing ports like molten tar.

"How about lights?" Jeavson muttered, his voice wavering.

"Leave them," Garrett snapped. He immediately regretted
his harshness. Couldn't blame Toby for feeling edgy. In such
awesome gloom, a man lost his sense of perspective, panic
became an ever-present enemy. Besides, Toby was his friend.

"I don't want to use the lights," he explained, "because I
want them to take us for the *Suchko*."

Jeavson didn't answer. Squatting at the viewing port, Garrett
could sense his fear.

Garrett did not see the ocean bed emerge, but he glimpsed
its proximity on the ANSAAD scanner, and his hands moved
deftly across the control panel, bringing their descent to a
halt. Their solitary ski blade dug gently into the silt, and
Garrett used the thrusters to settle the craft on an even keel.
Dense and impenetrable, the curtain closed around him,
blacker than pitch.

"What happens now?" Jeavson whispered.

"We wait," Garrett said grimly.

Malenov's skin felt clammy as he squatted inside the tiny
submersible, watching the seabed twisting and buckling. It
had been a long, nerve-racking haul from the security of the
support ship. Malenov struggled to hide his panic. He'd never
liked diving, never—tried to avoid it whenever he could.
Would have if it hadn't been for Garrett. Always, it was
Garrett.

Beside him in the cabin, Lieutenant Pertsovka hovered over
the instrument panel, his eyes trained on the elongated light
beam picking out the path ahead. Oh, he was a splendid
fellow, Pertsovka, followed instructions to the letter. Cool as
a cucumber when the need was there. But Pertsovka had one
big advantage. He lacked imagination. He didn't appreciate
the hazards they were facing in crossing nearly half a mile of
uncharted water three thousand feet beneath the surface.
Brains of a rabbit, had Pertsovka, but for the first time in his
life, Malenov had to admit that he envied the man.

His stomach jumped as something registered on the ANSAAD
scanner. He tapped it with his fingertips, his reverie forgotten. "We've got a reading," he said.

Pertsovka glanced at him, features tense. "Where?"

"Bearing one-three-seven."

Pertsovka engaged the motors and gently changed direction.

Garrett saw the light beam cleaving the water ahead, and heard Jeavson's quick intake of breath. Reaching out, he squeezed the young man's forearm. There was little to see beyond the approaching vessel's headlamp shafts. The hull itself was lost in the blackness of the ocean wall.

Garrett lowered his other hand, his fingers tracing the control console as the lights locked into position. Slowly and determinedly, the Soviet submersible was inching toward them in a direct line.

"We're going to collide," Jeavson warned.

Garrett's fingers bit deep into his forearm.

"Let them come."

Peering through the viewing port, Malenov saw something hovering directly in their path. It looked at first like a chunk of fallen ice or a buttress from the seabed, but drawing closer, his pulses quickened as he discerned a neatly beveled engine housing. The obstacle was the hull of some man-made machine.

"It's the *Suchko*," he breathed, squinting through the Plexiglas.

Fingers trembling, he watched the vessel take on definition as Pertsovka inched their submersible steadily closer. Something protruded from the vehicle's front—an elongated manipulator arm. He recognized viewing ports, a hoisting bit, a hydroplane.

"What kind of spacecraft is that?" Pertsovka whispered, his voice hoarse and strained in the clammy atmosphere.

Stupefied, Malenov felt a terrible weakness gathering in his limbs as he stared at the grotesque creature confronting them on the ocean bed.

"That's no spacecraft," he muttered. "It's the British submersible."

*"Now!"* Garrett bellowed.

Jeavson flicked the light switch. The Soviet vessel was transfixed in the dazzling glare.

Reaching down, Garrett engaged the thrusters, and their

craft surged forward, the water foaming around them. They soared toward the intruder's vulnerable underbelly, their screws chewing the chill Antarctic current. Garrett saw the vessel's titanium skin, saw the broad bulge of its hatch-turret and the flat parallel platform that housed its cameras and battery gear.

The Soviet craft seemed to hover motionless, like an inquisitive insect sensing a prey, then its bulbous hull tilted slightly to one side as the operator—panicked, probably—blew the trimming tanks in a desperate bid to swing to starboard. Filled with a fierce elation, Garrett held their vessel on a collision course, judging timings, movements, positionings.

At three thousand feet, the two submersibles did not move with grace through the inky water; they wallowed for position like a pair of drunken hippos. Garrett reached for the control unit governing the manipulator arms, feeling the chill touch of the handgrip cooling his fingers. The huge six-hundred-pound feelers wove clumsily through the eddying current, their mechanism filling the cabin with a heavy purring sound.

The pincerlike claws scraped across the Soviet hull, sending vibrations through its titanium shield. A terrible shock wave rippled along their deck, and to Jeavson, watching dry-mouthed, the Russian vessel seemed to rear backward, lurching over on its own axis, its screws thrashing the water in wild, impotent fury.

Garrett threw their craft to starboard, jockeying for position.

"Zach!" Jeavson yelled. "Have you gone crazy, for Chrissake?"

Garrett scarcely heard. Gripping the instrument module, he flung out the manipulator arms for a second try. His hands moved like pistons, switching from control panel to manipulator console, testing, aligning, activating. He could feel the shirt clammy against his chest, smell the sharp metallic odor of the submersible's rebreathing system, see through the viewing port the enemy vessel pitching and reeling.

This time, the steel claws caught the Soviet port headlamp, smashing its reinforced glass. In the arc lights' beam, Garrett glimpsed the severed lamp plummeting into the darkness. He swung the submersible into a lumbering broadside skid, and there was a deafening thud as the two hulls clanged together.

Peering up through the forward viewing port, Jeavson saw the Soviet vessel clip the corner of a craggy outcrop. The rock exploded outward in a starburst of silt and granite fragments, clouding the water around them. For a moment, the enemy craft was lost to view, and Jeavson heard Garrett cursing as he struggled with the controls. Then the sea swung into focus, and they spotted the vessel retreating desperately among a bristling forest of pinnacles.

Bellowing like a madman, Garrett engaged the thrusters, burrowing through the water in a wild pursuit. A rock reared up, and he swung the craft deftly to starboard, missing the projection by a breathless fraction.

Jeavson reached out, seizing Garrett's arm. "Forget it, Zach. Let them go, for Chrissake!"

Garrett glanced at him, some of the fury dying in his eyes. Jeavson saw reason and sanity returning to the craggy features as Garrett's gaze focused, losing its wildness. Abruptly, he slowed the submersible to a crawl. Jeavson felt a surge of relief as the Soviet craft vanished into the darkness.

"Sorry, Toby," Garrett said, his voice suddenly calm and sensible. "Did you do something unpleasant in your trousers?"

Jeavson filled his lungs with air. "That was the craziest thing I ever saw. For Chrissake, Skipper, do you want to start World War Three? You damn near killed the poor bastard."

"His headlamps were hurting my eyes."

Garrett blew the trimming tanks, bringing the submersible around in a gentle arc, and Jeavson gripped his chair, fighting to control the tension inside him. Something caught his eye through the starboard viewing port, a pale, faintly luminous outline amid the world of gloom. Jeavson felt his palms turn clammy as he squinted incredulously.

His voice was barely a whisper. "Look, Zach."

Twisting columns of rock traced the rim of a giant precipice, and here, balanced on the craggy edge, something swayed gently in the current. Jeavson discerned a titanium cone, porthole windows and numbers painted along its upper hull. A deep gash in its side indicated a collision of sorts, and more recent scratches suggested the vessel had rolled from its original position, hit by a rock, probably, dropped from the melting ice pack above. Caught in the headlamps' glare, the spacecraft looked like a relic from some forgotten age, its smooth shielding blending into the cliff top silt with no appreciable dividing line.

Garrett stabbed the telephone switch with his finger. "Submersible calling ship-con. Do you read me—over?"

A voice broke through the static, clearing as Garrett adjusted the background volume. "*Ashbourne*-con to submersible. Everything okay?"

"Everything's fine," Garrett said. "Mark our location and bring us to the surface."

He glanced through the Plexiglas, noting the vessel's delicately balanced position. The battered spacecraft looked as if it might plummet at any second, and Garrett grimaced as he punched the transmission switch.

"Tell Wesker we've found the *Suchko*."

# EIGHT

Trembling with emotion, Malenov climbed through the open hatch and dropped to the *Orlov*'s foredeck, watching as the submersible was cranked out of the icy water. Piotr Pertsovka stumbled against him, his cheeks pale, his body shaking. "Comrade Colonel," he croaked, "the Englishman is completely mad."

"Of course he's mad," Malenov told him irritably. "He's Garrett."

No one else, he thought, would have had the unbelievable gall to engage a Soviet vessel in a direct confrontation on the ocean bed. Malenov shivered, trying to control the fear that gripped him.

Dark clouds had gathered across the skyline, and freezing winds hurled stinging snow flurries into his face and throat. The weather was worsening, but what worried him more was the sight of the submersible's damaged hull: buckled and dented, wrecked almost beyond repair.

He waited impatiently as the chief mechanic, Grigory Nestiorov, gave the vessel a cursory once-over, pursing his lips like a doctor faced like a difficult patient.

"How bad is it?" Malenov demanded.

The man looked apologetic. "Bad enough, Comrade Colonel. The starboard strobe light has gone, the depth sensor is smashed, and the pressure housings for the electric controls have been punctured.''

"Will she function?''

"Up to a point, but without electrics, she cannot be manned. The ruptured tanks will have to be repaired before she can submerge again.''

"How long will that take?''

"At least a day, possibly two.''

Malenov swore, shivering as the rising wind bit through his padded diving jacket. Garrett, by his sheer hotheaded aggressiveness, had outmaneuvered him on the ocean floor. If Malenov returned to Moscow without the *Suchko*, his career could be ruined.

He watched the storm clouds strengthening as a daring thought occurred to him. The British hadn't a monopoly on recklessness.

"Tell me, is the machine still operable?'' he asked, eying the mechanic gravely.

Nestiorov looked confused. "Operable, Comrade Colonel?''

"Can it be controlled electronically, robot-style, from the support ship?''

"It can.''

"Then without a crew, surely the lack of electrics would be unimportant?''

"Correct, Comrade Colonel. Mechanically speaking, the vessel should still be seaworthy.''

Malenov glanced at Pertsovka. "Could you guide it into the search area without leaving the sanctuary of the iceberg?''

Pertsovka hesitated. "It would be difficult, Comrade Colonel, a slow, tedious process, but not impossible.''

Malenov turned to the captain. "You have explosives on board?''

"We do, Comrade Colonel.''

"What type?''

"CXThree, a combination of magnesium and white phosphorous. It carries strong 'blast probability' as well as a high incendiary potential.''

"Excellent.''

Pertsovka's eyes widened as he understood Malenov's intention. "Comrade Colonel, you can't destroy the submersible,'' he protested.

"My orders are explicit,'' Malenov explained patiently. "If

we fail to locate the *Suchko*, we must ensure no one else does. Since the British seem determined to carry on with their search, we are obliged to take desperate measures.''

He turned to the captain. In the biting cold, his lips were blue. ''I want the submersible turned into a floating mine.''

''The *Suchko*'s lying at a forty-degree angle,'' Garrett said, ''her lower half perched over a precipice. Try to move her, and she'll slide over the edge.''

''How far?'' Wesker asked.

''Can't tell. We have no way of judging how deep the chasm goes. All we do know is, if she falls, she'll be physically beyond our reach.''

In the *Ashbourne*'s control room, the soft purr of equipment hung in Lori's ears like the buzzing of distant insects. The air was heavy with cigarette smoke.

''Couldn't you fix grappling chains?'' Wesker suggested. ''Once the spacecraft's strapped into its cradle, we could hold her in position from the surface.''

''The angle's wrong. Because of the way she's lying, we can only get the chains around the upper nose cone. As soon as we try to lift her, she'll slide out of the harness. Of course''—Garrett cupped his coffee mug between his palms—''I can always try to enter her on the seabed.''

Wesker said, ''Is that possible?''

''Dangerous, but certainly possible. We have one of the new Belka diving suits on board. It's clumsy and unwieldy, but it can go anywhere the submersible can.''

''You're kidding. At three thousand feet, the sea will carry a pressure of two thousand pounds per square inch.''

''The Belka's armored,'' Garrett explained. ''It was developed for scientific salvage work and offshore oil operations, usually with a connecting line to the surface, though it can work just as effectively on its own. On land, it weighs almost five hundred kilograms, but once under water, the figure drops to twenty-three. The limb joints on its arms and legs contain fluid to prevent them seizing up, and it carries a rebreathing device which keeps recycling the air supply, adding oxygen and removing carbon dioxide for as long as forty-eight hours. It'll take anything the ocean has to offer and still remain pressurized, which means I can surface quickly without having to worry about the danger of bends.''

"How would you get inside?" Wesker asked.

"Well, there's a gash in the *Suchko*'s hull, which probably explains why the vessel sank so quickly, but it might not be wide enough to encompass something as large as the Belka. I'll probably have to use the entrance hatch."

"Easier said than done. If the *Suchko*'s balanced as delicately as you claim, you daren't risk blowing the shutter clamps, and they're probably too rusted to operate manually."

"True, but the submersible carries a high-speed drill on one of its manipulator arms. If we use it gently, the drill should cut through the *Suchko*'s shield like a knife slicing through butter."

"And if the spacecraft slides off after you enter?"

"I didn't say I liked the idea."

Garrett glanced at the faces surrounding him. "Well, what's it to be? Do we quit now and leave her to the Russians, or take a chance and board her?"

Silence fell in the crowded control room as the officers and technicians looked at each other worriedly.

Reaching into his pocket, Wesker took out a stick of gum and popped it into his mouth. "Let's go for broke," he said.

Snow flurries danced into Lori's face as she watched Garrett climbing into the bulky Belka. The suit's insulated armor turned him into a human robot, a bloated body and a pair of bulbous arms protruding from his trunk like clumsy insect feelers.

Despite the seriousness of the moment, Lori couldn't suppress a smile. "You look like the Pillsbury Dough Boy."

"It hasn't done much for my tango," he admitted, his voice muffled beneath the reinforced dome.

"How can you move in that thing?"

"It may look clumsy on the surface, but at three thousand feet, this straitjacket'll be little heavier than an ordinary overcoat."

"Will we be able to talk to you?"

"No, but I'll have a direct communications linkup with Toby Jeavson, so you can pass on messages via the submersible."

"The submersible?" She looked at him, puzzled. "You can't get into the submersible in that thing. You'll take up the entire cabin."

He grinned at her through his transparent face mask. "I'm

not going inside. Toby will hold me against the hull with the manipulator arms until we reach the seabed. After that, I'll be on my own."

The thought of descending into the ocean depths locked in the submersible's mechanical bear hug appalled her. Lori watched as Garrett took his place in front of the tiny hatch-turret, and Toby Jeavson engaged the controls, closing the manipulator arms firmly around him. At a wave from the crew, the crane operator swung the minuscule craft over the *Ashbourne*'s deck rail. Garrett's helmet vanished into the ice hole, descending rapidly amid a whirling cauldron of bubbles.

Shivering, Lori returned to the control room to follow his progress on the TV monitors.

In the fading sunlight, the Soviet submersible looked like an object from some exotic fairy tale, its fat body and blunt nose incongruous in the paleness of the Antarctic evening. As Malenov watched the hull maneuver delicately into position, Lieutenant Pertsovka made one last desperate plea.

"Comrade Colonel, I implore you. In destroying this vessel, you are throwing away years of painstaking research."

Malenov ignored him, turning to the captain. "How will the craft be detonated?"

"By a radio signal. Transmitted on the right frequency, it should blow the submersible into a million pieces. But—" the captain hesitated, "is this wise, Comrade Colonel? Apart from the political implications, think of the expense."

"The expense is immaterial. The *Suchko* must carry her secret to the grave."

Malenov stepped back from the rail, hugging his overjacket tightly around him. "Come, gentlemen, we've remained on deck long enough. We will track the submersible from the comfort of the control room. It would be a great pity to miss such a spectacular finale."

Garrett watched the ice pack vanishing steadily above him. Bubbles issuing from his helmet valve drifted around the plastic dome. Flowing through a filter and accumulator, the air from his compressor smelled curiously soporific. Surprisingly, there was no sense of stress inside his armored plating. The diving suit's roominess was quite remarkable. He was even able to withdraw his arms from the sockets if he wanted to.

He heard the radio linkup crackling in his ear; then Jeavson's voice echoed inside the bulky helmet. "We're down to two thousand feet, Major. Feeling good?"

"Better every minute. What's happening up top?"

"Weather's worsening. Could be a storm tonight."

"Just our bloody luck. Keep your fingers crossed, Toby. Let's hope we get this finished before the seas whip up."

Soon, the water deepened to a flat impenetrable black, and Garrett switched on his helmet lamp, cutting a swath of light through the gloom. There was nothing to see but the few square feet on which they moved. The ocean was like a velvet pad, drained of variation, wrapping itself around him in a smothering shroud. Something drifted through the shadows— gliding, hovering. It eased into the circle of lamplight, watching him ominously, its green scaly body tipped at the tail with a pinkish glow. A gulper eel. For a full minute, it swayed inquisitively in front of him, struggling to comprehend this curious intruder in the sunless ocean depths, then, having satisfied itself the newcomer offered no prospect of nourishment, turned with a flick of its tail and vanished into the darkness.

"I just saw one of your relatives," Garrett said.

"Good-looking, was he?"

"Striking family resemblance."

Jeavson chuckled dryly. "Almost there, Skipper. Twenty-eight hundred feet. What's the visibility like?"

"Thick as syrup."

In his lamp beam, Garrett saw the seabed emerge beneath them. The jagged silt-coated outcrops reared in the gloom like monsters from some half-forgotten nightmare.

"Coming down, Toby. Slow your descent. I don't want to bounce like a Ping-Pong ball."

"Easing off," Jeavson muttered reassuringly.

Garrett spotted the spacecraft balanced on the rim of the precipice. It looked like some ghostly apparition from centuries past. He could just discern the cavity in its hull where the American shrapnel had ripped it out of the sky.

He felt a bump as the submersible settled gently on the cliff top.

"All set to disconnect?" Jeavson murmured.

"Let her go, Toby."

"Disconnecting now."

The manipulator arms uncurled, releasing Garrett from the submersible's hull. There was no sense of discomfort as his feet touched the seabed. He stood for a moment, balancing carefully, getting the feel of the hardened magnesium-alloy shell encasing his body.

"Okay, Zach?"

"Feeling fine," Garrett confirmed. "Commencing walk."

Tentatively, he lifted his leg and deposited it two feet in front of him. The great limbs responded effortlessly to his movements, and he stepped forward again, tracing the slippery cliff top. The chasm loomed ominously at his side, and he tried to shut his mind from it, focusing instead on the gleaming outline of the spacecraft ahead.

He reached it at last, and leaning forward, ran the Belka's mechanical hands along the pale titanium hull.

"How does it look, Major?"

"It's about twenty-eight feet in diameter, I'd say. The retro-rockets are still intact. So is part of the communications antenna, though it seems incredible after crashing through the atmosphere."

"Any sign of an access point?"

Garrett stared dubiously at the ragged tear in the capsule's nose cone. It was too narrow to accommodate the Belka, that much was clear, and even if it could, one glimpse of those jagged shark tooth projections was enough to make his skin crawl. He ran his gaze down the smooth, shining hull.

"There's something here. Looks like a hatch cover."

Garrett tried it, but the release wouldn't budge. He turned, waving Jeavson forward. "Take it slowly, Toby. I don't want you pushing her over the edge."

Jeavson brought the submersible forward in a ponderous crawl while Garrett used his mechanical hands to mark the surface where the fastenings could be breached. Slowly, tentatively, the manipulator arm reached out, settling into position. Garrett watched the drill tips slot into place.

"Bull's-eye, Toby. Now hold it right there."

He stepped back as the twin blades sliced through the *Suchko*'s outer casing. The drill sent tiny slivers of metal spinning through the water, clouding Garrett's vision. The *Suchko* rocked gently, its conelike contours catching the fractured slivers of lamplight. When the blades had fully penetrated, Jeavson delicately withdrew, repositioning the manipulator arm. The operation had taken about twenty minutes.

"Here we go again," Jeavson said.

"Gently now."

Muck and grit floated around Garrett's helmet as the drill whirred steadily deeper and deeper. Garrett tried not to think about the consequences if the spacecraft toppled, tried to make his mind go blank, his nerves insentient.

When Jeavson had finished, he backed the submersible, giving Garrett room to maneuver. "Don't get too close, Zach. Once that cabin fills, she could tumble over the rim."

"My guess is, she's full already. That crack in her side looks like it reaches clean through to the interior."

Garrett reached up, hooking the *Belka*'s mechanical hand around the *Suchko*'s hatch clasp. He gritted his teeth, sucked in his breath. *Now,* he thought, and with a quick jerk, flung back the fastenings. The hatch cover exploded outward. The craft shuddered as a massive bubble emerged from its interior. Bits of chrome, leather, and other debris whirled out through the open hole and rocketed toward the surface. Muscles tense, Garrett watched the *Suchko* tremble, then gradually settle. His chest rose as he filled his lungs with air.

"We've done it, Toby. The hatch is open, and she's still in position."

"Easy, Zach. This is the tricky bit."

"I reckon there's just enough room to let me inside."

"Don't take any chances. If you feel it moving, get out quick."

"Fingers crossed, Toby."

Moving cautiously, Garrett approached the *Suchko*'s still-quivering hull. He hooked one of his mechanical hands over the hatch rim. With the other, he carefully touched his variable tilt control and engaged the electrically powered thrusters. The *Belka* lifted him through the water until he was directly level with the entrance. Then, leaning forward, he clamped his metal feelers around the insulation pipes and gently, gingerly, eased himself inside.

"Major Garrett is now entering the spacecraft."

Holding her breath, Lori followed Garrett's progress on the

TV screens. She hadn't wanted him to do this, had visualized talking him out of it, knowing she wouldn't, knowing she couldn't, but thinking about it anyway. He'd been so damned determined—that was the unnerving thing. Garrett was like a battering ram when his mind was made up. . . . She watched his boots vanishing into the darkened interior.

"He's done it," Wesker said.

A warning blip reached Lori from the scanning sonar.

"Something's approaching," the operator announced.

"How far?" Wesker demanded.

"Hard to say, but it's coming fast."

The man glanced up, his features slack with disbelief. "I think it's the other submersible, sir."

"It can't be!" Lori exclaimed. "Garrett knocked it out of commission."

She turned to Wesker. "If they catch Garrett inside that spacecraft, one quick push could topple him over the rim."

"I know," Wesker agreed grimly.

Lori turned to the radio operator. "Warn them," she snapped, her voice edged with panic. "Before it's too late."


"Major?"

Inside the *Suchko*, Jeavson's voice echoed in Garrett's ear.

"What is it, Toby?"

"We've got company."

"Russians?"

"Looks like. Ship-con says they're closing fast. Get out of there."

Garrett cursed inside his breathing mask.

"Zach, that's an order from the top."

"Sorry, Toby. My earpiece appears to be malfunctioning."

Balancing himself on the tilting deck, Garrett looked around the cramped little cabin. His lamp beam picked up the padding on the opposite bulkhead. The closeness was stifling, as if he'd entered some kind of tomb, as indeed he had.

He moved his lamp around, throwing the cabin into sharp relief, trying to visualize the vessel's final moments as the cosmonauts, locked inside their suffocating cocoon, made their last fevered dive through the planet's atmosphere.

"Zach, get out of there, do you hear me?"

"Keep your underpants on, Toby. I'll only be a minute."

"You're pushing your luck, Skipper."

"What's luck *for*?"

His beam picked out the flight deck and the instrument consoles, a million dollars' worth of hardware frozen at the point of destruction, encapsulated forever on the seabed.

"Everything okay, Zach?"

"Fine, Toby. I'm moving clockwise, exploring the cabin base."

"For God's sake, be quick. You haven't time to muck about. What can you see?"

"Pressure gauges, light indicators for checking inboard mechanisms, modular compartments for experimental apparatus."

"Anything else?"

"Food-storage cabin."

Garrett hesitated, his features tensing as he spotted an eerie shape strapped against the bulkhead in front. "Hold it, Toby. There's something odd here."

As he eased delicately through the gloom, the outlines focused, taking on shape and substance. Locked into a rack battened to the cabin wall hung a line of metal canisters. They were cylindrical in appearance, roughly one foot in length with an approximate diameter of six inches. Their lids were firmly sealed, and as if to ensure that they remained intact, heavy viselike devices gripped them both top and bottom. Garrett ran his mechanical hands along the row.

"What is it, Zach?"

"I don't know. Tubes of some kind—containers, I think. Must be something volatile. They've got them jammed against the bulkhead like rivets."

"Can you prise one loose?"

"I can try."

Garrett fumbled with the fastenings, but the metal screws jammed in his grasp, refusing to budge. He engaged the Belka's mechanical arms, and with a slight shudder, the handle relaxed and began to turn. Carefully, Garrett lifted the container. For its diminutive size, the tube felt remarkably heavy.

"How does it look, Major?"

"Solid as a rock. Clearly built to last. Whatever it's holding, I have a hunch they don't want any unexpected leaks."

"Can you bring it out?"

"Sure."

Garrett unzipped the specimen pouch on the diving suit's front, and squeezed the canister gently inside.

"What about the crew?" Jeavson asked.

Garrett swung his helmet beam around the cluttered interior. The dark shadows settled into identifiable shapes, and a faint chill rose inside him as he glimpsed the motionless figures, clad in bulky spacesuits, still strapped into the ejector seats. Three wore helmets. The fourth, for some indeterminate reason, had removed his.

"Crew intact," Garrett announced.

"Dead?"

"Naturally. Hold on a minute, I'm moving closer."

Garrett inched through the gloom. The face of the man whose helmet had been removed had completely decomposed. There was little to identify him as human. Clumps of ragged hair clung to his decaying bone structure, and something gleamed at the base of his throat, a tiny identity tag. Steeling himself against the grinning skull, Garrett leaned forward to study the disc more closely. His lamp picked out the spidery lettering, and a spasm of shock ran through him. The words were in English. Tearing the tag from the corpse's neck, he held it closer to his helmet dome, struggling to see as he read the inscription slowly. Softly, he whistled under his breath. "Toby, can you hear me?"

"Affirmative, Skipper."

"One of these characters was an American officer."

"An American? Are you crazy?"

"His name was Frank De Tabley, a major in the U.S. Army."

"What would an American serviceman be doing on a Soviet spacecraft shot down by U.S. military personnel?"

"That's a question that'll take some answering."

Garrett thrust the identity tag into his specimen pouch and zipped shut the top. Then he turned to the other corpses, examining each in turn.


"The submersible is not yet in position, Comrade Colonel," the Russian captain protested fiercely, standing at the radio console.

"We can't wait," Malenov said. "Garrett's already inside the *Suchko*. How far are we off target?"

"Impossible to say. Fifty yards, maybe a hundred."

Malenov turned to the radio officer. "Detonate," he ordered.

Lieutenant Pertsovka made one last desperate plea. "Comrade Colonel, I beg you, reconsider before it is too late."

Malenov brushed him aside and glared down at the headphoned operator leaning over the control panel. The man's face was pale, his eyes glassy. He too was reluctant to take the fateful step.

"Did you hear what I said? Fire, damn you!"

Without a word, the operator flicked the detonator switch.

Lori heard a roar to starboard, and whipping back the porthole curtain, saw a vast column of water spurting upward from the ocean bed. The ice cracked and buckled, its glistening surface splitting into giant floes that dipped and lunged on the boiling current. A thunderous echo wailed over the radio receiver, and she stared dumbly at the imageless screens, her muscles tense. Then the *Ashbourne* rocked as the swell hit it.

"For God's sake, get them up!" she shouted.

Jeavson saw the great wall of water hurtling toward him, felt the impact ramming the submersible's hull, throwing him backward to the rubberized deck. The vessel clanged against rock, rolling clumsily as the shock waves slammed it. The alarm bell clattered in his head, and blood streamed into his eyes. Struggling to his knees, he dragged himself toward the operator's seat, glimpsing through the viewing port the *Suchko* rearing from its perch like a sleek gray slug. With an air of almost weary reluctance, it tumbled over the precipice.

Jeavson watched the doomed spacecraft whirling downward in a graceful spiral, its empty hatch, like a toothless mouth, trailing wires, leads, and harnesses as it vanished steadily into the inky void.

*Zach*! he thought.

He flopped into the control seat, unable to think, unable to react. He scarcely heard the hoisting bit clank, scarcely felt the damaged craft lift from the ocean bed and with a gentle, barely perceptible rocking motion, slowly rise.

Garrett held his breath, battling desperately to maintain his equilibrium. Over and over he whirled as the vessel plummeted crazily downward. It was a curious sensation, like being trapped inside a washing machine. His helmet lamp picked out the spinning bulkheads flitting across the cabin like a laser beam. Objects floated through the water—pen lights and drink containers, instrument handles and oxygen packs. He felt no fear, that was the strangest thing. Instead, he struggled to realign his senses.

Think it out, he told himself, think it out.

He hit one of the corpses, feeling the blow ripple through his armor plating, and saw the decaying skull shatter into a million fragments. He didn't even know in which direction to turn, so insistently was the spacecraft rolling. Down, down, down—how much farther could he go before his diving suit popped open like a walnut shell?

Reaching out, his mechanical hands connected with the insulation pipes and he clamped on to them gratefully. Relief. Now, at least, he had an anchor.

The sense of descent was overwhelming; there seemed no end to it, as if the chasm into which he had plunged reached deep into the earth's innermost core. His stomach dissolved, and his genitals twitched in an involuntary spasm.

Directly in front, the bodies of the three cosmonauts strapped securely in their ejector seats floundered like a trio of rag dolls. The fourth had torn loose from its safety harness and was whirling around the cabin like a demented ghost.

Suddenly Garrett heard a clang, and with a spine-numbing jerk, the spacecraft shuddered to a halt. He hung for a moment, dazed, as the cabin swiveled into alignment. He could hear the sound of his breathing, magnified weirdly inside the bulbous helmet. Around him, the dancing objects slowed, hovering motionless in the eddying water. The *Suchko* had jammed on a projectile farther down the cliff. Like a bug on the side of a wall, it was clinging tentatively to the precipice—but for how long? He had to get his bearings.

Garrett eased to the deck, tensing his muscles as his feet touched the slanting incline; then, moving as quickly as he dared, he edged toward the exit hatch. One glance told him his escape route was blocked. The vehicle had come to a halt with its entrance jammed against the rocky buttress. There could be no joy that way.

Musn't panic, he thought. Think, think, think. There has to be another outlet—has to.

He recalled the endless briefings he'd conducted with Lori

Madden. The galley, he remembered. There should be an emergency chute in the vehicle's galley.

Garrett saw the ladder leading to the upper platform and headed gingerly toward it, gripping the rails in his mechanical fists. Raising one weighted boot, he pressed it against the first rung, paused for a moment, then moved to the second.

Inching upward, he scaled the ladder until his helmet emerged through the hole in the upper deck. His lamp picked out the galley's furnishings, and the beveled, clearly marked emergency hatch on the opposite bulkhead. Bending over the cover, he tried the handle. The hatch swung open, and he gazed into the escape funnel beyond. It was like looking along the barrel of a gun. The walls had been padded to facilitate access, and his lamp beam played among the folds, creating tiny spirals of light that glimmered back at him mockingly.

Garrett could see no end to it. The circular flanks looked far too narrow to encompass the dimensions of his bulky diving suit, but he had to give it a try.

Leaning down, he wormed his helmet and shoulders into the slender cylindrical opening. The tube gathered around him, pressing against his armored plating. He flexed his arm muscles, inching his way deeper and deeper, then rammed his boots against the padded sides as he maneuvered the Belka's awesome proportions toward the inky blackness of the exit hole ahead.

It was useless. The sheer size of the diving suit locked inextricably in the escape chute's center. For a moment, he lay panting, then, clenching and unclenching his shoulder muscles, wormed back the way he had come.

He felt exhausted as he popped out of the exit shaft; he leaned against the bulkhead, filled his lungs with air, a terrible lassitude gathering inside him. Speculatively, he examined the gaping tear in the *Suchko*'s hull. Jagged and uneven, the edges buckled inward like a series of savage spearheads, challenging him to pass. The size of the hole itself was depressingly small. He would find no passage that way.

Garrett gazed through the deck hatch into the cabin below. The three cosmonauts looked like a trio of drunks at a fancy-dress party. The fourth man, freed from his safety harness, drifted placidly beneath the cabin ceiling.

Garrett sucked in his breath as a thought suddenly occurred to him. It seemed a chance in a million that the spacecraft's internal workings might still be functioning normally, but he could think of no alternative.

Gritting his teeth, he moved to the companionway ladder and gingerly eased himself downward. The diving suit was like a second skin. He could hear it creaking and groaning as the armored plating inexorably contracted, driven inward by the relentless pressure of the surrounding water.

Reaching the deck, he inched his way toward the pilot's seat. The body of the first cosmonaut was straining forward against its harness, and Garrett placed his hands beneath the domed helmet, thrusting it back against the rear ejector plate. He tugged at the seat-belt buckle, dragging the waist and shoulder straps free. Released from constraint, the corpse floated eerily upward, its heavy boots scraping past Garrett's reinforced face mask.

Turning awkwardly, Garrett attempted to settle himself in the chair, but his hindquarters jammed on the padded arm-rests. He would have to hurry, he thought.

Fumbling with the safety harness, he struggled to clamp it around his bulging contours. The shoulder straps at first refused to meet, but after a good deal of tugging and groping, he managed to clip the seat belt into position. Leaning forward, he squinted hard as his lamplight picked out the dials and gauges. He prayed the heavy protective plates had kept their mechanism free from the chilly Antarctic waters.

He found the ejector-seat release button and primed it nervously. It's now or never, he thought, his skin crawling, his stomach tightening.

He pressed the tiny knob. He heard the explosive bolts opening up the *Suchko*'s rear, then was hurtling backward, turning over and over as he popped from the stricken vessel like a pellet from a peashooter. The water swirled around him, and he felt his brain swimming.

If I faint, I'm finished, he thought. If I pass out, I'll die.

His lamplight flickered and extinguished, and suddenly there was nothing to see, nothing to hear, almost nothing to feel. Reaching down, he tugged at the safety harness, releasing himself from the ejector plate and opening his variable buoyancy valve. He was rising or sinking, he couldn't tell which. The blackness around him was total, a debilitating shroud shutting off nerve and response patterns alike. Seconds drifted into minutes. Minutes elongated, stretched, blended. He had no awareness of the passage of time.

He longed for sleep, could feel it hovering somewhere just beyond his senses, but something kept him stubbornly awake. With sleep came death, and he was not ready to embrace it yet.

His teeth chattered in his helmet. The cold affected mind and body alike. He'd never known such incredible cold. He would be the freshest corpse in creation, he thought, his lips twisting wryly.

When he closed his eyes, he saw green fields and gentle pastures, smelled the deep-scented fragrance of a country June.

Suddenly, he blinked as something caught his attention. The sea was beginning to lighten. He glimpsed rays of sunlight penetrating the translucent current. Fish slithered by—a curious seal, a school of penguins.

Above his head, a jagged and luminous canopy began to take shape—the underside of the ice pack. His helmet was soon scraping across the heavily serrated bulges as the waves lifted him, turning his body around. A spasm knotted in his chest as he spotted the *Ashbourne*'s crusted underbelly beckoning him through the lifting current.

With a hoarse cry, he turned on his back and used his mechanical hands against the ice cap's rugged surface to drag himself painfully toward it.

Lori watched the A-frame swing the dripping submersible over the *Ashbourne*'s rail and lower it delicately to the deck. Water spurted from a dozen assorted leaks in its hull. Sailors tore open the hatch cover as Toby Jeavson, aided by a dozen willing hands, appeared in the narrow opening, his eyes blackened, his nostrils streaming with blood.

"What happened to Garrett?" Commander Henderson demanded.

Jeavson shook his head, and Lori felt a terrible chill settle in her stomach. It couldn't be true. Not the indestructible Zach Garrett.

Tears streamed down the steep curve of her cheeks, and she leaned against the deck rail.

She saw the ice pack below, the waves lapping against the

jagged hole where the submersible had operated. She blinked. For a moment, she imagined her senses were playing tricks as a helmet broke the rippling surface. It was a seal, she thought, a dolphin, a maverick whale coming up for air. Then she recognized the contours of the Belka diving suit.

"It's Garrett!" she shouted excitedly, and sailors came running from every direction.

Standing in the Soviet control room, Malenov heard Lori's exuberant cry and slammed his fist furiously against the instrument panel.

After all his cleverness and ingenuity, luck, like everything else, had turned against him. He wanted to cry aloud at the injustice of it. Yet despite the bitterness of the moment, he was filled with a sense of reluctant admiration.

That bastard Garrett, he thought bitterly, had more lives than a bloody cat.

# PART

## II

# THE QUARRY

# NINE

Jan Marisa Bowering was brushing her hair when her husband entered the bedroom. Clad in a velvet houserobe, his gray hair disheveled, Walter scarcely looked like the well-groomed businessman she had married.

"Caryl Brightman's here, kitten," he said.

Jan Bowering was genuinely surprised. "So early?"

A notorious nightbird, Caryl Brightman rarely surfaced before ten o'clock in the morning.

"He's waiting in the study. Says it's important."

Jan Bowering reached for her robe. Brightman was not a man given to exaggeration. When he declared something to be important, she knew his assessment could be relied on.

She found the deputy national security adviser gazing through the window at the dew-wet lawns outside. He looked a little more weary than usual.

"Good morning, Caryl. I thought you hated early rising."

He smiled faintly as he turned to look at her. "I haven't been to bed yet. I spent the night with some of our chemical research boys."

Jan Bowering fastened her belt. "Sit down, I'll get you some coffee. Have you breakfasted yet?"

Brightman flopped against the seat cushions.

"Forget coffee, Mrs. Bowering. I think it might be a good idea if we weren't disturbed for a while."

Jan Bowering settled into the armchair opposite. "What's this all about, Caryl? You make it sound very dramatic."

"You read the report I left on your desk last night?"

"Yes, I did. A remarkable escape, it seems, for Major Garrett. I trust he's recovering?"

"Major Garrett was virtually unhurt. The British submersible was damaged, but at least the crew came out alive."

"Thank heaven for that. What on earth did the Soviets think they were playing at?"

"We can't prove it was the Soviets," Brightman said, "although it does seem a pretty solid bet. A miniature radio transmitter was discovered in Miss Lori Madden's wristwatch, planted there by Colonel Sergei Malenov of the GRU. The Russians must have been listening to every word our people said."

"No wonder they were able to interfere so effectively. I see the body of an American officer was discovered in the *Suchko*'s cabin."

"Correct. And not just any American officer. Major Frank De Tabley."

"De Tabley's name seems to be creeping into this affair with alarming regularity."

"Right. How he got into a Russian spacecraft is puzzling enough. What he was doing there in a period when we were still in a state of contention with the Soviet Union and how he came to be wearing his U.S. identity tag staggers the senses. Sadly, the discovery of *Suchko Twenty-three* gives rise to a lot more questions than it answers."

"I take it you've examined the contents of the receptacle Garrett brought out."

"We have. What was left to work on. There was little more than a minute quantity of distilled liquid, but we discovered enough to offer a lead on what the drum originally contained."

Taking a handkerchief from his breast pocket, Brightman carefully blew his nose. "Fourteen years ago, that little cylinder, together with its companions, would have been filled with a fine liquid gas known as DDF Eight hundred. The gas contained a lethal toxin, probably the most dangerous element available to man. U.S. scientists were aware of its existence but at that time hadn't managed to produce anything quite so virulent. In those days, the Soviet Union led the world in the field of chemical and biological warfare."

"The toxin was a weapon?"

"A weapon, yes, though in realistic terms, not a terribly practical one. The problem with DDF Eight hundred lay in its power. It was, quite simply, uncontrollable. If I released a thimbleful in the middle of Central Park, say, practically the entire city of New York would suffer convulsions within three to four hours. Death would follow in varying degrees of alacrity, depending on the strength or weakness of the victims' metabolisms, but one thing you could count on—by the end of a fortnight, there would be few people left alive on Manhattan Island."

"That's horrific," she breathed.

"It's only the beginning. DDF Eight hundred is highly contagious. There is no known vaccine. What begins with a thimbleful in Central Park would spread throughout New Jersey and the eastern seaboard of the United States. Within a month, the entire area from southern Ontario to northern Florida would be one vast mausoleum. Within six months, nine—a year at the outside—two thirds of this country would simply cease to exist."

In the harsh sunlight, lines appeared around Jan Bowering's cheeks and eyes. "Are you telling me the Soviet Union has the capacity to wipe out the United States?"

"They do, ma'am, as indeed do we. At the end of World War Two, U.S. troops liberated a Manchurian death camp where the Japanese had been experimenting on Allied prisoners, exposing them to deadly diseases like bubonic plague, anthrax, and typhoid. We granted immunity to the people responsible in exchange for their findings. Since then, research has progressed on a more or less uninterrupted scale, until today, certain toxins developed by our own people would have a similar 'scorched-earth' effect were we to release them in Moscow, say."

"My God," Jan Bowering whispered. "What a delicate knife-edge our civilizations are balanced on. How long have we known about DDF Eight hundred?"

"Almost from the beginning. It didn't worry us too much in the early days. You see, biological weapons have one major disadvantage. Their agents can be carried by birds, people, even by the wind, to regions far beyond the target area. A toxin—that's a chemical produced by a living organism—is usually noncontagious; in normal circumstances, it cannot multiply. DDF Eight hundred, however, spreads with the fury of a prairie fire. So as a weapon of war, its handicap lies in its sheer potency.

"Few viruses can survive for long in hostile conditions, but DDF Eight hundred is the exception. It requires virtually nothing to sustain itself. It can't be suppressed, no matter how cold the atmosphere and how devoid of life or air. And should the United States be attacked, the toxin would scarcely recognize international boundaries. It would spread through Mexico into the Central American states. Within a year, two years, it would find its way around the globe. Therefore, it becomes a suicide weapon, a 'doomsday bug.' Use it, and you sentence to death not only your opponents, but a sizable portion of your own people as well."

"Will nothing stop it?" Jan Bowering asked, her cheeks unnaturally pale.

"Time will," Brightman said. "After a period of three to four years, the toxin liquidizes. That's what happened in this case. The substance we found inside the metal container proved to be harmless. But had the gas escaped at the height of its power..."

Jan Bowering sat back in her chair. A lock of hair had fallen untidily across her forehead, but she made no move to brush it away.

"I had no idea such toxins existed," she said.

"Well, most of our attention has concentrated on the threat of nuclear weapons. Few people know that East and West have for many years possessed the capacity to eliminate each other using microbiological warfare. The problem is—and this is what provides the built-in safety factor—employing an agent like DDF Eight hundred would be playing Russian Roulette with every chamber loaded."

"And this toxin was being transported inside *Suchko Twenty-three*?"

"For whatever reason, the Soviets were ferrying it to their space lab, *Salyut Fifty-six*."

Jan Bowering drummed her fingers absently on her knee. "If the substance is as lethal as you say, maybe they were using the space lab as a storage vault. It would make sense, wouldn't it, to remove the toxin from the earth's atmosphere in case there was some kind of leakage?"

"That's true," Brightman agreed. "But it doesn't answer

the question of why we shot the vehicle down. There had to be a reason, Mrs. Bowering, and in view of the lethal nature of the cargo, it would have to be a damned good reason. Maybe the Soviets weren't planning to stockpile DDF Eight hundred at all, but experiment with it instead. By using *Salyut Fifty-six* as a microbiological laboratory, they could forestall any danger of the toxin breaking loose. Until now, the safety factor has lain in the uncontrollability of DDF Eight hundred. What we have to face here is the question have the Soviets discovered a way of harnessing it, even directing it? If, for example, they could transmit a few drops into an American reservoir, then neutralize it at their leisure, they would have at their disposal the ultimate weapon of war. It would make nuclear missiles look like something out of the Dark Ages.

"I'm not saying they would choose to use it, you understand. After all, we no longer regard the Russians as our enemies, but we have to remember that the Communists have established a much more authoritarian regime in the Kremlin following the turmoil of the nineties, and even in the present era of goodwill, who knows what some of those hard-liners may be capable of? How can we conclude an agreement on international space cooperation, wondering if the Russians have a devastating new secret weapon tucked up their sleeves?"

"Well, we can't postpone the Centaur meeting, Caryl. It's too sensitive. The President will never agree to risk everything he's worked for on the grounds of mere speculation."

"Even if we could be turning ourselves into shorn lambs?"

"We've got six weeks before he travels to Moscow. Somehow, during that time, we've got to find the answer."

"That's a pretty tall order. We've damn little to go on, beyond the identity of Major Frank De Tabley, whose service record is alarmingly sketchy."

"You must know something about the man."

"Well, CIA has uncovered the name of a sergeant who served with De Tabley in Vietnam. He's a Navajo who lives down Albuquerque way. At the very least, he should be able to furnish the names of other De Tabley associates."

Jan Bowering was silent for a moment. "Caryl, I don't want you using any more intelligence people on this thing."

"Why?"

"It could be a conspiracy we're talking about, and we

don't know how deep it may go. We can't risk involving anybody who isn't one hundred percent.''

"That kind of limits our parameters. Nobody's that clean— you've said so yourself.''

"How about the people you used in the South Atlantic?''

"Well, Wesker's a good man, sound as they come. As a White House security consultant, he's already been subjected to a full-field FBI investigation.''

"And Garrett?''

Brightman looked dubious. "The British Defense Office has assigned Garrett to Wesker until the crisis is over, but let's face it, he's no investigator. He's a professional soldier.''

"He's SAS. There's a difference. Didn't the media used to call them the James Bond Brigade?''

"It's fieldcraft they specialize in—survival, tracking, infiltrating enemy lines. Hardly the kind of skills we're looking for here. The same might be said of Miss Madden.''

Jan Bowering was insistent. "At least we know they're reliable. They've proved their dependability and their trust. You could put Wesker in command and let the others operate under his control.''

"Are you serious about this?''

"You know damn well I'm serious. Remember, Garrett's the only man who's actually been inside that spacecraft.''

Brightman said, "Okay, I'll fly down to the South Atlantic and talk to him.''

"Good idea, Caryl. And thank Major Garrett personally for me, will you? Tell him how much the President appreciates the risks he's taken, and—'' she hesitated, "please impress upon him the critical nature of this affair.''

Ben Fleming, director of NASA's Cape Canaveral Space Complex, was eating breakfast in his office when Judd Cronin, his special assistant, looked in.

"May I have a word with you, Ben?''

Fleming eyed him impatiently. It was an important day at the cape. In less than two hours, a crew of astronauts would blast off from the launchpad on a secret Pentagon mission to re-man a spy satellite two hundred miles above the earth. Despite the new climate of collaboration, neither side had considered jettisoning its electronic surveillance network, and Fleming had no time for irrelevant issues.

"Is it that important?"

"Yes, sir. I think it is."

"Can't it wait until we get those astronauts into the sky?"

"Best not, Ben. This affects the astronauts personally."

"Okay, what's the problem?"

"The shuttle commander, Nelson Zahl," Cronin said. "He's been worrying me ever since he arrived here. There's something funny about him, Ben, something I can't put a name to."

Fleming looked surprised. Little had been said about the three-man shuttle crew who had arrived at NASA on the Pentagon's orders. Most of their training had been carried out under the strictest secrecy at Houston. Even NASA's most senior people had been kept largely in the dark about the true nature and purpose of the operation.

"Does he know his job?" Fleming asked.

"Sure, he knows his job."

"Then what the hell. He's not our headache."

"You're wrong, Ben," Cronin insisted. "He's very much our headache. You see, I took the trouble to check Zahl out. I have a cousin who works in the records branch at the Department of Defense. Two years ago, Nelson Zahl was discharged from the Air Force as unfit for duty."

"What are you talking about?"

Cronin fumbled inside his pocket and took out a sheet of paper. Unfolding it, he slid it across the desk toward Fleming, then sat down. "The information's right there. Read it. It's from his psychiatric officer. Zahl is a psychopath. He shows signs of severe mental disturbance. The recommendation is that he be released from the service with full rights and benefits."

Fleming glared at Cronin. "Judd, you realize this report is highly confidential?"

"I know that, Ben. But this is something that directly affects NASA."

Pushing his breakfast tray to the side, Fleming picked up the sheet and scanned it quickly. He whistled softly under his breath.

"What are you going to do about it?"

Fleming reached for the telephone. "Find out what the hell is going on, that's what I'm going to do."

"I already tried," Cronin said, looking faintly embarrassed.

"For some reason, I can't pin down just who authorized this mission."

Fleming looked puzzled. "Who've we been dealing with at the Pentagon?"

"Any one of a dozen sources. The people I talked to all disclaimed direct responsibility. Said they were taking their orders from higher up."

"Well, how high can the buck go, for Chrissake?"

Cronin lifted his arms in a gesture of bafflement.

Fleming considered for a moment. "Who's in charge of space projects generally?"

"I guess, if you pinned it down to a single department, that would be Major General Dan Connel."

"Okay, so I'll call Dan Connel."

Fleming leaned forward, punching out a number on his telephone. It took him almost twenty minutes to get through to Connel's private office. The general's voice was cool and polite.

"General, this is Ben Fleming at the NASA Space Center, Cape Canaveral."

"Good morning, Ben."

"We've got ourselves a bit of a problem here."

"What kind of problem?"

"You do know we have a shuttle launch scheduled for this morning?"

"Indeed I do. I've been watching your preparations on TV."

"Well, we understand from a certain unimpeachable source that Nelson Zahl, our mission commander, has shown signs in the past of mental instability."

There was silence at the end of the line. Fleming waited, glancing across the desk at Judd Cronin who was watching him impassively. "General? Are you still there?"

"Yes, I am."

"Have you any comment to make?"

"No comment."

"General, is the assertion true?"

"As I said, Ben, no comment. All members of the shuttle team have been cleared at the very top. Take my word, you have nothing to worry about."

"Nothing to worry about? What's that supposed to mean,

General? If this man Zahl is mentally unreliable, we could be placing the entire mission in jeopardy.''

"That isn't your concern. Whatever his faults, Nelson Zahl is the only man capable of carrying out our requirements satisfactorily. He's a specialist, and we need him up there.''

Fleming held his temper with an effort. "General Connel, have you any idea of the psychological pressures a man faces going into space?''

"I believe I do, Ben.''

"If he cracks under pressure, he'll endanger not only millions of dollars' worth of equipment, but also the lives of his fellow astronauts.''

"You have my word that Nelson Zahl won't crack,'' Connel told him evenly.

"Your word? I hope you won't take offense at this, but I'm afraid your word isn't enough.''

"It'll have to do,'' Connel answered in a clipped voice.

Fleming sucked in his breath. "Does the President know about this?''

"Indeed he does. In fact, Nelson Zahl was the President's personal choice.''

"You're kidding me.''

"Why don't you check with the White House?''

"There isn't time for that, and you know it.''

"Then hadn't you better quit fooling around and concentrate on this morning's launch?''

Fleming struggled to control his anger. "Just who are these people, these so-called astronauts?''

"In the interests of security, that is something you mustn't ask.''

Fleming's fist tightened on the receiver, his knuckles gleaming white through the skin. "General, when this is over, I intend to protest at the highest level.''

"Ben, please try to understand that this *is* the highest level.''

Fleming knew when he was beaten. He glanced across at Cronin. "I want you to know that I'm doing this under protest,'' he said into the mouthpiece.

"Your protest is duly noted,'' Connel replied. "Good luck with the shuttle launch. I'm sure your people will handle it with their usual efficiency.''

Two hours later, Ben Fleming stood on the observation

platform and watched the launch procedures with a heavy foreboding. In the early morning, the orbiter *Ulysses* looked practically alive, its hull quivering like the skin of an angry beast as thousands of gallons of water, released in a torrent to dampen the energy of its igniting thrusters, turned into steamclouds.

Fleming felt increasingly anxious as lift-off approached. Something about the mission disturbed him deeply, and he shivered, though the air was far from cold. Voices crackled on the overhead radio: "Orbiter, this is Control. H-two tank pressurization okay. You are go for launch—over."

"Roger."

"APU start is go. You are on your on-board computer—over."

"Roger, and out."

Fleming's stomach tightened as the shuttle's main thrusters began to spurt. Smoke belched around the lower fuselage, billowing upward like wisps of regal lace. He saw the vehicle shudder, visualized the tense scene in Flight Control. "Six, five, four, three . . . we have main-engine start . . . two, one, *zero* . . . we have lift-off."

It was a moment that never failed to move Fleming. No matter how many times he witnessed it, his reaction was always the same. The sheer power of an ascending spacecraft was one of the most exhilirating sights he knew. *Ulysses*, roaring deafeningly, rose from its perch with an almost languid elegance.

"The launch tower has been cleared," the voice crackled excitedly. "All systems look A-okay."

Then the engines, with their 430,000 pounds of upward thrust, swung into full momentum, and the vessel rapidly picked up speed, cleaving the sky like a signal rocket. Its main bulk was barely distinguishable; even its booster rockets seemed obscured by a fiery glare. Fleming watched the flames gradually diminish until, within seconds, *Ulysses* was little more than a pinpoint of light to the naked eye. It vanished into the atmosphere, its vapor trail dissolving rapidly in its wake. Fleming was always surprised at how quickly a launch could be completed—months of planning over in a few breathless moments. Too late now to voice his protests over the Pentagon's meddling. Whoever they were, the members of the shuttle crew were well on their way into orbit.

Fleming tugged his raincoat more tightly around him, and

clattering down the steps, walked slowly back to his waiting car.

The President sat in the Oval Office, running his fingers through his sleek gray hair. Standing in front of his desk, Jan Bowering and Secretary of Defense David Richner watched him worriedly.

"I just can't believe it's true," the President said. "Dammit, I've talked to Poskrebyshev. I *know* him. He's not the kind of man to unleash microbiological warfare on an unsuspecting country."

"With respect, sir," David Richner broke in, "that doesn't quite fit with the Soviets' track record. Look at Hungary in the fifties. Czechoslovakia. The Baltics. The Russians are willing to negotiate one day, then be as cold-blooded as they can when it serves their interests. The days of glasnost and arms-control treaties are over."

The President pursed his lips, leaning back in his chair. His fingers drummed the desktop restlessly. "This is a trick. I feel it in my bones. Somebody's trying to wreck the Centaur Program."

"That's impossible and you know it," Jan Bowering said bluntly. "Nobody's as committed to the program as I am, Mr. President, but Major Garrett brought that canister out of a spacecraft submerged for almost fourteen years. It *has* to be genuine."

"Godammit, Jan, I thought the power struggle was over. I thought the Russians had become, if not exactly our allies, at least our collaborators. But with die-hard Communists running the Kremlin again, we could be negotiating away our last avenue of defense. How can we open up space when space might be the only hope we've got of fighting back?"

"If what Mr. Brightman says is true, even that could be too late," Defense Secretary Richner said darkly.

"Where is Brightman now?" The President looked at Jan Bowering.

"On his way to the South Atlantic. He's meeting Wesker and Major Garrett. We're trying to keep this under wraps as much as possible."

"Sound policy, Jan. We don't want to spark unnecessary panic. But we must be certain in our own minds just what it is we're facing here. A situation like this—who knows how it might escalate?''

"What do you want us to do, Mr. President?"

"Form a special ad hoc committee, comprising Vice President Guthrie, the secretary of state, the secretary of defense, and the director of Central Intelligence." Clayman thought for a moment, then added: "Better include the attorney general, the national security adviser, and the Chairman of the Joint Chiefs of Staff, Admiral Reeves."

"What about Hal McCafferty, Director of NASA? He was in on the *Suchko* affair."

"Okay, him too. The group will meet once a day in the Situation Room to discuss implications and developments. I want no surprises. If trouble is coming, we need to be good and ready. This crisis is too volatile to leave to providence."

When Garrett awoke, the roar of engines echoed in his eardrums. For a moment, the strangeness of his surroundings confused him; then his features relaxed as his memory came flooding back. He was on a heavy transport plane, bound for the capital of the Malvinas, formerly the Falkland Islands.

The effects of his near-lethal dive had already disappeared; even the details seemed hazy in his mind, for Garrett rarely dwelled on the past, especially in matters relating to his personal welfare; he'd learned from experience that too much agonizing and analyzing whittled away a man's nerve, made him prone to irrational fears and phobias.

He glanced down. He was lying on a narrow bunk, a canvas safety harness strapping him in. He unclipped the buckle and rose to his feet, running his fingers through his tousled hair.

The cabin was small, scarcely the size of a rail-car compartment, but he found a tiny shower cubicle tucked behind the miniature dresser. When he emerged several moments later, all traces of sleep had vanished from his body.

He was shaving in front of the mirror when he heard a knock at the door, and Louis Wesker entered, carrying a breakfast tray. Wesker was dressed in slacks and a turtleneck sweater that made his body look more roly-poly than ever.

"It's your friendly neighborhood steward," he said, "bringing you service with a smile."

"I'd prefer one with boobs," Garrett commented darkly.

"I can put on my frilly apron if you like."

"Forget it. I'm just old enough to remember when the nearest thing to a transvestite was Doris Day in a cowboy suit."

Wesker placed the tray on the tiny bedside table, removing the covers from the plastic dishes. "I have scrambled eggs and crispy bacon, orange juice and buttered toast. Also, a moist, sweet-smelling cloth for drying the hands thereof, and a disposable toothbrush complete with an effervescent mouthwash tablet."

"You think of everything, Louis."

"We aim to please," Wesker said, fussily laying out the plastic cutlery. "I'd have made a terrific restaurateur. I exude a perfect blend of Epicureanism and sophistication."

"Not to mention your modesty."

"You've noticed?"

"Nothing about you ever goes unnoticed, Louis."

"Well, I do have a certain presence."

"Trouble is, it takes up twice as much room as anybody else's."

Garrett sat at the table and ate voraciously. His escape from the *Suchko* had left him with a permeating exhaustion, and he had slept like a man in a coma for nearly twenty hours. Now he was just beginning to feel alive again.

Wesker settled himself on the edge of the bunk, watching Garrett scoop scrambled eggs onto his toast. "I have a request."

"What kind of request?"

"A plea for sanity. Moderation. The Argentine authorities have kindly placed Punta Tula at our disposal, and it would be embarrassing if we abused their hospitality in any way."

Garrett grinned at him. "Afraid I'll misbehave?"

"You fought in the Falklands conflict. I guess you wouldn't be human if you didn't feel a certain resentment at finding the islands now under Argentine control."

"Forget it, Louis. It was a job, that's all. I like the Argies."

"Is that why you spy on their drilling rigs?"

"A little healthy competition is good for the soul."

"I hope the Argentines appreciate that," Wesker said.

"Anyhow, am I not a paragon of sobriety and tact?"

"About as tactful, I'd say, as a gorilla with a bellyache."

Garrett groped for his coffee mug and took a deep swallow. The bitter liquid sent a glow of warmth through his empty stomach. "Where's Lori?"

"Eating, like you. I always serve the ladies first."

"You're getting to be a regular mother hen, Louis."

"Zach, the pilot says we'll be landing in twenty-five minutes. After that, let's make this a nice friendly visit, okay?"

"Scout's honor," Garrett said cheerfully. "I promise I'll be good as gold."

Eighteen minutes later, Garrett caught his first glimpse of the islands through the porthole window. They looked gray and barren in the South Atlantic sunshine, reminding him of his home in the wild Northumbrian border country. Craggy inlets framed the endless sweep of hills, and in places, he spotted the sprawl of tiny farmhouse settlements. There were no roads and no fields, and the only sign of human habitation lay around the bays and coastal areas. Seven years had passed since the British government had formally surrendered the Falklands to Argentine sovereignty, and during that time, most of the original inhabitants had departed. The Argentines had converted the islands into an offshore penal colony.

Garrett felt no sense of regret as he gazed down on the tawny slopes where, as a nineteen-year-old second lieutenant, he had taken part in the historic march on Port Stanley. The past belonged to the past, he thought. As a soldier, he had little room for personal sentiment.

Humming softly, he plucked his tunic from the bulkhead peg and stepped into the main compartment. His spirits lifted as he saw Lori Madden coming toward him along the companionway, dressed in a pair of slacks and a woolen sweater. She looked dazzling in the sunlight, and his senses suddenly raced. They'd seen little of each other during the two-day voyage back to Port Shackleton—he'd been crashed-out in his cabin, too exhausted to care about human contact—now, meeting her again, he felt suddenly rejuvenated.

"How did you sleep?" she asked with a smile.

"Like the dead. I think the strain of the past few days mentally dismembered me."

"Breakfasted yet?"

"Louis brought me some scrambled eggs and dry toast. I

think he likes to see people eating. It's what they call sublimation of guilt.''

"I heard that," Wesker said, glancing through the flight-deck door. "Please refrain from making personal remarks. And take your seats. We'll be landing in seven minutes.''

They circled twice before commencing their final approach. The pilot descended in a series of graceful sweeps and taxied to a halt on the narrow runway. Garrett flinched as he followed Wesker and Lori through the exit hatch and felt the wind battering his face and throat. Things hadn't changed much, he thought wryly; whether they called the islands the Falklands or the Malvinas, the gales seldom stopped blowing.

A portly man in colonel's uniform strode toward them from a waiting limousine. After shaking hands with Wesker and Lori, he turned to Garrett, smiling. *"Hola, compañero!"* he said in a booming voice.

"Everisto!" Garrett exclaimed, hugging the Argentine warmly. "My God, I thought you were dead.''

"I am not an easy man to kill, amigo," the colonel said. "You, of all people, should appreciate that.''

Garrett told the others: "Colonel Jenofonte and I are old antagonists. During the British march on Port Stanley, he became my prisoner for a while.''

"We played chess to pass the time," Jenofonte confirmed. "Major Garrett usually lost.''

"My mind was on other things," Garrett said. "Besides, you always cheated.''

"It is a loser's privilege to cheat. And if my memory serves me correctly, you still owe me one hundred fifty-seven pesos.''

"I hate gamblers with long memories.''

Jenofonte threw his arm around Garrett's shoulder, steering him toward the waiting staff car. "It's good to see you, compañero. I am happy to discover you have changed little since the old days. Me—'' he patted his stomach meaningfully, "I still have a fondness for overindulging.''

"No fun doing things in moderation, Everisto.''

"That's what I like about you, Zachary. You're the only man I know with stronger appetites than my own. How are they treating you in Antarctica?''

"My life would be a lot more peaceful if your countrymen would learn to behave themselves.''

"Keeping you on your toes, Zachary. You know how bored you get when there is no enemy to fight."

They drove across the desolate windswept moor, with nothing to see in any direction but open moors and rolling summits. Garrett gazed out at the feathery rock crests, recalling with a strange dispassionate clarity, the spume bursts of artillery peppering the hillslopes as he'd led his men in a headlong charge against the Argentine positions.

He spotted the familiar outline of the radio masts ahead; then the buildings began to gather around them. The town looked much the same as he remembered, the houses flimsy ramshackle affairs, brightly painted and set out in meticulous rows.

A few residents stood watching them through blank, dispirited eyes—convicts, clad in dungarees and padded overjackets. There was no sign of guards, no sign of high-wire fences or machine-gun turrets, and little need for them either since there was nowhere for the prisoners to run.

They turned past the tiny pub—now a *boliche*, or cheap grocery store—and swung left along the seashore. A group of Argentine soldiers watched them curiously from the cathedral gates.

"You've taken down the memorial," Garrett observed, noticing the empty spot on the promontory where the stone obelisk had stood.

"We've built a new one," Colonel Jenofonte explained. "It's at the other end of the sound where Moody Brook Barracks used to be. It's dedicated to the dead of both nations."

"I'm sure Whitehall will be pleased."

"We are completely self-sufficient here," Jenofonte said. "We still run sheep on the open campo, and we've reclaimed some of the land for agricultural purposes. We're also foresting many of the mountain slopes, and we've built a fish-freezing plant to utilize the area's sea harvest. You have to admit that's a damn sight more than the British ever did."

"It does seem a shame though," Garrett countered cheerfully, "that the only people benefiting are your miscreants and dissidents."

A cluster of rhododendron bushes lined the roadside, and beyond them rose the familiar outline of Government House. Though the structure remained basically the same, the glass-fronted conservatory had been removed, the walls and roof garishly repainted. Argentine colors fluttered from the whitewashed flagpole, and heavily armed troops patrolled the entrance drive and the footpath leading to the spacious front lawns.

"We've changed the building's name to Casa Rosa," Jenofonte explained, noting Garrett's expression of surprise. "It's still the islands' administrative center, but today it houses the prison warden rather than the governor. However, our ministers felt it more appropriate if its exterior resembled the president's palace in Buenos Aires."

The limousine halted and Colonel Jenofonte escorted his visitors across the forecourt and through the narrow side entrance, saluting casually as the sentries snapped to attention.

"Mr. Brightman is waiting for you in the warden's office," he said. "Tonight, we've arranged a little entertainment to keep us amused, and who knows, compañero, we might even manage a chess game or two. It will be interesting to see if your technique has improved over the years."

"My technique would improve immeasurably, Everisto, if you'd only stick to the rules."

"Ah yes, the rules." Colonel Jenofonte raised his eyebrows expressively. "I am a great believer in such things, but sadly, I find they take all the fun out of playing."

A uniformed sergeant showed them into the prison commander's office where two men sat waiting. The sergeant introduced them as Señor Caryl Brightman, the U.S. deputy national security adviser, and Señor Joseph Wyatt, his assistant.

Brightman wasted no time in getting down to business. "We've studied your report, Major, and we've carried out tests on the canister you recovered. Unfortunately, it's presented us with an even more serious dilemma."

"What's the problem?"

" 'Problem' is an understatement. 'Crisis' would be more accurate."

Briefly, Brightman described the scientific analysis of the canister's contents. "There is no vaccine and no known cure," he concluded. "Released into the atmosphere, DDF Eight hundred is the deadliest element known to man."

"My God," Lori breathed. "Can it really do all those things?"

"Sadly, it can, Miss Madden."

Garrett was silent. As an SAS officer, he already knew the chilling reality of biological warfare. Never, however, had he encountered a toxin as potentially devastating as DDF 800.

"We have no idea why the Russians were transporting the gas into space," Brightman continued, "or indeed why we took such dramatic action to prevent them. All we do know is that in six weeks' time, the President travels to Moscow to finalize details on the proposed Centaur Program. The program, of course, will lose its point if the Russians have some new biological weapon so revolutionary it makes nuclear warfare virtually obsolete."

"Can't you postpone the meeting?" Garrett said. "Just for a month or two?"

"The President is against that. He's worked too hard to set it up. He's given us six weeks to come up with an answer. After that, all bets are off."

Wesker said, "It's difficult to know where to begin."

"We do have one lead," Brightman allowed. "Our computers turned up the name of a sergeant who served under De Tabley in the Vietnam War. As far as we can gather, he also worked for De Tabley's intelligence network after hostilities ended, a Navajo named Jules Belino. We'd like you to check him out when you get back to the U.S."

"Sounds like a hell of a long shot," Wesker commented.

"We're clutching at straws and I know it, but the truth is, we've damn little else."

Garrett was silent for a moment as a startling thought occurred to him. It was a crazy idea, a wild, crackpot, incredible idea, but there was just a chance—a slim chance.

He sat up in his chair, his pulses quickening. "There is one man who can tell us about that *Suchko* mission," he said.

"Who's that?"

"The undercover agent who tipped off U.S. intelligence."

"Alexandr Zystev? He was arrested by the KGB. No one's seen or heard of him since."

"They probably executed him years ago," Wesker said.

"But supposing they didn't? Supposing they stuck him in cold storage? Even the Soviets don't go around executing people out of hand—not any longer. Maybe he was too valuable to shoot."

"What difference does it make? Even if he's still alive, he could be anywhere inside the Soviet Union."

"The KGB would know," Garrett insisted. "They keep strict tabs on the whereabouts of dissidents."

"What do you want us to do, tell them we've lost our Christmas-card list?" Wesker said.

"That won't be necessary. I have a contact."

"What kind of contact?"

"Someone who works in the KGB computer department."

Boots creaked in the corridor outside, and a truck clattered along the highway into town. They heard a clock strike in the office next door.

"You know a KGB computer operator?" Brightman echoed.

"That's what I said."

"How?"

"*My* business. But if Zystev's still alive, my contact should have personal access to his computer file."

Brightman looked at the others. "What makes you so sure this man will be willing to play ball?"

"For the record, this 'man' happens to be a lady, and if you mean will she betray Mother Russia, the answer's no with a capital *N*. If, however, I can persuade her that finding Alexandr Zystev is vital to the interests of both the United States *and* the Soviet Union, there's just a chance she might cooperate."

Brightman studied him shrewdly. "This lady, you mention— is she in love with you?"

"Past tense." Garrett hesitated, realizing how preposterous his words sounded. "As a matter of fact, she's married to Colonel Sergei Malenov of the GRU."

Garrett heard Brightman's sharp expulsion of breath. "Are you out of your mind? The man is a leading figure in Soviet intelligence. If he gets just a whiff of what we're after..."

Garrett leaned forward in his chair, his eyes piercing. "Trust me, I know what I'm talking about. Whatever else she might do, Elke Malenov would never betray me to her husband. Oh, I can't guarantee she'll collaborate either, but I'm the one person in the world she'll listen to. Especially if I provide her with some kind of guarantee."

"What guarantee?"

"Something incriminating she could use against me if she discovered I'd been lying."

There was a long silence as Brightman sat rubbing his cheek. Somewhere upstairs they heard a radio playing.

"Major Garrett," Brightman said curtly, "I hope this isn't some wild attempt to renew a romantic association."

Garrett looked at him stonily. "It took me four years to get over that relationship, Brightman. I'm not in a hurry to get on the same merry-go-round again."

"That means nothing. I've seen plenty of men, intelligent men, making fools of themselves in their relationships with women."

"Well, I'm not one of them."

"Don't get sore. I just need to clear the air."

"I'm not sore. However—there *is* another problem."

"What's that?"

"I'm banned from entering the Soviet Union. The Russian authorities have both my picture and fingerprints, and if I show my face inside Soviet territory, they'll arrest me like a shot. Malenov himself would regard my capture—or death— as a personal triumph."

Brightman got to his feet and strolled to the fireplace. He stood for a moment, one hand on the mantelpiece, looking into the empty grate. When he turned, his face seemed unusually flushed.

"There might be a way. It's hardly ideal, but in the circumstances, we can't afford to quibble. There's a trade delegation leaving Washington for Moscow on Wednesday. We could replace one of the existing members with Major Garrett. It's tricky—and let's face it, we'll have precious little time to arrange a cover story—but if Garrett is willing, there's just a chance that as a visiting diplomat, he might not be scrutinized too intently."

Wesker objected. "Malenov tried to kill Zachary down in the Antarctic. If he discovers he's back in the Soviet Union, he'll do his damnedest to finish the job, you can bet on that."

"Malenov's my problem," Garrett said. "Get me into the country, and let me handle the rest."

Lori sat up straight, her face pale and anxious. "Even if you do manage to evade the security forces, and even if your sympathetic computer operator proves every bit as sympathetic as you claim, how in God's name do you expect to reach Zystev, assuming he's still alive? He could be anywhere in the

Soviet Union. You can't spirit him out, and the chances of getting near enough to make contact will be one in a million.''

''I didn't say it was a perfect answer,'' Garrett conceded, ''but desperate circumstances call for desperate measures, and from what Brightman says, these circumstances are about as desperate as we can get.''

''He's right,'' Brightman confirmed crisply. ''Aside from the identity of the Navajo Jules Belino, Major Garrett's computer operator is the only lead we've got. If the good Major is prepared to risk his neck, then by God it's our duty to give him all the support we can.''

For the rest of the afternoon, the intelligence team remained locked in the warden's office, making arrangements via telephone with Washington, D.C., and Lori took the opportunity to walk around the tiny settlement of Punta Tula, once Port Stanley, capital of the Falklands. The houses were bright and colorful, but at a cursory glance it seemed hard to believe their clapboard walls could withstand the fury of the South Atlantic gales. Their tiny gardens were well tended. There were few flowers, and most of the plots had been devoted to vegetable growing; it was clear the inhabitants employed every opportunity to supplement their monthly consignments from the supply ships.

To Lori's annoyance, she was filled with a sense of deep unrest. She knew the symptoms; she'd experienced them before.

She was jealous.

The sheer illogic of her emotions angered and bewildered her. She'd already made a fool of herself once on this trip. Wesker had discovered the bug Malenov had implanted in the wristwatch he had given her. Lori felt cold hard anger when she thought how the Russian colonel had betrayed her trust. She'd been so gullible. So naive. Hadn't even dreamed of checking. The damned Soviets had probably listened to every word she'd said, right through the entire *Suchko* search. And now, infuriatingly, she was letting her emotions control her again.

Garrett was risking his life going into the Soviet Union, yet it wasn't fear for his safety that troubled her most; it was the unbearable notion that the person he was going to meet was Elke, Malenov's wife. . . .

That night, the Argentines arranged a banquet in their visitors' honor. All the leading officers of the penal colony were there, their ladies resplendent in jeweled evening gowns. They dined on mutton served pampa-style, the ribs splayed like the wings of soaring birds.

Colonel Jenofonte sat next to Garrett, teasing him unmercifully about his chess game, his painting, his army career, and his childhood in the Northumbrian border country. Garrett took the leg-pulling in good part, tossing in humorous comments of his own.

Afterward, the guests withdrew to the drawing room, where an evening of entertainment had been arranged. Lori scarcely listened to the succession of singers and musicians. Her thoughts drifted infuriatingly toward Garrett's forthcoming meeting with Elke Malenov. Was he looking forward to it? she wondered. Did he regard any danger a trivial consideration against the prospect of meeting Elke again? Most men, most sane men anyhow, would feel subdued at the thought of such perils ahead, but not Garrett.

During Verdi's "Celeste Aida," sung by a notable soprano from the Buenos Aires Teatro Colón, Lori saw the singer falter as a strange droning noise filled the room. Her cheeks flushed as she recognized the cause.

Garrett was snoring.

# TEN

Suspended in space, the satellite looked like a model from a child's erector set. It bore no recognizable shape, beyond its cylindrical metallic core, from which conical antennae and field detectors sprouted like leaves on some extraterrestrial plant.

Seated in the approaching shuttlecraft, Nelson Zahl studied it intently through the forward viewing port. The great shroud of the firmament hung like a pall of endless night, its blackness impenetrable; only the earth's curve offered relief— blue in places, violet in others, it lay swathed in clouds, the rippling waves of the Pacific Ocean visible to the naked eye.

Zahl's face was expressionless as he ran his hands along the instrument panel. He was a handsome athletic man whose clean-cut face belied his lack of emotion. In the Air Force, where he had spent six years, he had been known as an officer of questionable temperament. Zahl absorbed ideologies with the devotion of a true fanatic, but human contact left him cold.

"Switching to manual controls," he declared.

Crouched at his side, Josey Hentoff looked mildly bemused. Unlike Zahl, he found it difficult to conceal his feelings. As a younger man, he had served at the White Sands missile base, becoming part of the SDI "Red Teams," developing and evaluating strategic defense countermeasures. The *Ulysses* flight was his first venture into space.

"Why bother?" he said. "The computer will take us in."

"That station's been uninhabited for almost fifteen years. We don't know if the docking bay's still functioning. I'm switching to manual."

Zahl braced himself for the difficult maneuver. Only in recent years had shuttlecraft been provided with a docking capability, and it had taken him weeks to master the tricky piloting procedures. Using the special control handles, he gingerly guided the shuttle toward the floating space station in a move calling for delicate split-second precision. For several anxious moments, Hentoff and his fellow crew member Mitch Finnegan waited nervously as their leader homed the vehicle into the hovering landing bay. They watched the great hulk growing larger and larger, gradually expanding until it completely filled their viewing ports.

Hentoff saw the bay approaching, held his breath. The satellite's grotesque sensors gave it a microbelike appearance. Against the disk of the earth, it looked infinitely remote. He counted silently as Zahl, measuring distances, eased the anchor pins into position. A muffled click ran through their quivering vessel, and he clamped shut the latches, locking the craft firmly together.

"We're in." Finnegan breathed with relief. "Slick as a whistle."

Hentoff peered through the viewing port, his face flushed with excitement. "Can we board her?"

"Not yet," Zahl said. "First, we check for atmospheric pressure."

"After fourteen years? Are you kidding?"

"We must make sure the platform's still tight. Open one of the valves, Mitch."

Finnegan stared at him for a moment. "That damned satellite will suck out all our oxygen," he protested.

"Don't argue with me, dammit, just do it."

Finnegan glanced at Hentoff and without a word, fumbled with a valve in the shuttle's hatch. A low hissing sound filled the vehicle's cabin, and worriedly Finnegan licked his finger, holding it against the tiny aperture.

"We're losing air, Nelson, losing it fast."

"Shut up," Zahl growled.

"You want to turn us into a vacuum?"

"Shut up, damn you. Unless the platform's properly sealed, our mission's finished, can't you understand that?"

Finnegan stared morosely at the narrow opening where the shuttle's oxygen was rushing into the transfer module. For several moments, the hissing continued; then, as abruptly as it had started, it faded into silence.

Hentoff glanced at the instrument gauges. "Pressure's stabilizing."

Zahl said: "What did I tell you? We'll repressurize the atmosphere with the consumable packs. In the meantime, we'll use oxygen masks to check inside. Josey, stay here. Mitch, bring the flashlights."

There was little point in arguing with Zahl. Finnegan pulled on his oxygen mask and waited for Hentoff to unlock the hatch cover. Free from the earth's atmosphere, the two men floated through the transfer module into the narrow airlock leading to the space station's living quarters. Finnegan felt no sense of apprehension at the idea of switching vehicles in space; his principal thought was that Zahl was crazy, a conviction he'd harbored for more than a month now.

There was something almost inhuman about Zahl. It was nothing Finnegan could put a name to. On the face of it, Zahl looked a perfect specimen of Nordic manhood, blue-eyed, blond-haired, muscular, and sinewy. But there were times Finnegan had the unpleasant notion that nothing at all existed inside Zahl's skull.

He watched Zahl slide open the entrance door and followed him into the satellite interior. A dazzling array of instruments confronted them, covering in some places almost the entire wall. The bulkheads had been padded to protect occupants' clanging against them in their weightless condition. There was little light apart from their flashlight beams and a cluster of sunrays penetrating the viewing ports.

Finnegan's immediate impression was the overpowering silence. He had never encountered such silence in his life. The central cabin was like a capsule frozen in time. Ice coated the bulkheads, glistening on the jogging treadmill where crew members exercised to avoid muscle atrophy.

Finnegan shivered. "Jesus, it's like a glacier in here."

"What did you expect? Damn thing's been derelict for almost fifteen years. No heating, nothing."

Zahl pulled off his oxygen mask and sniffed at the air. "Stinks a bit, but not bad. I think we're in business."

Finnegan didn't want to remove his mask, but with Zahl

watching, he knew he had to. He tugged loose the straps, and his breath froze in a cloud of vapor around his head. He gazed bleakly around the ice-glazed cabin. "Think we'll ever get it habitable again?"

"Sure we will. First thing we've got to do is recharge the batteries. We'll have to bypass the connections to the solar panels, but once we get the voltage rising, we'll be able to restore heat and ventilation."

Finnegan rubbed his glove across the tip of his nose. "When this ice starts melting, we'll have ourselves one hell of a humidity problem."

"We can work in the station and sleep on the shuttle, at least until we get the living quarters dried out."

"We'll never make it in time, Nelson."

Zahl patted him lightly on the shoulder. "Trust me, Mitch. We'll do it."

The Situation Room was stiflingly warm. Despite the air conditioner, the atmosphere had grown sultry with the emanation from a dozen excited bodies. The President's ad hoc Executive Committee faced each other across the oval table. The meeting had been a stormy affair, exacerbated to some degree by the seriousness of the matter under discussion.

"Let's keep a clear view of just what we're dealing with here," Secretary of State Dan Edwards said. "If the Soviets *have* been experimenting with DDF Eight hundred, our entire defense system could become antiquated."

"Don't exaggerate," the President answered. "We have no actual proof. There's no reason to believe the Russians regard us as a potential enemy. After all, why should they suddenly change the policies of an entire decade?"

"Mr. President, the implication is real. With dedicated Communists back in the Kremlin, we have to regard the threat as a possibility."

"Nobody's disputing that. But keep your speculating within a factual framework."

"How lethal are our own microbiological agents?" asked Gil Edwards, the attorney general.

"Just as deadly as anything the Soviet Union has to offer," Jan Bowering said. "But there's one major difference. We can't control ours."

The President's face was lined and tired, and one strand of

his usually immaculate hair dangled inelegantly across his forehead. "I suppose it's unrealistic to imagine we can generate enough security to prevent the Russians releasing their toxin?"

No one answered, and the President sighed. "Then our only alternative is to discover how to neutralize the agent after they've employed it."

The director of Central Intelligence, Phil Howell, shifted uncomfortably as he felt the President's eyes upon him.

"Is that possible, Phil?"

Howell struggled to keep his face impassive. He hated being put on the spot in front of the entire assembly. "Mr. President, at this moment in time, I have to confess I wouldn't know where to begin."

"Are you telling me that you employ more than fifty thousand people, and you can't carry out a straightforward espionage job?"

Howell glanced at the others with a pained expression. In the afternoon sunlight, his skin looked sallow. "I'm telling you, Mr. President, that this is the first intimation we've had of this affair. Nothing's surfaced in our field reports, not even a whisper."

"Well, the Russians are hardly going to broadcast it from the rooftops."

"That's not the point. Collecting intelligence isn't a simple business. It's a giant card game in which you fit together scraps of information like the pieces in a jigsaw puzzle. To date, there have been no indications of Soviet microbiological experiments."

The secretary of defense, David Richner, broke in: "Mr. President, aren't we sidestepping the issue here?"

"What are you talking about, David?"

"Until this matter has been resolved, any cooperation with the Soviets must be out of the question."

"We can't sever relations on the basis of pure conjecture."

Richner poured himself some water from the jug in the center of the table. "I'm not talking about severing relations, Mr. President. I'm talking about delaying the Centaur Program. In the light of what our people have discovered, surely it would be madness to continue with your space cooperation pact?"

The President's face hardened. "I'm not jettisoning years of work on a possible false alarm."

"Nobody's asking you to jettison. Just postpone."

"Negative. We've come too far to pull back now."

Richner looked exasperated. "Larry, that Centaur Program's getting between you and your wits."

"You're wrong, David. I know you've always been against the idea."

"Mr. President, I never said—"

"That's okay. I appreciate your feelings. A lot of people think the Centaur Program's an act of strategic insanity. I happen to believe they're wrong. Opening space to the nations of the world is the *only* way to prevent it becoming a battlefield. As long as it's an arena for the exclusive use of the superpowers, nobody's safe. That's why the Centaur Program must go ahead."

"Which brings us back to the starting line," the attorney general said.

"Not quite." The President looked around the table, his eyes glittering. His face carried the intractability of a battering ram. "We still have people in the field. Maybe they'll get lucky. Maybe we'll have an answer sooner than we bargained for."

"Within the next six weeks?" The Chairman of the Joint Chiefs of Staff sounded doubtful. "They'll have to be awfully good, Mr. President."

"They are, John. Believe me, they are."


Icy sunlight burnished Red Square and the turnip domes of St. Basil. Cloudless skies framed the endless tenement blocks which cluttered the city's suburbs. Though winter was officially over, Garrett wore rubber overshoes to protect his feet from the pavement slush as he mingled with sightseers drifting through the Armory Palace.

It seemed strange to find himself in Moscow again, stranger still when he considered the role he was playing. He'd never regarded himself as a devious man. He liked things up front where he could see them clearly, yet here he was, carrying another man's papers, another man's passport.

He'd spoken little on the long flight over, spending the time memorizing his cover story, preparing himself both mentally and emotionally for the difficult and delicate task ahead. At Moscow Airport, the U.S. party had been rushed through Customs with only a cursory document check. But afterward, as they'd toured the sights with their Kremlin guide, Garrett had noticed the Russians keeping them under rigid surveillance. He'd expected that to a certain extent—it was the old way; it was the Russian way—but he'd been unprepared for the stringency of the chaperoning. Ever since the early nineties, when Mikhail Gorbachev had paved the way for a more tolerant society, security restrictions had been considerably relaxed, but after years of ethnic upheaval, hard-line Communists had reestablished control of the Soviet government, and it was clear they were resurrecting many of the old practices. Agents were now shadowing Garrett's group in a multitude of disguises, from street vendors to traffic wardens, and he knew it would take every ounce of his ingenuity to slip unnoticed through their net.

He waited until the Armory guide had launched into a dry, toneless monologue, then edged closer to the delegation leader, a tall leathery Nebraskan named Piper. "I need your help," he whispered.

Piper regarded him with distaste. A punctilious man dedicated to the concept of improving international relations, he deeply resented Garrett's presence.

"I have to get out of here, and the place is crawling with Russian security men."

Piper said, "There's scarcely a cop in sight."

"Like hell there isn't. They've been shadowing us from the moment we arrived."

"You're crazy."

Garrett had no time for debate. "Listen, when you get back to the hotel, do you think you can cover for me?"

"What is this, some kind of screwball prank?"

"Just say you'll do it."

Piper looked contemptuous. "If you want the truth, Garrett, I was against you joining us from the beginning. This is a peaceful trade mission. It has nothing to do with espionage."

Garrett's eyes grew cold. "Piper, just give me a straight answer. Will you or won't you cover for me?"

"I'll do it, under protest. But I'm not jeopardizing relations with the Soviet Union on the strength of some ludicrous cloak-and-dagger exercise."

"Thanks. You're a real prince."

He glanced around, judging his moment. Most of the American delegates seemed absorbed in the tour guide's lecture. Garrett strolled to the door, following the stairway to the Armory lobby.

Almost immediately, two men detached themselves from a nearby tourist party, and hurried after him, their shoes clattering on the stone flags. So much for subtlety, Garrett thought. Glancing over his shoulder, he saw the men relax as he entered the lavatory and locked the door behind him.

Above the rusty cistern, the window had been reinforced with wire webbing. Stiffened by the winter's cold, its lock looked stubborn and inflexible, but he took out his penknife, and inserting it behind the metal clasp, dug and levered until he felt the handle budge.

The window swung open, and he glimpsed snow-covered lawns tracing the walls toward the Moscva River. He squeezed behind the water pipe and jumped into the muddy slush. Trying to look nonchalant, he began to walk toward the Borovitskaya Tower gate. A man clearing snow from the footpath threw his shovel into a wheelbarrow and followed quickly in his tracks.

The air felt chill against Garrett's cheeks, and he heard a factory whistle echoing plaintively over the nearby rooftops. Near the Alexander Gardens, he saw a *stayanka*, or taxi rank, and turned toward it, quickening his pace. He jumped into the only waiting cab and gave the driver an imaginary address on the Prospekt Kalinina. The workman sprinted toward a stationary car.

When the cab turned into Gogolevskiy, Garrett told the driver he had changed his mind, and thrusting a fistful of notes into the man's pocket, ordered him to halt at the nearest traffic light. Dashing across the street, he leapt on a passing tram and watched the Russian security car cruising doggedly in the taxi's wake.

Finding a seat, he sat gazing out at the city as the tram rattled northward. He felt a chill of apprehension at the prospect of meeting Elke again. He couldn't now, after all these years, make any sense out of what had happened. At Baikonur, there'd been no compromise; it had been in with both feet, all systems blazing. No wonder Malenov had been jealous.

A smoldering hatred gathered in Garrett's chest as he recalled those last fateful days—Malenov's letter calling him to the restricted "Section IV," the *militsoneryi* waiting in the darkness, the scraps of evidence planted around his quarters and in his clothes. Shipped back to England in ignominy and disgrace, the voices of his accusers echoing in his ears.

Questions in the House, questions at the Defense Office. For several weeks, his career in the balance. And from Elke, nothing. He had tried to contact her, but without success.

He got off the tram at Zubovskaya Place and walked up Smolenskiy Boulevard to the Metro station, then for the next two hours switched from one train to another, crisscrossing the city in a series of evasive maneuvers. Only when he was satisfied he was no longer being followed did he emerge on to the slushy streets and make his way to the nearest *stayanka*. He settled into the taxi and gave the driver Elke's address.

The apartment stood on the corner, overlooking the park. Elegant and comfortable, with iron balconies framing its tall French windows, it lacked the utilitarian air of the high-rise blocks of the Moscow suburbs, conveying instead the old-world charm of Paris or Rome.

Garrett ordered coffee at the buffet across the street and sat on the terrace where he could view the building clearly.

An hour passed, and still she hadn't come. People flocked along the busy sidewalk: a flower seller carrying a tray of spring blossoms, a couple wheeling a baby carriage, a father with his entire family in tow.

Then a slender figure emerged from the bobbing crowd, and something tightened in Garrett's stomach. Lithe, supple, achingly alluring, she walked with a cool and measured stride, clad in a light gray raincoat.

He rose to his feet and hurried into the street. "Elke?" he called.

She heard his voice, stopped in her tracks. He watched her eyes widen as a conflict of emotions swept across her face.

"Elke, it's Zach."

She started to back away, and he moved toward her, reaching out as the wind plucked at his hair. Turning, she tried to run, but Garrett seized her arm, and people stared curiously as they struggled on the pavement edge.

"Leave me alone!"

"Elke."

"Go away, damn you."

Glancing around, he pushed her into an empty doorway. "Pull yourself together. You're creating a scene."

Tears sprang to her eyes. "What in God's name are you doing here?"

"I came to see you."

"You fool. Don't you realize Sergei has me watched? He's pathologically jealous. I never go anywhere without some kind of surveillance."

"To hell with Sergei. I have to talk to you."

He shepherded her to the café terrace and thrust her into a booth while he ordered coffees at the self-service counter.

"Drink this," he said, placing a cup on the table in front of her.

She kept her eyes downcast. "I'd be sick."

"Get it down. Do you good."

He slithered into the booth and cradled his own cup between his palms, studying her silently for a moment. Her cheeks had gone pale, much paler than he remembered, but the wide mouth and enigmatic eyes hadn't changed a bit. She looked breathtaking in the early morning.

She raised her head, staring directly into Garrett's face. "I can't believe this is happening," she whispered. "Are you real, Zach, or am I simply imagining things?"

"I'm real, all right. Count on it."

"How did you know where to find me?"

"The British Foreign Office. I like to keep track of my rivals. I imagine Malenov does the same with me."

She studied him keenly, her eyes piercingly blue. "You don't look any different. I thought you would, but you don't."

"You're looking good yourself," he said. "Marriage must agree with you."

"Sergei's kind to me. He cares. That's more than I can say about you."

"We're not going to quarrel, are we, Elke? I'm risking my neck coming here. You know what Malenov would do if he ever got his hands on me?"

"Sergei's not a vindictive man."

"No? Who do you think got me thrown out of Baikonur?"

"You threw yourself out, Zach. You betrayed our trust."

"Don't tell me you actually believed that claptrap? Malenov set up the entire thing, didn't you know? He framed me on a trumped-up security charge."

"Sergei wouldn't. He's much too honest."

"Even honest men get jealous."

She glared at him. "Even if that were true, two years I waited. Two years, Zachary."

"They wouldn't let me come back. The only reason I'm here today is I'm traveling under false identity papers."

"You could have written."

"I *did* write. You never replied."

He saw the astonishment in her eyes and knew then the letters had never arrived. Was it yet another sin, he wondered, to add to Malenov's catalogue of crimes?

Through the terrace canopy, he saw a trio of Orthodox priests wandering by, their beards stirring in the wind.

"You know," he said, "for a while, I thought you were actually part of it."

"Part of what?"

"The scam. The plan. I thought it was some kind of political thing, engineered by Soviet intelligence. You and Malenov, working together to discredit an officer of the British SAS."

"You didn't really believe that?"

"It crossed my mind."

"Well, it makes little difference now. You had no right to come here, Zachary. I have a new life. The old one's finished. Everything's changed—the world, us, everything."

"I wasn't thinking about us, Elke. This is something far more important. I'm looking for a man, someone I need to talk to very badly. His name's Alexandr Zystev. He was arrested by the KGB fourteen years ago."

A hint of suspicion entered her voice. "The KGB?"

"We believe he might still be alive, locked in a high-security prison."

"So?"

"You have access to the KGB computer banks. You could check out his whereabouts for me."

She gave a brittle laugh. "You turn up on my doorstep after four years, asking me to spy against the Soviet Union?"

"I'm not asking you to spy, Elke. I'm not here to harm the Soviet Union. I'm trying to heal a dangerous diplomatic rift."

"You disappoint me, Zach. I thought at least you'd show some respect for my intelligence. Instead, you treat me like a fool."

"Elke, listen. Zystev is the only man alive who can stop the onset of another cold war."

"I can't believe what I'm hearing here. Did you imagine for one minute I would betray my country?"

"I'm asking you to help your country."

Reaching into his pocket, he took out an envelope and placed it on the table. She looked at it suspiciously. "What's this?"

"It's my guarantee. My marker if you like."

" 'Marker'?"

"Inside that envelope is a signed confession," he said. "It admits I've been infiltrating Russian bases on the Antarctic Peninsula."

Her eyes expressed shock and puzzlement.

"It isn't true," he told her. "I invented the whole thing. But if that letter gets into the wrong hands, it will not only cause embarrassment to the British government; it'll also ruin my career."

"Zachary, I don't understand."

"It's very simple. I'm putting myself at your mercy. If you find I've been lying, you'll have the power to destroy me. I'm demonstrating how much I trust you, and in return, I'm asking you to trust me."

She toyed absently with the envelope. "It must be something terribly important to make you take such a risk."

"It *is* important, Elke. More important than anything we've ever dreamed of before."

Patiently, he explained the circumstances, speaking as convincingly as he could. He took care to conceal specific facts, outlining instead the general background and the threat to the approaching space talks. A tremor of hope stirred inside him as he watched her expression gradually soften, watched the suspicion draining from her eyes.

"Unless I can get to Zystev," he concluded, "the Americans will pull out of the Centaur Program, and all the progress of the past few years will disintegrate."

She rattled her teaspoon against the saucer. "Why don't the Americans simply talk to the Kremlin directly?"

"Because they don't know who they can trust."

"And why should I believe you?"

"Because I'm giving you my word."

"Is that supposed to mean something, your word?"

In the hazy sunlight, his features froze into an icy mask. "If you don't know the answer to that by now, then I guess you never will."

\* \* \*

In a phone booth on the opposite side of the street, Andrejs Sergetov watched the conversation uneasily. He dialed Malenov's number and waited for the line to ring. It wasn't every day he had to tell a colonel in the GRU his worst fears had been confirmed. A dozen times during the past few weeks, Sergetov had followed the woman home from work, and on each occasion, his surveillance had proved fruitless. Now, to Sergetov's trepidation, he at last had something to report. His muscles jumped as he heard the receiver click. "Comrade Colonel? Andrejs Sergetov here."

"Where are you?" Malenov said curtly.

"On the corner of Lomonosovskiy and Leninskiy. Your wife is sitting in a buffet on the other side of the street."

Sergetov hesitated, choosing his words with care. This was always the difficult bit. Some husbands displayed their anger openly. Others tried to feign indifference. With a colonel in the GRU, who knew what the reaction might be?

"She is with a man, Colonel Malenov."

There was a long pause at the end of the line. Then Malenov said, "Do you recognize him?"

"No, Colonel, I have never seen him before."

"Description?"

"Tall, healthy tan, hair graying slightly at the temples, but athletic-looking. Dangerous."

" 'Dangerous'?" Malenov echoed.

"That is the only word I can think of, Colonel. He looks . . . dangerous."

Malenov's voice sounded empty. "Stay with them, Sergetov. Find out where they go and what they do. I want a full report on my desk in the morning."

"I understand, Colonel," Sergetov said.

Malenov's eyes were tired as he put down the telephone. Sergetov's profile had been flimsy but precise. He knew only too well the identity of the stranger on the café terrace.

It was Garrett.

# ELEVEN

A solitary fan sent a swath of cool air slicing through the stench of cooking grease and cigarette smoke in the roadside diner. Indians in jeans lounged beside an ancient jukebox, and Lori Madden felt their eyes upon her as she and Louis Wesker moved toward the counter. They had flown to Albuquerque early that morning and rented a car for the long drive across the New Mexico badlands.

"Hot day," Wesker commented to the proprietor, using a handkerchief to mop his glistening face.

The man glanced up from his morning newspaper, his sharp eyes noting Wesker's unimposing appearance; then, with an air of casual insolence, he turned a page and went on reading.

Wiping one of the stools, Wesker perched himself delicately on its edge. "I'm looking for a man named Jules Belino," he explained. "I understand he lives somewhere in this vicinity."

The proprietor ignored him, and Wesker glanced at Lori with a rueful grin. "I guess he thinks we come from another planet."

He raised his voice, addressing the group of Navajos who sat watching them around the battered jukebox. "Any of you guys know a man by the name of Jules Belino?"

For a moment, there was no response, then a husky-looking

giant with a cast in one eye cupped a palm to his ear. "What's that, fat man?"

Lori felt a tremor of uneasiness, and Wesker frowned. "We're looking for Jules Belino," he repeated.

The man turned to his companions, raising his eyebrows. "What's he sayin'?"

"I dunno, Chaco, I dunno what he's sayin'."

"Hey, ask him what he's sayin', Lee."

The Navajos watched the scene with malicious amusement. Lori said, "Louis, let's get out of here."

"He ain't sayin' nothin', Chaco."

"Maybe he's lost his tongue."

"You lost your tongue, fat man?"

Slowly, the giant rose to his feet. His huge head almost touched the ceiling. "Look at them clothes," he muttered. "He looks so neat, just like a little doll."

Lori felt her knees turn weak. It had been an act of insanity to enter this place alone. Wesker clearly offered an easy diversion to the Navajos' boredom. "Please let's get out of here, Louis."

Wesker's lips tightened. He rose from his stool, taking Lori's arm as he steered her toward the door. The giant moved to one side, deliberately blocking their path. He was grinning now, his lips drawn back to reveal a set of broken teeth. Even with his shoulders hunched, he dominated the room.

"Hey, you can't leave, fat man. Not yet."

Wesker's face looked calm. "I understand you boys are just having a little fun, but I'd appreciate it if you'd stand away from the door."

"You'd appreciate it?" The Navajo laughed, glancing at his companions. "Not yet, fat man. I'll tell you when you can go."

To Lori's horror, he pulled out a wicked-looking switchblade, then flicked it open. Wesker looked pitifully small. The Navajo moved his hand in a dizzy blur, and Wesker leaned back as the blade skimmed beneath his nostrils.

Then Wesker moved.

With the elegance of a ballet dancer, he spun on his heel, and to Lori's astonishment, his right foot swung sideways in a vicious arc, catching the Navajo on the side of the skull. The

Indian hit the ground like a fallen log, the knife spinning from his grasp.

A stunned silence fell across the diner as the man lay gazing up at Wesker, bewildered. Wesker seemed scarcely out of breath.

Bellowing with rage, the Indian scrambled to his feet. He lowered his head, charged like a bull. Dancing back, Wesker caught the man with a brutal jab to the face, knuckles extended. The blow found its target with stupefying force, and the Navajo's nose crunched as he crashed headlong into the counter, scattering the stools.

Wesker's eyes were bereft of emotion. The giant turned dazedly, blood streaming down the front of his shirt, and with a roar, lunged back into the fray.

The fight—short, savage, and bloody—was the most stunning martial-arts display Lori had ever seen. By the time Wesker had finished, the hulking Navajo lay senseless on the floor.

His companions watched open-mouthed as Wesker wiped his bloodied fingers on a handkerchief and took Lori's arm. "Let's move."

Numb with fright, she let him guide her toward the door. "Wait."

One of the Navajos stepped forward. He was little more than a boy, sixteen or seventeen, Lori estimated, with long hair and a lean sunbaked face.

"You're looking for Jules Belino?"

"That's right."

"Got a car?"

"It's in the parking lot."

"Follow me," the boy said.

Lori and Wesker trailed the battered Chevy along a network of rutted, unpaved desert tracks. She was still trembling from the tension of the fight, yet Wesker seemed totally unmoved.

"That was quite a show in there," Lori managed at last. "Where did you learn to fight like that?"

"When you look as absurd as I do, Miss Madden, taking care of yourself becomes an essential part of the survival process."

"I felt sure he was going to murder you."

"Well, I figured he wasn't going to ask me to dance."

"I thought you were terrific, Louis." Lori kissed him on the cheek.

Wesker's eyebrows lifted in surprise. "Hell, if I'd known you were going to react like that, I'd have taken on the whole damned tribe."

They saw the automobile in front skidding to a halt, and Wesker pulled up alongside as the youth leaned through his window. "That's Jules's place down by the wash. He's generally in most days. He don't have no place else to go."

"Thanks," Wesker said. "I appreciate this."

The youth waved his hand in acknowledgment and rattled off in a thick cloud of dust.

The walls of the ramshackle house were curiously out of alignment. Rusting refrigerators, truck tires, and worn-out engine parts cluttered the tiny garden. A man in rumpled dungarees stood on the open porch, watching their approach. His skin was the color of seasoned wood, his skull completely bald.

"Mr. Belino?" Wesker said, halting at the porch steps.

The man eyed him suspiciously. "Who wants to know?"

Reaching into his pocket, Wesker took out his ID card. The man studied it for a moment. "Are you joking?"

"No joke," Wesker told him.

"You don't look like any security consultant I ever saw."

"You don't look like Geronimo either."

Belino stepped back, opening the door. "Come on inside. It's cooler."

From the interior, the house looked less like a shack than it had from the road. There was a large cavelike living room with a stove, an unmade bed, and a wooden bench containing an assortment of metal plates. Long, rambling, dimly lit, it displayed little evidence of human comfort.

"Feel like a beer?" the Indian asked, stooping to open an ancient cooler.

"Thanks," Wesker said. "We'd like that."

Lori cast her eye across the well-stocked bookcase. She noticed Boswell's *Life of Samuel Johnson*, Couch's *Aspects of the Novel*, and several volumes of Shakespeare scattered among the paperback westerns and thrillers. "Have you actually read these?" she asked.

Belino glanced at her dryly as he tossed a beer to Wesker.

"What's wrong, lady, you think white people have a monopoly on culture?"

Lori bit her lip. "I'm sorry, I didn't mean to imply..."

"That's okay," Belino said, placing two more beer cans on the table. "I stopped feeling sensitive years ago."

He threw himself on the battered old couch, examining them curiously. "Well, what can I do for you?"

Easing gingerly into a rocking chair, Wesker came straight to the point. "Mr. Belino, during your army days, you served with an officer named De Tabley."

"Sure, I remember Major De Tabley. What's he done?"

"Nothing, as far as we know. This is just a routine matter, but if you would, I'd like you to tell everything about the man you can remember."

"What's to tell? He was running our operation in Nam."

"What kind of operation?"

"We mobilized the Hmong tribesmen in the Laotian highlands, trained them as guerrillas against the Pathet Lao troops keeping the Commie supply routes open."

"Was De Tabley part of any particular military outfit?"

"No, he was working directly for the CIA. He was only a lieutenant in those days, but he carried a lot of clout. Frank De Tabley saw Nam like the World Series."

"What kind of man was he?"

"Sharp-witted. Ruthless. Didn't show his feelings much. But he could talk it and he could walk it."

"Am I right in thinking you served together after the war was over?"

"Sure. Frank stayed in the army for a while and got me transferred to his platoon. We went to Texas and started experimenting with short-range attack missiles. SRAMs were cruise warheads with built-in guidance mechanisms which could be carried by B-Fifty-two and FB-One-eleven bombers. Frank was really into stuff like that. After a while, we moved from SRAMs to intercontinental ballistic missiles—ICBMs. We stayed in Texas almost eighteen months until Frank finally pulled out of the army altogether and started his own intelligence network, working hand in hand with the CIA."

"Then what?"

"We lost touch. I got transferred to China Lake, and Frank

went to the Fort Myers Institute in Florida to work on the Canby D-Five.''

''What was that?''

''Some newfangled defense system. I never found out the details.''

Wesker took out a notebook and scribbled something on the inside page.

''Mr. Belino,'' he continued, slipping the book into his jacket pocket, ''fourteen years ago, you were with De Tabley at Cheyenne Mountain. Can you recall what you were doing there?''

Belino said, ''Officially, checking out the security system, but that was only a cover. Our real purpose was to track and destroy a Soviet space mission.''

''The *Suchko Twenty-three*?''

Belino looked surprised. ''Correct.''

''Why? Why did the *Suchko* have to be destroyed?''

''I don't know,'' Belino admitted. ''Nobody ever questioned De Tabley's orders.''

''The spacecraft was shot down on De Tabley's say-so?''

''Well''—Belino leaned back, crossing his legs—''the authorization came from CINC-NORAD, but the scuttle around the base was that Frank himself originated it.''

Wesker said, ''Fourteen years ago, CINC-NORAD was General George Weir. How could De Tabley, a mere major, tell Weir what to do?''

''Apparently, Frank had some kind of lock on the General.''

''What lock?''

''I don't know that either. It was just De Tabley's way. He never felt comfortable unless he had a hold over people.''

''He sounds like a real pain.''

''Well—'' Belino shrugged, ''he had his good points. He was very patriotic, for instance. I never saw a man so obsessed with his country. He ran a patriots' club, sort of an exclusive society made up of top brass, colonels, generals, people like that.''

''What was the name of this club?''

''It didn't have any name that I know of. It was just a patriotic organization, dedicated to the 'American way.' ''

''Let's get this straight. Are you telling me that inside the armed forces there was an inner circle of high-ranking officers completely removed from—and presumably unknown to—both the Pentagon and the joint chiefs of staff?''

"That's right—unless they were in it too.''

Wesker was thoughtful as he placed his beer can on the tabletop. "Mr. Belino, do you by any chance have a picture of Frank De Tabley?''

"I think I have.''

Belino got up and rummaged through a drawer at the side of the bed. "We had one taken in Saigon, the bunch of us together.''

He straightened after a moment, clutching a tattered photograph. "I knew it. Here it is. That's Frank, third from the left.''

Lori looked over Wesker's shoulder as he studied the picture in the window light. It showed a group of young men posing on a sun-drenched street. Though they were smiling happily, their faces were riven with the rigors of war. De Tabley looked lean, hard, and angular, his dark hair swept back from his forehead, emphasizing his elongated features. Something about him looked strangely familiar. His eyes, Lori thought. Flat and cold, bleak. For a moment, she felt sure she had seen the man before, though his face belonged to a total stranger.

"Could Major De Tabley have changed his appearance before he died?'' she wondered.

"Frank was always changing his appearance,'' Belino said. "He kept growing beards and shaving them off, dyeing his hair, cutting it in different styles. He had some kind of hang-up about covering his tracks. Once, he even burned off his fingerprints with acid.''

"His fingerprints?'' Wesker echoed.

"Something happened to him in the early part of his life—seemed to haunt him in a funny kind of way.''

"Something he was ashamed of?''

"I guess so. He never talked about his past. What he did before Nam was a total void. The only thing that registered was this feeling of something terrible in his youth. I guess that's why he was so obsessed with looking different.''

Wesker was thoughtful for a moment as he studied the photograph. "Would you mind if I held on to this for a couple of days? I can get it copied and sent back to you, if you like. As far as I know, it's the only picture of De Tabley still in existence."

"You're welcome to it, Commander," Belino said. "Always happy to help the Great White Father in Washington, D.C."

The Institute for Strategic Defense Research was housed in an unpretentious building on the outskirts of Fort Myers, Florida, overlooking the Caloosahatchee River. Lori and Wesker left their car in the parking lot, and after passing the security desk, took the elevator to the second floor. They were met on the landing by a slim attractive lady who showed them into the chief scientist's office.

Red Brody rose to his feet as his visitors entered, a tall man with a freckled face and an unruly thatch of ginger hair. "Come in, Mr. Wesker. My secretary told me you'd be calling."

"Sorry if we're late," Wesker said as the two men shook hands. "We got held up at the airport."

"No problem. As a matter of fact, it gave me a little more time. I've been arranging a little demonstration for you."

"This is my assistant, Miss Lori Madden."

Brody took Lori's hand. "Clearly the intelligence business has improved immeasurably since my day."

"Sadly, Miss Madden is only a temporary fixture," Wesker told him. "Did my phone call make any sense?"

"You want to know about the Canby D-Five? Well, you've come to the right man. I'm the one who instituted it, to my everlasting embarrassment."

Brody shepherded them into a large laboratory cluttered with magnets and laser machines. "The Canby, I'm afraid, while revolutionary in theory, proved to be a dead duck in practice. I'm still trying to live down the amount of time my department invested, to say nothing of the government grant."

"What went wrong?" Lori asked.

"Costwise, the device became untenable. In certain conditions, the Canby could prove invincible in defense terms, but unfortunately, those conditions need to be unique."

Brody stopped at a large glass display case approximately four feet high. Inside, two metal blocks faced each other on the sand-coated deck. One was built like a shoebox, the other the size and shape of an ordinary paperback novel.

Brody handed them each a pair of dark sunglasses. "Put

these on. The Canby D-Five is invisible to the naked eye. You need Polaroid screening to distinguish it effectively."

He indicated the display case. "I want you to imagine this is a battlefield. The large dun-colored object is a fortress or defense installation. The smaller is an attacking tank or aircraft. Please watch carefully."

Moving to the rear of the cabinet, Brody flicked a switch and instantly a strange purring sound issued from the glass container. Lori saw the larger of the two blocks beginning to glow. A wave of incandescent light surrounded its surface like a second skin.

Smiling, Brody fumbled with a rotator knob, and the smaller block began to inch forward, crabbing across the cabinet bottom. Closer and closer the metal block edged until it had almost reached the dazzling light beam surrounding its companion's exterior. Then, as it shifted tentatively into the glare, a startling thing happened. The smaller block disintegrated. It happened so quickly, so suddenly, that both Lori and Wesker blinked.

"Jesus," Wesker whispered.

He gazed down at the mangled remains littering the tank bottom.

Brody said, "The attacking vehicle made the mistake of entering the Canby D-Five's defense shield, virtually destroying itself."

"What is it?" Lori asked. "Some kind of laser?"

"Not a laser, Miss Madden. A neutral particle beam, using accelerated negative ions as a disabling energy force."

He stepped back from the display case, wiping his hands with his handkerchief. He seemed pleased by his visitors' reaction. "There's nothing new about particle-beam technology. The first linear accelerator was developed as far back as 1931.

"What happens is that streams of protons or electrons are whipped up by meticulously tuned magnets to speeds approximating that of light. Unlike a laser, the particle beam does not burn a hole in an approaching target but actually passes through it, which means that sometimes a vehicle can be neutralized without being destroyed, simply by disrupting the electronic equipment on board. In the case of the Canby D-Five, however, where the particle density is high, the particles tend to pull the atoms apart, ripping holes in the target's atomic structure. The result, as you can see, is total devastation."

Lori stared down at the shapeless wreckage on the cabinet floor, and Brody moved behind the case, flicking off the light switch. "Unlike a laser, which has to be focused on its target," he went on, "the particle beam kills in fractions of a second, and was originally designed as a kind of science-fiction 'death-ray.' Then we developed the Canby. In effect, it 'splays' the electromagnetic force so that the beam forms a protective shield around the defense installation.

"You can see the potential at a glance. By equipping our war machines with their own electronic armor, we could render them virtually unassailable. On approaching his target, all a pilot would need to do would be to switch on his Canby, and anything passing within range of his defense shield—including nuclear missiles—would simply disintegrate on contact, from the inside out."

"Incredible!" Wesker exclaimed.

"Unfortunately, the Canby has two major handicaps. The first is that, like all particle-beam weaponry, it requires an immense amount of electrical power. Of course, it might be possible to conserve its energy, but the second handicap is more difficult to accommodate. It lies in the earth's magnetic field. Our planet's atmosphere distorts the shield, causing the changed particles to repel each other and lose power intensity. The experiment you've just witnessed was carried out in a vacuum. Were I to open this glass container, for example, it would render the Canby virtually impotent."

"Is that why you abandoned your research?" Lori asked.

"It wasn't entirely abandoned, Miss Madden. During the eighties and early nineties, the Canby became an integral part of the so-called Star Wars defense system, until the concept was eventually dissolved. However, in its original role—that of protecting ground installations—the device proved, sadly, impractical."

Wesker brushed his jacket absently. "Dr. Brody, among the officers assisting in your experiments was a man named Frank De Tabley. I wonder if you recall him?"

Brody thought for a moment. "De Tabley. It's an unusual name. However, we had such a turnover of Pentagon people in those days, it was difficult to keep track of them, and I'm afraid as a scientist, I do tend to be somewhat tunnel-visioned."

Wesker reached into his pocket. "I have a photograph here which might help to jog your memory."

Taking out a pair of wire-rimmed reading glasses, Brody examined the picture curiously. "Ah yes, the face does seem familiar. I'm sure the man was here, but I'm afraid I don't remember anything about him."

He handed the photograph back, looking apologetic. "I'm sorry, Commander, I feel I've let you down in some way."

Wesker was careful to disguise his disappointment as he slipped the photograph into his wallet. "Not at all, Dr. Brody. As a matter of fact, you've been an enormous help."

Secretary of Defense David Richner and Willard Shaw, special assistant to the President for national security, left the White House by the West Gate. The gate itself had been locked and barred to dissuade unwanted intruders, but there was a pedestrian walkway skirting the lighted guardhouse. Both men were weary after a day of heated argument in the Situation Room.

"Clayman's really got his mind set on this Centaur thing," Shaw said as they showed their passes to the sergeant on duty.

"Understandable. It's been Clayman's baby from the beginning. The Russians only came in as an afterthought."

"Maybe." Shaw's voice was almost obscured by the roar of a helicopter zooming over the Ellipse. "But if the Soviets really have managed to harness DDF Eight hundred, the Centaur Program would be the perfect way to halt any possibility of a new Strategic Defense Initiative."

Richner made no comment as they crossed Seventeenth Street, hurrying through the rush-hour traffic. He knew Shaw was right. The Soviet strategy seemed too obvious to ignore, yet Clayman surprisingly refused to acknowledge the fact.

"You were quite correct to speak up in there," Shaw said. "Somebody has to make Clayman see the truth. We must halt all cooperation with the Soviets until this situation has been clarified."

"Why tell me? I'm only the secretary of defense. Clayman's the one who makes the decisions."

"That could be corrected," Shaw said, his face bland.

"What are you talking about?"

"A man who sticks rigidly to his course, irrespective of danger—does that sound sane to you?"

"For Chrissake, Willard, Clayman may be stubborn, but he isn't crazy."

"Well, I'm no psychiatrist, but it doesn't take much imagination to realize that emotional instability can constitute grounds for possible removal from office."

Richner couldn't believe his ears. "If you think I'll go along with mutiny, you've come to the wrong man."

"I realize that, David."

"I may not agree with all Clayman's policies, but he's still my President. I offered him my allegiance when I took this job, and I'm damned if I'll do anything to betray him now."

"Of course not," Shaw said, his face a picture of innocence. "I wouldn't suggest such a thing. It's a theoretical observation, that's all."

He slapped Richner lightly on the arm. "Still, it's an interesting concept, isn't it? See you in the morning, David."

# TWELVE

Elke's fingers bounced over the computer keys, her listless eyes studying the name lists drifting by on the monitor screen. Three hours she had sat here, switching methodically from program to program, checking the locations of prisoners who'd vanished into the penal labyrinth.

Behind the circular reception desk, the library director watched her curiously, intrigued by her persistence. Elke's previous visits to the computer bank had been rare. As a rule, she worked at the Research and Analysis Section on the second floor.

Elke felt numb, as if some essential part of her body had abruptly ceased to function. Garrett's arrival had unsettled her deeply. She had loved him once, but it had been in a different world, a different existence. Now she scarcely knew what she was doing here.

She froze as a name on the videoscreen caught her eye. She leaned forward, her tiredness suddenly forgotten. She'd found it. Alexandr Zystev—born April 17, 1954. Elke noted the program reference and tapped it out on the computer keys. The screen changed, the lists dissolving into an outline of Zystev's arrest report. Pressing the "scroll" button, she sped through the document and began scribbling feverishly.

For the rest of the morning, she went through the preparatory procedures in a daze. The documentation was easy—she had access to forms and authorization stamps—but the turmoil in her mind proved a different matter. Supposing Garrett had been lying? Supposing the entire thing was nothing more than a cynical ploy to trick her into betraying her country? But Garrett had never lied in the past—and besides, she had his confession.

When lunchtime came, she stood for a moment on the lobby steps, watching the traffic roaring around Dzerzhinsky Square. The moment she stepped from this building, she knew, she could never step back. She was jeopardizing her career, her very life. But she had to trust him. She had given her word.

She took the Metro to Kuskaja and found him waiting on the café terrace as arranged. Her heart skipped as she glimpsed his long muscular body draped casually across the wicker chair. He was everything she felt a man should be. You never knew what Garrett was going to do next, and that, in a way, was the most fascinating element of all.

There was no sign of strain in Garrett's eyes as Elke hurried to the table and flopped into an adjacent chair. She waited until the waiter had withdrawn before speaking. "I want you to tell me again," she whispered. "I want you to look into my eyes and assure me—on your life, on everything you hold sacred—that what I am doing will not harm my country."

"Elke," he said patiently, "I've given you my word. This is for your people as well as ours."

"Very well. They have him at a mental asylum near Riga on the Baltic. Here is the address."

"An asylum? I thought they'd stopped the practice of assigning political prisoners to mental institutions years ago."

"Old habits die hard," she said.

She slid the paper across the table, and he examined it thoughtfully.

"Riga's in Latvia. That's quite a trip."

Elke fumbled in her purse, taking out the documents she had prepared during the morning. "You'll need these," she told him. "This isn't England. When you move about in the Soviet Union, you must be ready for identity checks. Latvia may be an independent country now, but it still operates under Russian influence. Here is a KGB visitor's pass made out in the name of Ilyich Zystev, the subject's brother. It'll get you past the asylum gates. Don't worry about security guards. The hospital authorities won't dare argue with such credentials."

Garrett took the papers from her. "You've been busy this morning."

"I made you a promise."

"I don't know how to thank you, Elke."

"Then don't try."

"I wish things could have been different," Garrett said. "I wish Baikonur could have gone on forever."

"Nothing goes on forever."

She was silent for a moment, then from her purse took Garrett's "confession" and laid it on the table.

"I don't need it," she explained.

"Of course you do. It's your guarantee."

"I don't need it."

Her eyes glistened and she seized his hand. "Do you think I would have done this if I didn't trust you?"

Across the street, the Soviet security men watched Elke's gesture in stony silence. Malenov winced, glancing at Rykov, his assistant. He hated being confronted by his wife's infidelity in the presence of subordinates. He found the experience demeaning.

"Are the men in position?" His voice was husky.

"They are, Comrade Colonel."

"Then we have him."

He felt no sense of triumph at the thought, only a dark and smoldering hatred. As he watched the tête-à-tête at the café table, his eyes glittered.

"Order the men to move in," he commanded harshly.

Garrett heard a screech of brakes and glanced through the terrace window. He saw cars skidding to a halt at the curbside. Men spilled onto the crowded sidewalk—security police, without a doubt.

Leaping to his feet, he reached for Elke's arm.

"No," she said, her eyes blazing.

"I'll get you out of here," he promised. "Out of Russia."

She shook her head. "This is my home. You go. I can look after myself, I promise."

"We go together, or we stay together," Garrett stated flatly.

"Can't you understand?" Elke's voice was strangled. "Sergei would never hurt me. You, yes. You he hates more than anything in the world. But he'll do everything in his power to protect me, I know it."

Garrett hesitated. What she said was true. Sergei Malenov was hopelessly besotted with his wife. And what about DDF 800? With Garrett in custody, who would track down Alexandr Zystev?

He came to a swift decision. Leaning forward, he kissed her lightly on the lips.

"I'll never forget you for this."

The customers watched in astonishment as Garrett darted away between the tables, colliding with a waiter coming through the swing doors, sending the man's tray crashing. He tore into the kitchen, dancing around the startled chefs as his pursuers burst through the opening at his rear. They yelled at the staff to hurl themselves on the ground.

A tub of soup simmered on the stove. Grabbing a kitchen towel, Garrett seized the cauldron, hurling it in the security agents' direction. Cries of anger and alarm echoed under the vaulted ceiling as the scalding liquid splattered across the walls, missing Garrett's pursuers by inches.

He rocketed into a narrow passage and down a dusty stairway. He'd almost reached the bottom when a man lunged into his path, pistol drawn. Garrett cursed under his breath. He should have realized Malenov would plug the building front and rear. Without pausing, he delivered a running dropkick at the gunman's unprotected jaw. There was a distinct crack as his shoe connected, and the man catapulted backward, the pistol clattering across the bare linoleum.

Garrett spun to the side and barged into an empty office. He dragged a filing cabinet across the entrance, jamming it tight. Footsteps echoed in the corridor as he ran to the window and swung it open. Squirming over the rim, he dropped lightly into a tiny yard, flanked on all sides by blank implacable walls.

A solitary drainpipe, rusty and dilapidated, led toward the sloping roof. Sucking in his breath, Garrett seized the metal tubing in both hands and began to climb. He tried not to look down, his eyes scouring the conduit ahead, watching for weaknesses, watching for small imperceptible signs of wear and tear. The drainpipe creaked alarmingly beneath his weight, straining away from the concrete wall.

He was sweating badly, and the tension in his stomach made his vision waver. He heard voices in the yard below.

Then a shot rang out. A bullet chipped the stonework slightly to his left, ricocheting into the stillness.

Not far now—fifteen or twenty feet to the roof above. The drainpipe was holding, but just. He redoubled his efforts, focusing his strength into his wrists and ankles, his body swaying dangerously. His fingers closed on the drainage chute, and he felt a wave of relief as he wriggled, gasping, onto the concrete summit.

Another shot. Then another. The security men below opened fire in a frenzy of frustration.

Balancing his palms against the tiles, Garrett edged cautiously toward his right. He could see the line where the building ended and beyond it, the flat rooftop of an adjacent warehouse. Lowering himself from the drainage funnel, he dropped carefully to the lower level.

A water tower rose from the center of the roof. Garrett spotted a door leading into the building below. The door was locked, but he forced it easily and moved down the spiral staircase.

He paused in his tracks as he saw men trotting up the steps toward him. With a murmur of alarm, he retreated back to the open rooftop, and sprinted across the slippery tiling to the concrete parapet on the opposite wall. One glance told him there were no drainpipes, no fire escapes, no exit routes to the lower floors. He was trapped.

A railroad track skirted the building's base, and as Garrett watched, a freight train clattered by, pulling a line of coal cars. The battered cars were piled high with fuel.

He looked over his shoulder as the security squad burst on to the roof, running hard. Garrett clambered onto the narrow parapet, calculating the building's height. He heard shouts echoing as he sucked at the smoky air. The train seemed miniscule, rattling by beneath him.

Clenching his teeth, he leapt wildly from the roof. He caught a fevered glimpse of the city, its spires and rooftops framed against the sky, and his senses spun as his body dropped in a breathless perpendicular line. Down, down, down, he plummeted, his velocity increasing as the space shortened. He saw the track lines blurring, the cars shuddering. Then his feet drove into the shifting mattress of coal and he tumbled over as the train roared into a narrow tunnel.

* * *

Standing at the parapet, Malenov watched the vanishing freight with a sense of fury and frustration. "Radio ahead," he ordered Rykov. "Have the train halted and searched."

"Yes, Colonel."

Malenov clutched Rykov's arm, pulling him to a halt as a terrible thought occurred to him. So absorbed had he been in his hatred of Garrett, he hadn't considered the implications of this affair. Elke's guilt was painfully apparent. It was not the simple emotional guilt of a woman betraying her husband but the unpardonable sin of a citizen betraying the state. It wouldn't be easy, covering such foolishness. Though the security squad presented no problem—to them, the woman had been a total stranger—Rykov knew Elke personally.

Malenov disliked ingratiating himself with subordinates, but he had little choice. He needed Rykov's cooperation. "Georgi," he said, softening his voice.

"Yes, Colonel?"

"This is . . . an extremely embarrassing matter."

"You have my sympathies, Colonel." Rykov's face was empty of emotion.

Malenov struggled for words. "I'm sure my wife had no concept of the dangerous company she was keeping."

"Naturally," Rykov said.

"It would be unthinkable if she were prosecuted for something which, after all, was little more than an affair of the heart, a harmless flirtation."

"It would also," Rykov added with devastating insight, "be extremely damaging to her husband's career."

"Georgi, I need to interrogate Elke, but I'd like to do it unofficially, understand? No paperwork, no arrest reports, nothing on file. This is"—he forced himself to smile, "strictly between you and me."

Rykov appreciated his chief's dilemma, welcomed it. He was an ambitious man, ready to seize any advantage in his struggle for promotion. Compliance would give him a useful hold over his commanding officer.

He nodded gravely. "I understand, Colonel."

It was still light when Garrett woke up. The train had stopped. Shivering under his flimsy raincoat, he peered cautiously over the cargo of coal. There were flat fields on both sides of the track. Beyond lay a drab expanse of open pastureland.

Snow formed patches among the hollows, and a line of trees traced the bank of a distant river.

He saw the engineer lounging beside the stationary locomotive, then his senses quickened as he glimpsed troops moving methodically from car to car. This was no orthodox halt, he realized. The train was being searched.

Cursing himself for his carelessness, Garrett clambered over the side and ducked beneath the heavy couplings. A wire fence separated the embankment from the fields. Wiping his face with the back of one hand, he scuttled down the grassy slope, burrowing head first into a narrow drainage ditch. Its bottom was covered with mud, and he grimaced as moisture oozed through his rumpled clothing. The odor of damp soil filled his nostrils, and the ground felt bitterly cold.

The soldiers called to each other as they worked their way toward the rear. Boots crunched on the cinders, and Garrett's stomach cringed as a uniformed figure stepped abruptly across from the ditch opening. He heard the man urinating against the wire fence and tried to will himself invisible. There was a momentary pause, then the man went back, buttoning his trousers. Garrett sighed with relief as he trudged off to rejoin his companions.

For almost forty minutes, the troops checked the freight from front to rear, digging into the coal heaps, peering beneath the underbraces. At last, satisfied it carried no passengers, they signaled the engineer to continue.

Chattering good-naturedly, the soldiers wandered back to their waiting trucks and drove off along an unpaved track bordering the northbound line.

Garrett waited until they had vanished from sight before wriggling out and stamping his feet in the chill. His body felt numb from a combination of strain and cold, and he was covered from head to foot in coal dust and mud.

The land looked gray and featureless. On all sides, drab meadows mingled with patches of misty firs. He climbed over the fence and with no clear idea of where he was heading, set off in a westerly direction. For almost an hour, he moved listlessly across ploughed fields and open pastureland until at last, nestling in a hollow ahead, he spotted a tiny farmhouse.

A tremor of hope stirred inside him. A farmhouse meant people. He had to get out of his disheveled clothing. It was his only hope of survival.

Detouring to the left, he followed a line of pine clusters, approaching the house from an easterly direction. Washing fluttered from a rope in the outside yard. A truck stood beside a ramshackle barn.

Garrett eased gently forward, studying the farmhouse windows for telltale flickers of life or movement. The building looked deserted, but as he drew closer, he detected the strains of a radio playing music.

He took his time—pausing, moving, pausing, moving— until he reached the clothesline. For a moment, he crouched perfectly still, watching the farmhouse warily. A metal knocker in the shape of a bear's head decorated the door panel, and a slender column of smoke issued from the single chimney. But there was no sign of the inhabitants.

Breathing hard, Garrett got to his feet and sprinted along the row of washing. He tore loose the garments, gathering them in a bundle against his chest. He seized everything in sight and clutching the damp assortment in both arms, went on running until he reached the battered old truck. Hurling the clothing into the passenger seat, he quickly connected the battery leads, grunting in satisfaction as the engine purred into life. A sound echoed in the paddock behind, and glancing over his shoulder, Garrett felt his skin crawl as he spotted three enormous mastiffs bounding toward him across the muddy ground. Their teeth were bared, and muscles rippled beneath their shaggy hides.

Leaping into the cab, he slammed shut the door as the first of the animals crashed against the truck's body. The second dog lunged onto the vehicle's running board, snarling and baying at Garrett's right elbow.

Engaging the gear, he slammed his foot on the accelerator, and the truck roared across the cobbled yard and onto the highway beyond.

Inside the interrogation room, Malenov gazed moodily at his wife, seated in the solitary chair. Though her cheeks were pale, there was a gleam of defiance in her beautiful green-flecked eyes.

She made no attempt to disguise the derision in her voice, and Malenov flinched uncomfortably at the idea of Rykov witnessing his embarrassment. She knew how belittling it was for a man to be berated in the presence of inferiors. God knew, he'd behaved decently. Hadn't arrested her, hadn't reported her to her chiefs at the KGB. Instead, with Rykov's help, he was handling the matter with delicacy and discretion. For that, at least, he deserved some gratitude.

"Let's go through it all again," he said, strolling across the bare stone floor. "You say Garrett appeared out of the blue, that this was the first time since his expulsion from Baikonur the two of you met?"

Elke stared silently at the opposite wall. Malenov paused in his stride and looked down at her. "Will you please answer me? Can't you see you are in serious trouble?"

"What is the point of repeating myself? If you refuse to accept my explanation, you are what I always imagined you to be—a fool."

Malenov winced. There was no reaction in Rykov's features. He might have been carved of stone.

"It was an essentially . . . romantic rendezvous then?" Malenov's lips twisted at the phrase.

"You didn't give me a chance to find out. We'd only just sat down when your bulldozers arrived."

Malenov stood in front of her, delicately brushing the hair from her face. "You're lying," he said, almost sadly. "This wasn't the first time you and Garrett had met. You were seen in each other's company only yesterday."

Elke's features tightened involuntarily. Malenov gently massaged the base of her neck. "You do realize Georgi and I are doing our damnedest to save you. But you must meet us halfway. Help us locate Garrett. Help us discover what he's doing here."

"If you choose not to believe me, I have nothing more to say."

Malenov paused as someone knocked at the door. There was a brief exchange, and Rykov glanced over his shoulder. "It's Leonov. He wants a word with you."

Leonov was Malenov's contact in the KGB. Since the civilian secret police and the GRU were bitter rivals, he had been obliged to use a paid informer to keep watch on Elke during working hours. Malenov didn't trust informers. A man who would sell his soul to one side could just as easily sell it to another. But in the circumstances, he had had little choice.

He went into the passageway. Leonov was a thin man with a pale pockmarked face. He always looked nervous, a trait

Malenov attributed to his inherent shiftiness. "What is it?" Malenov demanded.

Leonov's eyes darted around the corridor walls. "Colonel, it's about Mrs. Malenov. I don't know if this is significant, but I understand she spent the entire morning in the central computer bank, on the basement level."

"So?"

"It was somewhat unorthodox. The section director says he has never known her to remain so long."

"Why not? She's a computer operator, isn't she?"

"Only in the Research and Analysis Department. The basement level deals with political investigations, the SPU."

Malenov pursed his lips, feeling his instincts sharpening. "Does the section director know what Mrs. Malenov was looking at?"

"He has a list of the disks in his record book. She had to sign the register before he could release them into her care."

Malenov glanced at the door behind him, and taking Leonov's arm, steered him farther along the passageway. "Listen to me," he said gently. "You must bring those disks here as quickly as possible."

"But, Colonel, I have no authority."

"Leonov, this is important. I must examine those computer programs and discover what she was looking for."

"Impossible," Leonov protested. "If they knew I was even in this building, they would place me under immediate arrest."

Malenov pinched Leonov's cheek, squeezing the flesh until it turned white. "What do you think they would do to you, my tricky little friend, if I told them some of the information you've been passing to me over the years?"

Leonov swallowed hard. "Please, Colonel, I implore you, don't make me do this. If I am caught with the disks in my possession . . ." His voice faltered.

Taking out a handkerchief, Malenov wiped his fingers with a fastidious air. "You will have those disks on my desk within an hour. Otherwise, a full report on your dealings with this department will be sent to the chairman of the KGB."

A hint of humor showed in Malenov's eyes as he opened the door of the interrogation room. "I wonder how you'll find summer in Siberia," he said.

# THIRTEEN

The truck shuddered to a halt. Garrett had been nursing it along for miles, teasing the engine through one spluttering hiccup after another. Now, as he tried to pump the ignition, the fuel gauge remained depressingly dead. He looked through the window at the fir-studded landscape outside. All night, he had driven hard, following the signposts toward the city of Riga, and with the first flush of dawn, the land lay locked in the grip of a breathless stillness. Mist hung over the glistening spruce trunks, and in places, the trees blended into the flickering fog as if they were floating on some weird gossamer ocean.

Garrett pulled the bundle of clothing from the passenger seat and examined the garments earnestly. They were slightly damp to the touch, but he chose a thick khaki boiler suit and a heavy wool jumper—hardly ideal for a man trying to look inconspicuous, but he could buy fresh clothing as soon as he reached the nearest village.

He transferred his money and identity papers from his jacket pocket, abandoned the truck at the roadside, and set off along the icebound highway. The sun climbed steadily as the morning lengthened, dispelling the mist. Though the air remained cool, the countryside lost some of its austerity, and Garrett found himself working out perspectives and color harmonies in his mind. In the hollows, snow still lingered.

As the hours lengthened, the road filled with people. Cars, many of them ancient relics lovingly restored, mingled with horse-drawn farmcarts from which the occupants regarded him with stolid faces. Toward nine, he spotted a bus approaching, its bodywork coated with dust and grime. Waving the driver to a halt, he bought a ticket to Riga.

For the next two hours, the landscape changed little, the monotonous pool-table flatness meandering into the sky with no discernible dividing line, and Garrett tried to ignore the hunger pangs in his stomach, focusing his mind on the pitfalls ahead.

Finding Zystev would be the easy part. The difficulty would lie in getting home again. Returning to Moscow appeared out of the question. Malenov was no fool. He would seal off Garrett's escape route. At least in Riga he would be only a handful of miles from the Swedish coastline. But he had few illusions about the hazards of crossing the Baltic. It was probably the most heavily patrolled strip of water in the world.

He felt the bus drawing to a halt. A military truck stood at the roadside, and his senses quickened as he glimpsed armed troops waving the driver down. It was a routine identity check, the kind of thing that took place daily throughout the hinterlands. A group of *militsoneryi* entered the bus and began checking the travelers' credentials. Sweat broke out between Garrett's shoulders, running down his spine in an irritating trickle as the soldiers drew closer.

From time to time, they questioned one of the passengers, but their faces looked bored and disinterested. Pausing at Garrett's shoulder, a corporal snapped his fingers impatiently, and Garrett displayed the papers Elke had issued him, trying to appear casual and unconcerned. The man examined them, his pinched features inscrutable, and after a moment, handed them back with a curt nod. Garrett breathed a sigh of relief as the militsoneryi waved the driver forward and the bus continued its westward journey.

Malenov sat before the computer, wearily scanning the program lists. His spirits flagged as the letters blurred and blended, forming a continuum of indecipherable print. He had no idea of what he was looking for. Or was he looking for anything? Had he merely retreated, cowardlike, from Elke's disdain and Rykov's scorn?

Three hours he had sat here, poring, puzzling, assimilating. He was nearing the end at last, thank God. He had finally reached the $Z$'s. He blinked lethargically as his fingers danced over the keys, scrolling the list steadily upward. A name caught his eye, and he frowned, examining it thoughtfully. Alexandr Zystev. Why should this man's document, of all the ones he had viewed today, strike such a chord in his memory?

Malenov went to the central records computer, typed out Zystev's name, and pressed the control button. The screen hummed for a moment; then the prisoner's arrest sheet emerged. As he read it, a spasm of excitement knotted in his stomach. Alexandr Zystev had been at Baikonur during the launching of *Suchko Twenty-three*. Zystev—it had to be Zystev. This was the information Garrett had risked so much to uncover. This was the message Elke had passed him on the café terrace.

Flushed with triumph, he sped through the rest of Zystev's file. The man was being held at a remote mental asylum on the Baltic coast, not far from the city of Riga. Malenov groped eagerly for the telephone.

The Pentagon corridors were strangely quiet as midnight approached. Only the murmur of housekeepers drifted from the deserted offices. Lori found the emptiness disorienting. The twenty-nine-acre complex was made up of five separate buildings, linked together by corridors radiating from an open courtyard in the center. There were no elevators, only stairways.

As she turned the corner, she spotted a familiar figure walking toward her from the opposite direction. It was Vice President Randolph Guthrie—to Lori's surprise, completely alone. She'd always imagined, though she didn't know why, that both the President and Vice President were accompanied by a security entourage twenty-four hours a day. Unchaperoned, Guthrie looked strangely isolated.

Physically, Randolph Guthrie was an attractive older man. His face was tanned, his hair fashionably styled. But there was something terribly cold about him.

Her breathing quickened as Guthrie drew closer. She felt idiotically tongue-tied. He broke into a smile. "Why, Miss Madden. What are you doing here at this time of night?"

Lori was surprised Guthrie remembered her. They had met only once, during her first visit to the White House. "I'm working with Louis Wesker," she told him. "We're checking out the *Suchko* evidence on the computer files to see if any of it cross-references. I'm on my way to pick up more disks."

"Mind if I tag along?"

Lori felt uncomfortable as they rode the escalator side by side. "I didn't realize the Pentagon came under your watchful eye," she said.

"Everything comes under my eye. One of the first things you learn in the vice presidency is that you're expected to be on top of the dirtier and more difficult jobs—anonymously, of course."

"It must be awfully important to hold you here till almost twelve o'clock."

"Somebody's got to keep this administration going. If we had a leader instead of an aging football star, I mightn't have to work so hard."

Lori was surprised at his candor. "You're talking about the President?"

Guthrie said, " 'President' is only a relative word. This nation ceased to have a president when Larry Clayman assumed office."

"But I thought . . ."

"You thought I'd be his strong right arm, to love and to cherish him in sickness and in health? Well, I am and I do, publicly at least. But there are things that go beyond the public image. Integrity, for example."

"I don't understand," Lori said.

"If Lawrence Clayman had listened to me in the beginning, we wouldn't be in the ludicrous position we are now. Phasing out SDI was an act of insanity. I tried to tell him, but he just wouldn't listen. He pays far too much attention to that idiot woman Jan Bowering."

Lori felt bewildered by Guthrie's frankness. She'd always assumed, though she couldn't say why, that the President and Vice President operated in harmony. It had never occurred to her the two might be diametrically opposed.

"You're extremely forthright in your views, Mr. Guthrie."

"I'm not as open as this with everyone," he confessed with a friendly smile. "Only people I feel to be . . . sympathetic."

"But you hardly know me."

"You're wrong. I've been watching you from a distance, Miss Madden, and I pride myself on being a shrewd judge of character. I can tell at a glance you are a highly unusual young woman."

He paused, and his voice softened. "You're also an extraordinarily attractive one."

Oh-oh, Lori thought, recognizing the inflection. She didn't relish the thought of having to rebuff a man as powerful as Randolph Guthrie. They reached the bottom of the escalator and continued along the empty corridor.

Guthrie stared at her, amused. "You needn't look so stern simply because a man pays you a compliment."

"You took me by surprise. It isn't every day I get flattered by the Vice President of the United States."

"I wish you'd call me Randolph."

"Wouldn't that be a little presumptuous? I mean, this *is* a business relationship after all."

Guthrie's tone softened. "It doesn't have to be business. I'm not as aloof and unapproachable as the gossip columnists make out. And I'd like to call you Lori, if I may."

With a wave of relief, she reached the filing-room door and turned to look at him. "I'm afraid this is as far as I go."

He stood over her, peering directly into her eyes. "Do you always run for cover just when things start to get interesting?"

"I told you—I'm working tonight."

He cradled her cheek in his palm. "Then maybe we could get together sometime when you're not quite so hassled? I have a feeling we'll find a lot in common."

"Why not?" Lori said. "You can bring Mrs. Guthrie too. We'll make it a cozy threesome."

Ducking away from his hand, she stepped into the room and closed the door quickly behind her. For a moment, she stood quite still, sighing with relief. It was only when she heard his footsteps echoing along the corridor that she realized an extraordinary thing. The Vice President's skin had the same texture as melted wax. It wasn't her imagination.

Randolph Guthrie had no fingerprints.

"We had no idea Zystev had a brother," the hospital director remarked as he walked with Garrett along the echoing corridor.

The director was a fussy little man who had displayed no

surprise at Garrett's KGB permit, expressing instead an earnest hope that his visitor would appreciate the asylum was doing all it could for his unfortunate relative.

Garrett paid little attention to the man's entreaties. Instead he noted the hospital's prisonlike interior. Cobwebs cluttered the plaster cracks, and the floor was heavily stained with dirt. There was a scent of antiseptic mingled with the odor of stale urine. The passageway in which they walked commanded an excellent view of the central courtyard, where barred windows gazed down from the surrounding stonework. The sloping roofs were framed with miniature observation turrets, accentuating the impression of some dour medieval fortress.

It would not be an easy place to break out of.

Shaved, bathed, and rested, Garrett now felt prepared to face the challenge ahead. Dressed in a new suit and overcoat purchased on his arrival in Riga, he was the picture of respectability. Under his arm he carried a small basket of fruit from the city market, a gift for the brother he had come so belatedly to visit.

"You must appreciate Alexandr is an extremely sick man," the director explained in his fussy theatrical way. "You may find him a little . . . unreceptive. He has to be kept sedated much of the time. Please understand, it is all part of his treatment. Your brother's dementia was quite advanced when he came to us."

Garrett grunted noncommittedly. He couldn't bear to participate in this ridiculous charade. He knew, as the director knew, that Alexandr Zystev was as sane as any man alive. Assigning him to a mental asylum was simply the KGB's method of disposing of a political embarrassment.

The director paused to unlock a heavy metal door. "The human brain can be a delicate instrument. Don't be surprised if your arrival produces no response. Your brother is no longer the man you remember."

The cell was small, cramped, and windowless. A soiled mattress lay on the floor, its single blanket tossed haphazardly aside. The only light came from a wire-bracketed electric bulb in the center of the ceiling.

The prisoner sat with his spine against a corner. He seemed the focal point of the entire room, as if the lines and contours of the walls had been drawn from his scrawny body. His hair hung almost to his shoulders, and his bony cheeks were heavily stubbled. Small and narrow-chested, he looked like a scarecrow in his inmate's uniform.

He gave no reaction as the intruders entered but sat gazing into space in the manner of a man absorbed in some deep spiritual meditation.

"Hello, Alexandr," Garrett said. "It's been a long time, my brother. You must forgive me for not visiting you earlier, but it is such a dreary way from Moscow, and you know how busy we get at the alloy plant."

Zystev offered no sign that he was conscious of Garrett's presence.

"You must give him time," the director explained. "He's had so little contact with the outside world. Your coming here will hold unseen terrors for him. It will remind him of a life he has almost forgotten. It will bring back the very elements which contributed to his malaise."

Garrett said nothing. He knew perfectly well why Zystev wasn't responding. The man was drugged to the eyeballs, but for the director's benefit, Garrett said, "I've brought you some fruit, Alexandr, a few oranges, apples, grapes. You used to like grapes back in the old days, remember?"

Zystev looked like a resurrected corpse. Spittle gathered on his lips, running in a glistening trickle to the tip of his stubbled chin.

Garrett was about to speak again when he heard a tap at the door and a muscular man in a nurse's jumpsuit appeared on the threshold. "Comrade Director?"

The director glanced apologetically at Garrett. "Excuse me."

He stepped outside and spoke to the newcomer briefly, then turned to Garrett in embarrassment. "You must forgive me. Vishnayev tells me I have visitors in my office. I'll return as quickly as possible."

Garrett listened to his footsteps clattering along the corridor, then squatting on his haunches, examined the prisoner more intently. As his brain registered the slack lips and the limpid facial muscles, he felt his spirits sink. The man was clearly under heavy sedation.

"Zystev," Garrett whispered. "Can you hear me? Blink if you understand what I'm saying."

Zystev stared vacantly into space, no reaction in his flat brown eyes. He would get little satisfaction from Zystev in his present state. Unpalatable as the idea was, Garrett could think of only one solution.

"On your feet, friend," he murmured gently, gripping the front of Zystev's uniform. "I'll just have to take you out of here."

The asylum director blanched when he saw the militia men waiting in his office. He disliked dealing with the authorities in any shape or form.

"Gentlemen," he muttered, unconsciously leaving the door half open, as if it might offer an avenue of escape.

The detective in charge of the contingent rose to his feet. He was a rat-faced man with beady black eyes. "You have a patient here named Alexandr Zystev?"

The director's lips fluttered. "Why yes, I—"

"We have reason to believe a foreign agent will attempt to contact him within the next few days. He may pass himself off as a colleague, a friend, even a relative. As a precaution, I am installing two of my men in Zystev's room until the emergency is over."

Ashen-faced, the director struggled to speak. The detective studied him, frowning. "What is it, man? What are you trying to say?"

"He's here," the director moaned.

"Here?"

"He arrived barely an hour ago, carrying a KGB pass."

The detective flinched, as if he'd received an unexpected blow. "Are you telling me he's actually with Zystev now?"

The director nodded.

"Alone?"

Again, the director nodded.

"Damn you!" the detective exclaimed. "Don't stand there like a fool. Take us to Zystev's cell immediately."

They tumbled into the corridor and stampeded along the linoleum floor. Suddenly the detective heard an engine roaring in the courtyard below and glancing through the window, spotted a vehicle racing toward the asylum gates. He saw the guards, recognizing the vehicle's insignia, step back to wave the driver through, and his lips parted into an exclamation of muted outrage. He could scarcely believe the insolence of what he was witnessing.

The arrogant bastard had stolen their police car.

* * *

The news reached Malenov by telephone barely an hour later. He listened in silence as the detective outlined the details, then slammed his fist furiously on the desktop.

"What are you running up there, a department of clowns? Don't you realize this man is making fools of us all?"

"I am sorry, Colonel Malenov. If we'd arrived only two minutes earlier—"

"Yes, yes," Malenov snapped impatiently, ignoring the detective's protests. Already he was thinking ahead, struggling to visualize what was going through Garrett's mind. If the Englishman had reached Latvia, he would hardly bother returning to Moscow. A far more attractive escape route lay directly to the west.

"He'll attempt to cross the Baltic to the Swedish coast," Malenov said. He hesitated. Officially, he had no direct authority in Latvia. Since the Baltic state had acquired its independence, even GRU officers were obliged to operate through official diplomatic channels. But Malenov knew—as the Latvians knew—that even in the present milieu of enlightenment, orders from a Moscow security colonel could not be taken lightly. His voice grew crisp. "Notify the coast guard, and double surveillance on all exit and entry points. I want those waters so infested with patrol boats, not even a salmon can wriggle through."

"Yes, Colonel."

"And, Lyudin?" Malenov's voice grew cold. "Don't let him slip through your fingers again."

Putting down the telephone, he looked at it for a moment in silence. The damned fools seemed to be bungling everything in sight. Maybe what this manhunt needed was a more personal touch. After all, he had pinned everything on witnessing his enemy's downfall. Shouldn't he be there to orchestrate Garrett's finale?

He went to the door and shouted into the passageway. "Rykov, call the airport and order me a plane. I am flying to Riga immediately."

The midget submarine nosed into the tiny harbor, its fiberglass hatch-turret catching the sunlight of the bright spring afternoon. A small group of spectators watched from the quayside as the vessel drew alongside and the three-man crew, members of the Riga oceanographic team, made fast the mooring ropes and clattered up the wharf ladder.

The submarine bobbed gently on the harbor swell, its beveled contours specially designed to render them more mobile beneath the chilly Baltic waters. Standing at the rear of the crowd, Garrett studied the tiny craft.

It looked smaller than the British submersibles, but he imagined its control system would be pretty much the same. The submarine was a civilian vessel, the property of the local university. If he could spirit it out of the harbor, it might get them across the narrow ribbon of water to the safety of the Swedish coast. Garrett had no illusions about the danger of his position. He had outwitted the militia men at the mental hospital, but he had seen the offshore patrol boats and understood their meaning.

The Russians knew he would try to reach Swedish waters, and had ordered the Latvians to shut off all potential escape routes. Nevertheless, there was still a slim chance that he could slip beneath the security cordon.

Shivering a little in the chill, Garrett left the quay and walked briskly out of the tiny fishing port. He felt desperately sorry for Zystev. Inhuman, it seemed, to take away a man's mind and turn him into a vegetable.

A mile beyond the town, he turned along a narrow track, his shoes crunching on the half-frozen mud. He came to a barn surrounded by trees, its tin-roofed walls buckled by the winter gales. Garrett circled the building twice before entering. The interior was drafty and smelled of linseed oil. On a mattress of straw, Zystev lay hugging his knees to his chest, his slender frame shuddering in a series of agonizing spasms. Even from several feet away, Garrett could hear his teeth chattering.

Deprived of his mind-bending drugs, the Russian was now enduring severe withdrawal symptoms.

Unbuttoning his overcoat, Garrett laid it over the man's still-quivering body and piled straw around his limbs in an effort to conserve his body heat. Zystev stared up at him uncomprehendingly, his features riven with misery. When Garrett had satisfied himself he could do no more, he found a position commanding a view through the open doorway and settled down in the straw to wait.

* * *

Night came early to the Baltic coastline. As the minutes lengthened, the shadows blended to form a barrier of impenetrable blackness.

Garrett dragged Zystev from his refuge, buttoning the overcoat tightly around him. Zystev had ceased his shivering and now moved like a robot, responding to Garrett's hand as a blind man might accept a sympathetic guide.

It took almost forty minutes to negotiate the few hundred yards of mistbound fields to the deserted highway, nudging Zystev step by step along the icy cart track. He could see the lights of the fishing port in the hollow ahead and steered Zystev toward the glow, propelling him forward like a bewildered drunk. They passed no traffic, and when they reached the little town, they found the streets completely deserted. Mishkin, on the western approaches to Riga, was hardly a bustling metropolis, and like Moscow, it settled into a pall of provincial gloom as the hour of midnight approached.

Garrett steered Zystev toward the harbor. The searchlights of patrol boats crisscrossed the gulf. The security web had intensified with the coming of night. To attempt a surface crossing would be an act of madness. Their only hope was to make the journey underwater.

He spotted the midget submarine nestling among the fishing boats and started toward it. Then he saw a small squadron of uniformed troops huddled along the concrete pier. Their breath steamed around their padded shoulders and fur hats in the misty darkness.

Garrett paused. He hadn't counted on the submarine being protected, had expected the security net to be engaged mainly at sea—a foolish assumption, he now realized, since it was only natural that the Latvians would put sentries on all vessels in the area. What he needed was a diversion.

He glanced around for somewhere to deposit Zystev. He spotted a shop doorway and pushed the Russian into it, resting him gently against the shutters. Two buildings down, he found a boat-builder's shed. He jimmied the door and eased himself into its darkened interior. Cans of paint cluttered the shelves above rolls of heavy tarpaulin. A fishing boat lay upside down, supported on a stilted frame.

On the ground stood a jar of methylated spirits. Breathing heavily in the chill, Garrett poured the pungent liquid liberally over the vessel's fiberglass body. The fumes pricked his nostrils as he tossed the bottle aside and with his cigarette lighter, set fire to his handkerchief.

When the material was properly ablaze, he flicked it deftly onto the upturned boat. *Whooooosh!* The flames spread along the full length of the hull, and within seconds, the entire yard was engulfed in smoke.

The sentries were shouting as Garrett hurried back the way he had come, keeping to the shadows.

He found Zystev standing exactly as he'd left him, gazing into space. Seizing the Russian by the shoulder, Garrett bundled him across the road and along the side of the concrete pier. Several of the soldiers had run to investigate; the others were watching the fire, mesmerized by the drama at the harbor's edge. None of them noticed Garrett propelling his stupefied companion along the quayside.

Garrett steered Zystev down the metal ladder to the submarine deck and kneeling at the hatch, fumbled with the metal lock. With a click, the lid slid back, and Garrett maneuvered Zystev into the cramped little control cabin. Releasing the mooring ropes, he followed swiftly, then slammed the hatch shut.

Switching on the cabin lights, he knelt to examine the instrument panel. This was the crucial moment. Unless he could handle the vessel's controls, he knew, their flight would be doomed. A bewildering array of switches and computer buttons confronted him, but to Garrett's relief, he found the functions relatively familiar.

There was no time to run a systems check. The turbines purred as he started up the engine, the craft bobbing on the incoming tide. Zystev lay on the rubber-coated deck, staring blankly into the semidarkness.

Garrett fingered the control panel, nudging the vessel into the center of the harbor. A shout reached him from behind, and glancing back through the viewing port, he saw troops galloping toward him along the narrow breakwater. He could see their lips moving as they bellowed at him to stop. One of the soldiers halted and raised his carbine to his shoulder, then fired.

Then Garrett flooded the ballast tanks, and the tiny vessel slid beneath the waves.

Malenov saw the lights of Riga through the aircraft window as the pilot began his final descent. They came down in the heavy darkness, taxiing to a halt by a row of darkened hangars. A limousine stood at the side of the runway, and as he undid his seat belt, Malenov spotted a group of uniformed officers waiting to greet him in the headlights' glow.

His cheeks flushed as he stepped into the chill night air. A major moved forward, saluting smartly. "Colonel Malenov?"

Malenov recognized Anatoly Kerensky, the Latvian officer in charge of Riga and the surrounding district. He was a medium-size man with a large head who wore padded overcoats to emphasize his shoulders.

Ignoring the welcome, Malenov eyed Kerensky coldly. "Garrett?" he demanded.

The major looked unhappy. "We believe he has stolen a midget submarine belonging to the university. He was seen escaping from Mishkin harbor. The prisoner Zystev is understood to be with him."

Malenov cursed angrily. "Am I surrounded by imbeciles? What was the vessel doing in the harbor in the first place? You knew Garrett would attempt to escape by sea. You should have had it removed from the water at once and placed under heavy guard."

"All the vessels in the harbor were guarded," Kerensky said. "Unfortunately, Garrett diverted the sentries' attention by setting fire to a builder's yard. However, the destroyer *Kuzneck* is standing by with antisubmarine devices, and I have ordered a helicopter to carry you out to join her."

Malenov grimaced, tugging his overcoat across his chest and shoulders. Thank God he'd decided to take command of things himself. Garrett was operating against a bunch of amateurs.

He fixed the welcoming committee with a withering stare. "Inform the pilot that I wish to board immediately."

# FOURTEEN

Garrett guided the submarine through the inky black water, his eyes focused on the unfamiliar control panel. He kept his speed to a minimum, using the scanning sonar to pick his way across the silt-coated seabed. He was afraid to employ the lights in case their beams were picked up by the patrol boats overhead. The effect of floating through a world of total darkness was disorienting, and though it was cold in the tiny cabin, Garrett's body was lathered with sweat.

They hadn't far to travel, he calculated, but there were a number of obstacles to surmount before they reached Swedish territorial waters. First and foremost, he had to negotiate the gulf that lay between Riga and the open sea; this was a simple maneuver in normal circumstances, but he was tackling it blind in an unfamiliar craft.

Garrett monitored the sonar screen, his hands light as thistledown operating the controls. The engines made a monotonous purring sound as they propelled the minuscule craft through a world without contours, without substance. Only the shuddering of the deck and the flickering gauges on the instrument panel told Garrett they were actually moving.

He looked back to see how Zystev was faring and was surprised to see the Russian watching him gravely. The vacancy had gone from Zystev's eyes, and for the first time, Garrett noticed a glimmer of awareness.

"Who are you?" Zystev demanded in a husky whisper.

Garrett smiled thinly. "You're sensible at last."

The Russian glanced around the tiny cabin, noting the night-lights, the metal bulkheads with condensation. "What is this thing?"

"Submarine. We're on our way across the Baltic. With luck—a good deal of luck, I might add—we should hit the Swedish coast in about two hours."

A flicker of hope replaced the confusion in Zystev's eyes. "You got me out of the hospital?"

"Well, we had a slight advantage. The local militia conveniently left their car running."

Zystev jammed his fist against his mouth. A trace of bile oozed across his tightened knuckles. "I feel terrible," he groaned. "My stomach's exploding."

"The aftereffects of the drugs they pumped into your bloodstream. Keep swallowing."

Zystev seemed surprised at the sound of a friendly voice. Garrett had a hunch he'd experienced little cordiality during the past few years.

"Your accent is strange," Zystev observed at last. "It is too pronounced, too deliberate, to be Russian."

"Major Zachary Paul Garrett, of His Majesty's Armed Forces. Special Air Service."

"You came all the way to Latvia just to rescue me?"

"That's right. You've suddenly become very important to us."

Zystev's lips twisted into a bitter smile. "It's a long time since I was important to anyone."

"Well, now you're back in demand again. We need information, and you, it seems, are the only man who can supply it."

Zystev sobered as he digested this statement. The glow of the nightlights accentuated the shadows around his eyes.

"And if I agree to cooperate?"

"I can offer you freedom, though I can't guarantee how long it'll last."

The hum of the ventilator sang in their eardrums, and Garrett focused his attention on the emptiness outside. No point in rushing the man. He'd clearly had enough over the years.

"Why don't you tell me what you are after," Zystev said at last. "Perhaps it will take my mind off how awful I feel."

Garrett blew the starboard tanks to inch the vessel slightly southwest.

"You remember *Suchko Twenty-three*?"

"Of course I remember. It was before I got arrested."

"Tell me about it."

"Tell you what? It was a special mission, organized by the military."

"The military? According to our records, *Suchko Twenty-three* carried a party of scientists destined for an orbiting space lab."

Zystev laughed shortly. "That's nonsense. *Suchko Twenty-three* was a wartime commando unit on a wartime operation."

"What war?"

"You wouldn't understand."

Garrett said, "Zystev, I have to know why it was carrying canisters of a toxin the Americans call DDF Eight hundred."

It was Zystev's turn to look surprised. "Who told you that?"

"I found one of the containers."

"You've been inside the *Suchko*?"

"Briefly."

"How? It finished up on the bottom of the Weddel Sea."

"Not quite. Thirty-two hundred feet, to be precise, though I can't account for its position now. But why did the Americans shoot it down?"

"That was De Tabley's decision. I worked for De Tabley."

"Frank De Tabley?"

Zystev nodded.

"I don't follow. De Tabley was on the spacecraft when it crashed."

Zystev chuckled dryly. "Wrong. De Tabley was never on the *Suchko*. The man you're talking about was an American named Hanson. He was dying of liver cancer and volunteered to take part in a suicide mission."

"Doing what?"

"Ensuring no word of the missile attack reached Soviet Ground Control. If the American rockets failed to destroy the spacecraft on impact, it was Hanson's job to disable the communications system."

Garrett considered the idea soberly. It sounded outlandish, but he had no reason to believe Zystev was lying.

"What about you?" Garrett asked. "Where did you come into it?"

"I was part of De Tabley's outfit. He employed me on a freelance basis, sometimes in the United States, sometimes in Moscow. At the time, I was working at the USSR Research and Control Center at Kaliningrad. Under the Drinov Agreement, we carried out frequent exchanges with NASA personnel, which gave me a useful corridor into the U.S.A. I took part in most of the space-oriented operations conducted by De Tabley's intelligence network. During *Suchko Twenty-three*, I was part of the launch crew at Baikonur. It was my role to substitute Hanson in the real cosmonaut's place. De Tabley asked me to give Hanson his personal-identity disk. He called it a dog tag."

"Why?"

"He was fanatical about covering his tracks. It was kind of a quirky thing he had. He liked to remain anonymous." Zystev's lips twisted into a humorless smile. "I worked a lot with De Tabley over the years, and I got to know him pretty well. Something happened during his youth—something he never talked about—but he carried it inside him like a secret affliction."

"Are you suggesting De Tabley might still be alive?"

"Damn right. Frank is the ultimate survivor. Last I heard, he'd had his features altered by a plastic surgeon in Memphis."

Garrett asked, "What about the *Suchko*? Why did he consider it so dangerous?"

"Ever heard of SOBS?"

"Sons-of-bitches?"

"Strategic Orbital Bombardment System."

"I remember. Banned by international treaty in the eighties. Space satellites armed with nuclear warheads that can be fired without warning at any target on earth. There's no defense against them. By the time the missiles enter the atmosphere, it's too late for the victims to react."

"I see they keep you up to date in the British SAS. However, it wasn't the international treaty that made SOBS unrealistic as an attack system. It was the fact that the satellites were so vulnerable from the ground."

"Correct. They could be blasted out of the sky, or even

snatched by some shuttle-style conveyor vehicle, which is why nobody took them seriously, even before the Americans abandoned their Star Wars project."

"The Americans took them seriously," Zystev said. "Fourteen years ago, they developed a new type of SOBS satellite. It was bigger and more sophisticated, and it carried something else—a built-in defense mechanism that made it virtually invulnerable to attack."

"What kind of mechanism?"

"A particle-beam device known as the Canby D-Five. The beams form a shield around the space platform so that anything approaching the vicinity, including enemy vessels and attack missiles, automatically disintegrates."

"That's impossible," Garrett breathed. "We've been trying to achieve that effect with particle-beam technology for the past twenty-years, and nobody's managed it yet."

Zystev laughed dryly. "That's because the earth's gravity weakens the electric-magnetic impulses, but in space, it's a different matter. The Canby D-Five produces a force field which effectively protects a satellite in all directions. The trouble is, the platform carries only enough power to operate the Canby for ten to twelve days, but if it's engaged at the first sign of an approaching intruder, the crew has ample time to retaliate with their own missile system."

"'Crew'?" Garrett echoed.

"The early models were triggered by radio signals or laser beams. To make the new version operational, it has to be manned. That's the drawback. It's highly expensive and essentially impractical. The Americans called it the *Devil's Stallion.*"

"And they built one?"

"Not only built it—they put it into orbit."

"What about the treaty ban?"

Zystev shrugged. "It was an experiment. A prototype. Remember, it was a different world then. SDI was still considered the defense system of the future, and the particle-beam Canby D-Five meant the SOBS had suddenly become a practical proposition, treaty or no treaty. Had it worked, the plan was to set up an entire network. Frank De Tabley was the man in charge of the project. Frank was an expert on nuclear missiles."

Zystev studied Garrett closely, his face the color of parchment. "Have you ever played polo, Major?"

"Polo? No."

"There's a move in polo called the inside reverse. That's when you think a rider's heading one way, when in actual fact he's going another. While I was working for De Tabley, he carried out a remarkable double switch. Using a bewildering array of forged documents and letters of approval from politicians who didn't exist, he switched satellites. He built what to all intents and purposes was a conventional spy platform and loaded the missiles and Canby onto that. The actual SOBS vehicle he installed with dummy warheads."

"Why?"

"So he would have at his disposal the most destructive power known to man—a missile arsenal capable of hitting almost any target on earth."

The sea grew darker, wrapping itself around their viewing ports. Garrett reduced the intake of water into the ballast tanks, adjusting their attitude angle. "But what about DDF Eight hundred?"

Zystev snorted. "The toxin's only a sideshow."

"The *Suchko* must have been carrying it for some reason."

"You're right. When the Russians found out about the SOBS, they were faced with a delicate situation. Either they could accuse America of violating the treaty—an action the U.S. would naturally deny—or they could take direct action. They knew an overt assault would constitute an act of war, so they decided on DDF Eight hundred. They loaded the *Suchko* with a specially designed spraying device, allowing them to emit the toxin in the form of gas."

"Why gas?"

"Because the Canby defense shield wasn't fashioned to repel gas. You see, the *Suchko* never intended to approach the satellite at all. It planned merely to spray DDF Eight hundred into its orbital path. Since the toxin is colorless, and undetectable on a radar screen, it's unlikely the American astronauts, even in their guarded state, would have noticed anything unusual. They'd imagine the *Suchko* was merely passing by on its way to re-man *Salyut Fifty-six*."

"But the American satellite would be sealed from tip to toe. Spraying it would have no effect whatsoever."

Zystev said, "Not immediately, I agree, but the DDF virus

is a persistent little fellow. Sooner or later, the Americans would have to use their docking bay. And as soon as an astronaut stepped out, he would carry the virus back inside, no matter how scrupulously he went through the safety procedures. It would not only wipe out the satellite crew but would render the platform uninhabitable for years to come."

Garrett was overwhelmed by the simplicity of the Russian plan. It was dazzling. Masterly. "So U.S. scientists would assume the virus had originated in space, and declare the satellite a write-off."

Zystev looked patient. "You're missing the point."

"What point?"

"The platform the Soviets took to be the *Devil's Stallion* wasn't the *Stallion* at all. De Tabley had already switched both the Canby D-Five and the nuclear warheads. When I warned De Tabley what the Russians were planning, he knew he couldn't allow the *Suchko* anywhere near that unoccupied satellite. If the cosmonauts had noticed its defense system hadn't been activated, they might have taken it into their heads to investigate. So he used Cheyenne Mountain to blast them out of the sky."

"De Tabley was only a major when the *Suchko* attack took place. How could he influence an organization as powerful as NORAD?"

"The head of NORAD at that time was General George Weir. Weir was part of a secret society within the armed forces, created and controlled by De Tabley himself. Most of its members were high-ranking officers. They were drawn to it for patriotic reasons. However, Frank had a curious perversion. He liked to blackmail people. He would go to considerable lengths to dig up dirt on anyone he came into contact with. He was a great believer in the old adage that when you have them by the balls, their hearts and minds will follow. General George Weir was on De Tabley's blackmail list."

"And the *Stallion*?"

"After official protests by the Soviet government, it was dismantled under the terms of the arms-ban treaty."

Garrett felt a tingling in his stomach. "You mean the *phony* satellite was dismantled."

Zystev nodded.

Garrett stared at him. "Are you telling me that for the past fourteen years, a derelict spy station has been circling the earth with eight nuclear missiles on board?''

"Correct. Thanks to De Tabley's resourcefulness, the *Stallion* still exists, though not in its original form. He knows if ever he needs to, he can re-man that satellite, engage the Canby defense system, and strike with impunity at any target on earth."

"My God," Garrett breathed.

A signature on the radar screen caught his attention, and he froze at the controls, his eyes anxiously scanning the readings.

Zystev sat up, his cheeks strangely greenish in the reflected hue of the instrument panel. "What is it?"

Garrett tapped the screen. The blip was drifting closer. "Something's up there. Not a patrol boat, something bigger. A battleship, I think."

"Can we lose her?"

"I don't know. If I cut engines and sit on the bottom, maybe she'll drift on by. But she's approaching fast. My guess is, she's already picked us up on her sonar."

He looked at Zystev. "I have a feeling they've got us cornered."

The atmosphere in the warship's command center was tense. Clad in white gloves and antiflash masks, the crew looked like creatures from another universe. Malenov watched Captain Fiodor Pakhovitch studying the screens in front of him.

"They're directly below," Pakhovitch said. "Sitting on the seabed."

"You're sure?"

"Quite sure."

Malenov closed his eyes as a savage elation filled him. Garrett's luck had played out at last.

"What do you want us to do, Colonel?"

Malenov looked at him calmly. The fever had gone from his cheeks, and his eyes were filled with infinite patience.

"I want you to depth-charge," he said.

Crouching in the stillness, Garrett's body felt hot and cold by turns. He could hear the low, ominous hum of the warship hovering above. Beside him, Zystev moistened his lips as the seconds lengthened. Garrett eyed the clock. He heard a scraping noise against the submarine's hull, and a terrible fear lodged in his chest.

"God," he croaked, reaching for the controls.

A thunderous explosion filled Garrett's ears as the ocean erupted around them and the submarine slewed wildly to port. An odor of diesel fumes filled the air, and their bulkheads buckled and twisted alarmingly. Garrett heard a hissing sound as leakage streamed into the cabin from the rear, and a second explosion followed the first, not quite so close this time, but powerful enough to send plates and rivets screaming in protest.

Then suddenly the entire shell seemed to open up. Garrett could think of no other way to describe it. Zystev screamed in panic as water crashed along the cabin floor. Cursing, Garrett blew the ballast tanks, engaging the forward hydroplanes. Warship or no warship, they had to surface quickly.

He felt the submarine rising, and studied the depth gauge, holding his breath. The ocean brightened, took on substance and perspective; then he saw lights glimmering above the wave crests as their craft emerged, dripping, into the full glare of the warship's searchlights.

Garrett groaned softly under his breath. The irony of the moment was almost more than he could endure. He looked at Zystev, his face stricken with emptiness and regret.

"Sorry, friend," he said tiredly, "I'm afraid the party's over."

Malenov's expression was bland as he poured himself a drink from the captain's cocktail cabinet. He tried to hide his jubilation at the sight of Garrett and the Soviet traitor Zystev facing him in mute submission. Their drenched clothing created pools of water on the deck around their feet. It was a moment Malenov intended to savor.

He rolled the brandy glass in his palm. "Quite a dance you've led us, Major Garrett. A pity it had to end in such an ignominious fashion."

He gazed down at the handwritten statement on the desk in front of him. He had taken it out of Garrett's pocket on arrival, and though the paper was saturated with seawater, both the writing and signature were exhiliratingly clear. Malenov could scarcely believe his luck. The letter amounted to a personal confession of spying offenses on the Antarctic

Peninsula. The damned fool had been carrying it around in his jacket.

"At least you have the grace to admit your guilt." Malenov tapped the letter gently with his fingertips.

"Don't be a fool, Sergei. You know damn well that confession's a phony. I just didn't get a chance to destroy it."

"Really? It looks extremely convincing to me. I have an idea the Bureau for State Security will think so too."

Garrett said, "You can't tuck me away like some unwanted dissident. I'm a British officer."

"But your papers say you are Zystev's brother. Birthplace—Karaveavo on the Peksha. When the British report you missing, naturally the authorities will conduct an exhaustive search, but in such circumstances..."

Malenov glanced down at the confession again, then on a sudden impulse, folded it up and slipped it into his tunic pocket. Garrett was already condemned, by his presence, by his actions. Shrewder perhaps to keep the statement as an insurance against the future. Should there be diplomatic meddling, it might prove a useful weapon.

He drained his brandy glass and calmly poured himself another. Strangely, his hatred diminished as he contemplated Garrett's bedraggled state. He might almost have felt sorry for the man—except for Elke. The thought of Elke thrust such nonsense from his mind.

"You do realize, Zachary, that kidnapping mental patients is a serious offense here? In fact, considering the implications of your case, it wouldn't surprise me in the least if our doctors decide your sanity also is a trifle suspect."

Garrett glowered. "What's happened to Elke?"

"What are you talking about?"

"Is she safe, Malenov?"

"Of course she's safe. Do you take me for a fool?"

"I wonder how she'll feel when she hears about this."

"Why should she hear about it at all? You, Zachary, are about to disappear. It will be as if you never existed. For a time, the British and American authorities may apply a certain degree of diplomatic pressure, but looking at the situation in the realistic sense, what can they do? To Britain, and to your allies in the United States, you are a monumental embarrassment. As soon as the immediacy of the moment has subsided, they will be more than happy to forget you."

"You're such a bastard, Sergei," he said. "You were a bastard the day you got me thrown out of Baikonur, and you haven't changed a bit."

Malenov's cheeks flushed hotly. He was about to reply when a seaman appeared in the cabin doorway. "Colonel Malenov, you are required in the radio room at once. General Suivesky wishes to speak to you on the ship's telephone."

With a conscious effort, Malenov held his temper. He followed the seaman along the companionway, entering the crowded radio room. The operator handed him the telephone, and Malenov raised the mouthpiece to his lips. "Malenov here."

General Suivesky's voice sounded hollow and distorted. "Sergei, I understand you've arrested Major Garrett."

"That is correct, General. We also have the traitor, Alexandr Zystev. Garrett was trying to smuggle him across the Baltic to Sweden. I am interrogating them now."

"Is Garrett hurt?"

"Hurt?" Malenov was puzzled by the question. "No, General. Apart from being wet, he appears to be in surprisingly good shape."

"Splendid. He is to be released at once."

Malenov's lips opened and closed in an agony of astonishment. "Released?" he stammered. "I don't understand."

"I am making you Garrett's personal custodian, Sergei. You are to bring him back to Moscow immediately. Treat him with deference and respect. There will be a plane waiting at Bykovo airport, ready to depart the moment you arrive."

Malenov saw the room spinning dizzily, and nausea engulfed him as his lungs strained for air. "General, may I inquire Major Garrett's destination?"

"Washington," Suivesky said briskly, and hung up the telephone.

# PART
## III

# THE CHASE

# FIFTEEN

The taxi dropped Garrett at the White House gate. He breathed in the early spring air as he paid off the driver and peered through the railings at a group of Secret Service men staring unblinkingly back at him. Sightseers thronged the sidewalk, and several demonstrators wielded placards protesting the Centaur Program.

The tension of the last few days, and the long flight across the Atlantic, had drained him both physically and emotionally, but his arrival at the White House made him forget his discomfort, revitalized him in some extraordinary way.

Louis Wesker was waiting for him by the guardhouse.

"Laying out the welcome mat, Louis?"

Wesker ignored the greeting. His plump face creased with distaste as he stared at Garrett's clothing. "Where in God's name did you get that suit?"

"Tiny place in Latvia. The tailor lengthened the sleeves at no extra charge."

"What did he use, a knife and fork?"

"Did it ever occur to you, Louis, that I might be sensitive about the way I dress?"

"If you can wear a suit like that, nobody could ever accuse you of sensitivity."

Wesker escorted him past the security desk and along a maze of corridors. The floors were polished, the ceilings

arched, and paintings adorned the walls. Shirtsleeved security
guards watched them impassively from discreet vantage points.
Garrett felt slightly awed at finding himself in such presti-
gious surroundings.

"So this is where you work," he said.

"No," said Wesker. "I'm based in the Executive Office
Building next door. This is where my boss works, the
President of the United States. He's the one who got you out
of the Soviet Union, by the way. He decided you'd suddenly
become indispensable."

"I wonder what gave him that idea."

"Well, it sure as hell wasn't your tailor." There was an
undertone of tension beneath Wesker's bantering manner.

"Where are we going, Louis?"

"To meet the President's chief of staff, Jan Bowering.
We've got a crisis here—the worst kind of crisis. Your phone
call from Moscow confirmed that. If what Zystev said is true,
we need your expertise, and we need it fast. Mrs. Bowering
will explain things. She's the lady you've been working for
these past few weeks."

Garrett was silent as they took the stairway to the second
floor. When they reached Jan Bowering's office, they found it
crowded with people.

"My God," Garrett exclaimed. "It's like Piccadilly Circus
in here."

"These are aides and special assistants," Wesker said.
"Jan Bowering is the quickest avenue to the President, so
when an emergency arises, she tends to get inundated."

Garrett felt his pulses quicken as he spotted Lori Madden
talking to a nervous-looking man with a college-boy hairstyle.
Clad in a leather skirt and turtleneck sweater, Lori looked
breathtaking.

She gave no visible sign she had noticed Garrett's arrival,
nor did her attention waver when the chief of staff herself
walked in a moment later. Jan Bowering was a striking lady
in her early forties, slim, dark-haired, and attractive. Her
arrival brought an instant hush to the crowded room.

"The cabinet meeting's still in progress, and I have to
return as quickly as possible," she told the gathering, "so I
want no interruptions while I talk to Major Garrett."

She stepped forward to take Garrett's hand, her warm eyes

examining him frankly. "Major, I'm delighted you were able to join us."

"I'd call that pleasure mutual. The Russians were beginning to show a disturbing interest in my mental health."

"Well, you can thank the President for getting you out of there."

"I'm grateful. But I wonder if the President could extend the same courtesy to Alexandr Zystev? If the Russians get their way, they'll send him straight back to that monkey farm."

Jan Bowering considered for a moment. "I'll talk to Mr. Clayman this afternoon. Maybe he can telephone the Soviet president. We may be able to arrange something."

She appraised Garrett shrewdly from head to toe, and he recognized a hint of toughness beneath her friendly exterior. "You're quite an operator, Major Garrett. I believe we owe you our thanks, not only for finding the *Suchko*—at some risk to your life, I'm told—but also for what you managed to uncover in the Soviet Union. Zystev's disclosures create an alarming scenario. In fact, it's because of that scenario that we were able to get you released so promptly, in spite of the *Suchko* affair. Louis told you about our predicament here?"

"He hasn't had time to get around to it."

"Well, during the past few hours, the matter has taken a completely new turn, one that threatens not only the United States but the stability of the entire world. Please step over here. I have something I'd like you to see."

Garrett followed her to the window bay. Reaching up, she pulled the drapes, then turned to the nervous-looking man standing at Lori Madden's side. "Nicky, for Major Garrett's benefit, will you please run the videotape again."

As the aide leaned forward to operate the TV set, Jan Bowering explained: "This tape was delivered anonymously to the White House early this morning. According to the statement accompanying it, similar tapes have been sent to TV stations in twenty-one different countries. The message speaks for itself."

Frowning, Garrett watched a picture appear on the television screen. He recognized it instantly as an atomic blast. A violent flash burgeoned into the now-familiar mushroom cloud hovering over the distant horizon. Somber music accompanied the pictures. After a moment, newsreels of Hiroshima, leveled into rubble, flashed across the screen, and the camera lingered on a handful of survivors picking their way dazedly through an ocean of devastation.

Suddenly, the scene changed. The music became jaunty and invigorating, and Garrett saw a montage of paintings reflecting America's turbulent past. The montage ended with a shot of the Lincoln Memorial, the camera moving slowly up the steps to where the statue rose like a vision of God.

As the music reached a crescendo, the image dissolved into the outline of a man sitting in precisely the same position, framed by an American flag. He was totally inert, as if, like Lincoln, he had been carved out of stone. His face was concealed behind a molded rubber mask, and his shirt was open at the chest, revealing a pendant of some kind dangling at his throat.

He began to speak as the music faded. His voice was raw and rasping. Garrett assumed it had been mechanically distorted.

"Criminal mismanagement," the man declared without preamble, "has brought the United States to its knees."

The speaker exuded a powerful hypnotic presence that dominated the entire room. His words were slow, measured, ringingly clear. "This proud country, once the flagship of freedom and Western democracy, is about to take the irrevocable step into an abyss of self-destruction. When we make space accessible to the entire world, peace as we know it will cease to exist. The power balance, which has maintained our stability for the past half century, will disintegrate. Like many weaker nations, the United States will be subject to the fluctuating pressures of petty despots and tyrants, capable of launching terrorist attacks whenever and wherever they choose."

"We have decided—reluctantly decided—to take an unprecedented course of action. We have in our possession, eight one-megaton nuclear missiles, serial numbers two-two-two-four, slash, AMC-three, slash, eleven-oh-one to eleven-oh-nine. We are prepared to use these missiles to save the world from the chaos and disorder that the eroding international power balance will engender. With this end in mind, we are making the following demands.

"First, that all members of this patriotic community—what some will call a conspiracy—be granted an immediate and unconditional pardon, a guarantee that no retaliation will be taken against us for doing what we see as our duty. Second, that the Centaur Program, set up with the Soviet

Union and already the cause of much dissension and unrest, be terminated forthwith and forever. Third, that the President of the United States, Lawrence Clayman, resign from office immediately. Fourth, that a covenant be drawn up, to be honored by every future president, establishing the United States' superiority in space as a symbol of its strength, authority, and determination to preserve world peace.''

The man paused as he approached the crux of his statement. ''The United States has twelve days to comply with these terms. If they are not met to the letter, on Friday, April twenty-nine, seven major world cities will be obliterated from the face of the earth. No warning will be given. There will be unprecedented loss of human life.''

A murmur of shock rose from the crowded room. Almost as if he had heard it, the speaker raised his hands in a conciliatory gesture. His voice took on a softer tone.

''It is not our desire to destroy people. A nuclear holocaust is the ultimate nightmare. But we are determined to demonstrate the insanity of the road along which our leaders are steering us. So that there can be no misunderstanding, no foolish miscalculation of our capacity to carry out our threat, we will precede it with an illustration of our power. On Wednesday, April twenty, at four P.M. Eastern Standard Time, we will destroy the oasis village of Bir Hamada in the central Sahara. We earnestly urge the Algerian authorities to evacuate without delay both the village and the neighboring city of Abeidi. The blast will carry radiation and toxic effects over a six-to-ten-mile radius, and we cannot be responsible for any citizens who have not been transported to safety.''

The speaker lowered his voice as he reached his conclusion. ''After the explosion, President Clayman will have nine days to return the world to order. We trust and pray that reason will prevail. This is the end of our message.''

A series of still frames showed the devastation of Hiroshima after the 1945 bombing. This time there was no music. The pictures were delivered in total silence, and the effect was brain-numbing.

As the screen went blank, an aide stepped forward to flick the control switch, and Jan Bowering pulled back the drapes, flooding the room with light. To Garrett, she said simply, ''Well?''

Garrett breathed deeply. Suddenly, Zystev's revelations had

taken on a new and terrible meaning. "You say that message has been delivered around the world?"

"By now, I imagine it'll be leading the news bulletins in twenty-one countries."

"Have you checked the serial numbers of the missiles listed?"

"According to our records, they were dismantled almost twelve years ago, but who can believe the records any more? If what Zystev says is true, we have people at the very heart of our military machine who are capable of diverting anything—including nuclear missiles—by forging signatures and fabricating end-use certificates."

"So we have to assume the threat is genuine?"

"We do. It looks as if the conspirators, whoever they are, are using this nuclear satellite as a sophisticated weapon of blackmail."

Garrett thought for a moment. "Well, the first thing we've got to do is establish precisely where the *Devil's Stallion* is."

"We already know that. A Pentagon shuttle mission sent three astronauts to a derelict spy platform named DVT Twenty-four nine days ago. They're occupying it now, with the shuttle *Ulysses* still locked in the docking bay. They've cut off all communications with Ground Control."

"Who ordered the mission?"

"Nobody knows."

"And what does the President say?"

"Nothing, at the moment. If the *Stallion* proves as invulnerable as you claim, he may have no alternative but to resign. The platform's particle-beam defense shield makes any kind of military action impracticable."

"What about copying the Soviets, spraying toxin-carrying gas into its orbital path?"

"The astronauts are already conscious of that possibility. They'll take damned good care to stay inside the sealed doors."

Garrett pursed his lips, his face creased in thought. "How feasible would it be to calculate the orbital incline needed to hit the village of Bir Hamada on the morning of the twentieth?"

"Perfectly feasible. In fact, it's already been done. Our people at NORAD are hoping to shoot down the missile the minute it appears. However, I must tell you the chances of success aren't very strong. The advantage of the SOBS system is that coming in from space, it can hit almost any target on earth before defense systems can be activated."

She moved behind her desk, leaning forward to rest her weight delicately on her fingertips. For the first time, Garrett noticed the deepening lines in her face. "Major Garrett, we are considering two possible courses of action, and as a particle-beam expert, your opinion on their virtues is needed."

The others in the room watched Garrett closely, as if they imagined he might by some extraordinary circumstance offer a simple solution.

"When a nuclear warhead explodes," Jan Bowering went on, "the blast gives off a pulse of electromagnetic energy. If we fire our missiles and detonate them just outside the Canby D-Five force field, will the impact be powerful enough to alter or damage the satellite's solid-state electronics?"

"I'm afraid not," Garrett said. "Particle beams require a tremendous amount of energy to speed them up to the required velocities. The Canby D-Five will simply absorb the pulse beats, rather like a blotting pad mopping up spilled ink. The detonation may slightly alter the satellite's orbital position, but in general terms, will have very little practical effect."

"But I'm right in thinking the terrorists will have to switch off their defense shield in order to fire their own missiles?"

"Correct. Particle beams are indiscriminate. The Canby D-Five may stop rockets coming in, but it will also prevent them going out."

"In that case, supposing we send up a fleet of missile-bearing satellites, ready to hit them the minute they deactivate?"

"You'll never get close enough. They'll pick up your hardware on their radar scanners and blow you out of the sky."

"We could always dispatch decoys. Draw their fire. Make them waste their precious warheads."

"Dodgy. You'd run a serious risk of having them launch their entire salvo in a retaliatory strike against the earth. The only sensible answer, it seems to me, is to apprehend the man masterminding the conspiracy, Frank De Tabley."

Jan Bowering looked skeptical. "In twelve days?"

"Well," Louis Wesker said, speaking for the first time, "we're not starting entirely from scratch. We do have a rather sizable amount of raw information now. Maybe if we put it all together, look for a common denominator, we'll get lucky."

"Lucky?" Jan Bowering drummed her fingers wearily on the desktop. "It isn't luck we need. What we need is an old-fashioned miracle."

* * *

Frank De Tabley lay on the riverbank gazing at the azure sky. The sun bathed his cheeks, sending ripples of warmth through his body. The scent of blossoms hung in his nostrils, and a bee droned lazily among the foliage.

Frank heard his father calling, and raising his head, saw De Tabley senior standing up in the tiny rowboat, brandishing a fish he had just caught. The fish was wriggling and fluttering on the hook, and Frank's father grinned in triumph, his crooked jaw slightly out of alignment. Frank's father was not a handsome man, but he *was* an arresting one; his rawboned musculature, earnest eyes, and tousled hair captured the attention of everyone who met him, and he could talk intelligently about almost every subject under the sun. Frank would watch with pride as his father dominated a dinner gathering or fielded arguments from the cracker-barrel philosophers who gathered on Marty Sturvenant's porch.

De Tabley senior eased the slippery creature off its hook, and picking up the oars, began to paddle toward the adjacent shoreline.

A cool wind fanned Frank's cheeks, and he glanced up, frowning, as a dark cloud passed across the sun. In the twinkling of an eye, the lazy brilliance of the summer morning gave way to the menacing gloom of an approaching storm. Frank scrambled to his feet. He had never known the weather to change so quickly.

The trees swayed and groaned as the wind caught them, ripping at their branches, bending their trunks. Rain flecks peppered Frank's face, drenching his shirt till it clung to his body. The river whipped up, its placid surface churning into a cauldron of foam-tossed spray.

Frank's father turned, balancing himself on the gunwale as he prepared to leap for the shoreline. Suddenly, he lost his footing, toppling into the bubbling current. Frank's heart pounded in his chest.

"Dad!" He sprinted along the muddy riverbank.

His father rose from the water, laughing crazily. Frank's senses reeled. There was something terribly strange in his father's laughter. It was no longer the voice of the man he loved. It was taunting, mocking.

And then, as Frank watched unbelievingly, his father's body exploded. His flesh peeled outward like the skin of a decaying orange, and Frank cringed as he saw a monstrous creature taking shape beneath. It was a demon dredged from the depths of hell, eyes bulging, teeth thrashing.

He screamed. Unable to help himself, he screamed and screamed until he thought he would never stop. Then someone shook his shoulder, and a voice whispered urgently in his ear: "Frank, Frank, what's wrong, Frank?"

He opened his eyes, jerking spasmodically. He was lying on a narrow bed, his body drenched with sweat. General Connel was leaning over him, his eyes filled with concern. Sunlight streamed through the open window. Frank De Tabley swallowed hard.

"Are you okay, Frank?" Connel asked.

De Tabley wiped his glistening cheeks with his arm. He was shaking all over, like a man in a fever. "What time is it?"

"Almost noon. Kozani will be phoning shortly."

De Tabley pushed himself up, swinging his feet to the floor. His body felt weak, his knees wobbly. "I must've fallen asleep."

"You were dreaming, Frank. I thought you were going out of your head."

De Tabley looked up at him. "Did anyone hear?"

"Only me."

"I'd appreciate it if—" De Tabley hesitated, the sentence lodging in his throat.

Connel said, "Don't worry, Frank. I won't say a thing. Take a few minutes and pull yourself together. I'll wait for you in the library."

De Tabley sat for a moment after Connel had left the room, then rose shakily to his feet and shuffled across to the washstand. Peering into the mirror, he examined his face nervously. His cheeks looked flushed, his eyes feverish, and sweat beaded his sunbaked skin. But he didn't look like his father, he thought. No, by God, the plastic surgeon had seen to that. There was nothing left of his father at all. The monster he'd turned into existed only in Frank De Tabley's dreams, and with God's help, they too would fade in time.

He was still shaking as he turned on the tap and splashed cold water over his face and neck.

The President strolled across the North Portico of the White House, accompanied by Jan Bowering, the attorney general, and the secretary of defense. His eyes were tired as he gazed past his Secret Service detachment at the foliage in Lafayette Park. He was a resilient man, but the endless meetings were beginning to exhaust him. "My head's pounding like a sledgehammer," he remarked to no one in particular.

Jan Bowering shuffled the papers on her clipboard. "The press secretary's asking for another statement. He's holding a media conference at four o'clock. He can handle it, Mr. President, if you're feeling under the weather."

"No, Jan, it's my job. I need to relax for a few minutes, that's all."

The attorney general cleared his throat, trying to inject a note of optimism into the proceedings. "There's still a chance, Larry, that this is just an elaborate bluff."

"You don't really believe that," the President said.

"Why not? It's beyond credence that these characters will actually carry out their threat and murder millions of people."

Clayman stretched painfully, his features twisting as he felt his joints creak. "Gil, they've gone to an enormous amount of trouble to get those astronauts into space. Men so fanatically dedicated aren't going to hesitate when it comes to pressing the button. I think we can assume they mean what they say." He looked at the secretary of defense. "Any word from Algeria, David?"

"They appear to be taking the threat seriously, Mr. President."

"Hell, they'd better. Tell me again what will happen if that bomb goes off."

Richner rubbed the back of his neck. "Well, first there'll be the blast, probably a fireball about three or four miles across. Everything inside that area will be razed to the ground. Unless the inhabitants have been evacuated, the impact will travel along the drainage pipes, killing people on the outer fringes. Then there'll be the fallout—dust sucked up from the earth and made radioactive."

"How serious?"

"In a place like the Sahara, whipped-up sand could prove a monumental hazard. It'll carry radioactivity over an immense area."

"Strong enough to kill?"

The defense secretary said, "They'll have three different types to worry about—alpha, beta, and gamma. Alpha particles only travel a few inches and can't infiltrate the human skin. Beta particles travel about twenty or thirty feet. The most dangerous of all are gamma. They can penetrate matter like an X-ray, and they're extremely poisonous if inhaled.''

Clayman grimaced. ''Jesus, David, that sounds terrifying.''

''I guess the best we can hope for, Mr. President, is that the Algerian authorities get their people out in time.''

Prime Minister Howard Bowen flew into London on the morning of April 17. He had cut short his Caribbean holiday following a phone call from the home secretary, Richard Mills. Now, still clad in tropical clothing, he bustled through the line of security men, and hurried out to his official car. Accompanied by police vehicles, the cavalcade sped along the M.4 motorway and through the bustling London outskirts. At Downing Street, the prime minister left his wife in the lobby and made his way to the emergency cabinet room on the second floor. Inside, the cabinet ministers rose to their feet as their premier entered.

Waving impatiently, he walked around the conference table to his empty chair. ''Is it true?''

Defense Minister Gavin Menzies said, ''The Americans seem to think so.''

''No possibility of a hoax, then?''

''There's always a chance, Prime Minister, but''—Menzies shrugged—''Washington's convinced the threat is genuine. The terrorists' information is too accurate to be a bluff.''

''God.'' The prime minister thought for a moment. ''What's the reaction in Algeria?''

''Initially, very little. In fact, people generally seem unimpressed. I think they've lived so long under the nuclear threat, they refuse to believe in it anymore. News bulletins, like soap operas, come from a different world.''

''What about the United States?''

''Well, the State Department claims the nuclear warheads listed on the videotape were dismantled almost twelve years ago. However, they've discovered evidence of a dangerous conspiracy within the Pentagon, so it's quite possible the missiles still exist.''

''And Algeria?''

''For safety's sake, they've decided to evacuate not only Abeidi but also the towns of Timimoun, El Golea, and Ain Salah. I spoke to General Meki, the man commanding the operation, earlier this morning. Clearing Bir Hamada was easy enough. The oasis was closed nearly six years ago due to the increasing salinity of the water, and the only occupants are a group of local herdsmen who were airlifted out yesterday. The city of Abeidi, however, is another matter. The residential areas are being vacated in sections, with military units escorting the inhabitants in convoy to reduce congestion. The problem is, people simply don't want to go. Some aren't taking the threat seriously. Others are angry at being turned out of their homes. There've been violent scenes, especially in the outlying areas. They've had to ring the approach roads with armed troops.''

"Don't tell me there are idiots actually trying to break *in*?''

Menzies answered, ''You'll always find the cranks who want to be around when something happens, no matter what the cost. There are even a few demented souls who see it as a divine opportunity to join Allah.''

Opening his briefcase, the prime minister took out a small battery-operated electric shaver and ran it over his cheeks and throat. ''Bring me the panic howler,'' he ordered.

Without a word, an usher unlocked a cupboard and removed the telephone that connected the prime minister directly to the White House. Placing it on the table, he stepped back discreetly as the prime minister picked up the receiver.

After a moment, Lawrence Clayman's voice came on the line. ''Howard?''

"Larry, I've just got back from Barbados. Any news?''

"No further progress on last night, but we *have* had one small breakthrough. We now know where the missile is coming from. It's being launched from a satellite which, according to our records, should have been dismantled years ago. The satellite's carrying eight nuclear warheads. Presumably, one of them is being directed at Bir Hamada.''

"Larry, are you telling me this nightmare is actually happening? There's a platform orbiting the earth with eight nuclear missiles on board?''

"I'm sorry, Howard, I'm afraid that is the unpalatable truth. The satellite was a prototype for a network of Strategic Orbital Bombing platforms launched into space fourteen years ago.''

"My God,'' the prime minister breathed.

"The satellite is equipped with a Canby D-Five particle-beam defense shield, rendering it invulnerable to attack.''

"What does that mean?''

"It means we can't touch it," the President said. "It's beyond our reach."

"Beyond our reach, rubbish. We can blast it out of the sky."

"Negative. Our rockets would simply disintegrate. The Canby destroys from the inside, pulling atoms apart."

"A commando raid then."

"Same answer. You can take measures against a laser, like ablative coating or reflectors, but there's no defense against a particle beam. It kills in fractions of a second."

"So while this thing prepares to take potshots at us, we just sit here twiddling our thumbs?"

"Well, it's not quite as hopeless as it sounds. Since we now have the satellite's position, our people at Cheyenne Mountain are hoping to intercept the incoming missile and blow it up above the earth's atmosphere."

"Can they do that?"

"Nothing is guaranteed," Clayman said. "Our antimissile units are the most sophisticated in the world, but countering an attack from outer space poses a monumental problem. Whether they can lock on to the warhead accurately enough we'll just have to see."

In the morning sunlight, the prime minister's face was ashen. "Are you aware that we're contemplating the first nuclear blast to be carried out in anger since World War Two?"

"This is why I've worked so hard to implement the Centaur Program. We always knew that unless something was done to halt the military exploitation of the skies, sooner or later a major catastrophe would be inevitable."

The prime minister understood the terrible strain Clayman was under. "I don't envy you, Larry."

"Well, I'm not beaten yet. I'm going to lick these sons of bitches at their own game."

"I wish you luck, sir."

"Thank you. I appreciate that. I'll call you again as soon as I have any news."

"Good-bye, Mr. President."

"Good-bye, Prime Minister."

"The White House wanted to stick you in a hotel," Wesker said, "but I figured you'd be better off at my place. Lori's been staying there since we came back from Antarctica."

"You're very charitable, Louis," Garrett said.

"I have a generous personality."

Through the windshield, the gray waters of the Chesapeake looked peaceful in the sunset. The dying rays glimmered on the shiny surface, giving it the appearance of polished metal. Sitting in the passenger seat, Garrett watched dusk gather among the flat treeless islands.

He glanced at Lori in the rearview mirror. She was gazing moodily across the bay, her eyes somber, her cheeks drained of color. He wondered if he had upset her. He'd been looking forward to seeing her again, had been counting off the hours in his mind, yet she'd scarcely spoken a word since his arrival. Every look she gave him, every gesture, seemed like a warning: Don't touch.

The road dipped into a thatch of woodland, and Garrett spotted a river glistening among the trees. It ran directly into the bay. Reeds cluttered its grassy banks. There was a narrow drive, with an open gate and a metal sign: Albatross.

"This is it," Wesker announced, swinging off the highway. "Home sweet home."

"You're in for a shock," Lori warned, speaking for the first time.

Garrett saw a line of polished lanterns tracing the track along the riverbank. Suddenly, the trees fell away, and there, moored against a narrow quay, was a full-size cargo submarine. A spiral staircase led to its oblong conning tower, where plants and flowers framed the deck and beveled underbelly. Garrett blinked as Wesker drew the car to a halt.

"Louis, you live in *this*?"

"It's not operational," Wesker explained. "In fact, it's not even seaworthy. But it reminds me of my navy days. I got so I just couldn't stand living in the city."

Garrett shook his head in wonderment. "But, Louis—pink? Whoever heard of a pink submarine?"

"It's my boat," Wesker said. "I can have it any color I want."

Garrett gathered his things from the trunk and followed Wesker into the vessel's interior, whistling softly in admiration and disbelief. The entire inside had been redesigned in the manner of an eastern temple. Slender columns supported the frescoed bulkhead where inlaid panels showed hunting scenes from Jaipur. Chandeliers hung from the ceilings, and red carpets adorned the floors. The lights, skillfully concealed the tiny alcoves, cast delicate slivers across the gold door moldings and exquisitely carved furniture. Everything exuded an air of elegance and style.

"I can't believe this," Garrett murmured. "It's like staying at the Ritz. Where did you get it, Louis?"

"Bought it from the navy for a song. I gutted the interior and did the place up myself."

"It's a regular palace."

A man came toward them along the narrow companionway, his slender body clad in a silken kimono, his Asian face composed into a mask of utter impassivity. He bowed deeply from the waist. "Welcome," he said.

"This is Gendun," Wesker explained. "He's not only my manservant, he's also my guru, karate teacher, and spiritual adviser."

A stranger vitality emanated from Gendun's features. He smiled gently at Garrett. "Mr. Wesker desires to become an Enlightened One. He seeks the experience of universality, which extends between space and motion, substance and emptiness. He wishes his spirit to be light and elusive as the air."

"He'll never make it with that waistline," Garrett commented.

"Such a concept has no meaning in the doctrine of enlightenment. The true believer seeks only the liberation of the body and the path of spiritual harmony," Gendun replied.

Wesker took Garrett's arm. "This is your cabin," he said, opening a door. "It's a bit on the small side, but you can always step outside when you feel the need to stretch your legs."

Garrett looked around the tiny room. A mirrored wall added space and light, and the gallery-level sleeping area was reached by narrow stairs from the laminated deck.

He spotted the picture of a woman on the rosewood dresser. She was dark-haired and good-looking, with a hint of willfulness in her high-boned features. "Who's this?"

"My ex-wife. I put her in here so I don't have to look at her anymore."

"She's very attractive, Louis."

Wesker grimaced. "It was a disastrous marriage. She figured I was the wrong shape, so she stuck me on a slimming course."

"Did it work?"

"Damn right it worked. I lost nearly ninety pounds. Trouble was, as soon as she saw the streamlined model, she took off with an oil engineer from Galveston, Texas.''

"That's too bad."

Wesker shrugged philosophically. "It's life, I guess. Anyhow, dinner's in half an hour. We can talk while we eat, okay?"

"I'll look forward to it," Garrett said.

Dinner proved to be an exceptional meal. Wesker cooked it personally, rejecting every attempt by Lori to offer assistance. "Women in the kitchen make me nervous," he said.

They sat around the Regency table while Gendun, still clad in his elegant kimono, brought in the various dishes with an air of oriental reverence. The food smelled succulent and delicious.

"Try the pirozhi," Wesker recommended. "Tell me if you find it crisp enough."

Garrett popped a morsel into his mouth and began to chew.

"Well?" Wesker queried.

"Louis, you're a marvel."

Wesker looked gratified. "You'll find none better on the North American continent. I get the ingredients from Svoboda's in Tacoma Park. He imports them directly from the Soviet Union. He also keeps the source a strict secret. We could do with Svoboda's security at the White House."

When the meal was over, Wesker steered their conversation to more businesslike lines. Sitting back in his chair, he carefully lit a large cigar. "Let's take a look at what we've got here," he said.

"We haven't got a damned thing," Garrett told him bluntly.

"Oh, I wouldn't say that." Wesker blew smoke toward the ceiling. "We know there's a man named Frank De Tabley, and we know he started a secret society within the armed forces. We also know it's a pretty good bet that that society is responsible for the threat we're facing now."

"Nothing but conjecture, Louis. Who's going to believe it?"

"What's to believe? There's nothing new about soldiers forming secret societies. It's a practice that dates back to Spartan times when the corps d'elite of the emperor's army kept the lower ranks from getting out of line. Even Napoleon has his covert group of hard-liners, and Mussolini's troops founded the notorious *Ascesa Quinto*."

"But an organization like this—at the highest level of the American defense establishment . . ."

"Perfectly feasible," Wesker maintained. "It wouldn't require many members, merely influential ones. We're so accustomed to military coups in distant countries, we tend to ignore the possibility of one in our own. But the Centaur Program has become an intensely political issue that's split the country as violently as the Vietnam War. The military community, especially De Tabley's fanatics, regard space cooperation as a direct affront."

"To the extent of launching nuclear weapons on a defenseless world?"

"Fanatics come in all shapes and sizes, Zach. The fact that they are Americans doesn't make them any less ruthless or determined."

"I can't believe we're talking like this," Lori said. "All my life I've heard about the danger of nuclear warfare. Now suddenly it's right here on our doorstep."

Wesker examined his cigar tip. "Got anyone at home to worry about, Zach?"

"I have a ten-year-old son in England. Fortunately, his school is in the country."

"You're lucky. I wouldn't care to be a city dweller once those missiles start falling."

Garrett shifted uncomfortably in his chair. "What are the chances of us combing the Pentagon in time?"

"You mean a witch-hunt? Forget it. There are thirty thousand people working there. Let's stick to what we've got. De Tabley."

"Louis, we know nothing about the man. We don't even know what he looks like, for Chrissake."

"Wrong," Wesker said. He took out a photograph and pushed it across the table. "This is the only picture of De Tabley in existence. We got it from a Navajo named Jules Belino."

Garrett glanced at him with surprise. He took the photograph, studying it thoughtfully. "Where was this taken?"

"Saigon."

"Then it's obviously out of date. According to Zystev, De Tabley has since had his features altered by plastic surgery."

"He also burned off his fingerprints with acid."

Lori felt a breathlessness in her diaphragm. She jerked upright in her chair, a sudden sickly look entering her eyes. "His fingerprints? My God, I'd almost forgotten."

"Something wrong?" Wesker muttered.

"Louis, Randolph Guthrie has no fingerprints."

Garrett looked surprised. "The Vice President?"

"His skin's as smooth as silk. I've felt it."

"How?"

"Never mind how. I've felt it, that's all."

"Hold on a second. What are you suggesting?"

"I'm suggesting nothing. All I'm saying is that Randolph Guthrie has no fingerprints."

Wesker frowned, tapping ash from his cigar. "Why didn't you tell us this before?"

"Because it didn't mean anything before. We thought De Tabley was dead."

Garrett looked at Wesker. "Is it possible? Could the Vice President of the United States really be Frank De Tabley?"

Wesker looked unconvinced. "Randolph Guthrie had an automobile accident twenty-one years ago. He burned his hands trying to haul a companion out of the blazing passenger seat. There was a lot of publicity about it during the last election."

"Did anybody investigate that accident?" Lori asked. "Find out if it really happened? Are there medical records to substantiate Guthrie's claim, or has the story been taken completely on trust?"

Wesker sat back in his chair. "What the hell are you handing me here?"

"I know it's only circumstantial," she said, "but look at how the pieces fit. Item one, the fingerprints—a hell of a coincidence, you have to admit. Item two, Guthrie's physical appearance—he's long and bony, just like the man in the photograph. True, his features are different, but that could be the plastic surgery. Item three, Guthrie was in Vietnam at approximately the same time as De Tabley. He was also employed by the CIA for a while. Item four, he hates Lawrence Clayman and everything Clayman stands for. He only agreed to be his running mate to further his own political career. He resents Jan Bowering's influence, and he's wholeheartedly opposed to the question of international space cooperation."

"He told you all this?"

"His feelings were kind of difficult to ignore."

Wesker looked at Garrett. "It's a crazy idea, but these

people have known every damned move we've made, at the highest level. They must have a plant in there somewhere. Guthrie could be the man.''

He whistled softly as he leaned forward to stub out his cigar. ''Wow, what am I supposed to do with this? I can't go to the President and say, 'Your Vice President is suspect number one.' We need evidence, something concrete.''

''Turn him over,'' Garrett suggested. ''Check his background, his army record, see if anything cross-references. Look in the CIA files. If he worked for the agency, there'll be documents bearing his name. Maybe they'll link him to De Tabley's network. If there's nothing, that'll be an indication in itself. Dig out his laundry tags, his garbage—anything. Find out how many times a day he goes to the john.''

''We'll have to handle this delicately,'' Wesker said. ''Guthrie is a hell of a big fish to fry. But if we've linked him to Frank De Tabley—'' he reached for the bottle and deftly filled their glasses, ''then I think the occasion calls for a toast.''

For a long time after he had gone to bed, Garrett lay on his bunk staring at the ceiling. Lori's behavior during the evening had baffled him. He hadn't been imagining things—something was different about her. The way she'd looked tonight, the way she'd treated him; not icily, but with a haughtiness that didn't make any bloody sense. Though he'd attempted several times to penetrate her composure, she'd stubbornly refused to unbend.

Well, he thought, maybe he'd expected too much. Built up his hopes, the way a child might, looking forward to some long-awaited treat. But surely he'd had good reason. Before he'd gone, she'd indicated with every look and gesture that she wanted him back safely. Yet now he might have been a stranger. No warmth, no friendliness—nothing. Just that damned bewildering indifference. He decided it was time to get things settled.

Throwing back the bedclothes, he tugged on the robe Wesker had lent him, and slipped into the passageway. He tapped lightly on Lori's door. She opened it after a moment, gazing up at him with the same impersonal expression she had worn all evening.

''Feeling tired?'' Garrett asked.

''Not particularly.''

"I guess I slept myself to a standstill on the plane."

"Well, you can always try counting sheep," she said.

Garrett's jaw tightened. There it was again, that infuriating aloofness. "As a matter of fact, I had something far more interesting in mind."

Seizing her in his arms, he kissed her hard on the mouth. It was like the releasing of some powerful tension, and he was conscious of the softness of her body, the warmth of her flesh. He felt a throbbing in his temples, an urgency in his blood.

Suddenly he realized she was standing rigid as a statue. When he released her, she looked at him coolly. "You're extremely sure of yourself, Major Garrett."

"'Major'? How did we get so formal?"

"Since you decided to go back to Moscow."

Garrett blinked. Her reasoning escaped him. "Hold on a minute. You think I wanted to go back?"

"I don't know what you wanted. As a matter of fact, I don't know anything about you."

"Hey, what are you getting so het-up about?"

"I never felt calmer in my life."

"I was only trying to help," Garrett protested.

"In that case," Lori answered primly, "you'd better save your energy for your little computer operator."

"Lori, for God's sake," Garrett exclaimed.

But he was too late. She stepped back and closed the door in his face.

Angrily, Garrett returned to his own room and tore off his robe. Bitter and disgusted, he stormed into the bathroom and turned on the shower. The needle-sharp spray scoured his skin, chilling his body with icy droplets.

Women, he thought. They were the same the damned world over. Incomprehensible.

# SIXTEEN

Major General Nathan D. Kincaid, commander in chief of the North American Air Defense Command, pushed his electronic ID card into the slot on the computer console. The door slid open with a soft metallic hum. Air conditioners purred in his ears as he strode through the maze of corridors leading to the subterranean war room buried deep inside Colorado's Cheyenne Mountain. Unlike many of his countrymen who regarded the threat of nuclear attack with skepticism, General Kincaid knew the danger was very real. He had been head of NORAD for almost seven years, and during that period had kept the elaborate 4.5-acre defense complex on a continual wartime footing, Now, he was anxious to discover whether his constant practice exercises had been worth the effort.

Major Tony Evans met him at the war-room door. Like Kincaid's, the major's cheeks were flushed with excitement. "Is it true, General? Is this the real McCoy?"

Kincaid said curtly, "Straight from the President's mouth."

His eyes scanned the bristling array of computers, weapon consoles, and surveillance gear. "Is everything ready?"

"All systems A-okay," Evans confirmed. "All we need is the word."

Kincaid lowered his voice. "Tony, I want the doors sealed, and two highwaymen placed near the exit hatch."

"Highwaymen" was the name given to armed MPs who

239

had instructions to shoot down any man who panicked during emergencies.

"Is that necessary, General? Everyone's eager and ready to go."

"No offense, Tony. It's just a precaution. When this thing breaks, I don't want to look back afterward and think, Why didn't I follow the rule book? This operation is too damned important to fail."

"Okay, sir, I'll see to it at once."

Jan Marisa Bowering sat in her living room watching television pictures being relayed by satellite from the mountains above Abeidi. The city looked deceptively tranquil in the sunlight, its buildings flanked by a wide desert *reg*. It was not so much a city as a moderate-size town, brown and arid as the land in which it nestled, its outline tempered by the white domes of mosques and the squat ugliness of European-style apartment blocks. Government helicopters zigzagged the streets, looking for signs of movement or life that might denote the presence of human beings.

The voice of the network anchorman Allen Morris imposed itself over the stark images. "Our correspondent Tim Reynolds has been following developments with members of the Algerian armed forces. What's the position now, Tim?"

"Well, Allen, as you can see, helicopters are carrying out a last-minute check to ensure no stragglers remain behind. Abeidi is now awaiting the first nuclear attack since Nagasaki."

"Clearly the Algerian government has taken the terrorist threat very seriously."

"I think the extent of the evacuation confirms that. It's been a remarkable feat all around. One of the major problems has been the fact that this is the home of the Kel Ahaggar Tuareg, a nomadic people who could be wandering virtually anywhere in the surrounding area. The army has done its best to clear out the various scattered bands of tribesmen."

"What about Bir Hamada itself?"

"The oasis lies about six miles to the west, on the fringe of the Grand Erg Occidental, in a sea of rolling sand dunes. There's a genuine fear here that a nuclear explosion could have an unprecedented geological effect."

"And the Abeidi evacuees—where are they being held?"

"The lucky ones are in tents behind Mejouda Mountain.

Public-health experts, together with the International Red Cross, are busy laying latrines and transporting emergency water supplies, but there's been so little time to prepare that a large section of the populace has been left with virtually no shelter at all. Almost as fast as the tents are erected, they're being occupied.''

''How do the residents view the prospect of seeing their city on the nuclear hit list?''

''Well, there's an air of unreality about the whole affair here, Allen. I think most people expect the crisis to fizzle out. They're hoping to return to their homes either later this evening or first thing tomorrow morning. But if the terrorists do succeed, if radioactive fallout renders the city uninhabitable, what the citizens of Abeidi are facing is not a temporary inconvenience but the loss of everything they possess.''

Muttering softly under her breath, Jan Bowering switched off the television set and went to the window. She stood with her arms crossed, gazing moodily into the street. She was still there when her husband, Walter, came into the room.

''What's wrong, kitten?''

Jan Bowering spoke without turning her head. ''Walter, do you think this is all my fault?''

''What are you talking about, your fault?''

''Was it *my* program, *my* insistence that created this madness? Have I been too tunnel-visioned?''

Walter's features softened sympathetically; crossing the room, he put his arms around her, hugging her close against his chest.

''You're talking crazy, kitten,'' he whispered. ''The President wouldn't have gone along this far if he didn't believe in the program too.''

She clung to him. ''Sometimes, I have to remind myself it's not a dream.''

Pulling out a handkerchief, Walter mopped the tears from her cheeks. He had never seen her so emotional before. She looked weary and dispirited, as if her body had suddenly aged beyond its years. Easing out of his arms, she moved again to the window. People scurried along the sidewalk below.

''Look at them,'' Jan Bowering said. ''You'd think they hadn't a care in the world. The TV reports are too unreal— they come from a distant universe. Don't they understand that by the time this evening's over, nothing in the world can ever be the same again?''

"How long have we got?" Walter asked.

Jan Bowering glanced at her watch. In the light from the window, her face was a milky hue. "If our calculations are correct, approximately three hours and seventeen minutes."

"And then?"

"Then God help us all," she said.

For the umpteenth time, Josey Hentoff checked his calculations on the instrument panel. Within the next few minutes, he knew, they would reach the window into the atmosphere, the precise orbital position from which their missile should be launched for a successful hit. He glimpsed the earth drifting by peacefully below. It looked tranquil in the sunlight, its violet surface swathed by wisps of feathery clouds. Even at this distance, he could discern the snow-capped tips of the Himalayas.

He rose from his seat, floating effortlessly. The sensation of weightlessness had lost some of its novelty during the past few days, and now he moved with ease around the satellite's interior.

"It's almost time," he announced.

Finnegan glanced at him from the apogee motor, his cheeks pale and strained. There was no sign of emotion on Finnegan's face, but Hentoff noticed a tremor in his voice as he spoke. "Better wake Zahl."

Nelson Zahl had zipped himself into his body pad and was dangling from the bulkhead, snoring peacefully. As Hentoff floated across the open deck, Zahl opened his eyes, peering up at him. "What time is it?"

"Seven minutes to go."

With a cough, Zahl zipped loose his covering and kicked himself from the cabin wall. His body drifted gracefully through the air. His voice was cool, piercingly alert.

"Prepare missile one," he said.

Deep inside Cheyenne Mountain, General Nathan Kincaid watched the intercept procedures taking place. The men looked calm and capable as they went through the systems check. They'd conducted the sequence a thousand times, and the fact that this time the threat was real, the target tangible, did nothing to impede the smoothness of the operation. Kincaid approved.

"Launch keys inserted," a voice declared. "Function select switch to Off."

"Cain-and-Able switch set to Enable," a second voice announced. "Cain-and-Able switch down and locked. Initiation switch actuated counterclockwise."

"Actuated counterclockwise one thousand and one."

The weapons officer moved his hand across the console, displaying little emotion as he carried out the deadly ritual. His face showed a nonchalance created by many months of familiarity.

Kincaid looked at the clock on the chamber wall. The second hand was approaching the hour mark. If their calculations proved correct, the terrorist missile should be appearing on their scanning screens at any moment now. Kincaid felt his muscles twitch as a blip emerged on the radar console. Bang on, he thought wryly.

"Target identified," the operator stated. "Interrogation commencing."

His hands flipped across the panel, engaging the interrogation computer that assimilated data issued by the incoming missile. Kincaid watched the signature speeding into the atmosphere.

The console screen flashed out the words Target Acquired.

"Release Key-line and Commit-line," the weapons officer commanded.

Hands sped across the keyboards. This was the moment, the point at which Kincaid, no matter how many times he watched it happen, felt his limbs go weak, his stomach tighten. When the WO spoke again, his voice sounded unnaturally strained: "Three . . . two . . . one . . . *mark*."

Blast-off, Kincaid thought. Gazing at the scanning console, he flinched as eight new signatures appeared on the radar screen.

"Launch in progress," a voice declared. "Missiles away."

Dry-mouthed, Kincaid watched the rockets homing steadily on their target.

Garrett and Lori were sitting in Wesker's office when the telephone buzzed. They waited in silence as he picked up the receiver. He listened for a moment, his face composed, then said in a hushed voice, "I see. Thank you, Mrs. Bowering."

Putting down the telephone, he looked at them calmly. High on his left temple, a tiny pulse had begun to throb. "That was the Oval Office. Our missiles have missed their target. The terrorist warhead is approaching Bir Hamada now."

They turned to the TV screen where the commentator was still intoning calmly. From the heights above Mejouda Mountain, the city of Abeidi looked disarmingly peaceful, its sun-scorched buildings, minaret towers, and ancient *souk* marketplaces toylike in the shimmering heat. There was no inkling of calamity, nothing unusual that Garrett could see.

Then suddenly, almost as if the set had begun to burn from within, a blinding flash filled the screen. The newscaster fell silent as the picture began to shudder. The brightness seemed to splash against the clouds, sizzling and shimmering in a violent magnesium flare, changing from orange to yellow, then a brilliant white. For several seconds, it blotted out everything in sight—the sky, the *reg*, the city.

So white did the screen become that for a moment, Garrett thought it had gone completely blank, but he knew the impression was illusory, the lightness a heat more searingly destructive than anything man could imagine.

Gradually the blast diminished, began to take on dimension and perspective. The *reg* swiveled into focus, its entire horizon masked by a bulging black ball. Smoke belched into the sky, churning upward in a breathtaking column, then billowing outward in an expanding cauliflower of flame-tinged fumes.

It spread across the desert floor, its creeping tendrils never still—twisting, writhing, multiplying.

The city swung into alignment, but now the buildings that had baked so pleasantly in the African sun seemed lit by a demonic light, as if the earth had erupted in some unimaginable cataclysm, pouring out oceans of fiery pus. Flames danced on the building walls, and through the camera's telescopic lens, the watchers saw trees hurtling along the empty thoroughfares like clumps of macabre tumbleweed. Abandoned cars sailed through the air as if tossed by an invisible hand. Some exploded on impact, spraying out feathery fingers of flame.

Above Abeidi, the great cloud hovered, its twisting columns extinguishing the sun, filling the screen from corner to corner, and Garrett's stomach turned as he saw, far out beyond the horizon, a wall of sand, two hundred feet high, hurtling toward the defenseless city. He gazed at the thundering whorl, billions of granules churned up from the dune bed—boiling, tumbling, spewing, spuming, engulfing everything that lay in their path. On and on they came, picking up speed as the fuming ferment sucked up sustenance from the desert bottom.

The newscaster's voice echoed dimly through the speaker: "Holy Jesus . . ."

The barrier reared up like the prow of some incredible galleon, and without a pause, crossed Abeidi's suburbs and fell headlong upon the empty city. Buildings crumbled as the pulsating rampart wiped out entire districts in a blinding avalanche of dust. It swirled across the rooftops, devouring boulevards and market squares with a greedy thunderous roar. Then, as it reached the mountain's lower slopes, its momentum seemed to falter, and it roared to a halt, turning back on itself in a roiling somersault, its powdery grains shimmering like heat waves glimpsed on a summer day.

Garrett and the others stared numbly at the TV screen. Nothing existed but the blinding curtain of dust, the awesome canopy of the desert floor, and the ominous billowing mushroom cloud above.

Nick Koster drove tearfully through the teeming Washington streets and onto the Capital Beltway. Headlamps formed an endless ribbon of light, trundling through the darkness in a slow, infuriating crawl; horns blared, and voices rose angrily as the inhabitants made their laborious exit from the endangered city. In places, motorists desperate to escape Washington's confines had abandoned their automobiles altogether, aggravating the confusion still further.

The complacency that had greeted the terrorists' initial videotape had escalated into widespread panic. Seen by an estimated one billion people, the Algerian pictures had sent shock waves throughout the entire world. In all the major U.S. cities, authorities were reporting unprecedented levels of traffic congestion as residents, desperate to escape the impending holocaust, headed for the relative security of the open countryside.

In Portland, Maine, a family man had shot dead three neighbors trying to force their way into his fallout shelter. In Stockholm, Sweden, fourteen yachtsmen had disappeared after setting out across the storm-tossed Baltic.

The panic had become a virus, and as the cities emptied, those left behind—the poor, the alienated, the disaffected— had begun taking to the streets in an orgy of looting and violence.

At Forest Glen, Maryland, Koster ran into a police road-block. The uniformed officers examined him carefully with their flashlights. "No sense heading any farther," one told him. "Beltway's blocked for the next fifteen miles. Only way out of the city is on foot."

Koster displayed his ID card. "I have to reach Ashton. It's important."

The officer was impressed by the White House stamp. His voice took on a deferential tone. "It's no good this way, Mr. Koster. If I was you, I'd take the next exit and follow Cedar Lane and Knowles Avenue through the park. Most people are heading north, so I guess you should make it without too much trouble."

Pulling off the congested highway, Koster picked a tortuous route through the suburban streets. He had never seen anything like it. The entire metropolitan area had gone crazy. All the fear-stricken populace could think about was reaching the comparative safety of the rural areas, and after what he had seen on TV, Koster didn't blame them. It had been a terrible thing, an unimaginable thing, and he had been partially responsible. He had allowed it to happen, and that made him as guilty as the man who pressed the button, as guilty as Frank De Tabley himself. If he didn't put a stop to it quickly, millions of people could be incinerated; millions more could die from radiation.

When he reached the big house, the security guards waved him through the metal gates. He left his car on the cindered apron and made his way to the conference room at the building's rear. A small group of conspirators were gathered in front of the TV set.

De Tabley himself, dressed in a velvet smoking jacket, glanced up as Koster entered. "Nicky, what are you doing here?"

Koster struggled to control his breathing. In the past, De Tabley had frightened him, but not anymore. Now he was filled with a desperate fervor. "We've got to stop it."

"Stop what?"

"This madness. We've got to stop this madness."

De Tabley glanced at his companions. "What are you talking about, Nicky?"

"It's gone too far, Frank. It's out of control. We've got to call it off before it blows up in our faces."

"Nicky, you're upset."

"Listen to me, godammit. Have you been out there? Have you seen what's happening in the city? The people are going crazy, for Chrissake. In Anacostia, they're setting fire to the buildings. It's anarchy, Frank."

"Of course it is. Anarchy's just what we need. It'll help the White House realize the only answer is to concede defeat. It's working in our favor, Nicky."

"Fourteen people died in Stockholm today trying to escape the devastation that *we* created," Koster said accusingly.

"We can't be responsible for the actions of individuals. Nobody said this would be easy, Nicky. Nobody said it would be pleasant either."

Koster balanced himself against the back of a chair. His eyes looked frantic, pleading. "Phone Kozani," he urged. "Tell him to radio Zahl. Tell him the operation's been canceled."

"You think Zahl will listen?"

"He'll listen to you, Frank. Tell him the President's agreed to stand down. Tell him any damn thing you like, but for God's sake, get him back."

"How?"

"He's still got the shuttle, hasn't he? You can do a deal. No missiles, no charges. An unconditional pardon, signed by the President himself."

"As simple as that?"

"Of course as simple as that. Why not?"

De Tabley got up and examined Koster sympathetically. "What's wrong, Nicky? Getting cold feet?"

"Not cold feet. Sanity, Frank. Sanity's what's wrong with me. What we are doing here is crazy."

"Have we misled you in any way? There isn't a man here who wasn't told, a thousand times over, what this operation would entail."

Koster was exasperated. "You think that makes everything okay? You think it absolves us, Frank? For Chrissake, you saw those pictures this afternoon. We've wiped out an entire city. Even after the sand's removed, God knows how long it'll take to make Abeidi habitable again."

"Nicky, remember your promise when you came to see me seven years ago?" De Tabley's voice was soothing and insistent. "That was a sacred promise, Nicky. Every man here made that promise, and every man has honored it. We watched those pictures today, and we didn't like them either, but we're trying to save the world, not destroy it. We're offering people a taste of what the ultimate horror can mean. Our sacred goal is to ensure that this battered old earth of ours will never see such devastation again."

Koster shook his head wearily. Once, De Tabley had moved him, inspired him. But now he said, "You're crazy, Frank."

De Tabley slipped his arm around Koster's shoulders. "Nicky, we've achieved something momentous today. We've proved the *Devil's Stallion* is a viable proposition. We've demonstrated the very real dangers that exist in outer space. If President Clayman persists with the Centaur Program, it'll be suicide we're talking about, Nicky, not murder. The blood will be on Clayman's hands, not ours."

"How can you say that?"

"Because I know the *Stallion* will never be used. Clayman will have to give in. He'll have no choice. He'll be removed forcibly if necessary. The people aren't fools. They'll realize when their backs are against the wall. Take my word for it, Nicky, we're going to win."

Koster breathed deeply, his flash of rebelliousness dissipating. "I don't know, Frank. I just don't know anymore."

"I'm telling you the truth." De Tabley gently patted his shoulder. "Count on it."

"I used to think everything was so simple," Koster muttered, rubbing the back of his neck. The fire in his eyes dwindled. He glanced at the others with embarrassment. "I guess I'd better be getting back. All White House staff are expected to remain on call tonight. Emergency procedures."

"That's right." De Tabley smiled. "Go keep an eye on things. We'll handle the dirty stuff—it's what we're good at."

Nodding at the little group, Nick Koster made his way to the door. De Tabley's features hardened as he watched him go. He glanced at his companions, and against his florid cheeks, his eyes looked like chinks of frosted glass.

"Take care of the gutless bastard," he ordered.

* * *

Nick Koster drove through the darkened suburbs. Car horns blasted on the nearby freeway, but the streets here were silent and deserted. Rarely had he seen it so totally devoid of life, even in the early morning hours.

Koster's brain was in turmoil. He felt that his body and head had somehow separated, each operating independently of the other. He knew he had to stop the horror, but how? He wasn't a courageous man. He couldn't face the prospect of confession, the ignominy of arrest and disgrace. There had to be another way, something that wouldn't directly involve himself.

He drew to a halt at a public phone booth and sat for a moment, fiercely gripping the wheel. He couldn't do it. He couldn't become an informer. How could he betray a man he had once so admired? But maybe if he handled things right, informing wouldn't be necessary. Maybe all that was needed was a quiet word, a subtle pointer in the right direction.

Swallowing hard, he got out of the car and called Wesker's private number. He heard the line ring for a few moments before the receiver lifted and a female voice answered. It was Lori Madden.

Koster spread his handkerchief over the mouthpiece. "Is Louis Wesker there?"

"I'm sorry. Mr. Wesker is out at the moment."

"How about Major Garrett?"

"Major Garrett too, I'm afraid. Can I help in any way?"

Koster hammered his palm against the booth door in frustration. "I'd like to leave a message. It's very important."

"Go ahead."

Somehow, the words seemed to lodge in his throat. "Tell them if they're looking for Frank De Tabley, maybe they should try speaking to Frank's lady."

"His lady?" Lori's voice was suddenly taut.

"Her name's Bonnie MacAnally. Her address . . ." Koster fumbled in his wallet, taking out a slip of paper. He squinted in the dim lighting. "It's the Strobel Building in Falls Church. Apartment one-twenty-one."

"Just a moment," Lori said. "Who is this?"

Koster's hand trembled as he hung up the phone. He stepped from the phone booth and crossed the street toward his car, filling his lungs with air. For the first time in weeks, his head was clear, and he could feel the tension draining from his body.

He didn't notice the automobile bearing down on him from behind. By the time he glanced over his shoulder, the car was almost upon him, its headlights pinning him in a dazzling glare.

With a cry of alarm, Koster tried to throw himself clear, but the vehicle caught him in the base of the spine. His body catapulted forward, hitting the pavement with a sickening thud. Dazed and bloody, he lay moaning softly.

The car screeched to a halt, and a man came out, fitting a silencer to a semiautomatic pistol. Striding toward Koster, he removed the slip of paper from the injured man's hand, placed the pistol against his temple, and fired three shots in quick succession.

He looked down at Koster's corpse in silence, then hurried back to his car. He drove off swiftly into the night.

Gendun came into the room as Lori was scribbling a note for Garrett and Wesker. He studied her keenly, noting the flush in her cheeks, the excitement in her eyes. "What are you doing?"

"Gendun, I have to go out for a while. Will you please see Mr. Wesker gets this message the instant he arrives."

"Leaving here would not be wise. There are bad omens in the air tonight. You must try to attain quietude and serenity."

"Gendun, you're a sweetie, but I've just had our first real lead. There isn't time to wait for Louis and Zach. I have to move now."

"The streets are dangerous tonight. Can't you call someone at the White House?"

"There are too many people involved already. Besides, we don't know who we can trust any more. Here"—she handed him the note—"give Mr. Wesker this and tell him it's the address of Frank De Tabley's mistress. Tell him I'm on my way there now."

"Miss Madden, you must not act so hastily. Remember, only by conquering impetuousness can we achieve the true harmony of mind and body."

"You said it, Gendun," Lori echoed as she grabbed her handbag and headed for the door.

# SEVENTEEN

Garrett stood at the hospital reception desk, watching the ambulance arrive in a continuous convoy. White-coated orderlies ferried the casualties across the marbled lobby into the emergency room—victims of the street violence erupting in the poorer quarters of the city. It was like a war zone, Garrett thought.

A doctor walked by, his smock coated with blood. The man looked harrassed and drawn.

"What's happening out there?" Garrett asked.

"It's crazy," the doctor said. "You'd think the bomb had already dropped. Washington's like a gutted animal tearing at its own entrails. The city's gone completely wild—street riots, lootings, random violence. In Anacostia, the police have pulled out altogether. They're calling it a no-go area. Word is, the army's on its way to establish martial law, but this isn't an isolated incident. According to the radio, it's going on all over the country."

"Bad as that?"

"'Bad' is an understatement." The doctor hurried off, shaking his head.

Through the windows, Garrett saw flames flickering on the distant skyline. In places, the police said, entire blocks had been set ablaze.

He heard footsteps ringing in the corridor and saw Wesker

hurrying toward him, carrying a folder under his arm. Wesker's plump cheeks were flushed, and a thin strand of hair dangled loosely across his forehead.

"Any luck?" Garrett asked.

Wesker spread the papers on the reception counter. "The accident happened on September four, 1977. Randolph Guthrie suffered minor abrasions and a hairline fracture to his right collarbone. He also contracted severe burns to his palms and lower wrists."

"And his fingerprints?"

"Nothing," Wesker said.

"What do you mean, nothing? You mean there's nothing on the file, or nothing on his fingerprints?"

"I mean there's nothing in the file. No diagnosis, no observation sheets, no X-rays, nothing."

Garrett felt a flicker of excitement. "Louis, that's a hell of a coincidence."

"My feelings exactly. The accident report is there, plus a summary of Guthrie's main injuries. Otherwise, zero."

"Somebody's been tampering."

"That's what it looks like. It's the De Tabley syndrome all over. The question is, what do we do now?"

"Take our findings to Jan Bowering of course."

"What findings? We don't have any findings. All we've got is speculation."

"For Chrissake, Louis, we haven't time to muck about. We've got to act now."

"Zach, we're talking about the Vice President of the United States. If we're going to make this stick, we need something positive in the way of proof."

"And how do you figure on getting that?"

"By watching and waiting. If Randolph Guthrie really is Frank De Tabley, sooner or later he'll need to contact his fellow conspirators. When he does"—Wesker's eyes gleamed with flinty determination—"then we'll grab him."

Driving south along the Anacostia Freeway, Lori found the traffic almost choked to a standstill. Cars lined bumper to bumper like segments of a monstrous earthworm, getting nowhere. Fuming with impatience, she took the exit to Fort Dupont Park.

People surged everywhere on foot as she picked her way

through the baffling labyrinth of side streets. Raucous voices filled the air, and the crash of splintering glass made a discordant symphony. Discarded cars lay wrecked and burning where their owners had abandoned them.

Looters drifted by, carrying stereos, microwave ovens, VCRs, anything they could get their hands on—even, Lori noticed at one point, a tailor's mannequin, the evening gown and costume jewelry still intact. She saw a man kick in a store window and emerge a moment later with a TV set under his arm.

Several buildings were ablaze, turning the night sky into a sea of shimmering fire.

A jeep came hurtling out of a side street, its headlights, smudged by soot, carving twin cones of light through the smoke-tinted gloom. A chanting mob, nearly a hundred strong, sprinted in its wake. Glimpsing Lori, the panic-stricken driver jammed on his brakes, skidding across the highway and ramming into a fire hydrant with a thunderous crash. To Lori's horror, the mob was upon him in an instant, dragging him from his seat.

She swung her vehicle into reverse and set off in a different direction through the swirling smoke. She'd been crazy to come here. She was a stranger in this city, the districts and street names meaningless to her: Berwyn Heights, Hyattsville, Blandensburg, Silver Spring. She had no idea where she was going. She should have waited for Garrett and Wesker. She should at least have requested assistance from the White House. Now she was alone in a Washington gone mad.

Lori saw a man, his face bloody, stumbling along the sidewalk, pursued by a ragged gang wielding knives and chains. Where were the police, for God's sake?

A group of rioters appeared in her headlight beams, their eyes crazed, their features twisted with hate. Lori saw pickax handles, tire irons, heavy clubs. A man tore at her door and finding it locked, smashed the side window with his fist. Lori stabbed the accelerator and the car leapt forward, scattering the mob in every direction.

She drove madly down a side street, flames dazzling her eyes. The slipstream from the broken window fanned her fevered cheeks. Her hands were slippery with sweat, and her chest ached.

Out of nowhere, a barrier of battered furniture rose in front of her, blocking her way. Gritting her teeth, she braced herself for the impact, her skin icy as she counted the seconds. With a shriek of buckling metal, her car drove headlong into the makeshift barricade, jerking her savagely against the seat belt.

For a moment, she felt too stunned to move. A throbbing pain lanced her chest, but there was no sign of blood. She heard a hiss of escaping air; steam spiraled from her buckled hood. She tried the ignition. No response. I'll have to get out of here, she thought. Coughing and spluttering, she pushed open the door and staggered toward the nearby streetlights.

Through the smoke, she saw something waver, like a mirage on a hot summer day. A group of scarecrow figures advanced toward her in a disorderly line. They were almost indiscernible against the gloom, their grimy T-shirts blending into the swirling smoke, their movements measured and controlled.

"Come here, sugar," a voice crooned.

Lori edged back toward an alley as the gang spread out, fanning her on both sides. "Come here, sugar-baby."

Like predators, the men homed in for the kill. She smelled their pungent body odor. Something nudged at her thighs, bringing her to a halt—a garbage can.

The leader paused, his lips parting to reveal a line of broken teeth. He reached out, gently cradled her cheek with his palm. "We going to make your bells ring tonight, sugar-baby," he declared huskily, trailing his hand down the steep curve of her throat to her breast.

Reaching back, Lori's fingers closed on the garbage can lid, and she swung it. With a resounding clang, the metal slammed into her tormentor's face, hurling him backward. Lori flung the lid at the man's startled companions and darted frantically into the alleyway. With shouts of fury, the men followed.

An entrance opened on Lori's right, and she turned into it, slamming the door and sliding the bolt shut. Half-crazed with panic, she scurried, panting, through the darkened building. It was a warehouse of some kind, its stone floors scattered with wrecked equipment. Obscene graffiti had been spray-painted on the walls. Water dripped from the fractured heating pipes.

Following a stairway to the upper floor, Lori shuddered as she heard the door collapse under her pursuers' weight. A window opened onto a balcony, and she slithered across the narrow sill.

The balcony twisted to the right, following an indentation in the wall. Here an upright pillar several inches wide led from the roof to the ground below. Lori clutched the support post. She had to reach the street, give herself another avenue of escape.

She hooked one leg over the balcony rail and began to wriggle precariously downward. The pillar's surface felt chill against her fingers and she heard it creaking softly as she transferred her weight in measured stages.

She felt a wave of relief as her feet touched the pavement. Then a whoop echoed on the smoky hot air, and she heard a voice crooning gently, "Hey, sugar, come here, sugar-baby . . ."

Almost demented with terror, she huddled shivering in the refuge of a darkened doorway.

The submarine was dark as Garrett and Wesker drew to a halt on the concrete landing. In the warm spring night, the blossoms on its deck looked faintly luminous. Even at that distance they could smell the pungent odor of drifting woodsmoke.

Garrett eyed the surrounding treeline worriedly. "Something's wrong here, Louis. It's far too quiet."

He ran up the spiral stairway and entered the submarine's conning tower. Switching on the lights, Garrett hurried from room to room. "Lori?" he shouted. "Hey, Lori?"

Gendun met him in the companionway. He bowed deeply from the waist and handed Garrett Lori's note. Holding it to the light, Garrett read it.

"What is it?" Wesker asked, running up behind him.

"The little fool." Garrett showed Wesker the slip of paper. "She's gone off to find De Tabley's mistress. She'll never get across the city. Not tonight. Not alone."

Wesker examined the message, then asked Gendun, "Couldn't you have stopped her?"

"The lady would not listen."

Wesker checked his watch. "It's an hour's drive into town. She wrote this at eleven-oh-five, and the freeway's jammed to a standstill. If we cut through the backstreets, maybe we can overtake her."

Garrett thrust the message into his jacket pocket, and they hurried back to the car.

Lori moved through a world of darkness. Terror had made a vacuum of her mind—that and the strangeness of the city around her. Hours had passed, it seemed, since she'd evaded the would-be rapists, or was it only minutes? She had little sense of time.

Here, the streetlights looked impotent, their lifeless globes framed by wisps of smoke. In places, the glow of blazing buildings lent a curious sheen to the battered apartment blocks where looters surged among the shadows, smashing windows, kicking in doors, swarming through the rooms and passageways. Distant sirens wailed on the wild night air, and from time to time, Lori heard the crackle of gunshots beyond the smoke-seared rooftops. Her body felt disjointed. Her limbs had lost all feeling.

A line of warehouses opened on the right, and she saw skeletal cranes, deserted wharfs, abandoned freight cars. The river. She shuffled toward it. The river offered an anchor, a point of reference at least.

Her heart fluttered as something emerged among the shadows—a telephone booth. Tugging open the door, she groped for the receiver, but there was no dial tone. The line was dead.

Sobbing with disappointment, she stumbled dazedly on. Rotting timbers rose from the river's edge. There was a scent of garbage, the odor of burning wood. She saw someone sprawled in the darkness and stopped, clutching her handbag defensively against her chest. The body lay on the concrete flags, a man, she realized, his lips framed in a silent cry of protest and pain. The front of his shirt was drenched in congealing blood, and rats, drawn by the unexpected nourishment, were feeding on the corpse's gore.

Suddenly Lori wanted to be sick. The events of the past few hours had driven her to the point of exhaustion, and the sight of the gutted body seemed to push her over the brink. She jumped violently as a specter moved out of the shadows and came drifting toward her, wreathed in smoke. It was a woman, her bedraggled clothing splattered with blood.

"Don't be nervous, honey. I won't hurt you. Just happy to see a friendly face."

"Who are you?" Lori whispered.

"Meg Fairfax is my name."

She pointed at the body on the ground. "Tried to take advantage, he did. Tried to take advantage of old Meg."

Lori stared at her, petrified. "You killed him?"

"Sure I killed the son of a bitch. He was aiming to rape me."

Lori swallowed hard. The woman looked shriveled and witchlike.

"Got a cigarette, honey?"

"I'm sorry, I don't smoke."

The woman looked disappointed as she scanned Lori appraisingly, noting the frightened features, the tangled hair, the defensively clutched handbag.

"What you doing on the waterfront?"

"I got lost."

"Where you trying to get to, honey?"

"Falls Church, Virginia."

"Falls Church?" The woman cackled. "Why, Lordy, you're about six miles in the wrong direction."

"My car crashed. I got confused. There was so much smoke. Some men tried to attack me. I ran . . ."

The words bubbled from Lori's lips. She felt as if a dam had broken, releasing the pent-up emotions.

The woman seized Lori's arm. "Easy, honey. Relax. We ladies got to stick together, protect each other."

Her hand tightened on Lori's wrist. She had a grip like a prizefighter. "Come with me. I've got a place at the end of the wharf. You can rest up and leave in the morning. My neighbor Charlie'll take you anyplace you want to go."

Propelled by the stranger, Lori staggered along the waterfront. She could smell the woman's unwashed body, see the dirt in her hair. Across the river, flames danced into the glowing sky, setting the buildings in sharp relief.

Lori spotted an alley between the warehouses, its narrow walls cluttered with cartons. "Almost there," the woman murmured in her soft hypnotic way, patting Lori's wrist reassuringly.

Drawing closer, the cartons gradually took shape. They had been built into a series of ramshackle shelters, the roofs covered with plastic garbage bags. They formed a flimsy anthill beneath the gaunt buildings.

A dwarf crawled out of one of the hovels and ran toward them. "Meg," he wheezed, "What you got here?"

The woman cackled, and her grip tightened suddenly on Lori's arm, flinging her without warning against the alley wall. Lori gasped as the breath was driven abruptly from her body. She tasted the salty sting of blood on her lips and realized she had bumped her nose. Startled, she turned to see the woman wielding an ugly knife. Its blade flashed, inches from Lori's nose.

"The purse," the woman snarled. "Give me the purse."

Lori hesitated, whimpering in fear as other figures emerged from the shadows—derelicts, addicts, dropouts.

"The purse," the woman hissed again.

Lori fumbled with the shoulder strap, a feeling of anger starting inside her. I'm not a helpless cripple, she thought. I'm damned if I'll let this old bitch intimidate me. She swung the bag wildly, sending the knife spinning.

The woman seemed startled by Lori's aggressiveness. Lori pushed her backward into the dwarf and ran. No one stopped her.

She tore up the alleyway. A flight of stairs appeared, and she took them as fast as her heart and body would allow. As she burst into the open, her breath caught in her throat. Swarming toward her along the deserted street was a ragged gang of looters, their faces glistening with sweat. They whooped with delight when they spotted Lori. Several men started in her direction, and with a stifled sob, she scrambled back along the sidewalk, darting into a nearby apartment house. Blackened and dilapidated, the hall was shrouded in darkness.

Lori sprinted along the empty passageway, fighting for breath. She saw the elevator standing open and with a sob of gratitude hurtled into it, jabbing the button for the upper floor. Nothing happened. Footsteps clattered in her wake, and she punched each button in turn. Again, no response.

Sucking at the air, she glanced swiftly around. A bolted hatch in the ceiling led to the cubicle's roof. Jamming her feet against the narrow walls, she eased herself up on the handrails, throwing back the trapdoor cover. Panting, she wriggled through the opening as the first of her pursuers, a sinewy black man, thundered into the elevator below. She heard a scuffling noise as the looter attempted to follow her. She slammed the hatch cover down on his fingers and stomped on it with every ounce of strength she could muster. She heard a cry of pain as his body hit the elevator floor.

Summoning her strength, she groped through the darkness, her fingers touching the slippery, heavily greased cable. The shaft looked like some interminable chimney. A line of girders crisscrossed the walls, and she braced her toe on a metal rung. Settling her other foot against a narrow crossbeam, she switched her weight delicately, easing her body upward.

She fumbled along the rails, locating holds, testing them gingerly before inching on. As her confidence grew, she climbed more quickly, picking her way through the oppressive curtain of gloom. It wasn't so difficult, a virtual staircase really, as long as she kept her courage.

Below, she heard feet clanging on the metal girders—her pursuers. She didn't look down. She knew if she looked down, her nerve would shatter completely. Instead, she fixed her gaze on the few square feet through which she climbed. The smell of oil filled her nostrils, and dirt peppered her hair and clothing.

She reached the second floor, but to her alarm, the elevator door refused to budge. For a moment, she wrestled with the fastening, then, hearing the feet clanging steadily louder, went on climbing, trying each of the doors in turn.

If only Garrett were here, she thought. He would know what to do. Garrett always knew what to do. She'd made a fool of herself with Garrett, behaved like a headstrong schoolgirl. It had been jealousy, pure and simple. She'd frozen him out—and for what?

Reaching the final door, Lori jammed her fingers into the narrow crack and pulled with all her strength. Slowly, unwillingly, the door rattled open. Lori uttered a cry of relief as she stumbled over the threshold into an empty passageway. Done it, she thought. But she had no time to rest. Her pursuers were approaching.

She darted across the deserted landing and pounded wildly on an apartment door. "Please let me in!" she cried.

There was no response. She hammered again. "For God's sake, don't leave me like this. I've nowhere else to run."

There was a moment's pause, then a voice said tersely, "Go away."

Lori began kicking and punching the door in a fit of incoherent rage. "Let me in!" she screamed. "They're trying to kill me, can't you understand?"

The door eased slightly open and through the narrow aperture, Lori saw a black face gazing at her. A slender chain secured the look. "What you want?" a voice demanded coldly.

"I want you to help me," Lori pleaded, tears streaming down her cheeks. "I want you to save my life. Is that too much to ask?"

The face looked at her in silence for a moment. Then, with a muffled clink, the chain was removed, and the door swung open. With a sob of gratitude and relief, Lori stumbled inside. She saw a man, a woman, and two small children.

Her pursuers clattered along the corridor, hammering on each of the apartment doors in turn. For several minutes, they continued their frenzied clamor, then their feet rattled on the outside fire escape, their voiced faded, and Lori and her rescuers relaxed.

The woman took Lori's arm, stroking it reassuringly as she guided her into a tiny kitchen. "You look done in, honey," she said, helping Lori into a chair.

The man went into the other room and returned a moment later with a drink, which he pushed into Lori's hand. Lori tossed it back in a single swallow, choking as the liquid burned her throat.

"Better?" the woman asked, patting Lori's knee.

Lori struggled to hold back the tears. After the horrors of the night, such a simple act of kindness was unnerving.

"Thank you," she stammered. "Thank you so much. I'm really... very... grateful."

Unable to contain herself any longer, she began to weep.

# EIGHTEEN

Wesker drove through the darkness. "City's gone crazy," he muttered.

Wrecked cars cluttered the roadway, and people swirled across their path. Many were drunk, brandishing bottles looted from liquor stores. Fear lodged in Garrett's chest as he thought of Lori wandering alone out there. She was probably frightened as she'd never been frightened in her life.

"Stop worrying, Zach," Wesker said. "Lori will be okay."

"How can you be so sure? The streets are alive, for Chrissake."

"She knows how to take care of herself."

"Louis, if anything happens to her, anything at all . . ."

They spotted a square ahead, and Wesker eased his foot onto the brake. The entire enclosure was ablaze. Police cars were arranged in a cordon under the trees. A line of riot police wearing helmets and carrying shields faced a mob of several hundred people. Missiles flew through the air—rocks, cans, bricks. Molotov cocktails shattered across the side-walks, and a policeman danced crazily, flames licking up his trouser leg.

The mob surged forward, but the police squadron stubbornly held its ground. A fire truck drew up, and uniformed figures leapt into the street, trailing out ribbons of canvas hose. As Garrett and Wesker watched, twin columns of pressurized water burst from the metal nozzles. The crowd tumbled back in drenched confusion.

Wesker halted at the police barricade, and a battle-weary lieutenant peered at him coldly. "Where the hell do you think you're going?"

Wesker flashed his ID card. "We have to get to Falls Church, Virginia. I know it's a rough night, but this is important."

The lieutenant seemed relieved at the sight of a friendly face. "You'll have to take a detour. The square here's a battle zone. Try the streets around Benning Heights. Some of them are still open. I can't guarantee it, but you might get through."

Wesker slipped the card into his pocket. "You've got your hands full tonight." He threw the car into reverse.

The lieutenant wiped sweat from his face with the back of one hand. "It's like watching the end of the world."

"Let's hope that isn't too prophetic," Wesker said darkly.

He and Garrett cruised warily northward. A brick bounced off their roof, shattering the rear window, and Wesker swore under his breath. "Getting nasty."

"Keep your head down," Garrett warned. "Some of these maniacs might be armed."

Through the smoke they glimpsed a line of rioters spreading the full width of the roadway, jeering and gesticulating as they dared Wesker to approach. Wesker jammed his fist on the horn and drove the vehicle steadily forward. The mob surged to meet him. A chain swung through the air, smashing the windshield into a thousand pieces as the car slithered to a halt.

"Let's get the hell out of here," Garrett said.

He threw open the door, ramming it into the rioters' faces. A figure swayed into his vision and he lashed out, feeling a crack as his fist connected with a stubbled jawline.

A fierce elation filled him, and he went to work with a vengeance, hitting, ducking, kicking, butting, feeling the familiar stretch of muscle and sinew as he lashed out furiously.

Someone seized him by the throat. A pair of thumbs dug savagely into his larynx, shutting off his windpipe.

Seizing his assailant's elbows, he twisted violently to the right, jerking his knee up into the man's crotch. His victim groaned in pain, and Garrett flung him headlong into the surging crowd.

Wesker was leaping, kicking, and jabbing, his plump body hurtling through the rioters like a tiny whirlwind.

Garrett saw a heavyset man edging in toward him, wielding a murderous-looking pickax handle. Ducking to the right, Garrett drove his fist into the pit of his attacker's stomach. It was a devastating blow, carrying the full weight of Garrett's body behind it. Eyes bulging, the man collapsed over the car.

The mob fell back under the expert offensive, and Garrett and Wesker took the opportunity to retreat down a narrow side road. Garrett's fists were raw, his face bloody.

"I thought security agents were supposed to carry guns," he accused breathlessly.

"Only in the movies," Wesker choked. "I'm a lover, not a fighter."

"I wouldn't say that, Louis. You're a regular Nijinksy."

"Yeah, I'll bet it's the first time you've seen a plum pudding doing the *sokuto fumikomi*."

Amid the swirling smoke, Garrett spotted a lighted sign ahead—a Metro station. "Maybe we can take the subway. Even if it isn't running, we can follow the tunnels underground."

"You're right. The Blue Line'll lead us at least as far as Rosslyn. By then, we'll probably be clear of the riot areas anyhow."

They rattled down the stairs, and the corridor gathered around them, its ceiling lamps forming a beckoning flare-path toward the open entrance lobby. Smoke hazed beneath the high arched ceiling.

To Garrett's surprise, the place was completely deserted— not a soul in sight, not even a Metro guard. Ticket stubs littered the floors, and the dispensing machines winked at them in silent welcome, the only signs of life in the abandoned concourse.

"Where the hell is everybody?" Wesker wondered.

As if in answer, a shot rang out, reverberating beneath the ornate ceiling.

A jolt of alarm whipped through Garrett's body, and he hurled Wesker to the floor. The two men crawled behind a nearby bench. Garrett was panting hard, and his skin felt slippery with sweat.

Cautiously, he raised himself to his knees, peering across the row of turnstiles. A black Metro guard sat clutching a rifle. The guard's eyes glowed with fury. At the man's rear, huddling fearfully under his solitary protection, Garrett spotted a cluster of beleaguered travelers.

The guard took off his cap, waving Garrett and Wesker forward. "Damn near blew your fool heads off!" he shouted. "That was a crazy stunt, coming through the portico like that."

Garrett glanced at Wesker, and the two men rose, emerging into the open. They jumped inelegantly over the turnstile.

The guard studied them nervously, and it was clear to Garrett he was terrified out of his wits.

"How long have you been trapped in here?" Wesker demanded.

"Couple of hours," the guard said. "Damned crazies keep trying to break in."

"Called the police?"

"Sure, I called. Last time, only twenty minutes ago. They say the cavalry's coming."

Something was odd here, Garrett realized. There was no sound from the lower levels. Even the escalators had ceased running. "No trains?"

"Nothing. Lines are dead all the way to Takoma and Cleveland Park."

"Listen," Wesker said, wiping his dust-covered hands on his handkerchief, "we can't wait for the cavalry."

"Where you figure on going, man? That's enemy territory out there."

"We've got to get to Falls Church. Are the tunnels open?"

"Sure they're open. But they're off-limits to civilians."

"We're not civilians," Wesker told him, displaying his ID. The man studied it. "How about that? A spook."

"Can we use the tunnels now?"

"I guess you can, man. Power's off, so you should be safe."

"Got a flashlight?"

The guard jerked his head at the rear. "You'll find one in the office. But anything goes wrong, it's *your* ass, understand?"

"Sure." Wesker patted the guard's shoulder. "Good luck, Captain."

The guard fingered his rifle meaningfully. "I don't need luck. I got my insurance policy right here."

Wesker and Garrett found the flashlight and ran down the motionless escalator. Wesker shone the light at the track below, and jumping off the platform, they ventured cautiously into the silent tunnel.

"I have to go now," Lori said softly.

Sitting across the table, the woman said, "It's a madhouse out there."

Lori knew she was right, but she knew too that somehow she had to find De Tabley's mistress before the whole damned city went up in flames.

"Is there a police station nearby?"

"There's a precinct house about two blocks west," the man said.

"I'll ask them for protection."

The man led her into a tiny room where stars glimmered through a ceiling fanlight. Standing on a chair, he helped her through the narrow opening. The roof's surface was bordered by a three-foot wall. The man came up behind her and directed her to a metal fire escape clinging like a limpet to the rear of the building.

"Take care, lady. When you reach the alley, follow the avenue west. The precinct house is on the corner. You can't miss it."

"Thank you. You've been very kind."

The tunnel was an endless artery leading nowhere. There was no sound other than the hollow clatter of their feet against the concrete drainage channel.

Garrett followed Wesker's flashlight. Hours, it seemed, since they'd set off on their subterranean march, and he could scarcely think straight anymore. How could Wesker stand it? Wesker seemed indefatigable, undeterred by either the dark or the damp. Nothing stopped him; nothing slowed him down.

With an irritating persistence, Garrett's mind kept drifting to the same old theme: Lori. Was she safe? Had she, by some miracle, managed to evade the perils in the streets above?

He heard Wesker draw to a halt and jerked himself upright. "What is it, Louis?"

"Something's out there."

Wesker shone the flashlight into the tunnel ahead, and dimly, Garrett sat two people crouching at the side of the track, a woman and a boy. They were both black, the woman in her early forties, the boy about eleven or twelve. The woman lay among the cinders, her hat tilted crookedly over one eyebrow. The boy, clad in jeans, watched the two men approach through flat defiant eyes.

"What happened here?" Wesker asked.

"My mother's sick," the boy said. "She can't walk. She keeps falling down."

Garrett knelt to examine the woman. She was breathing hard, her ebony face creased and tired. Spittle framed the corners of her mouth.

"What are you doing in the Metro?" Wesker asked the boy.

"Trying to get home. The city's a battlefield up there."

"That's no excuse for walking along the line. Supposing they started the trains running again? You'd be in big trouble."

The boy said: "You too, man."

"It's different with us. We're on government business."

Garrett felt the woman's pulse, pressing his fingertips against her carotid artery. He touched her temples and forehead, and she gazed up at him with an air of weary entreaty, her face hollow beneath her cheekbones.

"She's not sick," Garrett said. "She's just exhausted."

"Well, we can't leave her here."

Garrett nodded grimly. "We'll have to do it the hard way."

Slipping his arms beneath the woman's spine and legs, he lifted her as if she were a doll. She clung to his neck, as he eased her against his chest. He could feel the sharpness of her bones through the flimsy material of her clothing. She weighed practically nothing at all.

"Let's go, Louis."

"Give me your arm, young man."

The walls around them were damp and suffocating, and as they resumed their trek, Garrett began to wonder if the tunnel would ever end. Then he saw something glowing directly ahead.

"Lights," Wesker said. "A station."

As they approached, they saw passengers crowding the narrow platform, settling down for the night, wrapped in overcoats and blankets. Somewhere, a child was crying.

"Louis, it looks like a scene from the London Blitz."

A Metro guard came to the platform rim. "What are you folks doing down there?"

Switching the flashlight to his other hand, Wesker displayed his ID card. The man studied it warily for a moment, and his attitude marginally relaxed.

Wesker stared at the passengers huddled like laundry bundles along the narrow platform. "You look kind of crowded here."

The guard grimaced. "The streets are going wild, man. Most of these people have decided to sit tight till the army arrives."

Delicately, Garrett deposited his slender burden on the platform edge. "Can you take care of this lady?"

The guard leaned forward. "Is she ill?"

"No, just whacked. Find her a spot in the corner, and she'll be okay."

"Leave it to me, mister."

The woman smiled at Garrett as the guard helped her to her feet and guided her toward the platform wall.

Wesker looked at Garrett, patting his stomach meaningfully. "Have you any idea the effect this exercise is having upon my waistline? I'll be a shadow of my former self by morning."

Garrett grinned as they pushed on wearily into the tunnel. "Don't worry, Louis. Just think of the fun you'll have putting it all back on again."

Lori saw the mob as she moved into the open. The besieged police had barricaded the windows, and the space in front of the lobby steps was cluttered with bricks and bottles. Lori realized that her chances of breaking through the rabble would be terrifyingly slim, but she had to give it a try.

Bodies swirled around her as she moved against the tide, battling to maintain her balance. Keep your head, she told herself wildly. A mob isn't people. A mob is a creature on its own.

Somehow, she forced her way to the forward ranks and scrambled across the open ground. A hail of missiles followed her as she hammered breathlessly on the barricaded door.

"Let me in!" she yelled.

The door swung open, and she stumbled across the threshold. Armed policemen looked at her in amazement. Several wore helmets and bulletproof vests.

"What the hell do you think you're doing?" an officer demanded. "Can't you see we're under siege here?"

"The whole damned area is under siege," Lori told him. "I need protection. That's your job."

"Who are you?"

"My name's Lori Madden. I'm a special aide at the White House."

"Okay," the officer said. "You can wait here till the army arrives."

"That's no good. I have to get to Falls Church. I need an escort."

"Lady, you're out of your mind."

Lori looked around impatiently. "Who's in command?"

"Why don't you talk to the Sergeant?" the officer said. "He'll help you, if anybody can."

Lori found the sergeant sitting at his desk, a portly man in his early forties, wispy hair framing a high-domed forehead. He displayed no surprise at Lori's sudden appearance. She hesitated, choosing her words with care. "Sergeant, I realize how preposterous this may sound, but I must have someone to accompany me to Falls Church."

"Why don't you ask for the key to Fort Knox? That, maybe I can arrange."

"Please. I'm on a special mission for the White House. Here is my identity card."

"Lady, I don't care if you're the illegitimate great-great-granddaughter of Abraham Lincoln. This is the Little Big Horn, and right now, I'm General Custer."

Lori held her temper—with difficulty. "You're right, of course," she said patiently. "But unless I get where I'm going, that madness out there is going to increase."

"Is that a fact?"

"Please listen to me, Sergeant. I nearly got myself killed tonight. Getting here wasn't exactly a picnic, and what I'd really like to do is sit tight until the army and the National Guard arrive. But I can't. The reason I can't is that unless I get to Falls Church, what we're witnessing here will be only the beginning."

A detective in rolled-up shirtsleeves heard Lori and moved toward her. He was in his early thirties, with a thin freckled face and sandy hair. "Can I help you, ma'am? I'm Detective Dan McCord."

Lori turned to him gratefully. "My name is Lori Madden. I'm on special assignment at the White House. My car crashed, and I've been trying to explain to your sergeant that I must have an escort to Falls Church.''

McCord's lips twisted wryly. "A man would be crazy to be out there tonight."

"I know. Believe me, I know. But there's a woman in Falls Church I desperately need to interview."

"For what purpose?"

She hesitated. "I can't tell you that. It's classified."

"Yeah?" The detective shrugged. "Now that you mention it, so is my hide." He turned away.

"All right," she said hastily.

He glanced back at her, and Lori took a deep breath.

"I have reason to believe this woman is connected with today's missile attack."

"The Algerian blast?"

Lori nodded, and he studied her thoughtfully. "I hope you're not hustling me. If I risk my neck out there, it better be for a damned good reason."

"It's the truth."

"If you find her, what then?"

"Maybe we can stop this madness."

"Okay," McCord said crisply. "I may live to regret this, but if you're dumb enough to try, I guess I'm just crazy enough to take you."

Lori followed him down the stairway to the basement parking lot. Stone pillars supported the building's understructure, and wire-bracketed bulbs cast pools of orange light across the silent rows of vehicles. There was a smell of gasoline and diesel oil.

"An automobile's no good," Lori protested. "They're stopping everything on wheels."

"I wasn't thinking about a patrol car," the detective said, steering her across the basement. An old-fashioned motorcycle stood propped against the wall.

She said, "Are you still using these things? I thought they phased them out decades ago."

"This one's a museum piece. We keep it around for nostalgic reasons." He plucked a helmet from the vehicle's handlebar, jamming it firmly over Lori's skull. "I used to race during my misspent youth, before I got culture and enlightenment."

McCord kicked the starter pedal and Lori hooked her leg

over the saddle as the engine roared into life. He cruised through the electronic eye that raised the massive exit portcullis. Opening up the throttle, he thundered into the street above.

The mob scattered as the motorcycle came at them. A man leapt at the vehicle's handlebars, but McCord kicked him away. Within seconds, they had broken free of the square and were zigzagging through a baffling complex of alleys. Lori held on to the detective's torso with all her might, the wind hammering her face and throat.

The suburban homes of Falls Church were framed by trees, manicured shrubbery, and clipped lawns. After the turmoil in the poorer districts, Garrett found the silence unnerving.

They had hired a cab in Culmore. In the outlying towns, services continued more or less as normal. However, as they drove along Hillwood Avenue, Garrett noticed a curious absence of cars. Many residents, he assumed, had joined the exodus farther into the countryside; others, alarmed by reports of the unrest, had probably barricaded themselves in their homes.

"Where's the Strobel Building?" he asked.

"Next intersection," the driver said. "Directly opposite the park."

Surrounded by quiet residential houses, the Strobel Building towered above green lawns and stately sycamores.

Wesker paid the driver. "Aren't you afraid of the missiles falling?"

The driver spat through the open window, his eyes contemptuous. "The way I figure it, this is probably the safest spot in the country. Those terrorists will want to save Washington till last, and by that time, Clayman'll be out of office."

"You may have a point at that," Wesker said.

There was no sign of a security guard in the lobby. They checked Bonnie MacAnally's name on the wall register and took the elevator to the seventh floor. Garrett felt uneasy as he pushed the bell button. Supposing Lori wasn't here?

They heard the apartment floor creak, and a voice said softly, "Who is it?"

"Garrett and Wesker."

The door swung open. Lori's eyes were huge, their luster dimmed by terror and exhaustion. Her hair was unkempt, her forehead smeared with dirt. She threw herself into Garrett's arms, and he hugged her fiercely.

"Thank God," she choked, "thank God, thank God."

"I thought you were dead."

"I damned near was."

He tightened his grip, afraid to let her go, his relief almost paralyzing. After a moment, Wesker coughed politely.

Garrett released Lori and stepped into the luxuriously decorated apartment. The sofa and chairs were of fine white leather, the walls adorned in rococo latticework. A wet bar stood in one corner, and the windows opened onto an elaborate balcony.

A man was talking on the telephone. Tall and sandy-haired, his necktie dangled loosely around his throat.

"That's Detective McCord," Lori explained. "He brought me here."

"How did you learn about Bonnie MacAnally?" Wesker asked.

"An anonymous phone call."

"Did you recognize the voice?"

"I thought for a minute it sounded familiar, but I couldn't be sure."

Wesker said, "Where is she?"

Lori pointed to the bathroom door. "Somebody beat us to it."

The body lay near the washstand, gazing sightlessly at the ceiling, a smudge of mascara on the left cheekbone, a trickle of blood at the side of the mouth. Heavy bruises marked the neck and throat.

Garrett felt no shock at the grisly discovery. His emotional responses, like everything else, had been blunted by the rigors of the night. But he did have a sense of sadness at the cruel waste of a human life.

"Strangled?" Wesker asked.

"Yes," Lori said. "Detective McCord estimates she's been dead about an hour. I guess they knew we were coming."

Wesker glanced around the living room. "Anything been disturbed?"

"Well, Mr. McCord thinks the apartment may have been ransacked. A professional job—clean, slick, nothing shifted out of place. Except—" a glimmer of triumph shone in Lori's tired eyes, "even professionals can make mistakes. Look at this."

She led them to a picture hanging on the wall. It was a neatly framed print of Van Gogh's "Sunflowers." Lori turned it back to front. Taped to the cardboard rear was a tiny package.

"Detective McCord spotted it," she said. "It was a chance in a million."

Wesker opened the package. Inside were two plane tickets dated May 2, the destination Buenos Aires. He whistled softly. "So De Tabley's planning to take off as soon as his little escapade is over."

"That's not all." Lori fumbled inside the envelope, removing a small gold chain with a broken coin on the end. The coin was a Spanish doubloon. It had been snapped neatly in half.

"What is it?" Garrett asked.

"It's a love token," Lori explained, "a declaration of intent. Instead of giving your lady a ring, you break something in two, and each takes a piece."

Garrett was silent for a moment. He knew he had seen the ornament before. "The man in the videotape," he exclaimed. "He was wearing a pendant exactly like this one."

"Probably the other half," Lori said.

Wesker turned the pendant over in his fingers, examining it thoughtfully. "So find the coin that corresponds with this, and we find Frank De Tabley?"

"That's about the size of it."

Wesker flipped the coin in the air, and slid it into his jacket pocket. "You know Randolph Guthrie collects antique coins?"

Garrett said, "Guthrie? You're sure?"

"I remember an article about it in the *Washington Post*."

"Guthrie keeps popping into this with the regularity of a cuckoo clock."

"Nevertheless, it's only circumstantial."

"Circumstantial, hell. It's got to be more than just coincidence."

"Use your head, Zach. Even if we're on the right track, who's going to believe us? Guthrie's beyond our reach."

"Are you suggesting we let the bastard get away with it?"

"No. We'll get him. Sooner or later, we'll get him. But first we need solid proof."

McCord called to them from the telephone, cradling the receiver against his chin. "Message from headquarters. The army's moving in at daybreak. They want us to remain where we are until they get some kind of order restored. I guess there's not much they can do anyhow before morning."

Garrett walked to the bathroom and closed the door. He stood with his back to it, looking around the lavish apartment. "Well, except for poor Miss MacAnally, I can think of worse places to spend the night."

Lori wandered onto the balcony before dawn. The skyline looked disarmingly peaceful. Only the occasional glimmer of a distant blaze betrayed the turmoil still raging on Washington's streets. Smoke lingered in her nostrils, and the wind molded the blouse against her body.

The French window swung open, and there stood Garrett, his thick hair tousled from lying on the apartment sofa. "What are you doing out here?"

"Getting some air," she said.

"It's still dark, for God's sake."

"I couldn't sleep."

He stepped outside, closing the window gently behind him. "Me neither."

He leaned against the metal rail. In the darkness, his body looked lean and fit. "Been quite a night."

"It's been horrible."

She gazed over the woodlands that framed the suburban streets. "I wonder what's going to happen when those bombs really start falling."

"It'll never come to that."

"How can you be so sure?"

"Common sense. The President will have to resign."

"It'll make a mockery of everything we believe in."

"It's the way of the world."

She knew he was right, that was the awful thing. The Algerian explosion had been only a demonstration, a sick and histrionic display. When the real attack came, the horror would be unendurable. Her body felt limp. The old familiar things had lost their substance, and she was filled with a sudden yearning for the comforting world she remembered in her youth.

"Zach?" she whispered.

He looked at her, and she hesitated, the words sticking in her throat.

"I want to forget," she breathed, "just for a moment. I want to be away from all this."

Garrett's eyes burned behind the smoke-grimed mask of his face. He took her in his arms, kissing her hard on the mouth, and she felt her brain swimming, her senses reeling.

Somehow, they were back inside, and she was lying on the floor. The cool air touched her naked skin as his hands fumbled at her clothing. In the darkness of the early morning, they performed the timeless ritual of love.

# PART

# IV

# THE KILL

# NINETEEN

Around the Situation Room table, the members of the President's Executive Committee sat dispiritedly. The rigors of the night had affected them all. In Washington, as in most major cities throughout the United States, National Guard forces together with the regular military had at last restored order, but the memory of the havoc and destruction lingered like the vestiges of some half-forgotten dream.

"Where's Jan Bowering?" the secretary of state asked, glancing at her empty chair.

"I don't think she'll be joining us this morning," the President said. "Her aide, Nick Koster, was found murdered last night."

"Murdered?" The secretary of state was startled.

"That's right."

"Dear God, what happened?"

"He was shot. Three slugs from a thirty-eight. No witnesses and no apparent motive."

"Somebody killed him just for kicks?"

"You saw what happened last night, Dan. I guess Nick Koster was another victim of the random violence sweeping the city."

The secretary of state shook his head sadly. "How's Jan taking it?"

"She's understandably upset. She'll be joining us later."

"Please give her my condolences."

The President turned to the assembly at large. "What's the general picture? Do we have the situation contained at last?"

"Pretty well," the defense secretary said. "Garfield Heights and Anacostia look like battlefields, but most of D.C. is peaceful again at the moment, thank God."

"It's difficult to believe what happened last night."

"Believe it, Larry," the attorney general said quietly. "It's only a foretaste of what we can expect when those missiles start flying. We're sitting on a powder keg."

"Any estimates on the damage done?"

"We're still working on that," the secretary of state answered. "It'll probably run into billions."

"What about casualties?"

"The army reports thirty-two dead so far, thousands injured. There could be more, of course. The situation's still pretty confused, especially around Twining and Benning Heights. The police have set up an emergency number, and they're asking people to phone in details of any relatives unaccounted for."

"And nationwide?"

"There's still rioting in Los Angeles, but the army expects to have it under control within the next couple of hours. The worst unrest took place in New York and Detroit. Both those cities are now under martial law. The biggest problem at the moment is in the countryside where motels and campsites are flooded with refugees. There are people squatting on every inch of available space, and with no proper sanitation, the health authorities fear some kind of epidemic."

"It's like a nightmare," the President said.

"It *is* a nightmare," the attorney general corrected.

The President sat back in his chair, squeezing the bridge of his nose with his fingertips. His face looked tired but calm. "One simple decision would resolve this crisis," he said, "and I guess I'm the only guy who can make it."

The prime minister's car passed through the police barrier and halted outside 10 Downing Street. Howard Bowen was met in the hallway by an usher carrying a portable telephone. "It's the President of the United States, sir."

Bowen dismissed his retainers and, stepping into an alcove, lifted the receiver. "Larry?"

"Good morning, Howard. What kind of night have you had?"

"Horrendous. London's like a war zone. I've just now got back from a tour of the riot areas. The streets are peaceful for the moment, but God knows what the price tag's going to be when it's time to clean up the mess."

"I sympathize with you. I've had to declare martial law in the District of Columbia."

"Is it working?"

"Temporarily. But something tells me it's merely the calm before the storm. After what we witnessed last night, I can't allow such madness to continue."

Clayman was silent for a moment, and when he spoke again, his voice was terse and strained. "Howard, I wanted you to be the first foreign ally to know. I've decided to resign."

Garrett stood under the shower at Wesker's home, letting the water cool his fevered skin. He turned off the spray and walked naked into the bedroom, toweling himself vigorously. Lori lay propped against the pillows, listening to the news reports on her portable radio. Most of the items dealt with the previous night's unrest.

"Property damage is estimated at tens of billions of dollars," the radio announcer said. "In Europe, the principal cities are now quiet. And in India, our correspondent reports that government tanks have reestablished order in Calcutta and New Delhi. In countries throughout the world, heads of state are calling for calm."

Lori looked better in the daylight, Garrett thought. She'd come through the experience with flying colors, which didn't surprise him a bit. She was a girl in a million.

He smiled as he dried his hair. "You intend to stay there all day?"

Lori stretched herself luxuriously. "Why not? Can you think of anything better to do?"

"How about work. We're running out of time."

"I hate work. I've finally decided there's only one sensible occupation, and that's making love."

Garrett laughed. "That's fine. In fact, I'd say it was one of my favorite occupations. But somebody's got to start doing something."

"We *are* doing something. We're keeping in touch with the situation by listening to the news bulletins."

She hesitated as a disembodied voice broke in on the radio announcer's broadcast. "C-for-Charlie Company, C-for-Charlie Company, do you copy? Over."

"Those damned National Guard people." She fiddled irritably with the knobs. "They've been interrupting the newscasts all morning."

"They're cutting in on your frequency."

"Why can't they go back to old-fashioned semaphore?"

Garrett paused as the idea suddenly hit him. It was like a bolt of lightning, startling in its impact. "Jesus!" he breathed.

"Something wrong?"

He slammed the bulkhead with the side of his fist. "Why didn't I think of it before?"

"Think of what before?"

"The answer's been staring me in the face, and I've been too damned thick to see it."

"Zach, what are you talking about?"

"Electronic interference—it's the obvious solution."

"Solution to what?"

"The *Devil's Stallion*. We're not as helpless as we think. Not by a long shot."

Struggling into his clothes, he hurried into the main room where Louis Wesker, clad in a blue jumpsuit, was standing on his head under the antique clock. Wesker looked ridiculous, his toes pointing at the ceiling, his plump belly merging into his chest like an overweight robin's.

Despite his excitement, Garrett paused. "Louis, what are you doing?"

"Meditating," Wesker told him.

"Come down from there. I need to talk to you."

"I can't. My psychic and physical functions have blended into a radiant harmony. I am on the path to enlightenment."

"I've already found enlightenment."

Even upside down, Wesker could see the triumph in Garrett's face.

"I know how to disable the *Stallion*."

The secretary of defense was in the gymnasium when Garrett and Wesker arrived. Despite the crisis, David Richner believed in a regular exercise regime. Clad in a blue sweatsuit, he sat pumping rhythmically at an elaborate rowing machine, his skin glistening, his eyes bulging. He paused as his visitors entered, and with a sigh of relief, groped for a towel. "Gentlemen?" he said, rising awkwardly to his feet.

Wesker eyed him with amusement. "Sorry to interrupt your training schedule, Mr. Secretary."

"Forget it. Working-out may be good for the metabolism, but it's the nearest thing I know to medieval torture."

Still breathing heavily, he led them to a juice bar in the gymnasium corner. "No alcohol, I'm afraid, but I can offer you crushed orange, pomegranate, or natural spring water."

Garrett settled for the water. Wesker had nothing.

The secretary of defense poured himself a drink, and sweating freely, perched on a high stool at the bar, mopping his cheeks with a handtowel.

"Now what's this all about?"

"The *Devil's Stallion*," Wesker told him. "Major Garrett thinks he may have a solution."

"Why come to me? I thought Jan Bowering was handling this affair."

"Nobody can get near Mrs. Bowering since the Algerian blast. She's with the President night and day. At least you're available, Mr. Secretary."

Richner drank his fruit juice and wiped his lips with the back of one hand. He said, "Well, I'm sorry to disappoint you, but I'm afraid Major Garrett is a little late. The President has already decided to step down."

"Since when?" Garrett said.

"Since just under an hour ago. He'll make his announcement on television this afternoon."

"That's crazy. We've still got a week to the terrorist deadline."

"The way he sees it, the longer he drags this out, the greater the chance of those idiots pressing the wrong button. The President doesn't intend to take that risk."

Garrett said, "If he quits now, he leaves the world open to nuclear blackmail."

The secretary of defense disagreed. "The world has always been open to nuclear blackmail, Major Garrett. From the moment such weapons became a reality, it was inevitable that one day they'd end up in the wrong hands. What we're facing here is the legacy of 1945. There aren't any superpowers anymore, not in the strategic sense. From this moment on, it's a game of chance, and we play our hands like everyone else, waiting for the moment when some maniac loses his head.''

"It isn't going to happen yet," Garrett told him determinedly, "not if we handle this right. Those terrorists up there think they're invulnerable. They think they're so far removed from interference by man or machine, they can do as they damn well like, but they're wrong. There *is* a way. It's dangerous, and it's delicate, but the *Stallion can* be neutralized.''

The secretary tossed his towel onto a nearby stool. "Go on, Major.''

"Remember back in the eighties when the Russians tried using electromagnetic impulses to interrupt the homing mechanisms on American missiles?''

"I remember," Richner said. "As it happened, their efforts were only partly successful.''

"Then they switched to particle-beam technology. Particle beams, properly applied, can penetrate a target, and immobilize it by disrupting its electronic launching devices.''

"I know all that. That's why we fitted our missile systems with foolproof coding. Even a neutral particle beam is powerless against present-day launching technology.''

" 'Present-day'," Garrett echoed fiercely. "That's the point, Mr. Secretary. The missiles on the *Stallion* have been orbiting the earth for more than fourteen years. They're antiques. Gnooche solid-propellant rockets, still deadly maybe, but vulnerable to interference by a skilled particle-beam operator. Their guidance antennae are notoriously delicate. The Gnooche post-boost computer has to make thousands of calculations in the first ten minutes of flight to bring the warhead onto its precise course. An error of just one second in cutoff velocity could result in a target miss of over ten miles.''

The secretary of defense straightened on his barstool. "What are you saying?''

"We can't dispel the satellite's particle-beam force field, but if we get close enough, we can use the ANSAAD RFQ to knock its missiles out of action. The *Devil's Stallion* will be like a tiger without teeth.''

Richner considered for a moment. "That means launching a crew into space.''

"Exactly.''

"Do you realize what the cost would be?''

Garrett looked exasperated. "For God's sake, the cost is negligible compared to the price we'll pay if those maniacs fire their rockets."

The secretary's lips tightened. He strolled to the window and looked out. "There *is* a shuttle launch scheduled," he said at last. "It was due to blast off tomorrow morning. It's been delayed because of the current crisis."

"Could you alter its coordinates?"

Richner turned. "How close would we need to get?"

"Three or four miles should do it."

"They'll pick us up on their radar, blow us out of the sky."

"And waste one of their precious missiles?" Garrett shook his head. "They'll hang on a bit, see what our intentions are. By the time they decide to press that button, we'll have rendered their Gnooches inoperable."

"How long would it take our crew to learn how to handle the ANSAAD?"

"Too long, Mr. Secretary. Particle beams are mercurial and difficult to control. A mission like this would call for split-second precision. It would require a great deal of skill and experience."

"In other words, you are volunteering?"

"It's the only answer," Garrett said.

The secretary shook his head. "NASA would never agree. They insist on a minimum hundred-fifty-day training schedule, even for people traveling as passengers."

"I've already been through the training," Garrett told him. "At Baikonur, we did the lot from A to Z."

"On simulators?" Richner looked unconvinced. "You were using different equipment, different techniques. NASA has its own way of doing things."

"I know what I'm talking about," Garrett said fiercely. "I've studied the American space program for years. I'm not pretending I can pilot an *Apollo* shuttle, but I understand enough to tag along for the ride. Besides, whether NASA likes it or not, I'm the only one who can operate that ANSAAD effectively."

Secretary Richner walked back to the counter. "I don't know. I can't make the decision alone—it's beyond my authority. Go back to Wesker's place and wait until you hear from me. I'll talk to the President, and contact you as soon as I have his answer."

* * *

The Oval Office was filled with people when Garrett, Lori, and Wesker entered. Lori recognized Randolph Guthrie; Jan Bowering; Hal McCafferty, the director of NASA; and Willard Shaw, special assistant to the President for national security.

The President wasted no time in getting down to business. "The decision is unanimous," he said. "If there's any chance to neutralize those missiles, we must take it. Can the ANSAAD accelerator really do the things you say?"

"Handled properly, there's no question," Garrett told him.

"What if the terrorists decide to shoot you down before you get within operable range?"

"It's a chance," Garrett admitted. "On the other hand, they'll feel pretty secure behind their defense shield, and they'll want to avoid squandering their warheads on an unnecessary target."

Jan Bowering said, "They may think you're waiting for them to switch off their Canby D-Five before opening fire with missiles of your own."

"Not if we stay out of immediate striking range. They'll be suspicious, yes, but they'll be cautious too. And by the time they figure out what we're up to, it'll be too late."

"How long will the ANSAAD take to operate?" the President asked.

"It's almost instantaneous once I get the pulses under control."

Lawrence Clayman was silent for a moment, fingering the papers on his desk. Sunlight lit the potted plants under the furled flag at his rear. "I must tell you," he said, "I'd already made up my mind to resign."

"That would be a big mistake. Once you give in to nuclear blackmail, it'll go on and on. These people will never be satisfied."

"Well, I'm willing to postpone my decision if you think there's a genuine chance."

"Mr. President, I give you my word."

Hal McCafferty, the director of NASA said, "Major Garrett, how do you know that you're even capable of traveling into space?"

"Because I've already trained for it. I was part of the United European space team at Baikonur."

"But you never actually went into orbit."

"There's got to be a first time for everything, and you know as well as I do, that any normal healthy person can fly on a shuttle."

"But if you fail, if anything goes wrong, the consequences would be unthinkable."

"They're already unthinkable," Garrett said mildly.

"Very well, Major Garrett," the President said. "You will join the crew of the *Arrowhead*. It is scheduled to launch in five days' time. That cuts our safety margin pretty thin, but Hal here refuses to send you into orbit without at least a minimal training period."

Lori felt her senses quickening. She knew she had to speak now, before she lost her nerve completely. She'd thought it all out, gone over and over in her mind what it was she really wanted, knowing she had to try, because—godammit—it was her domain as much as it was Garrett's. "Mr. President?"

Clayman turned. "Yes, Miss Madden?"

"I—" Lori hesitated, conscious that everyone in the room was looking at her, "I want to go along."

"No," Garrett protested.

She ignored him, focusing her attention on Clayman. "Mr. President, I've been involved in this operation since the beginning. It was my department, you may remember, that picked up the *Suchko*'s signals in the first place."

"Indeed, it was, Miss Madden."

"Nobody's more capable of commanding the *Arrowhead* than me. I've been into orbit twice, once as a shuttle pilot. I've spent my entire career working on the space program, and I'm personally familiar with every detail concerning the *Devil's Stallion*."

"She's crazy!" Garrett exclaimed.

"Mr. President," Lori said, "Major Garrett belongs to the old school of masculine philosophy that believes women should know their 'place.' "

Despite the seriousness of the moment, the President's eyes twinkled. He turned to McCafferty. "What do you think, Hal?"

The NASA director looked at Lori. "You mentioned the word 'command.' Isn't that an ambitious concept for someone who's been out of commission for the past four years?"

"Not entirely out of commission," Lori insisted. "I've

been ground-based, it's true, but I've still been working for NASA.''

"Nevertheless, a lady shuttle commander would be something of a novelty, would it not?"

"Innovative, perhaps. But maybe at a time like this, a little innovation is exactly what we need."

"I'm inclined to agree with you, Miss Madden," the President said.

He raised his hand as Garrett started to object. "Sorry, Major, it's not Miss Madden's inclusion that worries me here. She's already proved her suitability for space travel on at least two occasions. You, on the other hand, are an unknown quantity. It's four years since that training course at Baikonur. Even then, you were operating with Soviet and European equipment. We have no way of telling how you'll respond once you get into orbit. Supposing you become disoriented? Space sickness is a common affliction among first-time astronauts. Who handles the ANSAAD then? You've said yourself it's a delicate and complex instrument, and this launch is too critical to entrust to just one man, no matter how resourceful he may be."

He looked at Garrett earnestly. "I want another ANSAAD specialist to accompany the mission."

Garrett knew Clayman was right, knew it was the only sensible way to operate, but he felt a coldness starting up inside him as he said, "There's only one man qualified for the job, Mr. President: Colonel Sergei Malenov of the Soviet GRU."

Inside the conference room, Frank De Tabley watched the circle of faces as he outlined the White House decision. "The President has given the go-ahead for a shuttle launch on Wednesday. Its target will be the *Stallion*. It will move into orbit and seek a position several miles from the Canby D-Five's periphery. From there, Major Garrett will attempt to use the ANSAAD particle-beam accelerator to disrupt the electronic launch-and-guidance systems on the satellite's missiles."

The meeting was silent for a moment; then a man shifted nervously on his chair. "Is that possible?"

De Tabley inclined his head with an expression of regret. "Difficult, but possible, certainly. The *Stallion*'s missiles were designed before the new coding system came into effect. They are, I fear, vulnerable to particle-beam interference."

"Then we'll have to fire now. One warhead—one city."

De Tabley said, "Fire now, and we disclose my identity. Only a handful of people were privy to that meeting today. Let's not lose our heads, gentlemen. We've retained our anonymity this far. It would be crazy to throw it away on what, after all, would be a highly irrational response."

"In that case," Admiral Tyre said, "let's blast the shuttle as soon as it leaves the atmosphere."

"And deplete our arsenal? No, I'm not wasting precious warheads on an impudent intruder. General Connel has contacts at Cape Canaveral. He's taking steps to see the mission is subverted."

He glanced around the silent assembly, smiling confidently. "You may rest assured, gentlemen, the *Arrowhead* will never reach its target."

Wesker stood on the submarine deck, staring across the river bank. Stars hung above the trees, forming a misty halo that illuminated the entire sky. The water was black.

He heard a movement behind him. Gendun approached and placed a blanket over Wesker's shoulders. "It is cold tonight."

"Cold? Yeah, I guess it is."

Somewhere an owl hooted twice, its cry low and mournful on the misty air. "Gendun," Wesker said, "I want to ask you something."

Gendun inclined his head. "The true believer should always ask."

"There is a man, a very powerful man, so powerful that his integrity is above reproach. This man is threatening our very existence. I know it, I feel it, but unless I can offer some proof, nobody will believe me."

"He is in the government, this man?" Gendun's eyes glittered.

"Very high up in the government. So high, in fact, that if I denounce him, I will be publicly ridiculed. The problem is, he's switched identities, and I can find no reference to his previous life anywhere in the computer files."

"You are thinking only with your mind," Gendun said. "It is a common Western failing. Just as the lotus turns toward the sun, you must turn toward the source."

"The source?"

"Go back to the beginning. There you will find the path of true enlightenment."

Wesker stared at him, then nodded shortly. "Thanks, Gendun. Maybe you've got a point at that."

The morning air was chill as Garrett and Lori crossed the airport concourse. A private jet stood on the apron, waiting to take them to Cape Canaveral. Garrett saw Louis Wesker stamping his feet near the aircraft's fuselage, his hands pushed into his overcoat pockets.

"Come to see us off, Louis?" Garrett grinned.

"I've come to cheer you up," Wesker said, falling into step alongside them.

"Good. I could do with something like that."

"We've had a breakthrough on the De Tabley investigation."

"What kind of breakthrough?"

Wesker said, "It was Gendun's idea. I don't know why I never thought of it before. Remember how De Tabley's name kept drawing a big fat zero in the computer banks?"

"Sure."

"Well, Gendun suggested I go back to the beginning—1944. The big genesis, nuclear fission."

"And?"

"Bingo."

Garrett said, "But in 1944, De Tabley would be only a kid."

"Right. You remember the Gemrose case?"

"How old do you think I am, Louis?"

"Harry Gemrose was one of the scientists working at Los Alamos on the original atomic bomb. He helped formulate the Hiroshima and Nagasaki explosions in 1945. Two years later, he was convicted of leaking secrets to the Russians."

"A traitor?"

"One of the notorious 'atom spies.' But Gemrose didn't do it for money. He did it because of his beliefs. He thought atomic power too terrifying to rest in the hands of only a few. He hoped, by spreading his knowledge, to even up the international balance of power."

"What happened to him?"

"He died in prison in 1953. But here's the interesting thing. Harry Gemrose married a girl from his hometown,

Oskaloosa, in Iowa. Her name was Martha De Tabley. They had a son, an only child. They called him Frank.''

Garrett felt the breath catch in his throat.

"After Gemrose's arrest, Martha reverted to her maiden name. She severed all contact with her husband, refusing even to visit him in prison. Four years after his death, she married again. She died in 1990, in her eightieth year.''

"What about the boy?''

"I dug up some old newspaper reports from the time. Young Frank, by all accounts, was a regular patriotic American. He couldn't believe what his father had done.''

"Try to picture the period, Zach. The United States had just defeated the most powerful enemy in history. It had at its disposal a weapon more devastating than anyone could visualize. It was entering a period of unprecedented prosperity. Gemrose's son wouldn't have been human if he hadn't been affected by that. He was proud that his father had helped build the first atomic bomb. Imagine his disillusionment when the truth finally emerged. Young Frank denounced his father bitterly. He was only ten at the time, but the newspapers ran extensive interviews with the entire family, including Gemrose's four sisters. You could feel the boy's shame, his sense of betrayal. I guess he never got over it.''

"And you think he's been trying to make amends ever since?''

"That's my guess. Because of his father's treachery, his sense of patriotism probably reached psychotic proportions.''

"The question is, can you link that boy to Randolph Guthrie?''

"I'm working on it. I'm checking out new leads. And I've got a man named Dunlap watching every move Guthrie makes. Dunlap's an old pro, ex-CIA, now running his own private surveillance company. He knows the business inside out. Sooner or later, Guthrie's going to make a slip, and when he does, we'll be waiting.''

Garrett paused as they reached the aircraft steps. Lori climbed into the cabin, and the two men shook hands. "Good luck, Zach. Don't try to be Flash Gordon up there.''

"If there's one thing I've learned in the army,'' Garrett told him, "it's never be 'flash' anything.''

Wesker's eyes shone humorously. "Has it occurred to you

that if I was part of your shuttle crew, we'd be practically the same weight in orbit?''

"If you were part of the shuttle crew, Louis, we'd never get off the ground.''

"Hey, it may interest you to know a lot of women find heavyset men very attractive.''

"I wasn't challenging your sex appeal, Louis, just wondering how you manage to find it.''

Wesker chuckled softly as Garrett trotted up the aircraft steps.

It was almost lunchtime when Garrett and Lori arrived at Cape Canaveral. They were met by the director of the Space Center, Ben Fleming, who showed them to the new astronaut accommodation blocks built at the south end of the complex, replacing the spartan quarters originally located in the Operations and Checkout Building. Here, he explained, they would be virtually isolated from the outside world to guard against colds and debilitating germs.

Garrett had little time to contemplate Wesker's discoveries. Every ounce of his attention was absorbed in preparing for the mission ahead. After a quick lunch in the Space Center canteen, Fleming delivered them to the medical block where NASA doctors put Garrett and Lori through a stringent physical. As soon as it was over, they were conducted to the Flight Crew Training Building and, clad in coolant-fluid space suits, immersed in deep water tanks to experience the sensations of body weightlessness. When the instructor was satisfied they felt reasonably comfortable, they were driven to a nearby inlet and made to practice emergency escape procedures on a mock-up spacecraft bobbing on the incoming tide.

After a short break for coffee, they were given a detailed tour of the shuttle interior while NASA experts lectured them on the simple day-to-day problems of living in outer space. They were taught how to eat (the absence of gravity made it impossible to keep food on the plate), how to sleep (one crew member utilized the underside of the bunk mattress, his body literally floating above the floor), even how to use the lavatory, where a complicated system of suction pipes carried away human fluids and wastes.

When evening came, they were driven back to a hasty supper, then for the next four hours put through a punishing routine of launch takeoffs and aborts on the orbiter simulator pad.

, By the time they returned to their quarters, Lori's body felt as if it were breaking in two. Her brain seemed numb from the information she'd absorbed. Her muscles ached, and her bones creaked. Rarely had she felt so physically and mentally drained. Had she really been so clever, talking her way into this madness? she wondered. Why was she putting her life on the line when it actually didn't matter a damn whether she went along on this mission or not? She had so much to relearn, so much to assimilate. How could they pack six months of training into the space of a few short days?

Utterly exhausted, she was brushing her hair in front of the mirror when Garrett tapped lightly on the door. She eyed him with amusement. He looked like a man who had just completed a six-day route march. His shoulders were stooped, his features etched with weariness.

"I should've listened to the first rule in the soldier's handbook," he said. "Never volunteer."

"That makes two of us. If they keep this up, I'll never make it to the launchpad."

He stood behind her, looking at her reflection in the mirror. "Feeling crocked?"

"Like I'm coming apart at the seams."

"You shouldn't be doing this. You're out of practice."

"Is that what you really mean, Zach? Or are you trying to say it's because I'm a woman?"

"I'm being realistic, that's all. I don't want anything to happen to you."

"Thanks for the vote of confidence. It's okay if it happens to you, right? Since when did men have a monopoly on danger? Am I supposed to sit here twiddling my thumbs while you risk your neck hundreds of miles above the stratosphere?"

"It's what I get paid for."

"That's not why you're going, and you know it."

She paused, her chest rising and falling rapidly. She might as well tell him, she thought. "You're crazy, Zach. I knew it the first minute I set eyes on you. There's a wild streak in you that makes you do crazy things. Sometimes you don't care whether you live or die. All that matters is the thrill of the moment."

Her eyes held his in the dresser mirror, and her gaze carried the obstinacy of raw steel. "That's why I'm coming with you. Because somebody has to keep an eye on you for your own damn good."

His features softened, and he reached down, toying gently with her hair. "Well, I have to admit you're the best-looking bodyguard I ever had."

"I mean it, Zach."

She felt his lips against her throat, the rasp of his beard on her cheek. That was Zach all over. He could never take anything seriously.

"Wait," she said.

He pulled back, surprised, as she rose to her feet.

"Let me shower first. I've been sticky all day."

She stood beneath the ice-cool spray, letting the water flush the weariness from her body. Where did Garrett get his energy? she wondered. After the rigors of the afternoon, she felt utterly exhausted. The man was a medical marvel.

She dried herself, and combed out her hair. As an afterthought, she sprayed perfume over her throat and breasts. Her eyes were smoldering as she slipped into the other room. Garrett lay beneath the bed covers, snoring softly. She ran her fingers over his chest, but he was oblivious to the world. *Men,* she thought with exasperation. Then she snuggled in beside him and promptly fell asleep.

# TWENTY

Vice President Randolph Guthrie came out of his bedroom and saw his son Ralph walking across the hallway with a rolled-up tracksuit under his arm.

"Where are you going?" Guthrie asked.

"Running, Dad. I've got to keep up my training."

"You've finished your schoolwork already?"

"I can do it later, after I get back. Right now, I have to hurry to catch the light."

"For God's sake." Guthrie was exasperated. "How do you expect to get to West Point if you won't even take the time to study?"

"I'll study, Dad. Later, I promise. But I need to be fit for the Winchester game on Saturday."

"The way things are going, what makes you think there'll be any game on Saturday?"

"You mean the missile crisis? You'll fix it, Dad, I know you will. You always do."

Randolph Guthrie watched his son trudging down to the cellar where he kept his sporting gear. Kids, he thought, they always figured the future would look after itself. He went back into the bedroom, and pulling the drapes, looked across the manicured lawns at the distant framework of the Chesapeake Bay Bridge. Guthrie had refused to move into the Vice President's house on the grounds of the U.S. Naval Observatory, opting instead to remain in his elegant colonial-style home on the outskirts of Annapolis.

The house stood in an elevated position, commanding spectacular views of the surrounding countryside, and from the window, Guthrie could see wooded inlets and the billowing spinnakers of racing sloops. Secret Service squads roamed the grounds.

As he glanced toward the neighboring highway, his breath caught sharply in his throat. The car was still there, parked in a thatch of scrub where its driver could watch the house undetected. The vehicle had been shadowing him for days now, and the realization filled Guthrie with anxiety and alarm. Was he under surveillance? Had someone, however unwittingly, discovered the truth? It was a dangerous game he was playing, and sooner or later, the facts were bound to come out—but not yet, he pleaded silently. Not at such a critical moment. Discovery would ruin everything.

Guthrie let the drapes fall. With a worried frown, he picked up the telephone and punched out a number. "It's me," he said.

He paused, glancing through the window at the stationary car. "We've got a problem here. I'm being followed. Yes, I know it'll make things difficult, but not impossible. I'll join you as quickly as I can. Just stay calm and make no attempt to contact me. It's simply a question of keeping our heads and not panicking."

His fingers were trembling as he hung up the receiver. He'd waited so long for his masquerade to be discovered that now that the inevitable had happened, he felt surprisingly cool and calm.

He crossed the landing and stepped into his son's room. Photographs of football stars covered the walls, and a mini gym stood in the corner, flanked on one side by a stereo disk player and on the other by a papier-mâché model of an *Apollo* space shuttle. Articles of clothing lay strewn across the unmade bed.

Guthrie picked up a woolen sweater bearing the colors of Ralph's college fraternity and tugged it over his head. He plucked Ralph's baseball cap from the dresser top, and pulling it on, examined himself in the wall mirror. It wasn't much of a disguise, but with luck, it should prove effective at a distance.

Guthrie found the keys to Ralph's car and went downstairs to the garage. He opened the doors and climbed behind the wheel of his son's battered jalopy. HIs heart was thumping as he started the engine and cruised slowly down the exit drive.

Sitting in the parked sedan, Vince Dunlap reached for the thermos flask and poured himself a mug of tepid coffee. Five hours he'd been here, shadowing Guthrie on Wesker's instructions, and he was bored out of his mind. Surveillance he could handle any day—dodging, weaving, backtracking, sidestepping helped to keep a man on his toes—but hanging about aimlessly numbed the brain and stultified the senses.

Dunlap tensed as a car appeared in Guthrie's drive. The guards stepped forward to open the gates, and Dunlap recognized the Chevrolet belonging to Randolph Guthrie's son. He caught a glimpse of a baseball cap through the windshield and relaxed.

The driver spun onto the highway and set off toward Washington, D.C. Dunlap fiddled with the radio knobs, whistling softly as he picked up a country-and-western station. He drained his coffee and screwed back the thermos top. Then he tensed as someone trotted down Randolph Guthrie's drive, and he recognized the athletic physique of the Vice President's son. The boy was setting out on a jog.

Dunlap moaned softly as he realized he had been duped. "Jesus Christ," he exclaimed, and reached for the ignition.

At Cape Canaveral, there was little respite; as the days passed, the training intensified.

Clad in bulky EMU suits, Garrett and Lori practiced using the manned maneuvering units, or MMUs—small gas-propelled power packs that conveyed astronauts bodily through space. They went through, for the umpteenth time, the prelaunch systems check and the post-lift-off procedures, and Garrett's head swam from the incessant lecturing. Despite his training course at Baikonur, it seemed an awesome amount of information for a man's brain to absorb at one go.

On the second day, they were introduced to their fellow crew members, both young men in their early thirties. Clean-cut and athletic-looking, they reminded Garrett of professional tennis players.

"I'm Brad Delaney," the first man said with a friendly smile. "This is my idiot son, Joe Bamberger."

Garrett and Lori shook hands with them.

"How did they talk you into this?" Bamberger wanted to know, eyeing Lori approvingly.

"They didn't. I gave them an ultimatum."

"A volunteer? My God"—Bamberger rolled his eyes at his companion—"we've got ourselves a Joan of Arc."

"I think Bette Midler might be more appropriate," Lori said.

Garrett was impressed with their fellow crew members. He could tell at a glance the two young astronauts knew their business.

He was less sanguine about the prospect of their third associate, Sergei Malenov, scheduled to arrive in the late afternoon. President Clayman had made a direct appeal to the Soviet leader, who had agreed to send Malenov, accompanied by a fully trained team of Soviet observers. Tensions on the ground promised to be high, but Garrett knew they would seem trivial compared to the ones he would have to accommodate in the sky. In theory, Malenov's inclusion made absolute sense, but it seemed an explosive mixture—sworn enemies locked together in the stifling confines of an orbiting spacecraft.

When evening came, Garrett joined the reception committee at Titusville Executive Airport. His heart raced as he watched the Russian aircraft coming in. A detachment of U.S. Marines snapped to attention. Then the aircraft door swung open, and a uniformed official carefully lowered the trestle steps. The marine band struck up the Soviet national anthem, the music strangely flat and discordant on the moist Florida air. Pelicans watched from the fence posts as the team of Soviet observers, some uniformed, others in civilian dress, filed slowly down the metal stairway.

Ben Fleming and the marine colonel greeted the newcomers on the apron, shaking hands with each of the visitors in turn. The Russians maintained an air of frosty composure.

Garrett felt his spirits chill as Sergei Malenov appeared in the aircraft doorway. He looked resplendent in his colonel's uniform, and he stood for a moment at the top of the steps, haughtily observing the scene below.

Then Garrett froze as a slender figure, dressed in a light cotton jumpsuit, stepped out of the semidarkness and stood at Malenov's side. She looked dazzling in the early evening, her blond hair catching the pastel rays of sunlight.

"Who's that?" Lori asked.

"Malenov's wife."

Lori looked at him sharply. "Elke?"

"That's right."

"What's she doing here?"

Garrett turned to a NASA official as the visitors filed toward the waiting bus. "Why has the Colonel brought Mrs. Malenov along?"

"The Russians insisted. She's part of the observer team."

"Malenov's idea?"

"I don't know, Major. Ask Ben Fleming. I'm only the hired help around here."

As they drove back to Merritt Island on the NASA bus, the Americans did their damnedest to make their visitors feel at home, but the Russians remained cool and unresponsive.

Neither Malenov nor Elke cast so much as a glance in his direction, but Garrett knew Elke had noticed him. And he sensed Lori's resentment.

At the Space Center, the new arrivals were escorted to their quarters and given a tour of the complex. Afterward, they were taken to the mess hall where a welcoming dinner had been arranged. Garrett realized the moment must come when he would have to confront the Russians face-to-face. Neither Malenov nor his wife displayed recognition as they shook hands with each of the team in turn, including Garrett. Garrett looked hard into Elke's face, but she greeted him indifferently, and he moved on.

"I want to know what's going on," Lori said.

Garrett shrugged helplessly. "Why don't you ask Malenov? He's the idiot who arranged this."

"Do you take me for a fool, Zach? I want you to understand something. I don't play games. I mean, if you like to dabble a little, renew old acquaintances, that's okay, but I've already gone that route. The last thing I need in my life at this moment is a man who thinks he's Casanova."

"Hold on a minute," Garrett protested. "Have I given you any reason to talk this way?"

"I just want it understood between us, that's all. I've been hurt before. Badly. I made up my mind it wasn't going to happen again, and I mean that, godammit. I hope you're not lying to me. She's got to be here for a reason."

"The Russians sent her. That's the reason."

"I thought you said Malenov was pathologically jealous? Well, he sure as hell doesn't look jealous to me."

"Maybe he just can't bear to let her out of his sight."

"So he brings her to Cape Canaveral, knowing you'll be here?"

"What are you getting so worked-up about? I'm as upset by it as you are."

"That's what I'm mad at," she told him.

After a torturous dinner during which the Russians remained icily polite and Lori resisted all Garrett's attempts at small talk, Garrett returned to his quarters in disgust. He tugged off his shirt, filled the washbasin with water, and plunged his head into it. He heard a click as the door opened softly; face dripping, he straightened in surprise. Elke was standing just inside the threshold. There was a hint of color in her beautiful face, and he could see her breasts rising and falling beneath her light khaki jumpsuit.

"Zachary," she whispered.

"Elke, for God's sake."

He glanced around desperately for a towel as she came toward him, running her palms across his naked chest. "Zachary, I had to come. Sergei didn't want me to, but I talked General Suivesky into it. I had to see you again."

"You're crazy. Don't you realize how delicate this situation is?"

Her eyes were fevered and intense. "Zachary, when you came to Moscow, I thought, in the beginning, you were lying. I thought you were using me, but I was wrong. Everything you said was true. When I understood that, I knew I had to come."

"Elke, listen. What happened in Moscow had nothing to do with you and me. It was part of my job, that's all. It was necessary."

Her lips separated, and he saw the pale outline of her teeth. "Forget what happened in Moscow. Remember what happened at Baikonur."

She slid her arms around his neck, kissing him passionately on the mouth. For a moment, he was too stunned to react. He felt her hair brushing his face. "Elke," he protested as their lips parted.

Her hands slid down his spine, clawing at his skin, her mouth warm and moist against his ear.

Garrett scarcely heard the door opening. A waft of salt air

reached him from the night outside, and he blinked at the sight of Lori framed against the starlight.

"How touching," she said coolly. "I was always a sucker for emotional reunions. I even cried at the end of *Showboat*."

God, he thought. He couldn't believe the absurdity of this. "Don't jump to conclusions," he warned.

"Of course not," Lori said. "You're just comparing notes on past experiences. In the interests of Anglo-Soviet cooperation, I assume."

"Lori, you're making a terrible mistake."

"You're right," she agreed, eyeing his naked chest. "I should have known from the beginning you carry your brains between your legs, Major Garrett."

"This is childish," he said.

"If you consider fidelity childlike, I guess it is. But then, I lack your finesse in worldly matters."

"Listen," Garrett pleaded, "nothing happened here. Whatever you think happened exists only in your mind."

"In that case, there's nothing at all to worry about, is there, because I intend never to let you into my mind again."

Her face was cold as she stormed from the room. Elke looked at Garrett quizzically. With a moan, he picked up a towel and began to pummel his dripping hair.

Elke walked slowly back to her quarters in the dark. Cicadas were humming in the swamp, and the air felt soft against her fevered skin. She had made a fool of herself tonight. She'd wanted so desperately to see Garrett again. Those few hours in Moscow had awakened emotions she'd thought long dead and forgotten. It had never occurred to her that Garrett might have changed. She knew now the past was over. It was the American girl Garrett really wanted. She had risked everything—her career, her reputation, even Sergei's devotion—on some wild fantasy.

Reaching her quarters, she found Sergei waiting, his face taut with anger. "Where have you been?" he demanded.

"Walking."

"You're lying. You went to see Garrett. I followed you."

To Elke, the situation seemed too grotesque for words. "Leave me alone, Sergei. I've had a bad night, and I really couldn't face another quarrel."

She moved into the bedroom and took off her shoes, and he

watched moodily as she loosened her hair, letting it fall around her shoulders.

"You deceived me," he whispered. "You deceived General Suivesky. You didn't come here to support the space mission. You came to see Garrett."

"It's not true," she insisted weakly.

"Don't treat me like a fool. It's always been Garrett."

"You're wrong, Sergei. Quite wrong. Garrett doesn't want me anymore."

"Doesn't want you?" His lips twisted into a disbelieving sneer. "Garrett's an animal. What he wants changes with the moment."

He picked up her lacy blouse, turning it in the light. "I wonder what Suivesky would say if he knew you'd met Garrett in Moscow, given him Alexandr Zystev's address, even—" his voice rose accusingly, "even provided him with forged documents."

"Please, Sergei. You promised you wouldn't refer to that again."

"Have you any idea what it cost me—in terms of dignity, of personal prestige—to put things right?"

"I'm sure it was an expensive bargain."

He showed her an envelope, smiling coldly. "It may interest you to know that I still have a souvenir I took from Garrett in the Baltic."

A sudden coldness swept through her. "His confession?"

It was clear from Sergei's eyes that he was desperate, and Elke knew that a desperate man was capable of anything.

"What are you going to do with it?"

"Ruin him."

"How long have you had this."

"All the time."

"You never showed it to General Suivesky?"

"Never."

"Why?"

"I thought I might need it one day."

"You're crazy. The SOBS satellite changes everything."

"Wrong. It changes nothing. Garrett admits he was working against the interests of the Soviet Union, and I intend to make that public."

"You'll destroy his career."

Malenov laughed, his voice low and deadly. "Don't you

understand? Garrett doesn't *have* any career. I'm talking in the 'posthumous' sense. The one crew member who will not be returning from this mission is Major Zachary Paul Garrett.''

The air in Wesker's office smelled stuffy. He rose from his seat and opened the window, frowning as the roar of traffic drifted in from the street outside. Flopping behind his desk, he examined Vince Dunlap keenly. "You lost him?"

Dunlap was embarrassed. "I couldn't help it. He went through the gate wearing his son's baseball cap and sweater. I trailed him two or three miles, but I found his car parked at the roadside."

Wesker was silent for a moment. Guthrie's behavior seemed unorthodox, to say the least. According to Dunlap, he had even spurned the protection of his Secret Service squad.

Wesker knew his instincts had been sound. "Guthrie's our man, I'm sure of it."

"I'm sorry, Louis. I feel like a fool."

"It wasn't your fault. You couldn't know he was on to you."

Dunlap fumbled in his pocket and laid a scrap of paper on the desk. "I found this in Guthrie's garbage. It's some kind of message, scribbled in his handwriting. Damn fool must have forgotten to shred it."

Wesker examined the message thoughtfully: *Aunt Grace can no longer come for tea. Cousin Porter is proving unexpectedly difficult. Tell Laughing Water to bring donuts and other essentials to the summer house, so our picnic may continue. And please check that the Dentist is still at the gondola.*

"Whom was this sent to?"

"There was no address," Dunlap said. "Does it make any sense?"

"It's 'antique-speak,' the kind of communication they used in the old days at CIA. It went out of fashion twenty, thirty years ago."

"But what does it mean, Louis?"

"Let's think for a moment. Aunt Grace probably refers to Guthrie himself. The fact that he can't come for tea may suggest that he's unable to join his companions."

"That's guesswork," Dunlap said.

"This whole thing's guesswork. Cousin Porter could be

one of the conspirators. On the other hand, it could also be Guthrie's code name for us.''

"Meaning he's changing the rendezvous?''

"Right. And he's telling the caller to bring something important to the new location, the summer house.''

"What about Laughing Water?''

"Christ knows. One of his associates, I guess.''

"And the Dentist at the gondola?''

"Could be the terrorists on the *Devil's Stallion*.''

"Nothing but conjecture, Louis.''

"Okay. But when Guthrie worked for the agency, this kind of thing would have been all the rage. If these cryptonyms refer to specific people, maybe we can identify them from CIA files.''

Dunlap looked doubtful. "You'll never get access. Not at that level.''

Wesker thought for a moment. He tucked the paper into his pocket and rose to his feet. "Maybe not. But I think I know somebody who will.''

The White House mess was bustling with people. Willard Shaw sat alone at a table, working on the morning crossword. His lips moved soundlessly as he made little jottings in the newspaper margin.

A shadow fell across his table, and he looked up to see Louis Wesker standing there, holding a tray. "Mind if I join you?''

Shaw was surprised. Folding the newspaper, he pushed it into his briefcase and waved at the empty chair. "Help yourself, Louis. It's a free country.''

Wesker settled himself at the table, and Shaw watched in wonderment as he placed a plate of steak, ham, eggs, and hash brown potatoes in front of him.

"Are you planning to eat all that at this time of the morning?''

"I have to look after my constitution.''

"No wonder your appetite's a White House legend, Louis.''

"Not any longer. These days, I'm on a diet.''

Shaw watched him tucking away the steak and dabbing at his lips with a paper napkin.

"I have a favor to ask,'' Wesker said.

"What kind of favor?''

"A delicate one. Something you may not like."

"Well, Louis, I'm always receptive to a direct approach."

Without a word, Wesker handed him the piece of paper. Shaw examined it briefly. "What is this, some kind of code?"

"Mean anything?"

"It's gibberish."

"Not quite. That was the kind of communication the agency used back in the old days."

"CIA?"

"They made a fetish of it. Nobody employed simple language when a cryptonym would do. It strengthened security, they claimed."

"I don't understand, Louis. Why are you giving me this?"

Wesker was silent for a moment as he sliced off a piece of steak. "That message was written by Randolph Guthrie to a person or persons unknown. We have reason to believe it has something to do with the terrorist satellite, the *Devil's Stallion*."

Shaw stared at him. "How can you know that?"

"I have my sources."

"Good God, you're talking about the Vice President, for Chrissake."

Wesker said, "I'm talking about the bastard who's going to blow seven world cities to kingdom come unless I can conjure up some kind of hard evidence."

"Louis, what are you handing me here? Are you saying Randolph Guthrie is involved in the *Stallion* conspiracy?"

"I'm saying Randolph Guthrie *is* the *Stallion* conspiracy. I've had a man watching him for days. Unfortunately, he's proving cleverer than I thought."

"This is the craziest thing I ever heard."

Wesker pushed away his plate as if he had suddenly lost his appetite. "That's how he's managed to get away with this for so long. Guthrie's the one man nobody would dream of suspecting. That message is the only hope we've got of earmarking his associates. I need somebody with direct access to CIA records."

Shaw frowned. "What about yourself? You're an ex-agency employee. You've got DOD clearance and plenty of clout in the intelligence community."

"It's not enough. I have to examine Guthrie's personal files. Oh, I can get authorization, okay, but it would take time, and time is the one commodity we haven't got."

"What are you asking me to do?"

"Check out that code. See if anyone in Guthrie's early years at the CIA used the same cryptonyms. Pinpoint those identities, and we'll be halfway toward stopping Guthrie dead in his tracks."

"You're asking a hell of a lot, Louis. Have you any idea what the consequences might be if I agree to go along with this?"

"I know what they'll be if you don't," Wesker said.

Shaw glanced at a nearby table, then picked up the paper and tucked it into his jacket pocket. "Leave it with me. I'll see what I can do."

For Garrett, the last few days' training proved an agony of frustration. Lori steadfastly ignored him, avoiding his presence during the rest breaks and keeping their communication to the bare minimum when the schedule demanded they work together. Malenov too acted with arrogant hostility. He went through the motions of cooperating, but tempered his manner with a veneer of barely concealed disdain.

Garrett saw nothing of Elke. He assumed she had locked herself in her quarters. Fortunately, the two Americans, Bamberger and Delaney, appeared not to notice the frosty atmosphere, but Garrett felt deeply apprehensive about the mission ahead. It would be tricky enough immobilizing the satellite's missiles with a crew working completely in unison, but when three members were actively hostile to each other, the prospects seemed hardly encouraging.

On the morning of the shuttle launch, he awoke feeling stale and dispirited. He had slept badly during the night, having made one futile attempt to gain admittance at Lori's door.

It seemed ironic, he reflected. All his life he had dreamed of reaching the sanctity of space, of experiencing for himself the last great adventure left to man. Now here he was on the threshold of realizing that ambition, and all he could think about was the unholy mess he had maneuvered himself into.

He breakfasted with the crew, then at six A.M. precisely, they boarded the NASA van for the short ride to the *Arrowhead* launchpad. Garrett's head throbbed as they cruised past the Vehicle Assembly Building. He could see the skeletal tower, and the huge planelike fuselage clinging to its booster rocket like a butterfly on a tree branch. The clouds had cleared during the night, and the sky looked dazzling as the sun rose. According to Control, the launch conditions were perfect.

The van rattled to a halt, and two minutes later, the center director, Ben Fleming, arrived to wish them luck. The ground crew shook hands in the traditional manner, and Garrett knew their expressions of goodwill were genuinely felt. There wasn't a man present who didn't know how much depended on the mission's success.

Technicians in lint-free coveralls escorted the crew to the tower elevator where a steel-grated catwalk led to the orbiter's already open hatch. The cabin was small, even smaller than Garrett had expected; from outside, the shuttle looked almost the size of *Concorde,* but much of its dimension was taken up by its massive cargo bay, and the two flight decks felt cramped and stifling.

One by one, the astronauts were strapped into their padded chairs by the ground launch technicians. Lori, Bamberger, and Delaney occupied the forward flight deck, with Garrett and Malenov seated in the rear. They lay flat on their backs, facing the heavens into which the shuttle would carry them, the best position to withstand the force of blast-off.

Around them, the vehicle was already rumbling and groaning, and as the technicians withdrew, Garrett's worries about Lori abruptly evaporated. Even his tiredness vanished in anticipation of what lay ahead. No more simulators, no more make-believe. This was the real McCoy.

For two long hours, the crew went through the complex preflight systems check, ensuring everything was in working order.

The radio console hummed. "*Arrowhead,* this is Launch Control. Let's try the abort routine."

"Roger. Looks good. Over."

"*Arrowhead,* this is Control. Initiate APU prestart procedure—over."

Garrett watched as Lori prepared the three auxiliary power units that operated the orbiter's hydraulic system. She checked the nine boiler switches, the three fuel-tank valves, and the two fuel-pump valves.

"Control, this is *Arrowhead*. Prestart fine. Procedure complete. Powering up APUs."

"Roger, over."

"*Arrowhead*, this is Control. Your H-Two tank pressurization looks okay. You are go for launch."

"Roger that. Go for launch, and over."

"*Arrowhead*, this is Control. You are on your on-board computer, over."

As the moment approached, the launch director ordered the crew to lower their helmet visors, and they felt the bulkheads vibrating as the main engines gimbaled into their final position. Garrett knew the procedure by heart, and pulses throbbing, he sat back in his chair, listening to the controller's voice: "Five, four, three . . . you have main-engine start . . . two one . . . SRB ignition . . . zero—*lift-off*!"

Garrett felt the paralyzing power as slowly, smoothly, the shuttle began to rise. He heard the brain-numbing roar of the solid-fuel boosters. By the time they had cleared the tower, they were traveling at a hundred miles an hour.

"The tower has been cleared," the controller's voice intoned. "We are instituting roll maneuver."

Arcing swiftly, the vehicle rolled 120 degrees, suspending the crew in a heads-down position. There was no fear in Garrett now, just a feeling of heightened awareness, as if never before in his life had his emotions been so keen, his senses so alert.

He was pinned helplessly against his chair as they reached maximum dynamic pressure, his face shriveling under the g-force strain. His body felt heavy, incapable of response.

The cathode-ray tube, used to display computer output, flashed a report that the solid-fuel boosters had burned out, and Lori's voice echoed over the radio transmitter. "Control, this is *Arrowhead*. We are ready for SRB separation—over."

"Roger. Hit boosters for separation."

Bamberger's fingers danced across the controls, and there was a distant rumbling sound as the solid rocket boosters parted from the shuttle vehicle.

Two minutes later, the voice of the controller droned again. "*Arrowhead*, a launch abort is no longer possible. Do you copy? Over."

"Roger, Control. Negative return. We are now single-engine press to MECO. We can reach orbit even if two main engines fail."

"Roger, *Arrowhead*."

Lori throttled down the main engines to hold acceleration below three g's.

"*Arrowhead*, this is Control. Go for main engine cutoff—over."

"MECO," Lori shouted, engaging the computer to stifle the main-engine thrust. The status indicators flashed to red.

"*Arrowhead*, this is Control. Go for external-tank separation."

"Roger—we have ET tank separation."

Explosive bolts disconnected the heavy external tank, allowing it to drop backward into the sea.

"*Arrowhead*, this is Control. You are go for OMS-one burn—over."

The orbiter's maneuvering engines mounted on each side of the fuselage fired a brief burst of hydrazine fuel oxidized by nitrogen tetroxide, and the vehicle rocketed into the firmanent.

The pressure was easing, dissipating. Suddenly the thunder ceased, and Garrett was conscious of an overwhelming lull. The astronauts relaxed. Looking through the viewing port, Garrett experienced a feeling of exhiliration as he glimpsed the earth's curve taking shape below. It looked incredibly blue, its cloud sheath tinged in places with shades of russet red. A wild tingling sensation rippled through Garrett's body.

They were up.

Sitting in the Mercedes passenger seat, Wesker stared wearily through the windshield at the entrance to the Hobart Building, headquarters of the multimillion-dollar Hobart business empire. A group of Secret Service men stood on the marble steps, watching the traffic drifting by. Two hours had passed since Randolph Guthrie had vanished through the revolving doors, and Wesker was becoming rapidly bored and irritable.

"Coffee?" Dunlap asked, brandishing his thermos flask.

Wesker looked at him. "Who made it?"

"My landlady made it."

"Shit. The last lot tasted like river mud."

"Close your eyes. You'll never know the difference."

Wesker glanced idly at the rooftops across the street. He could see the sky, piercingly blue, and he wondered suddenly how Zach and Lori were doing up there. A chance in a million, their prospects of putting the terrorist satellite out of action, though he'd bet on Garrett where tenacity and guts were concerned. A man like Garrett just wouldn't quit, no matter what, and Lori—Wesker's lips twitched—she could match Garrett eyeball-to-eyeball as far as stubbornness went. A hell of a pair they made.

Wesker tensed as a flurry of movement took place in the building entrance opposite. Randolph Guthrie appeared, talking animatedly to his security men. They looked deeply unhappy.

Guthrie walked down the steps, opened the door of his limousine, and said something to the uniformed driver. The man stepped from the car, saluting obediently.

Guthrie took his place at the wheel, started up the engine, and with the Secret Service men watching in silent disapproval, joined the traffic heading north.

Wesker nudged Dunlap with his elbow. "Looks like the cuckoo has left the nest. Scramble."

They trailed the Vice President through Trinidad and past Gallaudet College, and Wesker felt his senses quickening as they took North Capitol Street toward Rock Creek Cemetery.

"Don't get too close," he warned. "He'll be watching for a tail."

When Guthrie began to double back on his route, Wesker knew he hadn't been mistaken. Through Brookland, Petworth, and Mount Pleasant, the chase continued, a bizarre cat-and-mouse game in which Guthrie zigzagged and detoured, Dunlap hanging doggedly in his wake.

At last, Guthrie swung north on Connecticut and turned west through the suburban network of Randolph Hills. After nearly an hour, he drew to a halt at an elegant house framed on all sides by leafy woodlands. Plainclothes security guards opened the entrance gates, waving his limousine through.

Wesker ordered Dunlap to park in a grove of trees. He was almost dizzy with excitement. "This is it," he said. "It's got to be. The nerve center of the terrorist operation."

"You want me to put out a call for backup?"

"Not yet. If we get this wrong, they'll skin us alive. We have to be sure, cast-iron one-hundred-percent sure."

"What do you figure on doing?" Dunlkap's face was pale.

"I'm going in," Wesker said.

"For Chrissake, let me at least call the local police. If anything happens . . ."

"If anything happens, go to the secretary of defense and tell him what we've found. Let him make his own decisions."

Dunlap looked unhappy, but he nodded in agreement. "Don't take any chances, Louis. If it looks like trouble, get out fast."

"Don't worry," Wesker said. "My mother didn't raise any heroes."

He left the car and crossed the highway toward the outer wall. A thatch of woodland traced the estate's perimeter, and Wesker climbed over the fence, pushing his way deep into the thicket. The wall rose above him, twelve or fifteen feet. Flies droned from the surrounding foliage, gathering around his head in a maddening cloud.

He found a spot where a beech tree offered a makeshift ladder to the parapet above, and sucking in his breath, grasped the outspread branches with both hands, and began to climb. When he reached the wall's summit, he saw that the rim had been peppered with broken glass. Wedging himself against the tree trunk, he struggled out of his jacket and laid it carefully over the jagged slivers, then lowered himself to the top of the wall and dropped to the other side.

For a moment, he crouched in the underbrush, listening intently. There was no sound other than the faint humming of a distant radio.

Picking his way through the rhododendrons, bracken, and fallen branches, he came to an open lawn with a fountain at the center. Directly in front, the house rose against the sky, its walls dominated by a line of whitewashed pillars.

He took a detour, tracing the grassy verge and keeping to the cover of the luxuriant underbrush. A figure emerged from the bushes ahead and approached him warily. Wesker froze in his tracks, his stomach crawling. A Doberman.

The dog paused, puzzled by the presence of this unexpected intruder, and Wesker saw its shoulders hunch, its mouth draw back in a vicious snarl. Its growl grew louder, more challenging, and Wesker felt sweat break out between his shoulder blades. Gently, almost imperceptibly, he lowered himself to the ground. His squat body settled into the full lotus position, legs folded in front of him. Fixing the Doberman with his eyes, he began to hum. The sound was strange and disorienting, coming from deep within his chest.

The dog blinked, and its growling stopped. With a whimper, it settled on its haunches, resting its chin on its front paws. Silent and obeisant, it gazed at Wesker with innocent eyes.

Wesker rose to his feet and moved around the motionless animal. At the edge of the lawn, a line of greenhouses formed a protective barrier between the thicket and the house beyond, and Wesker tiptoed between them, ducking his head to avoid being seen by observers in the windows above.

He paused as someone crossed the timbered porch in front. It was a fleshy man with a mane of wiry black hair. His jacket was undone, and Wesker saw a pistol butt protruding from the leather holster at his waist. The man vanished into a side door, and Wesker waited a moment to make sure the area was clear, then skirted the outside of the house.

At the rear, a flight of steps led to an underground doorway—the cellar. Wesker found it locked, but using his penknife, jimmied the latch and stepped inside. Shafts of sunlight lit a massive garbage bin. Above, the tip of a rubbish chute protruded from the ceiling. Wesker examined the opening. It looked small, perhaps too small, but if he pulled in his stomach, he might just be able to wriggle his way into the building's interior.

He was halfway up the bunker when he heard a movement on the concrete floor below, and a pistol barrel dug savagely into the nerve center at the base of his spine.

"Move, and you're dead meat," a voice said.

Wesker's knuckles tightened on the metal rim. Footsteps clattered on the outside stairway as another man entered the cellar. "What you got here, Tim?"

"An intruder. Caught him trying to sneak up through the garbage chute."

A fist seized Wesker's belt, dragging him to the ground.

"Get your palms against the wall and spread those legs," the first voice commanded.

Wesker did as he was told, cursing himself for his incompetence. Hard hands frisked him expertly, going through the contents of his pockets, patting the outline of his body beneath the flimsy clothing.

"He's clean," the first man said at last.

He stepped back, waving Wesker forward. "Move," he ordered. "Not too fast and not too slow. Make a break, and I'll drop you where you stand. Understood?"

Wesker nodded.

They left the cellar and made their way to the front porch, Wesker leading, the two gunmen trailing at his rear.

His captors steered him across the lobby and into an elegant drawing room where a glittering chandelier dangled from the ornate ceiling. Paintings lined the walls, and around the hearth, a group of men sat warming themselves before a roaring fire. Wesker gave a start of surprise as he recognized Earl Hogan, assistant director of the U.S. Secret Service.

Hogan rose to his feet as Wesker entered. "What the hell are you doing here?"

"I might ask you the same thing," Wesker said, regaining his composure.

"Don't get snotty with me, Louis. If you want my advice, you'd better start explaining fast."

Wesker glanced at the men surrounding him. Three of the faces he recognized. They were all members of the White House security contingent. He felt a tremor of uneasiness. "What's going on here?"

"What does it look like? We're guarding the Vice President. That's our job."

"Since when did the assistant director take on nursemaid duties?"

"Since some dumb asshole began poking his nose into affairs that didn't concern him," Hogan answered.

Wesker looked at him angrily. "I've been trailing Guthrie for days. Don't you realize the bastard is Frank De Tabley?"

"Bullshit."

"I can prove it."

"You can't prove a damn thing. You're so wide of the mark, you might as well be in a different continent."

"Guthrie's here to meet with the *Stallion* terrorists. This is their operations base."

Hogan laughed humorlessly. "Call yourself a security man? Guthrie's here for one reason only. Listen."

He switched on a small receiving set, and the sound of heavy breathing filled the room. Wesker heard a woman moaning softly; then a man's voice interrupted, hoarse and inarticulate.

Hogan switched off the set, glowering at Wesker. "Guthrie's having an affair," he said. "In fact, he's been having affairs ever since the administration started. He doesn't like our people interfering, so we have to cover him the best we can—surreptitiously."

Wesker felt his legs turn weak. "You mean Guthrie came here simply to get laid?"

"The man's an inveterate womanizer. He can't help himself, it's in his blood. Keeping the news from the press and the public is a full-time job. Guthrie figured you must be a private eye, hired by his wife. We were afraid you might be something a little more sinister."

"But we have code messages in Guthrie's own handwriting."

"Just part of his scheme to outwit Theresa," Hogan said tiredly. "The damn fool thinks he's still in the CIA."

Wesker felt his cheeks beginning to flush. He glanced at the Secret Service men in an agony of embarrassment. "So all this is perfectly innocent?"

"Mrs. Guthrie may not think so," Hogan said. "But in terms of a terrorist conspiracy, I guess there's nothing more innocent under the sun."

The D.C. streets were almost empty when Dunlap pulled to a halt at Wesker's car. "Don't take it so hard, Louis. Anybody can make a mistake."

"We haven't time for mistakes," Wesker said. "In a few more hours, those maniacs will start pushing buttons. Then the shit will really hit the fan."

He climbed wearily from the car. "You've been a good friend, Vince. I'm sorry things didn't work out the way we figured."

"I'm sorry too," Dunlap said. "But at least we tried."

"The cemeteries are full of men who tried."

Wesker crossed the street to his own vehicle. The streetlights cast pools of orange light across the empty road.

As he reached the curb, he heard a screech of brakes, and a gleaming Volkswagen skidded to a halt at his rear. "Louis?" a voice said.

It was Willard Shaw. Wesker walked toward him. "Mr. Shaw, you're working late tonight."

"I'm on twenty-four-hour call. The White House is like a circus at the moment."

Shaw hesitated, tapping the driving wheel with his fingertips. "Those cryptonyms you gave me, I checked them out. I think maybe you might have something, Louis. Back in the seventies, Randolph Guthrie ran two field agents code-named Aunt Grace and Laughing Water."

Wesker gave a tired smile. "I appreciate your support, Mr. Shaw, but I'm afraid I wandered into the wrong track. Randolph Guthrie has nothing to do with the *Devil's Stallion*."

Shaw looked nonplussed. "You mean he isn't Frank De Tabley?"

"I guess not."

"Hell, I was just beginning to get excited."

"Me too. Now it's back to the drawing board."

Shaw hesitated. "Louis, I want you to know that I'm behind you all the way. Anything you discover—anything at all—please feel free to call me, night or day."

"That's very kind of you."

"Good night."

"Good night, Mr. Shaw."

Wesker watched him drive away into the darkness, then got into his own car. He set off, his mind in a turmoil. He'd behaved like an amateur tonight, wasted precious time and energy trailing a man whose only crime was a little extramarital dalliance. He felt weary and despondent as he stopped outside his home.

The submarine gleamed in the heavy darkness, stars framing its oblong conning tower. Gendun met him at the entrance. "Something is wrong," Gendun said shrewdly.

"I've done something today I haven't done in a long time," Wesker told him. "Made a fool of myself."

"Foolishness is relative."

Wesker flopped into a chair, bending to unfasten his shoelaces. Gendun poured him a drink from the cocktail cabinet on the bulkhead. "You remember the man I was telling you about—the evil one?"

"Mr. De Tabley?" Gendun queried.

"I've made a terrible mistake. I thought he was someone important in the government. I was wrong."

"In that case, you must look again."

"I wish it was that easy. If you want the truth, I haven't the remotest idea where to begin."

"Why not begin with Bonnie MacAnally."

Wesker looked at him, puzzled. "De Tabley's mistress?"

"Is she not your only genuine lead?"

"Right. But Bonnie MacAnally's dead. The coroner's keeping her on ice until after the inquest. That's the usual procedure."

"Surely a man of your intelligence can get around that."

"For what reason?" Wesker queried.

"When one lives like the fox, one must learn to think like the fox. By pulling a few strings, you could arrange to have Miss MacAnally buried tomorrow."

Wesker sucked in his breath. "You think De Tabley might show?"

"He may be a psychopath, but he wouldn't be human if he didn't feel at least a twinge of regret."

"By God, Gendun, you're a marvel." Wesker's eyes glowed with excitement as he slapped Gendun lightly on the shoulder. "I'm going to arrange the biggest goddamned funeral you ever saw."

Garrett adjusted effortlessly to space. He had thought about it so often, studied it so long, that the experience of being in orbit held few surprises for him. Even the sensation of weightlessness seemed familiar, not unlike diving in the *Belka,* though without the pressure of the surrounding water.

For a while, he amused himself like a mischievous schoolboy by floating around the cramped little cabin, until Lori, irritated by the distraction, ordered him to return to his chair.

"Where do you think you are, Disneyland? Can't you see you're getting in everybody's way?"

Garrett contemplated a final attempt at reconciliation but decided against it. A crowded shuttle deck was hardly the place for ironing out a lover's quarrel—and besides, as flight commander, Lori had more important things on her mind.

Hundreds of miles beneath them the globe's surface was swathed in fleecy ribbons of cloud. Garrett recognized the broad bulge of the Moroccan coast and the shimmering waters of the Mediterranean. Even at such a height, it was possible to discern the lacy spumes of wave crests as the sea danced in the throes of an early spring storm.

He took out his drawing pad and began to sketch feverishly in an attempt to capture his impressions, but the earth was moving by too fast, and the spacecraft cabin, though relatively silent after the thunderous roar of lift-off, was filled with a cacophony of distracting noises—gases hissing, bulkheads creaking, ventilators purring. He put away his sketch pad in frustration.

Now that they were effectively in orbit, there was little for

Garrett and Malenov to do since the handling of the vehicle fell largely to Lori as flight commander and the two experienced astronauts, Delaney and Bamberger. To fill his time, Malenov was moodily cleaning one of the five revolvers the secretary of defense had insisted they carry along as a precaution. Garrett watched as the Russian methodically oiled and wiped the firing mechanism. He knew it would be only a few hours before they neared their objective. Somehow, he had to shore up the gulf between Malenov and himself.

"Sergei?"

Malenov glared at him.

"I'm not asking you to forget the past," Garrett said, "but if we're going to work together, we've got to reach some kind of truce."

"Why?" Malenov demanded.

"Because we may have to depend on each other, that's why."

"Depend on you, Zachary? I'd rather depend on a nest of vipers. Certainly, we must put our personal quarrel aside until that satellite has been disarmed. But once it's accomplished, I intend to do something I've dreamed about for years."

"What's that?" Garrett asked.

Malenov's face was calm as he went on cleaning the handgun. "I am going to kill you."

In Houston, Mission Director Leonard Brody studied the multiplexor consoles that charted the spacecraft's progress. He was pleased at the way the launch was proceeding. During a shuttle flight, most people imagined the important activity took place within the orbiter itself, but it was here in the control room that the real drama unfolded. This was the hub, the brain center from which the tiny capsule was guided. Happily, the lift-off had been perfect, no problems—a blessed relief, considering two of the shuttle's crew were first-time flyers.

Under normal circumstances, Leonard Brody didn't approve of military spaceflights. To him, space was a hallowed thing, and people had no right to sully it with politics and diplomatic tensions. But this was a special case. The crew of the *Arrowhead* were trying to save mankind, and Brody hoped to God their mission succeeded.

The capsule-communication, or CAP-COMM, controller,

the man responsible for maintaining contact with the shuttle called suddenly: "Leo, we've got ourselves a problem here."

Brody moved toward him. The CAP-COMM was manipulating the control panel, his face taut with anxiety. Around him, his four assistants toyed with dials and switches.

"What's wrong?" Brody asked.

"We've lost touch with the *Arrowhead*."

"Lost touch? That's impossible. We ran a radio check just before launch. Everything checked out fine."

"Well, we can't seem to raise them anymore."

"Try the RRM," Brody advised.

The controller switched his attention to a separate console. Brody waited patiently as he fumbled with the instruments. After a moment, the CAP-COMM shook his head. "Negative."

"It was functioning normally on the launchpad. You're using the wrong frequency."

"I'm sorry, Leo, but what we've got here is a complete communications breakdown."

Someone called Brody from another part of the room. It was the reaction control supervisor. Brody moved toward him, a sickly feeling in his stomach. The man indicated his visual display unit. The electronic screen showed a skeletal sketch-plan of the shuttle's functionings.

"Trouble. The communications antennae have broken up."

"How?"

"Only one way. Somebody fixed it."

"Sabotage?"

"Right. And clever too. Whoever got into that shuttle knew exactly where to tweak so it wouldn't show on the instrument checks."

"Jesus. Can't we do anything?"

"Without those antennae, there's no hope of reestablishing contact. And who knows, maybe the communications breakup is only the beginning. There are eight hundred items on that shuttle that could spell disaster if they malfunction."

Brody understood the man's meaning. A saboteur who could disengage the radio so cleverly that they hadn't even noticed could just as easily have tampered with something more vital.

"My God," he breathed, moistening his lips with his tongue.

*   *   *

"We've lost contact with Houston," Lori said.

"Lost contact? That's impossible," Garrett said.

"Listen."

A crackling sound filled the cabin.

Delaney glanced at Bamberger sitting at his side. His tanned face looked unusually pale. "Try the secondary downlink."

Bamberger manipulated the dials. The crackling noise increased.

"What in Christ's name's going on?" Delaney muttered.

Malenov examined the flight-deck consoles over Delaney's head. He understood the seriousness of the situation. Without communications backup, they would have little hope of disabling their target, even less of making the dangerous return journey to the Cape. "What about Launch Control?"

"That's gone too," Lori told him. "There's nothing out there but frying eggs."

A terrible apprehension gathered in Garrett. "Communications worked okay during lift-off."

She agreed. "Which leaves only one logical answer. They've been got at."

" 'Got at'?" Bamberger echoed.

"Fixed. Somebody in the handover-ingress team, I imagine."

Prior to departure, the handover-ingress team had spent several hours inside the spacecraft preparing it for launch.

"Sabotage?"

"There's no other explanation. They've done something to the antennae."

Garrett glanced at Malenov as a terrible thought occurred to him. He could see the Russian had been struck by the same chilling idea. Together the two men rose from their chairs, floating into the aft compartment where the particle-beam accelerators were stored.

Garrett tore open the cupboard. The twin machines lay mocking him silently, their metal casings blackened and charred. He cursed softly under his breath as he dragged them into the light. Coated with charcoal, they were barely recognizable. The electromagnetic circuits had been blown apart by some form of mini timing device, damaged beyond repair.

"How could it happen?" Malenov breathed. "They were still intact when we boarded the shuttle."

Garrett indicated scorchmarks around the ANSAADs' inner casings.

"Somebody wired them with explosive. They probably detonated when we blasted into orbit. The roar of the engines would have masked the sound."

The Russian looked at him questioningly. "What happens now?"

"Nothing happens. Without the ANSAADs, we're sunk."

His fury deepened. It was hard to accept the ignominy of defeat, the humiliation of failure. He'd known from the beginning the mission would be a tricky one, but he hadn't reckoned on interference in their own backyard.

He jerked his head at the flight cabin. "Let's spread the good word."

Lori glanced up as they floated through the entrance hatch.

"The ANSAADs are knackered," Garrett announced.

" 'Knackered'?"

"From the Old English verb 'to knacker.' Demolished. Kaput."

"How, for God's sake?"

"Somebody used explosive charges."

Delaney's clean-cut face seemed to have aged markedly during the last few minutes. "Can't you improvise?"

"Impossible. It's the first time a particle-beam accelerator has been developed in portable terms. Without the necessary parts, we're stumped."

"Supposing you salvaged bits from each machine, joined them together?"

"You don't understand. We're talking about a total write-off."

"But how could it happen? The shuttle was guarded night and day."

"Clearly somebody got in. Somebody with enough influence to penetrate even NASA's security. Somebody who's been following every move we've made."

"What are we going to do?" Bamberger asked. "Retreat?"

"Run home with our tail between our legs?" Garrett was scornful.

"Let's take a vote on it," Delaney suggested.

"No need to vote," Lori said. "I'm the commander. I'll make the decisions."

Suddenly she looked very small and frail. Garrett couldn't blame her for panicking. Panic, however, was the last thing on Lori Madden's mind.

Her voice was crisp and authoritative as she said, "We're aborting the mission. We'll return to earth."

"Without support from Ground Control, that's going to be tricky," Delaney told her. "We'll have to wait for a window into the atmosphere."

"Supposing we don't bother waiting?" Malenov asked.

"Then we'll miss the Cape. We could land anywhere. Europe, Asia, Africa."

"Dammit," said Garrett, "there must be an emergency procedure for this kind of thing."

"There is. NASA has landing strips all over the world, but without radio contact, we've no way of putting them on alert."

"Okay, how long before we reach a suitable reentry point?"

Lori's fingers danced lightly over the computer keys. "One hour, forty-two minutes."

"We'll never make it, Coach," Joe Bamberger declared softly.

Lori looked at him. "What are you talking about?"

Bamberger indicated the system screen on the instrument panel. His eyed looked sickly. "There's a fault on the main oxidizer valve."

"There can't be," Lori said.

"See for yourself. It's coming apart. Whoever rigged the ANSAADs with explosive charges could just as easily have done the same thing someplace else."

"Can't you fix it?" Garrett asked.

"Hell, just getting into that combustion chamber would take a goddamn miracle."

"The fuel reburner's gone," Delaney announced suddenly, leaning forward to examine the system screens. "So has the low-pressure turbo pump and the auxiliary power units."

"My God," Lori breathed. In the fetid heat of the cabin, her voice was strained.

"What does it mean?" Garrett demanded.

"It means we're too late to trigger reentry. In fact, we're too late to do anything at all. Whoever fixed those function systems knew exactly what he was doing."

She looked up at him, her eyes stricken. "The shuttle's going to disintegrate," she said.

# TWENTY-ONE

In Mission Control, Leonard Brody stared incredulously at the multiplexer consoles where warning blips were flashing in at least a dozen places. "The vessel's coming apart at the seams," he muttered. "How in God's name did it stand up to the pressure checks?"

"Whoever fixed it did one hell of a job," said Pat Traumont, the deputy mission director. "He used explosive charges to blast the things apart after the vehicle got into orbit."

Brody's face turned ashen as he massaged his forehead with his fingertips. "My God," he breathed. "Those poor bastards haven't a chance up there. That shuttle's going to crumble like a stale cookie."

Inside the cabin, Lori's brain was beginning to function again. Deep down, something smoldered inside her, overriding the fear. Anger. She wasn't going to be disposed of like a piece of unwanted garbage. Think it out, her brain urged. There has to be an answer.

Like an inspiration, the idea came to her. *"Mayflower."*

*"'Mayflower'?"* Garrett echoed.

"It's a satellite. Or to be precise, two satellites. They were put up a year ago by the United European Space Program. One is a computerized laboratory for conducting experiments in orbit, the other its electronic support section, funded by the

United States. The *Mayflower*'s currently unmanned, but it carries a space capsule for ferrying material and equipment between the companion platforms. The capsule's large enough to carry eight fully equipped passengers, and the pressurized accommodation module contains life-support systems for approximately thirty days.''

"Are they within our orbit?''

"We're scheduled to pass them sixteen minutes before reaching the *Devil's Stallion*. If we use the MMUs, *Mayflower* should give us a breathing space at least.''

"Then what?'' Malenov demanded. "How do we know NASA can get us down again?''

"We'll worry about that later,'' Garrett stated. "If we buy time, we buy survival. We'll regroup and improvise.''

He looked at Lori. "Think this machine will hang together until we reach those satellites?''

"I don't know. Maybe. If it doesn't, this whole damn exercise is theoretical. The important thing is to try.''

"We're supposed to spend two hours breathing pure oxygen before any extravehicular activity,'' Bamberger protested.

"Forget the rule book,'' Lori told him. "We'll use what time we have. Get into the EMU suits, and let's hope our body systems adjust when we go out through the cargo bay.''

Delaney looked amused by Lori's crisp authoritative manner. Now that her fear had evaporated, she was totally in control.

"Anything else you'd like us to do, Commander?'' he asked.

"You might try praying,'' she said.

Wesker parked his car directly opposite the Garden of Remembrance, where he commanded an excellent view of the funeral ceremony. The priest's voice droned softly on the morning air.

Leaning back in his seat, he watched the mourners at the gravesite. Several of the ladies were weeping. It looked like a simple family affair.

Wesker watched a limousine pull up along the cemetery drive. The driver made no attempt to alight but observed the funeral from the seclusion of his seat, hidden from view behind the sun-reflector windows.

Wesker sucked in his breath. Was it possible Gendun had

been right after all? Had the mountain finally come to Mohammed?

He waited until the limousine started up, then, switching on his ignition, followed it cautiously, staying a good sixty yards behind. It joined the Capital Beltway, moving east, and Wesker picked his way in and out of the traffic, keeping a wary eye on the vehicle's roof. Through Silver Spring and College Park the two cars dipped and weaved, Wesker clinging like a limpet to the limousine's receding tail.

At the door of the Fremont Club, the great car slid to a halt, and Wesker waited expectantly as the steward came forward to drive it into the parking lot. A man emerged into the sunlight, looking at the sky, his face racked with desolation and pain. He said something to the steward, and crossing the marbled threshold, vanished into the club's interior.

"Jesus Christ," Wesker whispered in disbelief.

His fingers trembled as he reached for the radio.

Garrett huddled in the cargo bay, gazing calmly between the open hatches. He felt shaky at the thought of all that space out there—nothing between him and the whole damned universe. There was something unnerving about the idea of drifting through the heavens without a spacecraft. The emptiness was so total.

The EMU suit, or "extravehicular mobility unit," which consisted of three separate assemblies—upper torse, lower torso, and portable life-support system—and sported a chest-mounted microcomputer maintaining a constant status check on oxygen and battery power, plus a cooling and ventilation garment made from plastic tubing and Spandex mesh, was not unlike the *Belka;* it carried the same sense of constriction, the same overwhelming oppressiveness.

It was bitterly cold crouching in the cargo bay, and he was conscious more than anything else of the overwhelming silence. Somehow, it accentuated the emptiness, gave a man a chilling awareness of his true size.

He jumped as a cluster of shapeless contours emerged between the cargo-bay doors. Obscured by blackness, they were scarcely discernible to the naked eye, and he sensed rather than saw a merging of the shadows, a subtle thickening in the gloom. Something was up there—close, terrifyingly close—something huge and menacing, towering above them like an inquisitive giant.

Struggling to see through the dark, Garrett's eyes defined a cluster of elongated arms sprouting outward in every direction, cluttered with sensors and communications antennae. Beyond and slightly to the left, a similar object, shapeless and grotesque, floated motionless, devoid of symmetry, as if it had been designed not by man but some alien intelligence.

Lori's voice in Garrett's helmet was distorted slightly by the communications linkup. *"Mayflower."*

Garrett felt a dryness in his throat as he surveyed the twin platforms floating above. Never had he seen a more unwelcoming haven.

"Into the MMUs," Lori ordered crisply. "And stick together. We're not on the racing circuit at Le Mans. We move in convoy. That way, if anyone gets into trouble, there'll be immediate backup on hand."

Moving ponderously, Garrett unhooked his MMU from the cargo-bay wall and slotted himself into the narrow seat, fixing the safety fastenings with his gloved fingers. The MMU was a self-contained backpack that latched onto the astronaut's spacesuit. Nitrogen gas jets from twenty-four nozzles around its outer rim propelled him through space at a maximum speed of seventy feet per second, controlled by knobs on the armrest ends.

As a rule, shuttles carried only two or three MMUs apiece to economize on cargo space, but because the *Arrowhead* was flying empty, NASA had provided a separate unit for each crew member.

Garrett was glad about that now.

He was panting as he settled himself against the MMU's neckplate. Every movement, no matter how simple, required monumental effort. Peering through his helmet visor, he quickly checked the vehicle's controls. Left-hand-operated transverse movement, right-hand rotation. His brain went through the instrument sequence drummed into his brain during their crash course at the Cape.

Lori hovered above them, framed by the cargo-bay doors. "Okay," she commanded. "Keep together. No wandering. Let's go."

Garrett twisted the left knob. A faint hiss reached him through the helmet, and he rose obliquely into the air like a man on a minielevator. There was no sensation of movement. It was as if he were sitting motionless while density and perspective shifted around him.

He watched the shuttle falling away below. With its cargo bay open, it looked like a grotesque bird framed against the receding earth. Silence gathered, stifling and oppressive, the only sound the faint hissing of the gas nozzles as the astronauts glided eerily into the inky darkness.

The savage cold bit into Garrett's EMU suit, chilling his limbs to the bone. Never in his life had he experienced cold like it, not even in Antarctica.

The aluminized outlines of his companions picked up the refracted light from the earth below; locked in their tiny maneuvering units, they looked like a swarm of insects drifting through some inexplicable vacuum.

Gradually, the satellites took shape. Closer, it was possible to discern the skeletal framework of their extended arms and the tiny porthole windows that framed the living quarters. The platforms had been empty for months. Who knew what kind of shape they'd be in?

Suddenly, Malenov cried out in alarm, his voice reverberating inside Garrett's helmet. The Russian colonel was rolling wildly to starboard, his body performing a weird aerial ballet as he turned over and over in a series of graceless somersaults.

Garrett could see him fumbling frantically with the armrest controls. "What's wrong?" he barked into his accoustic microphone.

"Damn thing's going haywire."

"Use your right hand. Bring yourself upright."

"I can't. Nothing's responding."

Garrett cursed under his breath. Already, Malenov's EMU suit, framed by the earth's curve, was veering crazily into the darkness. Clearly, somebody had to go after the idiot.

He glanced at the others, hovering in a tiny cluster. "Head for the satellite. I'll fetch Malenov."

Without waiting to see if they obeyed, Garrett twisted his right-hand knob, bringing the MMU directly to starboard. He relased a spurt of nitrogen gas, propelling himself vigorously in Malenov's wake. Mustn't let the blackness unnerve him. Nothing out there to worry about but his own imagination.

As the darkness thickened, he struggled for glimpses of

Malenov's receding form. "Keep talking, Sergei. I'm losing sight of you."

The Russian's voice echoed in his eardrums. "I'm over to the right, directly below the satellites."

Garrett adjusted the direction controls. He fired another spurt of gas, his momentum quickening. "Hang on," he muttered.

Malenov had stopped rolling now and was floating helplessly on his back, his helmet tilted toward the earth. Garrett readjusted his attitude level, homing in on his target upside down. "Cut loose your MMU," he snapped into his microphone set.

Through his sun-shaded helmet visor, he saw the Russian glaring at him. My God, Garrett thought, he's angry at me for saving his life.

"Do it, Sergei. Don't be a bloody fool. This is no time to be standing on dignity. Cut loose the MMU."

Malenov's gloved hands fumbled at the fastenings, disengaging himself from the tiny space vehicle. Mumbling softly, he kicked himself free and seized Garrett's arm, clinging like a limpet to the Englishman's backpack.

"Secure?" Garrett asked.

"Affirmative," Malenov said in Russian.

"Hang on."

Swiveling the MMU backward, Garrett struggled to discern the spidery outlines of the twin satellites above. Dimly, he glimpsed their extended arms. Engaging the nitrogen thrusters, he propelled himself gracefully upward, Malenov clinging to his rear.

Somewhere behind, he heard an odd commotion. Glancing back, he saw the shuttle disintegrating. It happened slowly, like the peeling of a fruit. The entire vehicle appeared to be skinning itself, shedding bits of fuselage and scattering the wreckage in its wake. It somersaulted, its cabin crumbling, its cargo doors ripping, then, in a blinding flash, exploded violently outward, illuminating the night in a dazzling, mind-numbing glare.

In Mission Control, Leonard Brody stared dumbly at the multiplexer screens. There was no mistaking the telemetry signals. The orbiter was in its death throes. Brody watched the *Arrowhead*'s agony with horrified fascination. It was like witnessing the end of a dear and intimate friend.

Despite the pandemonium on the monitor units, no sound rose from the Mission Control operators. Speechless, they sat, like Brody, frozen.

At last, a terrible silence filled the room, and Brody felt his muscles contract. He stared in horror at the empty monitors. "Jesus God," he whispered.

Through the satellite's viewing port, Zahl watched the *Arrowhead* falling apart. He glanced at his radar scanner. The only signatures came from the orbiter's scattered entrails, floating through space on aimless voyages of their own.

At Zahl's side, Hentoff and Finnegan, watched the devastation with horror, but Zahl looked perfectly calm as he operated the communication console.

"*Stallion* to Control. Do you copy? Over."

There was a faint crackling on the receiver, then Kozani's voice broke through, crisp and clear. "This is Control. We copy."

Zahl looked again through the shaded viewing port. The only evidence of the orbiter remaining was a faint cloud of rapidly dispersing smoke and chunks of shapeless fuselage floating eerily through the void.

It was difficult to disguise the satisfaction in his voice.

"Tell De Tabley the *Arrowhead* threat has been eliminated."

Wesker stood in the defense secretary's office, staring through the darkened windows. Arlington Cemetery was lit by floodlights, the gravestones neat and regular, like precise, evenly set teeth.

David Richner looked at him worriedly. "You've got no proof," he maintained. "You're working on assumption only."

Wesker fumbled in his jacket pocket, tossed something on Richner's desk. "Here's your proof."

Richner picked it up, studying it in the window light. It was a broken Spanish doubloon on a thin gold chain, its beveled edges polished and irregular.

"You searched his home without a warrant?"

"It wasn't necessary, Mr. Secretary. We found a safe-deposit key in his office drawer. When we checked it out, the box contained a suitcase packed with overnight clothing and a phony passport in the name of John Wolfe. The coin was in the toilet bag. It fits perfectly the half we discovered in Bonnie MacAnally's apartment.''

"Where's De Tabley now?"

"We've trailed him to a house belonging to General Dan Connel. I've got the place sealed off and surrounded. All I need is the go-ahead."

"My God, I can hardly believe this."

"Believe it, Mr. Secretary. Give me permission to send in my men, and we'll argue about priorities afterward."

"In a moment," Richner said, steadying himself against the desk. "First I have to tell the President."

Elke smelled the moist tang of the adjacent sea as she crossed the complex, heading toward the accommodation block. Her body felt shapeless, like a piece of unfeeling fudge. She could scarcely believe the horror of what she had seen tonight.

She couldn't visualize Garrett's body ripped to shreds, floating through that unreachable vacuum. And yet, Garrett was only a symbol, an illusory fragment. He'd offered an anchor during the worst moments of her marriage, but love, like everything else, was an expendable commodity, and what had happened at Baikonur had withered with the passage of time.

Sergei, on the other hand, had been real. Now that he was gone, she was conscious of a soul-sickening emptiness. Human emotion was a funny thing, she thought; it blinded perception, distorted reality. She'd despised Sergei for his slavish devotion, but if she were honest with herself, really and truly honest, hadn't his loyalty kept them together? Without it, she was left with nothing.

Reaching her quarters, she stepped inside. Silent and functional, the room confronted her mockingly. It had been designed to prepare astronauts for the austerities of space, and somhow, its cell-like simplicity seemed to unnerve her.

Covering her face with her hands, she leaned back against the wall and cried.

The ice that coated the satellite's living quarters melted rapidly as Lori and Bamberger switched on the electrical heaters. Repressurized by portable consumable packs, the air supply was quickly becoming breathable, but they kept their helmets on while they checked through the platform's life-support system.

They had tried the communication console, but the transmitter remained depressingly dead. Marooned. That was what it amounted to. Though Garrett had found this tiny toehold of survival, he had few illusions about the precariousness of their position.

Delaney floated into the galley, looked around despairingly. "We're actually expecting to live in this thing?"

"We'll get it operational," Lori told him. "Don't worry."

"Operational, maybe. But will we make it habitable?"

"Sure we will, if we all work together."

Opening the galley dispenser, Malenov checked the plastic trays inside. "No shortage of food, anyhow. Plenty of packages and cans."

He picked one up, chuckling dryly as he examined its contents. "Six-day standard menu. At least it'll give us the right calories."

Lori tried the convection heater. "Oven's functioning normally. We can take turns preparing the meals. How about the water supply?"

"Water shouldn't be a problem," Delaney said. "If this ice keeps melting, we'll have more condensation than we can handle."

Lori's voice assumed a businesslike tone. "We'll work to a routine. Two hours a day on the exercise machine to avoid muscle atrophy. The rest of the time, we keep the satellite operating."

Bamberger stared at her with disgust. "This is crazy. NASA doesn't even know we're alive, for Chrissake."

"Not yet. But they will if we get the communications linkup working."

"And if we don't. What then, Commander?"

"Don't talk like that. We'll do it because we've got to."

"If there's one thing I can't stand, it's a cockeyed optimist."

It was clear that Bamberger was nearing the end of his tether. The loss of the shuttle had completely unnerved him.

Lori kept her voice calm. "If the linkup doesn't work, we'll engage all the systems, run them full blast as long as the energy holds out. Sooner or later, somebody on Earth is bound to realize we're up here."

"That's great," Delaney put in. "How do we know they're even capable of getting us off this thing?"

"Don't be so bloody spineless!" Lori exploded. "What do you want from me, a guarantee signed in triplicate? I don't know the answer, but there's no alternative except to lie down and die."

Garrett ignored the exchange. Peering through the viewing port, he spotted a faint glow in the western sky. When he raised his helmet visor, the glow disappeared. "Something's out there," he said. "I can see it clearly through the sunscreen, but if I lift it up, it disappears."

Lori floated alongside him. "It's the *Devil's Stallion*. The Canby D-Five is invisible to the naked eye. It can only be seen through Polaroids."

Garrett looked surprised. "So close?"

"Well, it's farther than it looks."

Garrett studied the glimmer thoughtfully. "Didn't you say there's a passenger capsule mounted on this thing?"

"Sure. It's used for ferrying equipment to the other platform."

"Will it carry us as far as the *Stallion*?"

Lori looked surprised. "Depends on how much fuel it's holding. It was never intended for traversing space."

"But could it make the journey, at a pinch?"

"Maybe. If the tanks are full."

"What are you getting at?" Malenov asked.

"The terrorist deadline is almost up," Garrett explained.

"So?"

"They'll have to switch off their defense shield to fire their first missile. There's just a chance that if we get close enough, we can occupy the platform while they're going through the preparatory checks."

Malenov looked astounded. "We'll have, at the outside, barely fifteen minutes."

"Maybe it'll be enough."

"'Maybe'?" Delaney echoed. "What the hell does that mean, 'maybe'? If you don't know, man, forget it. I don't intend to be vaporized just because we miscalculate by a couple of seconds."

"Besides," Bamberger put in, "they'll pick us up on their radar scan and blast us into bits, just like the *Arrowhead*."

"The *Arrowhead*'s what makes it all feasible," Garrett told him reasonably. "We'll be too small to register as a full-size orbiter, so they'll assume we're part of the wreckage from the disintegrated shuttle.''

Malenov looked dubious. ''It's a chance in a million, Zachary. We have no way of knowing if the capsule's capable of traveling such a distance, and even if it is, you're talking about a military assault in space, something which has never been attempted before.''

''Only because nobody *had* to attempt it before, but let's face it, we're in a jam. We've bought ourselves a little time, but as Brad points out, how do we know NASA can even get us out of here? We've got food and oxygen for approximately thirty days. What happens after that? Starvation? Asphyxia? I don't know about you, Sergei, but speaking personally, I'd rather go out in a blaze of glory. Besides—''

He paused, peering at them meaningfully. It was his trump card, and he played it with calculated skill. ''Those terrorists out there still have the shuttlecraft *Ulysses* locked in their docking bay. Take the *Stallion*, and we buy ourselves a ticket home.''

That did it. The shuttle was the one factor they could all relate to.

''It's a hell of a gamble,'' Bamberger said.

''So's entombment.''

''What if we get it wrong?'' Lori asked. ''What if the capsule doesn't have the right amount of fuel? What if they switch their force field back on before we reach the docking bay?''

'' 'What if, what if,' '' Garrett echoed exasperatedly. ''Then we die, that's what if. But at least it'll be quick. No hanging about watching the oxygen needle drop lower and lower. And we'll make sure the bastards know they've been in a fight.''

Nothing could stop Garrett now. His energy spread like a virus to everyone. Lori saw the excitement mounting in their faces, and she wanted to hug him.

''I say let's do it,'' she said.

Bamberger nodded. ''Me too.''

Delaney and Malenov agreed silently, and Garrett felt his spirits lifting. ''Come on,'' he snapped. ''We'll see if we can get that vehicle working.''

They found the capsule in the docking bay. Shaped like a narrow football, its beveled hull picked up the light from the inner cabin.

Malenov studied it anxiously. "Think we'll all get in?"

"We'll manage," Lori said. "But it'll never hold the MMUs."

"Then we'll ride double," Garrett stated. "Two to a machine. We can squeeze three into the aft section at a pinch, can't we?"

"I guess so."

The maneuvering units were stacked in the capsule's rear cargo hold, then the five astronauts wriggled into the cramped little passenger cabin. Clad in the EMU suits, they seemed to occupy every inch of available space. The bulkheads gathered around them like the walls of a constricting coffin.

Lori fumbled at the control console, but there was no sign of life from the dials and system gauges. She muttered softly under her breath.

"What's wrong?" Garrett demanded.

"I can't get the damn thing to operate. Nothing's responding."

"Are you sure you're using the right program?"

"See for yourself."

Again, she went through the preparatory procedure, engaging the capsule's inboard computers. Nothing. The instrument lights failed to glow; the screens remained alarmingly dead.

"Maybe there's a fault on the instrument circuits," Bamberger suggested. "Here, let me try."

Lori edged back, watching the young astronaut go through the preflight systems priming. Suddenly, the lights flickered, and Lori breathed a sigh of relief as the panel burst into life.

"Get the docking pins unlocked," Bamberger ordered, grinning triumphantly. "Then fasten your seat belts and extinguish all cigarettes. This flight is ready for departure."

The jangling of the telephone broke the stillness. Rising to his feet, Frank De Tabley picked it up, listening to the drone of a human voice. After a moment, he said, "Thank you," and replaced the receiver.

"The President has refused to resign," he announced to the gathering at large.

A faint murmur rose from the men who were sitting there.

"He's crazy," General Connel said.

"Of course he's crazy. Who but a crazy man would offer rockets to countries that could one day become our enemies?"

"You said he'd *have* to resign," another man accused. "You said he'd have no choice."

"I made a mistake. Lawrence Clayman clearly doesn't give a damn about what happens to the world so long as he retains his illusion of power."

"So we've lost our initiative, our impetus?"

"No," De Tabley said, unperturbed by the tension of the moment. "We'll have to show him we mean business, that's all."

There was a pause as the others considered his statement.

"You mean you intend going through with it?" a man said.

"Of course I intend going through with it."

"You're crazy, Frank. It's insane."

"Linus, you knew from the beginning what the operation entailed."

"But it was only a bluff. You said yourself it would never come to anything. The President would have to comply, you said. The country would force him to."

"And so they will, as soon as they see what we're capable of."

The protester's voice was strangled now as he said, "Abeidi was one thing, but you can't sentence millions of people to death."

De Tabley serenely picked up the telephone again. "Not me, Linus. I'm not doing the sentencing. That decision has already been made by Clayman."

"Frank, please, this isn't murder we're contemplating, it's wholesale genocide. We tried and we failed. Now it's time to cut our losses. Back off."

De Tabley hesitated, the receiver still in his hand. "As always, we abide by majority decision. What's it to be, gentlemen? Do we pretend this never happened, go back to our safe little lives, and watch the President turn the world into an international free-for-all? Or do we act now and stop this madness before it goes any further?"

For a long moment, the conference members sat silently, then a man said in a quiet voice, "Act."

Other voices joined the chorus, echoing faintly beneath the vaulted ceiling: "Act . . . act . . . act . . . act."

De Tabley punched out a number and waited as the line buzzed in his ear. After a moment, he heard a click.

"Trust might, trust constancy," he rasped. "Tell Zahl to fire one," he ordered. "The target will be Milan."

# TWENTY-TWO

Zahl experienced no trace of emotion as he inserted the firing key into the missile console. He had never questioned the legitimacy of what he was doing. The thought that millions of people would die when his finger pressed the button scarcely occurred to him. De Tabley had long ago recognized the young man's psychopathic tendencies and had carefully conditioned them. Zahl obeyed De Tabley's orders without question. His hands were cool as they drifted across the switches, carrying out the prefiring systems check.

At his rear, Hentoff and Finnegan watched the procedure in silence. "You're not going through with this, Nelson?" Finnegan said.

Zahl looked at him, surprised. "What the hell are you talking about?"

"I mean, you're not actually planning to fire that thing?"

"It's what we came for, isn't it?"

"Nelson, that's a city of people down there. You'll be killing them. *We'll* be killing them."

"Not us. We're only the instruments. It's Clayman who'll be doing the killing."

"Nelson, listen," Hentoff pleaded. "This isn't Abeidi anymore. Milan hasn't been evacuated. For Chrissake, they don't even know they're on the target list."

Zahl switched off the firing key and turned toward them, his eyes blazing. "What is this, some kind of mutiny?"

"Not mutiny, Nelson," Hentoff said. "Common sense. De Tabley promised we would never get to the firing point. He said the President would be forced to back down. I guess that hasn't happened, which means we've lost the gamble and we'll have to take the consequences. But let's not compound our guilt by murdering countless numbers of innocent people."

"You both swore an oath before we embarked on this flight," Zahl growled, "and there'll be no crapping out—not for you, not for me, and not for Lawrence Clayman either. De Tabley says destroy Milan, and we're going to destroy it if I have to shoot you both and finish the launch myself."

There was little doubt he meant what he said. Both men knew Zahl was dangerously unstable when the spirit took him.

"Take it easy," Finnegan said. "Nobody's trying to defy you here. We're simply pointing out how crazy it is, that's all."

"Not if we do what's expected. The guilt won't lie in our hands."

Finnegan felt like a man confronting an animal in its lair. There was no reasoning with Zahl. "Anything you say, Nelson. You're the boss."

Huddled inside the capsule, Garrett saw the satellite's orange sheath abruptly vanish. The effect was startling; one second, it was there; the next, there was nothing but blackness.

Garrett felt his senses tense. "They've switched off the Canby. They're preparing to fire the first missile."

There was little room to move or breathe in the tiny cabin as Lori engaged the maneuvering thrusters, propelling them upward. Garrett squinted through the viewing port, struggling to discern the satellite's outline.

"Listen to me," he said quietly. "When we get to the docking bay, we'll have to move fast. They will almost certainly be armed, so don't try to be gentlemen. Shoot first, and ask questions later. And remember—never squeeze your trigger without bracing your spine against a bulkhead. In zero gravity, it'll be like blasting off at the Cape."

Garrett could feel their nervousness and understood. They hadn't prepared for this. Danger, yes, that was an intricate part of the game—they'd taken an acceptable risk, simply by coming here. But armed combat in space seemed a strange and barbarous thing, and Garrett couldn't blame them for feeling apprehensive. Christ knew, he was scared himself.

The satellite's outline emerged at last. It floated above them in a grotesque welter of spidery tendrils and bristling antennae. Its windows gleamed in the darkness like a row of watchful eyes, giving it the appearance of a monstrous insect.

Garrett spotted someting pale in the portholes' glow, and leaned forward, narrowing his eyes. The contours merged into the form of a fat gray slug. It was the *Ulysses*, still locked in the docking bay.

"Open the hatch," Garrett ordered.

With a faint hum, the doors swung back.

"Into the MMUs. Move, dammit, we're running out of time."

They grappled the tiny units into position. Each knew his survival depended on split-second timing, and with a minimum of fuss, they segregated themselves two to a machine. Garrett clung grimly to Bamberger's backrest as the astronaut fired his gas nozzles, rising in a perpendicular line. Again, Garrett was conscious of the overwhelming silence. It was as if nothing existed out here, as if reality and everything connected with it had come unaccountably askew. He saw the two accompanying MMUs trailing in his wake and fixed his gaze on the underside of the massive platform above.

Bamberger struggled to guide his vehicle in an uninterrupted line, trying hard not to waste vital seconds in unnecessary maneuvering. The cold was an enervating force, though Garrett knew that when the sun came out, the heat would be devastating.

Above, the satellite solidified in the darkness, and Garrett saw the shuttle directly in front, its cargo bay open to lessen friction strain during its journey through space. Delicately, expertly, Bamberger guided his MMU in through the gaping hatch, and the others followed, heading toward the air-lock door.

Garrett made no attempt to remove his space suit. Releasing Bamberger's neck, he floated into the shuttle's interior, fumbling for his pistol in the zipped-up pouch at his thigh. He glanced back at Lori.

"Stay here," he ordered.

"No way. I'm coming with you."

"Don't be a fool. We need somebody to get the orbiter ready. When we leave this thing, we'll have to move like greased lightning. Without the Canby D-Five, NORAD will try to blast the *Stallion* out of the sky."

"You're right," Lori said, and headed toward the forward flight deck.

Garrett turned to the others. Clad in their bulky space suits, they looked like fantasy creatures from a forgotten nightmare. Despite the tension of the moment, he grinned as he waved them toward the transfer module. "Okay. Last man in buys the first round."

The bleeper sounded as Zahl was fingering the firing switches. He glanced up, frowning. A red warning light was flashing with urgent insistency.

"We have intruders on board," Zahl said.

Hentoff looked at him in astonishment. "That's impossible. The electrical system has probably short-circuited. It's a false alarm."

Zahl's face was bereft of emotion. "Switch the Canby D-Five back on," he ordered.

"You're calling off the launch?" Finnegan said hopefully.

"Just a postponement. We've got seven missiles to fire. I don't want unnecessary distractions."

Pushing himself up from his seat, he floated across the cabin to the compartment where the weapons were kept. He tossed two revolvers to Hentoff and Finnegan. The heavy magnums sailed gracefully through the gravity-free air.

Zahl pulled open the hatch leading to the lower deck. Below, a gridiron catwalk led across a metal well cluttered with boilers and instrument casings. The striplamps were diffused, and pools of shadow lay over the entire chamber, creating a confusing contrariety of light and shade.

At the far end of the walkway, Zahl detected a flicker of movement and squinted into the semidarkness. A figure emerged through the entrance hatch, eerie and unreal. Zahl saw another figure, identically clad, clutching a pistol in its thickly gloved fist. A feeling of unreality filled him. Where the hell had they come from? There had been no signals on the radar scan.

He watched the newcomers wriggling into the satellite chamber. "Delay them," he snapped.

Hentoff and Finnegan looked sick with fear. Zahl knew his companions had lost their stomach for the operation, would be happy to abort it if they could, but he was unflinching in his resolve. "Unless we fire now, we'll lose the window to Milan," he said. "Pin them down from the catwalk while I complete the missile launch alone."

Without waiting for their answer, he floated backward through the hatch, flicking the switch that governed the emergency sealing door. With a gentle, almost imperceptible purr, the heavy barrier slid into place.

Garrett saw the hatch click shut. Someone—the terrorist commander, probably—had locked himself inside the firing chamber. Already, their presence had been discovered.

As if in confirmation, a shot rang out, reverberating above the pipes and engine housings. The sound was like the hammer of God in the vaulted satellite well, and impulsively, Garrett and Malenov ducked behind a row of metal boilers. At their rear, Bamberger and Delaney, trapped inside the transfer module, returned fire through the entrance tunnel. The pandemonium was deafening. Each shot resounded a dozen times over, clattering backward and forward between the towering bulkheads.

Cautiously, Garrett peered around the boiler rim. Two men sat at the rear of the catwalk, their spines braced against the bulkhead. They commanded an excellent view of the entire area, including the narrow aperture that formed the only entrance opening. It was clear Bamberger and Delaney had little hope of gaining admittance as long as the defenders remained in position.

Garrett said to Malenov, "Unless we get inside that firing comartment within the next few minutes, we'll be too bloody late."

"What do you expect me to do, wave a magic wand?"

Their dilemma filled Garrett with frustration. The two terrorists, because of their superior position, were virtually untouchable from the lower deck. Though he could see their outlines, the metal railings presented a perfect body shield. It would take a miracle to score a hit against such difficult targets.

"They've got us pinned down. We can't move one bloody way or the other."

Malenov looked thoughtfully at the ceiling where a series of metal pipes ran like spaghetti across the entire area. Swiftly, he calculated angles and deflections. "Aim for the second coupling from the wall. If we hit the underside of the curve just right, maybe the bullets will ricochet."

"By Christ, Sergei, it's worth a try."

Garrett squeezed backward, ramming himself hard against the boiler. Gripping his pistol at arm's length, he took careful aim at the metal coupling above. It was only partially visible through the confusion of light and shade.

At his side, Malenov was also sighting his barrel. "Ready?" Garrett nodded.

Malenov took a deep breath. *"Now!"*

The roar was deafening as side by side they laid down a blistering barrage of fire. Flame spurts lanced the semidarkness, and bullets pinged against the metal pipe casing. Garrett could hear the ricochets whirring above them like deadly insects, the fusilade rolling thunderously across the empty chamber.

A cry rang out. Glancing between the boilders, Garrett saw a man topple from the catwalk, clutching his lower stomach. Wriggling and squirming, he floated inelegantly downward, a scarlet tendril of blood trailing on the microgravity air. As he reached the deck, his body began to rise again, his limbs motionless this time. Garrett felt a grim sense of satisfaction.

There was a frantic scuttling as the man's companion slithered along the catwalk, distancing himself from the underbelly of the pipe. They would not be so lucky a second time.

From his superior vantage point, the lone defender could hold off an entire regiment, at least long enough for his commander to carry out the missile launch.

Garrett studied the emergency door above. It looked heavy and impenetrable—electronically operated, no doubt; they would find little joy that way.

Then his eyes narrowed as he spotted a metal hatch cover on the opposite side of the facilities well. A warning sign blazoned out the words: *Do Not Enter Launch Tube While Missile in Position.*

Quickly, he glanced around. On the wall behind him, a

fireman's ax lay inside a glass container case next to a fire extinguisher. Garrett leaned up, smashing the cover with his boots. Malenov stared in astonishment as he tugged the extinguisher from its rack.

"What are you doing?"

"See that air-lock hatch?" Garrett said, jamming the ax against the boiler at his feet.

"I see it."

"It's the maintenance entrance to the launch tube. The missile has to be shifted into position electronically. If I can get through before that maniac completes his firing circuit, maybe I can knock it out of commission."

"How?"

Garrett patted the fire extinguisher. "By squirting foam through the missile's ventilator grills."

"What good will that do, for God's sake?"

"With luck, it might stop the homing computer. That computer has to make thousands of calculations a minute to get its warhead on a precise target. Just one second in cutoff velocity can cause a deviation of ten to fifteen miles. The guidance antennae lie directly behind the grate openings. If I can clog them up, there's just a chance the system will misfire."

"You're crazy."

"Maybe. But those Gnooches have been lying around this platform for over fourteen years. They were temperamental at the best of times. It shouldn't take much to knock them off-balance. Maybe we can deflect the warhead away from a populated area."

"If you're still in that tube when they press the launch button, you'll be burned to a crisp."

"Not if I move fast. That's a Smith & Wesson our friend is using. I haven't seen him reloading, have you? Maybe he came out of that firing chamber in such a hurry he forgot to bring any spare cartridges. If that's the case, he's only got three shots left."

"Three or twenty, what's the difference? The minute you move into the open, the bastard will blow your brains out."

"I'm going to draw his fire. Think you can keep his head down, Sergei, if I offer myself as a target? Not too vigorously, you understand. I want him to shoot. I just don't want him to hit what he's aiming at."

Malenov eased back against the boiler and balanced his pistol across his forearm. "Go ahead."

Garrett laid his own weapon on the deck at Malenov's side, ramming it beneath the metal cover.

"You may need this. I don't want you running out of ammunition while that son of a bitch is drawing a bead on me."

He placed the fireman's ax beside it. "This too."

Clipping the extinguisher to the metal ring on his EMU suit, he stretched out on his belly, and gripping the ground rail as an anchor, wriggled along the line of heavy boilers. The foam-packed tube seemed light as a feather in the gravity-free atmosphere, but he could feel his weightlessness plucking him away from the deck. It was a weird sensation, like trying to crawl underwater.

When he reached the end of the row, he paused, filling his lungs with air. A spiral of metal pipes sprang from the catwalk directly ahead. The distance between them was approximately seven feet, an easy jump in normal circumstances, but in zero gravity, Garrett knew it would take several seconds to span that innocuous little chasm.

Well, he thought, what are you waiting for? Applause? Are you showing off to Malenov, proving you've still got what it takes? You poor sad bastard, either move now, or forget the whole crazy notion.

Sucking in his breath, he lunged toward the sanctuary of the pipes, his body moving with desperate lethargic slowness.

Two shots rang out as he dragged himself into cover. The first came from Malenov, the second from the terrorist. The din echoed eerily inside the vaulted cabin. One down, Garrett thought, two to go.

Still clutching the fire extinguisher, he glanced around for another refuge. Beneath the walkway lay a narrow channel choked with electrical cables. If he could reach it, he would be effectively hidden from the sniper above.

Garrett estimated the distance. Five feet. Slightly less than the area he had just covered, but with one slight difference. In his first leap, he'd had the advantage of surprise. Now the man was watching and waiting.

Garrett gritted his teeth, hoping to God Malenov was on his toes. He thrust himself off, sailing crazily through the air. He saw the conduit looming up and reached out, grasping the cables. Shots rang out as he dragged himself, panting, into the sunken sanctuary. His body was trembling, and a terrible sickness had gathered in his stomach. He'd made it unharmed, he realized with relief. But he still had one more shot to go.

Hentoff sat on the catwalk, the revolver clasped in his sweaty palms. He watched the cable conduit where the intruder had disappeared. Hentoff's brain couldn't begin to assimilate what was happening here—where the attackers had come from, how they'd managed to infiltrate the satellite at such an impossible distance from Earth, was beyond his understanding. All he knew was that he was afraid.

He could see Finnegan's body drifting beneath the ceiling. Blood dripped from his companion's wound, but it did not fall to the deck; instead, it weaved and undulated like the tendrils of some macabre sea anemone.

Hentoff had never really known Finnegan. It would have been an exaggeration to call the two men friends, but he felt a smoldering resentment at the thought of Finnegan's death. Gazing down at the narrow ditch where he knew the intruder lay hidden, his hatred, fueled by fear, began to find a focal point. If Hentoff was destined to die, then as God was his witness, he would take the stranger with him.

Hentoff sucked in his breath as a thought entered his mind. He had been firing impulsively, terror guiding his instincts, his hand assuming a life of its own. Now he had only one round left. He felt even more isolated and abandoned. Zahl had vanished, and the attackers below were deliberately drawing his fire, counting his shots, waiting for the final squeeze of the trigger when they could rush his position and finish him off.

Hentoff looked around. Finnegan's revolver floated just above the catwalk. Finnegan had dropped it when the bullet caught him in the stomach. Hentoff snatched it and quickly checked the chambers. Three cartridges still in position. Time now to use his head. Catch the bastards at their own game.

Tucking the revolver in his lap, he balanced his own weapon across his forearm and deliberately loosed the final shot. For a moment, nothing happened. Then, to Hentoff's amusement, a figure rose from the cable trough and sailed through the air.

Hentoff's fear had gone now, replaced by the bitter humor of the moment. At this range, he couldn't miss.

Picking up Finnegan's revolver, he pulled back the hammer and took careful aim at the intruder's neck.

Crouching behind the boilers, Malenov spotted Hentoff's reflection in the polished fanlight above. The man had eased out of his original position and was leaning forward with both arms extended, his pistol fixed on Garrett.

Malenov thrust down with all his strength, his muscles bulging as he drove out with his legs, soaring into the air. He was conscious that he was rising more quickly than prudence demanded, knowing he would hit the ceiling with the impact of a cannonball, pushing the thought from his mind as he concentrated on what he had to do.

He saw Garrett in his space suit, tearing at the hatch-cover. He saw the catwalk where the terrorist crouched, protected from below by the metal railings. He saw the man gaze up at him, his features stricken with shock and astonishment. Then Malenov tilted forward, panting deep in his chest as he brought up his pistol.

The terrorist switched aim, swinging his weapon in a ponderous sideways arc, realizing he would never complete the motion in time, but doing it anyway, as if in the final seconds of his life, he wanted to offer a gesture of protest and defiance.

Malenov fired instinctively and saw the man's face vanish in a welter of blood. The recoil sent Malenov spinning backward, his shoulder catching the ventilation pipes. The impact was jarring, disorienting, and suddenly he was careening in the opposite direction, bouncing between the bulkheads like a billiard ball.

Garrett squirmed through the entrance hatch below.

# TWENTY-THREE

The lid slammed shut above Garrett's head, and the launch tube closed around him with a suffocating blackness. He was trembling all over, and sweat droplets, free from gravity, floated between his body and the EMU suit's inner lining. He longed to quit, to settle back and leave the responsibility to someone else, but he couldn't. In a few seconds, the unknown man in the missile chamber would complete the firing sequence and press the fatal button. When the Gnooche's rockets ignited, this slender tunnel would become a raging inferno.

He switched on his helmet light. The beam carved an elongated cone through the inky darkness, and he saw the dark curve of the missile's hull confronting him like an alien presence. Its bland shell looked deceptively innocuous, but Garrett's genitals moved in an involuntary spasm as he thought of the terrible destructive power encapsulated within its metal skin.

Floating downward, he clanged against the missile's tail fin, flinching as if his clumsiness might inadvertently detonate the warhead. There was just enough room to squeeze between the shiny casing and the outer wall. Hooking the fire extingusher under his arm, Garrett wriggled along the missile's length.

He found what he was looking for—a tiny ventilator grill in the side of the hull—and swiveled the extinguisher into position, thrusting its nozzle through the minuscule aperture.

Then he thumped the triggering plunger with his fist. With a hiss, foam spurted into the missile's interior, clinging like snow to everything in sight. Damp and fluffy, the substance formed a thick white fur over the Gnooche's inner workings, gradually building up on itself till it began to ooze back through the tiny openings.

When he was satisfied the sensor rods were suitably congealed, he wriggled toward the grill on the opposite side, a ribbon of foam trailing behind him like carnival bunting. Garrett jammed the nozzle into the second aperture and sprayed again.

He tried not to think about how long the process was taking. Time had no meaning—that was the message he kept forcing into his head. He didn't give a damn about time because if this little gambit didn't work, time for him would cease to exist. Perspiration was pouring off him now, but still the extinguisher spewed. Then the hissing sound grew stronger as the tube began to empty.

He switched off the pulsing jet and dragged himself across the curved hull, wriggled toward the exit hatch. Still attached to his EMU suit, the fire extinguisher clattered along behind him. A terrible chill seized Garrett as he saw that the air-lock lid had dropped back into position. The heavy cover confronted him mockingly. Though he pushed with all his might, its insulated undersurface remained stubbornly and intransigently in place.

There was no emergency handle to operate the security lock from the inside, and Garrett groaned as he realized the hopelessness of his position.

He was trapped.

In a fever of impatience, Zahl went through the final stages of the firing operation. It had been a long laborious job, carrying out the prelaunch priming sequence alone. For security purposes, the process had been designed for a three-man team operating in unison, and he had been obliged to float from one section of the compartment to another, flicking switches, inserting release keys, going through the motions like a man demented, his actions further hampered by the gravity-free atmosphere.

Through it all, he had been painfully conscious of the gunfight raging in the satellite well outside. The shooting had stopped now, and someone was hammering furiously at the entrance hatch. Zahl ignored that, forcing his attention on the myriad intricacies of the task in hand. It was the moment of culmination. He switched off the Canby D-5 defense shield, knowing that the satellite, deprived of its electronic armor, was dangerously vulnerable and exposed.

Zahl gazed out at the earth. In another minute, he would dispatch his angel of death. He felt no sense of uneasiness at the thought, only a fierce, exhilirating excitement.

His muscles tensed as he turned toward the launch switch.

Garrett hammered wildly against the underside of the escape hatch, making little impact. The launch tube had been soundproofed and bulwarked to protect the satellite's occupants, and he realized there was little hope of Malenov hearing him through the reinforced deck layers above. He had tried using his acoustic microphone, but that too had been silenced by the impenetrable walls. His only hope was to get out through the funnel's mouth before blast-off.

His light slid along the missile's shell. He could see the opening beckoning invitingly barely thirty feet away, but hampered by the absence of gravity, could he cover the distance in time?

Taking a deep breath, he moved backward, squirming into the narrow space between the rocket's curve and the launch-tube bulkhead. It was a tight, suffocating squeeze. There was nothing to grip, and he had to slide inch by inch along the hull, the fire extinguisher dragging remorselessly in his wake. Sweat streamed from his skin, floating in droplets inside his helmet dome as he concentrated on shortening the distance to the exit.

The missile's nose fin was directly in front, and he seized it, pulling as hard as he could, propelling his body toward the waiting aperture. He watched the missile's blunt nose float by under his helmet, its muzzle concealed by a disklike weather cover with mounting brackets indexed at ninety degrees around the hull.

Then the shaft seemed to widen, and Garrett hurtled helplessly through the opening, rolling over and over into space. Terror gripped him. He had pulled too hard and was somersaulting out of the launch tube. It was too late to clutch at life-saving projections.

The satellite reared above him, monstrous and grotesque. It

was only inches away, its tentacles beckoning, but without an MMU unit, he had no way of reaching it and no way of stabilizing his momentum. His body tumbled over and over, the platform flashing dizzily by. He saw the solar panels etched against the void, the porthole windows framing the module's living quarters, the vehicle docking bay where the shuttlecraft lay locked in position, its hatch covers open like the wings of a nestling dragonfly.

He was soaring upward, his impetus gradually slackening as the initial force of his thrust began to dissipate. I'm stuck, he thought. No way out.

His mind worked fast, pushing the ironies aside. If he was going to get out of this, he had to move now, this instant. No delays, no indecisions. Somehow he had to halt his momentum and steer himself back to the satellite. But how? There was nothing of substance to give him thrust.

Then something bumped against his shoulder, and Garrett felt a sliver of hope. It was the fire extinguisher, still clipped to his EMU suit. In the launch tube, the foam had practically emptied, but there might be just enough pressure left in the gas cartridge to propel him back to safety.

He looked down at the hovering satellite. One slender communication antenna trailed like a teasing finger almost directly in his path. If he could reach it, perhaps he could drag himself down to the accommodation module.

Throat dry, Garrett tugged the extinguisher against his body, clutching the triggering mechanism in his left glove. Gritting his teeth, he pressed the tiny plunger. For a moment, nothing happened. Then, with a hiccuping splutter, a jet of foam shot like a party streamer into the emptiness in front. He felt its recoil driving him backward.

He fixed his eyes on the approching antenna rod, measuring distance, timing, velocity. Reaching out, he felt his fingers clasp the metal girder and his body ceased tumbling, swinging sharply into alignment. Clutching his precarious handhold, he wrapped his legs around the elongated arm, and unclipping the fire extinguisher, let it drift off into space.

A tremor ran through the satellite's structure like the first warning of an impending earthquake. Smoke belched from the launch tube's mouth, and like a baby whale emerging from its mother's womb, the Gnooche missile soared through a halo of shimmering flame, its sleek body wreathed in fumes.

Clinging to his unstable refuge, Garrett watched as the terrible projectile turned implacably toward Earth.

Zahl watched the receding missile, feeling damp and drained. The banging on the entrance hatch brought him back to his senses. He heard the echo of splintering metal, and glancing over his shoulder, saw the lid buckling inward, a ragged tear appearing in its upper left-hand corner. Between the jagged edges, he spotted a crazed figure brandishing a fireman's ax.

Zahl reached for his revolver, his fingers closing on the ribbed Bakelite handle. Twisting sideways, he soared into the air, his hand struggling to bring his target into alignment. A spurt of flame lanced from the outside catwalk, and Zahl felt a paralyzing blow in the center of his chest. He rocketed backward, hitting the console panel with a stultifying force. As his body ricocheted, he saw suited figures coming through the ragged aperture. Then his vision clouded, and he drifted into the arms of death.

Garrett clung to the satellite arm. The missile flared in the darkness, its powerful thrusters pulsing. The rocket itself was practically invisible, etched against the earth's curve. Only the crimson glow of its booster rockets could be seen by the naked eye.

Apprehension gathered within Garrett. The missile seemed to be proceeding unerringly on course. Would it strike its target, or would his desperate sabotage bear fruit?

He clung grimly to his precarious perch. Against the violet haze of the earth's atmosphere, the Gnooche's tail fumes had become little more than a pinpoint of light. Smoke rings hung in its wake, forming a miniscule funnel across the sky.

Then Garrett blinked. The light had disappeared. Like an aircraft looping the loop, the missile was banking steeply, its blunt nose curving backward in a spectacular arc. Now he could clearly see the hull framed against the earth in a profile of exquisite beauty, its boosters belching flame as it sailed into an immaculate upward roll. Dry-mouthed, he watched the blunt nose swing toward him, its contours diminished now, its flanks forming a perfect sphere, smoke bordering them like wispy lace. The extinguisher foam had done the trick, all right, but the missile, instead of deviating, was now heading back toward the *Stallion*. Unless a miracle happened, the satellite, lying directly in its path, would be blasted into oblivion.

Garrett thought quickly. If Malenov turned on the Canby D-5, it might disable the warhead, but perched on the antenna arm, he would be torn apart. Then he remembered Lori sitting in the docking bay.

He spoke into his acoustic microphone, hoping to God that now he was clear of the launch tube, he might elicit some response.

Malenov lowered the fireman's ax and gazed with satisfaction at the mangled weapon console. He had smashed it to a pulp, shattering gauges and condensers alike. Severed cables sprouted incongruously from the tangled wreckage. Behind Malenov, Bamberger and Delaney surveyed the devastation with approval. The body of the terrorist floated against the ceiling above.

Malenov heard a crackling in his helmet, then Garrett's voice echoing earnestly in his ear. "Sergei, Sergei, can you hear me?"

"What is it?" Malenov said.

"Switch on the Canby D-Five."

"The Canby? Why, for God's sake?"

"Don't argue, Sergei, just do it."

"I can't," Malenov told him.

"What do you mean, can't?"

"I've just smashed the instrument panel."

"You've done *what*?" Garrett's voice was strangled with fury. "Sergei, that bloody missile's done a complete U-turn, and it's bearing down on us like the clappers. Without the defense shield, we're a sitting duck. In another minute, that warhead is going to blow this whole bloody erector set into kingdom come."

On the shuttle flight deck, Lori saw the missile approaching through the rear viewing port. When it hit the satellite, the entire platform would be vaporized in a spasm of unimaginable heat. She had to alter their position, use the orbiter's maneuvering engines to push to *Stallion* out of the missile's path.

She fed the instructions into the digital autopilot, pressing the vapor isol switch and the OHMS engine lever. On the computer keyboard, she pushed the Exec button to begin the countdown. The panel lit up, and the bulkheads trembled as the maneuvering engines mounted on each side of the fuselage flared suddenly into life.

Locked firmly in the docking bay, the shuttle remained depressingly still. Move, you bastard, she urged silently.

The vehicle shuddered, and she heard the clatter of objects breaking loose from their bindings as it pushed gamely against the satellite's massive framework.

Then slowly, imperceptibly, she felt the spacecraft shift. Sweat beaded her skin as she studied the gauges. She hadn't been imagining things—the shuttle was inching forward, propelling the platform in front of it.

Still clinging doggedly to the antenna arm, Garrett watched the missile skim harmlessly by. With remarkable presence of mind, Lori had used the shuttle to ease the satellite out of the projectile's way. Now the deadly payload was speeding into the icy vacuum of space.

Garrett watched it soar into the distance. It looked elegant in retreat, and he admired its symmetry as it sped toward the sun, glad now of the risk he had taken, glad that his skin-crawling moments in that suffocating coffin had proved so effective. A chance in a million, it had been, the extinguisher foam gumming up the guidance antennae, but it had worked like a dream, and he felt idiotically satisfied with himself.

His euphoria was short-lived, however, when he realized the missile was heading directly for the twin *Mayflower* laboratory satellites. There could be no sudden reprieve from that. Collision was a certainty, and though the distance was too immense to pose any appreciable threat, the explosion's electromagnetic pulses would, he knew, blast him clear of his flimsy perch. He had to get back to the accommodation module. He had to get under cover.

Garrett pulled himself down the extended metal column, grasping the narrow girders. He tried not to move too quickly, tried to ensure that his grip was secure before easing onto the next metal rung. It was a weird sensation, his limbs and torso threatening at every second to float off like a carnival balloon. He could see the main body of the satellite directly below, and slightly to his right, the open cargo hatches of the *Ulysses* still locked in its docking bay. The orbiter offered the closest avenue of escape, and he switched direction as he approached the satellite's core.

The space around him was lightening rapidly. The missile was almost lost to sight now. All he could see was the miniscule pinprick of its fiery thrusters. Soon it would reach its target, and the heavens would erupt.

Garrett moved with agonizing slowness; it wasn't so hard, really, as long as he had the heart and lungs for it, as long as he didn't lose his head, but he wished to God he could go faster.

The sunlight grew brighter, but Garrett ignored the heat beginning to sear his EMU suit's outer lining, concentrating instead on the slow, torturous downward haul. Never in his life had he known anything so strenuous. He was breathing hard, his heart hammering wildly against his rib cage. Reaching the shuttle's cargo bay, he dragged himself into the air lock with barely a second to spare.

As he slid shut the titanium hatch, the sky was lit by a blaze of demonic light.

The satellite cabin seemed to flare into life. Everything turned white, the details vanishing in a splurge of blinding incandescence, and Malenov closed his eyes, unable to believe his senses.

Then something rammed the platform with a stupefying force. Panels creaked and bulkheads shuddered as the great contraption turned over and over in a bewildering blur.

Malenov and the crew floated helplessly through the air, banging into each other as they were flung like confetti from one end of the compartment to the other. Out of control, the satellite whirled like a spinning top.

Crashing into the terrorist's bloodied corpse, Malenov pushed it away. Dimly through the viewing ports, he saw the earth's curve, lit by the rays of the emerging sun, flitting by dizzily in a stunning kaleidoscope of color. A great pall of smoke spread across the sky like a gigantic locust swarm.

The platform's elongated arms creaked and groaned under the strain, and Malenov seized one of the severed instrument cables, clinging to it fiercely as his body streamed outward. With a chill of horror, he realized what was happening.

The satellite, with six nuclear warheads on board, was being dragged inexorably into the earth's atmosphere.

\* \* \*

On the shuttle's flight deck, Lori struggled to fasten her safety harness, confused by the sudden switch in circumstances. Though she'd managed to ease out of the missile's flight path, the explosion's reverberations had started the satellite cartwheeling crazily.

Holding hard to the pilot seat, she managed to buckle the canvas belt as someone tumbled into the cabin behind her. It was Garrett.

"Fire the OHMS engines," he yelled.

"What for? We're ready for atmospheric reentry."

"We've got to stabilize the satellite first."

"To hell with the satellite. Let the satellite look after itself."

"We can't. It's being sucked in by the earth's gravitational pull."

"What?"

Through the viewing port, she saw the earth's curve looming terrifyingly close. Biting her lip, she leaned forward and began to operate the instrument console.

Deep in NORAD's Cheyenne Mountain, General Kincaid watched the monitor screens worriedly. For almost four hours, his missile crews had been standing by to intercept the incoming warhead. Now, to the general's consternation and alarm, he noticed the satellite blip beginning to move. Steadily and unmistakably, it was drifting toward the upper stratosphere. He had seen the flash of the earlier detonation, but the impact had taken place many miles from the *Devil's Stallion*. Was it possible its pulses had pushed the platform out of orbit?

"Sir?" The voice of the radar operator made Kincaid jump.

"The satellite is being pulled into the earth's gravity field," the man announced, confirming the general's worst suspicions.

"How many missiles are still on board?" Kincaid asked, already knowing the answer.

"Six, sir."

Jesus, Kincaid thought, this was a bigger threat than anyone had bargained for. As the satellite built up kinetic energy, it would flare into a monstrous ball of flame, and the effect of six exploding nuclear warheads directly above the earth's surface would be unimaginable.

"Is the defense shield still activated?"

"Negative, sir. The Canby D-Five has been disengaged for almost twenty minutes now."

Kincaid felt a flicker of hope stirring in his chest. He still had a chance if he acted quickly.

His palms felt damp as he turned to the weapon crew. "Prepare the missiles for firing," he ordered. "We're going to blast that satellite out of the sky."

The maneuvering engines roared in Lori Madden's ears. Gradually, she felt the satellite stabilizing. It was not a sudden process, but a slow, torturous disengagement, and tears of relief blurred her eyes. For the second time, the shuttle's thrust had pushed the platform back into orbit.

Garrett reached out, gently squeezed her shoulder. "Good girl. I think you've done it."

Malenov felt the satellite settling and cautiously released his hold on the severed cable. Hovering motionless, he watched the cabin swivel into focus. Bamberger and Delaney were bruised and battered from the pounding they'd received against the bulkheads.

"We've stopped," Bamberger muttered, his voice distorted.

Through the shaded face mask, Malenov saw the astronaut's lips swollen with blood.

"Are you all right?"

Bamberger ran his hands across his upper torso. "Smashed my skull against the bulkhead, but nothing's broken as far as I can tell."

"Lucky it was only your head," Delaney commented dryly.

Garrett's voice came over the acoustic loudspeaker. "Get back to the shuttle. We're about to commence the deorbit burn for atmospheric reentry."

"Give us a breather to pull ourselves together," Delaney protested. "We've taken a hell of a hammering here."

"Forget the breather," Garrett said tensely. "Our defense shield has been out of commission for almost twenty minutes, and you know what that means. The boys at Cheyenne Mountain are probably lining us up in their sights at this very moment."

# TWENTY-FOUR

Sitting in the police van, Wesker looked up as Lieutenant Sal Gassner entered through the rear door. "Any word yet?"

"Nothing," Gassner said.

Wesker slammed the side of the vehicle with his fist. "How much longer do we have to wait?"

For almost two hours, his men had been sitting outside General Connel's house, awaiting the go-ahead from the secretary of defense.

Lieutenant Gassner said, "You do realize that sooner or later, those security guards on the gate are going to get suspicious?"

"Why don't you tell that to David Richner?"

Wesker paused as the door opened, and a young detective looked in, blinking as his eyes adjusted to the dimmed lighting.

"Mr. Wesker?"

"That's me."

"Call for you on the automobile phone, sir. It's the secretary of defense."

Wesker glanced at Lieutenant Gassner and hurried to one of the stationary cars where a uniformed patrolman stood waiting with the telephone. His fingers were trembling as he took the receiver.

"Louis?" Richner's voice sounded strangely distorted.

"Mr. Secretary?"

"It's go for broke. You have the President's blessing."

Wesker's senses tightened. "Thank God for that," he said. "We're on our way, Mr. Secretary."

Thrusting the car phone into the startled patrolman's hand, he ran back to the radio van as Lieutenant Gassner emerged into the sunlight. "Are your men all set?"

"Just waiting for the signal," Gassner answered.

Tugging his pistol from its holster, Wesker checked its firing mechanism, and gestured fiercely across the road. "Then let's take them."

Lori eased the shuttle out of the docking bay. The massive satellite hovered above them, no longer obscured by darkness but lit by the blinding rays of the sun. Spindly and shapeless, it seemed to spread in all directions like the filaments of some grotesque protoplasm.

"Going for OHMs burn." Her fingers flicked across the instrument panel.

The cabin shuddered as the orbital maneuvering engines flared into life, slowing the shuttle's velocity and momentum. For almost three minutes, they hung suspended, looking out at the diminishing outline of the receding space platform, then Lori turned the shuttle over so that its nose was pointing directly toward the earth. The next maneuver would be the trickiest of all. They had to penetrate the atmosphere at precisely the right angle to prevent the vehicle blazing into a cinder.

"Entry interface," she declared grimly, trying to hide the nervousness in her voice. Everything depended on split-second timing.

"How about a window into the atmosphere?" Garrett demanded. "Shouldn't you check the computer?"

"Forget the computer," Lori answered calmly. "If that satellite blows before we clear the target area, the entire orbiter will go up in smoke. We'll just have to touch down where we can."

In the War Room, General Kincaid watched the signatures separate. Now there were two blips, one large and motionless, the other progressing slowly but determinedly toward the right-hand section of the monitor screen.

"Sir," the radar observer announced, "the shuttle has left the satellite and is approaching the earth's atmosphere."

General Kincaid breathed deeply, filling his lungs with air. Like rats, the terrorists were deserting their sinking ship.

"Prepare to fire," he commanded.

It seemed like nothing at first, a faint, almost indiscernible hissing sound, then the noise grew louder, became a low muffled roar. Garrett glanced at the g-meter. The needle was rising. They were reentering the atmosphere. The operation would be delicate, he knew. As the orbiter cannonballed against the air, the resulting friction would build up incredible heat, the shuttle's kinetic energy intensifying to temperatures of 2,500 degrees Fahrenheit. Their beveled black underbelly, coated with silica-fiber tiles, should offer protection against the blazing exterior but only if Lori could maneuver them in at precisely the right angle.

Bamberger and Delaney, seated at Lori's side, sped through the deorbit, entry, and landing checklist compiled from cue cards in the flight data file.

"Instruments show pressure of ten pounds per square foot," Bamberger said. "Deactivating roll thrusters. Elevons will now control roll."

"Pressure increasing," Delaney announced. "Pitch thrusters deactivating. Elevons now control pitch. It's up to you, Lori. Take her home."

Lori handled the manual control, little more than a pilot stick with pedals operating the rudder for yaw. Under normal circumstances, Lori would have fed the deorbit and landing programs into the orbiter computers, leaving the tricky homeward journey to the autopilot, but so abrupt had been their departure, so impromptu their descent, she had taken the responsibility entirely upon herself.

Garrett felt a subtle pride in her as she prepared for the precarious landing operation. She'd come through like a veteran.

He grimaced as his limbs grew steadily heavier. His body was losing its weightlessness, and though he experienced no actual discomfort, the feeling was hardly a pleasant one.

The roar of the slipstream reached an ear-shattering intensity, and through the viewing ports, Garrett saw their nose cone beginning to glow.

Bamberger spoke from the radar screen, shouting to make himself heard over the acoustic microphone. "We've got a cluster of signatures approaching."

Garrett felt his heartbeat quicken. "Missiles?"

"Looks like. Heading for the satellite. Cheyenne Mountain, probably."

"How long before contact?"

"I'd say almost immediate," Bamberger answered.

"Brace yourselves," Garrett bellowed, checking his seat straps.

The blast, when it came, felt as if the sun itself had exploded. A core of light pulsed outward to envelop them completely. So intense was its glare that for a moment it drained all color from the cabin's interior. Even through Garrett's sun visor, everything around him—the bulkhead, the instrument panel, the astronauts themselves—blended into a featureless magnesiumlike canescence.

Then the impact hit them like a meteor blast. There was a thunderous roar, and suddenly they were spinning through the stratosphere. Lori struggled to realign the handset. Through the viewing port, Garrett saw their fuselage sheathed in flame.

"Hold her steady," Delaney shouted.

Lori's voice was barely audible. "I can't."

"Of course you can. Hang on to the handset."

"It's jerking too hard. I'm losing my grip."

"Hold it, Lori, hold it. Keep it under control. Bring her nose up and belly-flap in on your thermal tiles. Try and poise her at thirty degrees."

The shuttle was completely wrapped in flame now. It was impossible to see anything through the viewing ports but fire.

"We're burning up," Delaney yelled. "Lift the nose, lift the nose. You've got to bring her in between twenty-eight and thirty-eight degrees."

Lori sobbed, wrestling with the handset as the orbiter went into a dizzy sideways roll. Garrett saw flames streaming to the left as their vehicle slewed across the sky. They were somersaulting. He glanced at the g-meter. Their deceleration had reached a force of 1.7.

"Bring her up, Lori, bring her up," Garrett said.

"I can't!" she cried.

"Sure you can. You can hold her if you really try. Use the pedals and get her altitude steady."

"She won't stop rolling—damn!"

"Use the pedals."

He understood the terror she was going through, tried to will confidence into her as she pumped desperately at the rudder, her thighs working in unison. Garrett held his breath, watched the fire licking at the heat-sealed windows. Then the vehicle slowly stabilized.

Good girl. She'd done it.

"Turn off the roll thrusters and pitch thrusters," Delaney said. "And move the speed-brake handle back to one hundred degrees."

Concentrating intensely, Lori swiveled the great machine into a precise reentry angle. The roar steadied, the flames flickered into a white-hot glow, and a cheer broke from the astronauts.

The Mission Control, Leonard Brody studied the multiplexer screens, frowning. He had seen the destruction of the satellite on the monitor set, but now a tiny blip was rapidly approaching earth.

Deputy Controller Pat Traumont stood at Brody's side, trying to make sense of the unfamiliar readings. "What the hell is going on, Leo?"

"It's the *Ulysses*," Brody explained. "It's reentering the atmosphere."

"But how in Christ's name did those bastards get off the satellite before it exploded?"

"Maybe they were already on their way."

"What are we going to do, Leo?"

Brody considered quickly. "Get me a fix on their landing spot," he ordered.

Traumont hurried to one of the computers and ran his fingers expertly over the keys. Leaning forward to examine the readings, he scribbled something on a piece of paper and pushed it to Brody across the desk. "Looks like the Mediterranean," he said.

Brody glanced quickly at the paper. "You're sure the longitude and lattitude are correct?"

"Give or take a couple of degrees. That's what the telemetry signals say."

Brody picked up the telephone and punched out a number.

His eyes were tense as he gazed at Traumont over the row of monitor sets.

"We'd better notify Washington," he said.

"It's the secretary of defense, Mr. President."

Lawrence Clayman looked up from his desk as David Richner was ushered into the Oval Office. Richner's face was flushed, his eyes gleaming with excitement.

"The terrorists have reentered the atmosphere," he said. "According to NASA's calculations, they're scheduled to splash down in the Mediterranean in approximately forty minutes' time."

The President had been on the point of drafting a congratulatory letter to General Kincaid at Cheyenne Mountain. "Do we have their position?"

"It's right here, Mr. President."

Richner placed a slip of paper on the President's desk. Clayman wasn't a vindictive man, he reasoned, not in the real sense, but men who could perpetrate nuclear blackmail were not to be taken lightly. What they'd accomplished once they could easily attempt again. The world required justice in this case.

He came to a quick decision. "We have a presence in the Med, David. The aircraft carrier *Zuni*."

"That's correct, sir."

Clayman handed back the paper. "I want you to contact the commander. Make it Operation Immediate."

"And?" Richner looked expectant.

"Tell him to blow that shuttle apart," President Clayman said.

Captain John Lennox strode into the $800-million Command and Control room on the U.S. aircraft carrier *Zuni*. In the subdued lighting, his combat team was already in position, assimilating data and readying their electronic weapons of war. No one spoke as the captain entered.

Lennox looked at Lieutenant Rob MacKenna. "Where's the message?"

MacKenna showed it to the captain.

"You're sure this is correct?"

"Yes, sir."

"No miscalculations in the decoding?"

"None, sir."

"God-*damn*."

Lennox rubbed his forehead with his fingers. He could scarcely believe the substance of what he was reading. Shoot down a NASA shuttle? It seemed unthinkable.

"I'm seeking confirmation," he announced to no one in particular, crossing the cabin to the radio console.

The query took thirty seconds to transmit, another thirty to corroborate. Its authenticity was indisputable. A secret code sign settled the last of Lennox's doubts. "Jesus," he whispered under his breath.

He straightened from the radio console and delivered the order to attack.

Lieutenant Mitch Schulman heard the sound of the alarm bell, and struggled slowly into consciousness. In the next bunk, Lieutenant Tom Rudd was sitting up, blinking in confusion. "What the hell is that?"

"Action stations," Schulman muttered. "I can't believe it. Jesus, we came off watch barely an hour ago."

"Maybe it's an exercise," Rudd said. "The old man testing to see if we're on our toes."

There was a clatter of footsteps in the companionway outside, then the door burst open, and Lieutenant Tank Anaka tumbled in. Anaka's tunic was open to the waist, his shirttails flapping. "What's up with you guys? Got your ears plugged with sealing wax?"

"What is it, Tank?" Schulman demanded. "Another balloon drifted into the old man's personal airspace?"

"Balloon, hell. We're going into action."

The two lieutenants stared at him. "Action? Who's the target, for Chrissake?"

"They'll give us that when the squadron's rolling. Right now, you'd better get your asses out of the sack."

Schulman and Rudd scrambled from their bunks and into their flying suits. Fifty seconds later, they were sprinting across the flight deck toward their waiting aircraft. In a daze, Schulman plugged in his g-suit attachment and fixed his torso harness to the parachute clips behind his ejection seat. At a signal from the crew chief, he started up his powerful Roffe and Schellbach engines, the roar of the squadron almost shattering his eardrums. The radio blared, giving him his flight-course coordinates, and he entered them into his navigational system.

"What is this?" he exclaimed into the transmitter mike. "Some kind of joke?"

"It's no joke, Lieutenant. That's the order."

"A shuttle? Why, for Chrissake?"

"Ours not to reason why, good buddy. Just get it done."

"God Almighty," Schulman said.

The deck crew, wearing heavy earmuffs, hand-signaled him into position, and he pushed his throttle forward, sending his aircraft thundering down the carrier runway. As he soared into the air, he slotted into formation and set out grimly on his mission.

# TWENTY-FIVE

Malenov was the first to spot the signatures on the radar scanner. After conducting several banking maneuvers to reduce the velocity of their descent, Lori was preparing for the delicate process of touchdown. The computer display screens, the CRTs, showed their approximate landing point to be somewhere in the Mediterranean, just north of the Morroccan coast, but now the radar blips indicated a new problem.

Malenov counted seven, approaching swiftly from the west. "We've got visitors," he said into his helmet microphone.

Garrett examined the signatures over Malenov's shoulder, a feeling of uneasiness starting up inside him. "Looks like aircraft. A squadron of fighters, judging by their speed."

"Maybe they've been sent out to escort us in," Delaney suggested hopefully.

Garrett didn't voice what he was thinking. There could be only one explanation for the squadron's determined approach.

"Try that radio transmitter again," he told Bamberger. "Let's see if we can make contact."

Lieutenant Schulman's cruise speed was 380 knots, the sea a dizzy blur beneath his nose cone. Spread out in abreast formation, the squadron thundered south of the Balearic islands. Schulman spotted a fuel tanker below, and his eyes swiftly checked his gauges. According to his navigation dial, he was right on course, his fuel burn more than ninety pounds a minute.

Lieutenant Schulman's heart thumped as he scanned the forty-mile range sector on his radar scanner. He felt little compunction about the strike ahead. He was doing the job he had trained for.

A blip appeared on his VD screen, and Schulman tensed. From the speed the signature was traveling, an estimated 320 miles per hour, it had to be the shuttle. He forced himself to remain cool as he spoke into his radio mike. "Target south about twenty degrees. Anybody spot her yet?"

"Affirmative, Mitch, affirmative."

"Speed three hundred twenty, altitude twenty-five thousand, now in descent. Level off here. I'll try and make radio contact."

Altering his frequency, Schulman spoke into the microphone attached to his helmet strap. "Fighter squadron to shuttlecraft. Please identify yourself. Repeat—please identify yourself, and state intention. Over."

The radio crackled, but no answering call came back. Schulman tried a different frequency, but the shuttle continued approaching, shrouded in electronic silence.

Schulman's tongue snaked out, moistening his lips as he switched back to the squadron. "Python One, Python One, I'm going in for a strike."

"Easy, Mitch, easy," a voice crackled. "You want to call the ship and reconfirm?"

"Reconfirm, hell. You heard the order. Pull back and assume defensive formation. I'll make the first sortie alone."

Schulman increased his speed to 600 knots, soaring up to 22,000 feet. Fourteen miles from the target, he back-pressured the control handle, banking starboard and drawing six g's. The bladders on his pressure suit automatically inflated, pressing hard against his stomach and legs to slow down the blood flow from his brain as he focused on the kill.

He switched the knob beneath the navigational instruments from position one to position two, and the aircraft made a slight turn to port, the blip moving into the center of the target zone. Schulman set the dials on the data processor to identical coordinates. His heart beat wildly as he moved the selector from Ripple to Single-shot. Patiently, he waited for the surveillance system to process its information to the missile launcher. The digital radar screen flashed out the words *Target acquired*.

"Master arm on." He spoke into his radio mike. "Shuttle is on my nose now. Centering up the T. Have tone, have tone. Select Fox One. Range nine point five miles."

Almost in a daze, he went through the circuit check, pressing the relay switched downward, his right hand clutching the control stick. The screen switched to the message *You have completed checks. Firing solution go*.

Schulman sucked in his breath, his nerves suddenly raw.

"Fox One, Fox One," he yelled, punching the little red button marked Fire.

Garrett saw a sudden spurt of flame, felt a jarring thud in the orbiter's fuselage, and knew they had been hit. He found himself wrapped in a cocoon of blinding light, like a camera flashbulb that went on and on.

They skidded dizzily sideways, the flight deck filled with choking black smoke, and somewhere near Garrett's feet, a hole opened up. The bulkhead peeled backward to offer glimpses of the ocean far below. A thunderous gale battered through the ruptured canopy as Garrett, forgetting he was still wearing his EMU helmet, raised his hand numbly to his skull.

His first thought was for Lori. Had she been hurt? He peered across the smoke-filled flight deck, feeling a surge of relief as he spotted her still wrestling gamely with the shuttle hand controls.

"What are you doing?"

She glanced at him over her shoulder. "Trying to right this thing."

"Forget it. We're crashing, for Chrissake."

"I've got to get the orbiter under control. If we hit the ocean at this angle, we'll smash into a million pieces."

"We'll never make it to the ocean. Can't you see we're being shot at?"

Malenov looked dazed. "You mean that was a deliberate strike?"

"Damn right it was a deliberate strike."

"Why, for God's sake?"

"Maybe they've mistaken us for the terrorists."

"What are we going to do?" Bamberger cried.

"The only thing we can. Abandon ship."

"Bail out?"

Garrett knew what Bamberger was thinking. The escape hatch was the final resort. Only when the orbiter was traveling at less than 250 miles per hour could a parachute drop be attempted with any chance of survival, and even then, it was a hazardous maneuver. The crew had to slide down an extended pole and hope to God it would sweep them clear of the orbiter's destructive slipstream. A fractional miscalculation, and the awesome backwash would rip their bodies to shreds. It seemed a cold and desolate prospect, but Garrett could think of no alternative.

"Grab the parachutes," he ordered. "We're going out of here the hard way."

Lieutenant Schulman's right hand nudged the throttle, his eyes scouring the INS and radar screen. He could still see every moment of the hit imprinted on his mind in vivid detail. According to the blip, his target was now in a 45-degree dive, hurtling toward the dancing wave crests.

Almost crazy with excitement, Schulman jabbed his finger on the radio switch. "Good kill, good kill. I'm going in for a second strike—over."

And without waiting for confirmation, he peeled off to starboard, focusing his eyes on his SNL-22-111 missile aimer.

Lori stood on the lower flight deck, watching Bamberger and Delaney preparing to exit. The pipe along which they would have to slide had been lowered into position and now protruded awkwardly through the escape-hatch opening. Lori could feel the awesome power of the vehicle's slipstream.

Through the drifting smoke, she saw Garrett. What would she have done without him? Garrett's voice placating her during the desperate battle for reentry, Garrett's presence sustaining her as she'd struggled to right the cartwheeling satellite, Garrett offering her confidence and comfort. Her petty resentments seemed irrelevant in the face of what they had endured together.

She eased back as Delaney gripped the slippery escape pole. She could see he was scared, but he scarcely hesitated. Stepping into the opening, he whipped through the gaping hatch with a breathless whoosh, vanishing instantly into the raging turbulence beneath. She did not see his parachute open, for he was whisked from sight by the cross-blast.

Bamberger went next. He moved into position, wrapping his arms around the gleaming pipe. There was no last-minute pause for reflection. One second he was there, the next he was sucked into the awesome void below.

Lori felt her stomach tense. Now it was her turn. Well, what was she waiting for? Did she expect to have her hand held? Win or lose, the step had to be taken. Holding her breath, she seized the pole in both hands and leapt into the narrow opening.

She felt her body falling, saw the slippery pipe whip past her face, sensed rather than saw the fuselage opening up around her, then something solid pounded her stomach and chest, driving the air from her shuddering lungs. She could scarcely believe the strength of it. Like a battering ram, it steamrolled into her, stunning her mind, blurring her vision.

She rolled over and over, unable to help herself, catching fractured glimpses of the sea far below. For a moment, she thought she was going to faint; then her brain reminded her there had been no time to set up a static line and anchor cable. She was free-falling.

Numbly, she groped for the release chord at her chest, experiencing a surge of relief as the chute cascaded out above her head. She felt her momentum slacken, the straps tugging gently at her thighs and armpits. She was floating earthward in a gentle, controlled descent. Below and to the right, she glimpsed the tiny umbrellas of Bamberger and Delaney's billowing parachutes.

Glancing up, she saw the *Ulysses* still plummeting earthward, its devastated hull belching out a column of thick black smoke. Then something fast and fiery streaked through the sky, and in front of her horrified eyes, the shuttle erupted in a blinding spasm of flame.

Malenov lay where he had fallen, struggling to realign his senses. Around him, the entire cabin was ablaze. Smoke wafted across his face mask, and he saw sparks dancing above the control console. A massive rupture had opened up the starboard fuselage, and tremedous pressure was sucking out everything in its vicinity. Malenov saw a chair, ripped from its deckbolts, sail through the gaping aperture.

Malenov's muscles were sore, but otherwise he was unharmed. He rolled onto his knees, dragging himself painfully to his feet. Braced against the tilting deck, he held the bulkhead rail for support. The suction tugged at his body.

Garrett was sprawled facedown on the deck, motionless. The entire instrument console had been ripped from the cockpit wall and lay across the Englishman's lower body. There was no hint of life in his chest or limbs.

Malenov stared for a moment at the prostrate figure of his fallen enemy. Strange, it seemed, finding Garrett vanquished at last. He had dreamed of it so long, worked for it so hard, and in a final irony, the task had been accomplished through nothing more sinister than circumstance.

Malenov felt no sense of triumph. His only concern was survival. He turned toward the escape hatch.

"Sergei?"

The cry was weak, barely audible in the roar of the slipstream. Malenov glanced back. Garrett's helmet was tilted toward him, and even through the smoke, he could see the Englishman's eyes.

Garrett is your enemy, he thought. Don't risk your life on a meaningless exercise. He shuffled on, his hands reaching out to grasp the descent pipe.

"Sergei?"

Again Malenov looked back. Well, what now? he asked himself. It's what you wanted, isn't it? You swore you'd kill him, so let him die.

But somehow he couldn't.

Swearing, he turned and eased across the sloping floor. Reaching the spot where Garrett lay pinned, he bent down and tested the weight of the insturment console. What he needed was a bloody crane, he thought.

Cursing Garrett silently, he dropped to his knees, squeezing his shoulder beneath the panel's outermost rim. Pushing hard, he focused the full weight of his body into the console's upper corner, his veins swelling, his lungs bursting. The panel shifted slightly to the right. Gritting his teeth, he prized it painfully upward, and Garrett rolled free across the rubber-coated deck. With a strangled cry, Malenov stepped back, letting the massive console crash back into position.

He turned just in time to see Garrett slide toward the gaping fissure, his gloved fingers clawing at the floor. Malenov

moved forward to help, and instantly his feet were tugged
from under him as the incredible force of the slipstream
caught him in its grip. He hit the deck with a jarring thud and
felt himself pulled along as if by an invisible hand.

Desperately, he looked around for something to cling to.
The deck looked smooth and uncluttered as far as the bulk-
head. His only chance was to use Garrett as a living prop.
Rolling over, he seized the Englishman around the chest.

"Ram your boots against the aperture rim!" he shouted.

Without waiting to see if Garrett had complied, he let
himself slide into the suction vortex, positioning his feet
against the opening's jagged perimeter. With a clump, his
boots thudded into the bulkhead. Using Garrett as a support,
he formed a living triangle, bracing himself against the
slipstream tug.

On the opposite side of the rupture he spotted the bulkhead
handrail. It ran the complete perimeter of the flight deck,
ending abruptly at the escape hatch. If he could reach it,
maybe he could maneuver Garrett as far as the emergency
pipeline.

"Jam yourself in position," he said hoarsely. "I'm going
to climb over you."

He wedged his feet on each side of the gaping hole, and
clinging to his companion, inched his way breathlessly across
the Englishman's torso. He could see Garrett's eyes laughing
at him through the shaded face mask.

"Sergei, I never knew you felt this way."

"Shut up," Malenov hissed furiously. Here he was struggling for survival, and all Garrett could do was joke.

He reached the opposite side of the aperture. Holding
onto Garrett with one hand, he groped out awkwardly with
the other. His fingers closed on the bulkhead rail, and he
gripped it hard. Still holding Garrett's arm, he wrestled
himself into a sitting position and staggered laboriously to
his feet. The awesome drag of the slipstream pummeled
him wildly, but he clung to the bulkhead rail, hauling
Garrett toward him.

For several seconds, they stood wheezing against the metal
bar, the wind howling around them. Then, hooking his arm
around Garrett's shoulder, Malenov maneuvered him awkwardly
toward the escape hatch.

\* \* \*

Dangling beneath her parachute, Lori watched the space-craft plummet like a meteor from some forgotten planet. A terrible wail accompanied its descent. Her stomach tightened as it hit the ocean. There was a thunderous roar, a blinding flash, and a roil of water. A terrible anguish gripped her. She felt her head spinning, as if every part of her body had suddenly disconnected. Her lips formed into a soundless protest—*no*, she wanted to shout, it was too cruel, too unjust.

Then twin parachutes blossomed in the wind. She blinked, scarcely able to believe her senses. Garrett. Against logic, against reason, he had somehow managed to escape. It seemed a miracle.

Her eyes filled with tears of gratitude and relief. She was still crying when far below she saw a fishing boat speeding across the water to meet them.

The great house echoed to the clatter of footsteps. In the oak-paneled corridors, armed detectives carried out a final check.

Wesker stood in the anteroom, watching the prisoners being escorted to the lobby. They walked stoically, their wrists handcuffed. It seemed hard to believe these eminent figures were the conspirators he had worked so hard to uncover.

He felt no elation that his search was finally over. He was conscious only of an underlying sadness, as if he had delved, unexpectedly and unwillingly, into some dark and contempt-ible secret. There were no winners when heroes were destroyed.

He watched uniformed patrolmen shepherding the captives down the marble steps to the outside drive where TV camera crews were trying to gain admittance.

The door of the conference room opened, and Lieutenant Sal Gassner emerged.

"That the lot?" Wesker asked.

"All we found, apart from De Tabley. There could be more, of course. We'll weed out their names during interroga-tion. De Tabley says he wants to talk to you. In private."

Wesker looked surprised. "Did he say why?"

"Claimed it was personal."

Wesker hated recriminations. On the other hand, they still hadn't found the terrorists' communications center. And mag-nanimity in victory was as important as courage in defeat. "How long have I got?"

"Five minutes. Best I can do."

Strolling up the steps, Wesker entered the conference room, signaling to the uniformed guards who stood just inside the doorway. Without a word, they filed into the passage outside.

Wesker looked at De Tabley across the mahogany conference table. He felt no sense of triumph, no sense of anything at all, except perhaps a reluctant curiosity.

De Tabley's sunbaked face was pale beneath its surface tan. There was a weariness in his eyes, but his shoulders were set, his bearing dignified. Wesker had to admit the man had style.

"Hello, Walter," Wesker said softly.

Walter Bowering smiled tiredly. "I knew it would take a miracle to surprise you, Louis."

"You surprised me, all right," Wesker admitted. "I realized De Tabley had high-ranking connections at the White House, but it never occurred to me he might be operating through his wife."

"You do appreciate Jan had nothing to do with this?"

"Isn't it a little late for loyalty?"

"Loyalty was what made me do it," De Tabley insisted.

"Walter, the charade is over. Your satellite no longer exists."

"How's that?"

"We've just had word that NORAD destroyed it with F-Twenty-two rockets."

"Impossible."

"You're thinking of the defense shield? Sorry, Walter, I'm afraid the Canby D-Five wasn't functioning at the time. The *Stallion*'s gone. But we still need the location of your communications base. Give us a chance to pick up your radio people and put an end to this sorry mess."

De Tabley was amused. In the sunlight, his silvery hair gleamed like polished ivory. "How earnestly you play your role."

"I'm just trying to tie up the loose ends. Don't let's drag this out to its miserable conclusion."

"I know what you're thinking. You think I'm a traitor, right?"

"It doesn't matter what I think," Wesker told him tiredly.

"I'm not a traitor, Louis. Everything I've done has been for the good of my country."

"You really believe that?"

"Of course I believe it. It's the truth."

"You're wrong, Walter. It was guilt that inspired you, not patriotism."

"What are you talking about?"

"Your father."

De Tabley wrinkled his nose as if something had just soured the air. "So you've dredged up the truth about my past?"

"We have. A little old-fashioned spadework."

"Well, I guess it had to happen sooner or later."

"Don't feel bad about it. You did an extraordinary shredding job. Rarely have I seen a man vanish so completely into the system."

"Switching identities can be an intricate business," De Tabley admitted.

"How did you do it? How did you fool even the security services? As the husband of a presidential aide, you must have known you'd have to stand up to an FBI full-field investigation."

"It wasn't easy. I had to create a new persona in Walter Bowering and make his background stick. It took months of painstaking documentation and research."

He looked through the window at the lawns of Connel's estate.

"You're wondering about my motive," he said. "Well, it wasn't self-interest, I can assure you. I love this country more than anything in the world. When I was a boy, America was a land of freedom. It was filled with a restless energy. My father betrayed all that, and I hated him for it. At the time, I would happily have acted as his executioner, not only for what he did to me and my family but for what he did to the United States. Now . . . now we're a nation of spineless bellyachers, tainted by the very corruptions we struggled so hard to conquer. Our society is sick, Louis. We've lost direction. We're surrounded by leaders who snipe at the very foundations of our culture, our freedom."

"I would hardly call President Clayman a corrupting influence," Wesker said.

"Clayman?" De Tabley laughed derisively. "A pussycat. A strong society demands a strong leader. Man craves order, just as he craves purpose, because order gives him identity and direction. We need to regain our dignity, our pride, our self-respect. Those things are part of our heritage."

"Don't tell me what it means to be an American," Wesker said softly. "You forfeited that right when you disregarded the Constitution."

"There's something I want you to do for me."

"It's a little late for that."

"It's my wife. She's innocent of any involvement. I used her, Louis—coldly and deliberately. I can't bear to see her name dragged through the mud."

"You should have thought of that a long time ago."

"Don't deny me a shot at nobility. Even a condemned man is granted a last request."

"What did you have in mind?"

"I'm willing to trade. I'll tell you how we maintained contact with the *Stallion*, but only for a price. Give me your word my wife will not be implicated."

"You know that isn't up to me. Mrs. Bowering will have to be investigated in the usual way. But if it's any consolation, I'll do my damnedest to see she isn't caused unnecessary distress."

De Tabley said, "That's good enough."

Leaning on the table, he scribbled something on a piece of paper. Wesker glanced over his shoulder. It was the address of a disused radio station near Magdalena, New Mexico. Wesker picked up the telephone and conveyed the details to Lieutenant Gassner. Replacing the receiver, he looked at De Tabley in silence. In the driveway outside, a police siren wailed as the first of the prison vans set off with its distinguished cargo.

"I've often thought of this moment," De Tabley said.

"It isn't easy to accept defeat."

"I don't know. I must have a touch of the actor in my blood. I rather enjoy being center stage. And I never could resist an extravagant gesture."

He pressed a hidden button beneath the table lid, and a drawer slid open with a muffled click. Wesker saw the pistol too late. He lunged forward, groping for De Tabley's wrist. "No!" he shouted.

De Tabley was smiling as he raised the barrel to his temple and gently squeezed the trigger.

\* \* \*

The Washington Mall teemed with people as Jan Bowering strolled slowly toward the Lincoln Memorial. People swirled across the open lawns, linking arms as they celebrated the news of the satellite's destruction. She saw a group of boisterous teenagers, fully dressed, splashing in the Reflecting Pool. Nearby, a trio of uniformed patrolmen watched their antics, smiling indulgently. The world had been made safe again, and for a few hours at least, the human race wanted to acknowledge that fact before going back to the drudgery of routine.

A terrible emptiness engulfed Jan Bowering. She simply couldn't believe what had happened. The way Walter had used her, betrayed her. And she'd never suspected, that was the awful thing. Love—it had a lot to answer for.

As she reached Twenty-third Street, a car pulled up alongside, and she heard someone call her name. Louis Wesker waved to her from the open window. "What are you doing?" he asked.

"Walking, Louis. I needed some air."

"Alone?"

"I have to think. Sort things out. I'm a little confused at the moment."

Wesker hooked his arm over the window frame. "Mrs. Bowering, I tried to stop him, I want you to know that."

"I do know it. There was nothing you could do."

Wesker was silent for a moment, his eyes dark and somber. "If you want to talk about it, call me," he offered.

"You're a good man, Louis. You believe in people. I wonder why some enterprising lady didn't snap you up years ago. But this is something I have to work out for myself, and I'm doing it the best way I can."

Wesker watched her vanish into the crowd, her head proud, her spine erect. He switched on the ignition and drove slowly back the way he had come.

"De Tabley had a direct linkup to a number near Magdalena, New Mexico," Wesker explained. "The number connected him to a disused radio station where a man named Eli Kozani was waiting. Kozani was a genius at electronic communications. Using equipment supplied by General Connel, he built an effective high-powered radio transmitter, establishing a connection with the terrorists in space. It was through Kozani that De Tabley controlled their actions."

Sitting on Wesker's submarine deck, Garrett and Lori listened attentively. Garrett's left leg was encased in plaster, propped on a kitchen stool. It seemed hard to believe it was really over, hard to believe they had actually been up there. It felt good, Garrett thought, to be back on Earth again. It felt good to be with Lori, for if there was one worthwhile thing to emerge from this whole sorry business, it was the discovery that he was not a hopeless misfit after all.

In front of the flower-bedecked conning tower, a pot of chili sat simmering on Wesker's cast-iron stove. It had been Wesker's idea that they should celebrate their victory with a barbecue. Now, his bulky frame clad in an apron, he was opening a bottle of Bordeaux.

"We picked up eleven high-ranking officers in the swoop on General Connel's house. De Tabley was siphoning off Pentagon funds to finance his secret organization. It was a master plan. Our investigators estimate it'll take years to unravel the full extent of De Tabley's scheming."

"He must have been something of a genius," Garrett said.

"He was the last of the dinosaurs. He spent his entire life trying to make amends for his father's treachery, and I guess it pushed him beyond the boundaries of reason."

"Why did he marry Jan Bowering?" Lori asked.

"He calculated that she was destined for the White House. Maybe he figured he could influence her outlook. If that was the case, he *mis*calculated. Jan has a mind of her own. Nobody, not even the President, can tell her what to think. However, she did provide De Tabley with a marvelous insight into what was going on at the seat of government."

"I still don't understand how he managed to change his appearance so radically," Garrett said. "He bore no resemblance at all to the man in that Saigon photograph."

"Well, first he had his face altered by plastic surgery—that we already knew. But merely looking different wasn't enough. De Tabley dreaded the thought of someone linking him to the fanatical young officer in the Mekong Delta, so he took steroids to build up his bodyweight. He changed his whole metabolism."

"And when the moment came—when he realized he'd lost—he proved he had the courage of his own convictions."

Wesker rolled his wine gently in the glass. "What will happen to you, Zach, now that it's all over?"

"Back to Antarctica, I imagine. I'm still an officer in His Majesty's service. However, there should be time for a little painting. In fact''—he reached out and slid his arm around Lori's waist—"with such an attentive nurse, I could be incapacitated here for months."

"What about you, Louis?" Lori asked gently.

"Somebody's got to keep the nation running. Besides, I have a new interest at the White House."

"What interest?" Garrett asked.

"It's personal."

"Personal, Louis? what are you talking about?"

"All right, if you must know, it's Mrs. Bowering." Garrett said, "Jan Bowering?"

"I think she likes me. We have a certain emotional empathy." Garrett glanced at Lori.

Wesker said, "It may surprise you to learn there are some women who appreciate refinement and sensitivity. They warm to a man who's fastidious and discerning, who exudes a sense of elegance and style."

"To say nothing of humility," Garrett quipped.

Lori's laughter sounded lightly on the soft night air. "If that's what she's looking for, I'd say she's come to the right department."

Wesker picked up the wine bottle and carefully refilled their glasses. "That's what I told her," he said.

Garrett and Lori stool on the airport concourse, saying good-bye to Malenov and Elke. Balancing himself on a pair of crutches, Garrett shook Malenov's hand. "I never got to thank you for saving my life."

There was no answering smile on Malenov's face. "I didn't do it for you," he answered bluntly. "If you want the truth, I was sorely tempted to let you die up there, but I find, to my regret, I suffer from that most virulent of human afflictions—a conscience."

"Sergei, you are incorrigible. Will nothing make you forget the past?"

"Some things never change, Zachary. We've hated each other too long to alter our attitudes now. However—" he hesitated, "there *is* something you should know. I had nothing to do with your expulsion from Baikonur."

"What are you talking about?"

"I mean it was a KGB operation from the beginning."

"But the note calling me to Section Four was in your handwriting."

"A forgery. The KGB rigged the whole thing. They wanted to embarrass the British government. You were proving too successful on the ANSAAD, and they considered you a threat to Soviet morale."

"But what about the evidence, the stuff planted in my quarters, on my clothing?"

"KGB agents put it there."

Garrett stared at Malenov in disbelief. "Sergei, are you telling me that for the past four years, I've been blaming you for something you didn't do?"

Malenov's cheeks flushed. "Not exactly, Zachary. I'm not pretending I'm completely innocent."

"What, then?"

"Those letters you sent to Elke . . ." Malenov's voice trailed away in embarrassment.

Garrett eyed him shrewdly. "So that's why they never arrived."

"I make no excuses about Elke. You were always wrong for her, Zachary."

Reaching into his pocket, he drew out a paper envelope and handed it to Garrett with a dismissive shrug. "It's your confession. If I may make a suggestion, destroy it as quickly as possible."

"Don't worry," Garrett told him. "I never make the same mistake twice."

Malenov turned to Lori, clicking his heels. "Goodbye, Miss Madden. You are a remarkable young woman. Should you ever visit Moscow, I would consider it a privilege to act as your host."

"Thank you, Colonel Malenov, you're very gracious."

He touched his cap, and strode toward the waiting aircraft. For a moment, there was an awkward silence as Elke stood uncertainly, embarrassed by Lori's presence. "I would like to apologize," she said. "I made a terrible mistake in coming here. I knew that, Zachary, when I saw the pain in your face the night Miss Madden caught us together. It was an absurd illusion on my part. I should have appreciated that you had your own life to lead."

Lori felt a choking sensation in her throat. She'd been so

angry at this woman, so unreasoningly jealous. She'd behaved abominably, allowing her emotions to get the better of her. Now she felt ashamed.

She held out her hand. "Good-bye," she said. "I hope you sort things out with the Colonel. He's really a most unusual man."

"I believe I'm just beginning to appreciate that," Elke replied. "May I wish you both much luck and happiness?"

She shook hands with Garrett, and Lori saw her eyes glistening. Then she followed in her husband's wake.

Lori was filled with a sense of warmth and gratitude as Garrett slipped his arm around her.

They watched the Russian jet roar down the runway and rise gracefully into the morning sky.

Defense Secretary David Richner examined the business card of the young lady sitting in front of him: *Marian Hepler, Political Analyst, The Washington Post.*

Richner had to admit she looked like no journalist he had ever seen. Her chestnut hair hung almost to her shoulders, and her emerald eyes were disarmingly direct.

He studied her over his thick-rimmed glasses. Rarely had he seen a girl so devastatingly attractive. "You're quite a novelty, Miss Hepler. Most of the political analysts who come my way are dull, stodgy, and invariably male."

She inclined her head at the compliment, her eyes twinkling. She carried her beauty carelessly, like an old glove.

"How may I help you?" Richner asked.

When she crossed her legs, his heart almost missed a beat.

"Trust might, trust constancy," she said.

For a moment, Richner wasn't sure he had heard correctly. He sucked in his breath, glancing around with an expression of alarm. Then, rising to his feet, he closed the connecting door to his secretary's office.

"Who are you?" He examined his visitor with a new intensity.

"My name—that is, my real name—is Nelia De Tabley."

Richner shook his head as if to clear it. "Frank's girl. He told me he had a daughter. He said she was living somewhere in the south of France."

He returned to his desk, and his voice grew husky with embarrassment. "I know what you're thinking. You're wondering why I didn't warn your father when I knew General Connel's house was about to be raided. Well, I couldn't. They already had the place surrounded, and the telephone lines were tapped. I delayed the raid as long as I could, but it was out of my hands. Your father always insisted that if everything was lost, it was the primary duty of each individual to protect his own position."

"Correct," she acknowledged. "The vital thing has always been to maintain the organization's survival. How many members are still at large?"

"Besides myself, only two. They're lying low while the investigations continue."

"But more could be recruited?"

"You're not suggesting we can actually continue?"

The young lady was silent for a moment, sunrays from the open window casting subtle nuances of light across her chestnut hair. Richner caught the fragrance of her perfume, and his senses stirred.

"My father was a great man," she said at last. "It would be unthinkable if everything he worked for was allowed to crumble after one defeat."

Her eyes held his across the desktop. "We may have lost the first hand, Mr. Richner," she said softly, "but the game itself has only just begun."

# THE INFINITY GAMBIT
# By James P. Hogan
## Author of *The Proteus Operation*

Bernard Fallon is that rarest of creatures: a master spy
with a conscience. After years in Britain's SAS and other
covert intelligence organizations, he realized he must
either deaden his conscience and risk becoming what
he'd spent his life fighting, or get out. He got out, went
freelance. Now no one owns him, no political system
holds him...only the idea that justice belongs to everyone.

It's not long before Fallon finds his services in heavy
demand. First by an African government seeking his
help in eliminating the rebel Zugendan Republican Front.
Then by the ZRF itself, whose leaders claim that the
government is the real terrorist group. But things get
really interesting when a third party comes to Fallon,
with an almost irresistable offer: an independant organization with no allegiance to any nation, ideology,
religion, or economic system, they stand for only one
thing: freedom. Its name: Infinity Limited.

Bestselling author James P. Hogan creates an intricate
maze of political doublespeak, betrayal, impersonation,
and violence in his most gripping novel to date.

On sale in March wherever Bantam Falcon Books are
sold.

AN213 -- 2/91

*Bantam Falcon Books presents the beginning of a brand new series:*

An ancient oracle...a scheming temptress...and a budding young archaeologist named Indiana Jones!

# INDIANA JONES AND THE PERIL AT DELPHI
# by Rob MacGregor

For sixteen centuries the Order of Pythia has awaited the reappearance of the ancient oracle of sacred knowledge of Delphi. An earthquake, rending the earth beneath the ruins, has now heralded her return. Dorian Belecamus, a beautiful and bewitching archaeology professor, sees this as more than an opportunity to dig into the past: This is her chance to seize control of the country's future -- by becoming the Oracle of Delphi! And she's found just the man to help her consummate her scheme. He's brash, he's reckless, and he's fallen under her spell. His name: Indiana Jones.

In an adventure that spans the globe, from Chicago to Paris to Greece, **Indiana Jones and the Peril at Delphi** is an epic story, written by the *New York Times* bestselling novelizer of *Indiana Jones and the Last Crusade.* For the first time we will learn the secrets of what shaped Indiana Jones into the man who found the Lost Ark, escaped the Temple of Doom, and survived the Last Crusade!

It begins here, in **Indiana Jones and the Peril at Delphi**. On sale in January wherever Bantam Falcon Books are sold.